A Curse of Ashes

OTHER TITLES BY SARIAH WILSON

Stand-Alone Novels

Falling Overboard

Party Favors

Hypnotized by Love

Almost Like Being in Love (novella)

The Hollywood Jinx

The Chemistry of Love

Cinder-Nanny

The Paid Bridesmaid

The Seat Filler

Roommaid

Once Upon a Time Travel

The Eye of the Goddess Series

A Tribute of Fire

A Vow of Embers

Praise for *A Tribute of Fire*

"Sariah Wilson demonstrates an [impressive] level of storytelling talent and originality."

—*Midwest Book Review*

"An incredibly captivating introduction to Wilson's new romantasy series."

—*Harlequin Junkie*

"Greek mythology, a strong heroine, found family, enemies to lovers. What more could you want? How about captivating world-building, mystery, action, romantic tension for days, and a cliff-hanger that leaves you gasping for more! *A Tribute of Fire* is a must-read book of 2024."

—Jennifer L. Armentrout, #1 *New York Times* bestselling author

"Sariah Wilson isn't just a master of the romance genre—with *A Tribute of Fire*, she proves herself a skilled writer of romantasy, too. I inhaled this story—rooted in Greek mythology but all new in its cocktail of stunning twists, fierce characters, sisterhood, magic, and enough heat to torch a small country. Don't mind me, I'll be here impatiently waiting for the next book in the series."

—Jodi Picoult, #1 *New York Times* bestselling author

"Sariah Wilson is in her element with this book! The intricate plot and sizzling romance grip you from the beginning and will not let you go. This is a must-read for romantasy lovers, and easily her most addictive book yet."

—Charlie N. Holmberg, *Wall Street Journal* bestselling author

The End of the Line Novels

The Friend Zone

Just a Boyfriend

The #Lovestruck Novels

#Starstruck

#Moonstruck

#Awestruck

The Royals of Monterra Series

Royal Date

Royal Chase

Royal Games

Royal Design

The Ugly Stepsister Series

The Ugly Stepsister Strikes Back

The Promposal

A CURSE OF ASHES

SARIAH WILSON

This is a work of fiction. Names, characters, organizations, places, events, and incidents are either products of the author's imagination or are used fictitiously. Otherwise, any resemblance to actual persons, living or dead, is purely coincidental.

Published by Montlake, Seattle

www.apub.com

EU product safety contact:
Amazon Media EU S. à r.l.
38, avenue John F. Kennedy, L-1855 Luxembourg
amazonpublishing-gpsr@amazon.com

ISBN-13: 9781662527487 (hardcover)
ISBN-13: 9781662534195 (paperback)
ISBN-13: 9781662527470 (digital)

Cover design by Elizabeth Turner Stokes
Cover image: © Nadia Murash, © Chorna_black, © colnihko / Shutterstock

Printed in the United States of America

First edition

For my nephew, Ben—your family loves and misses you.

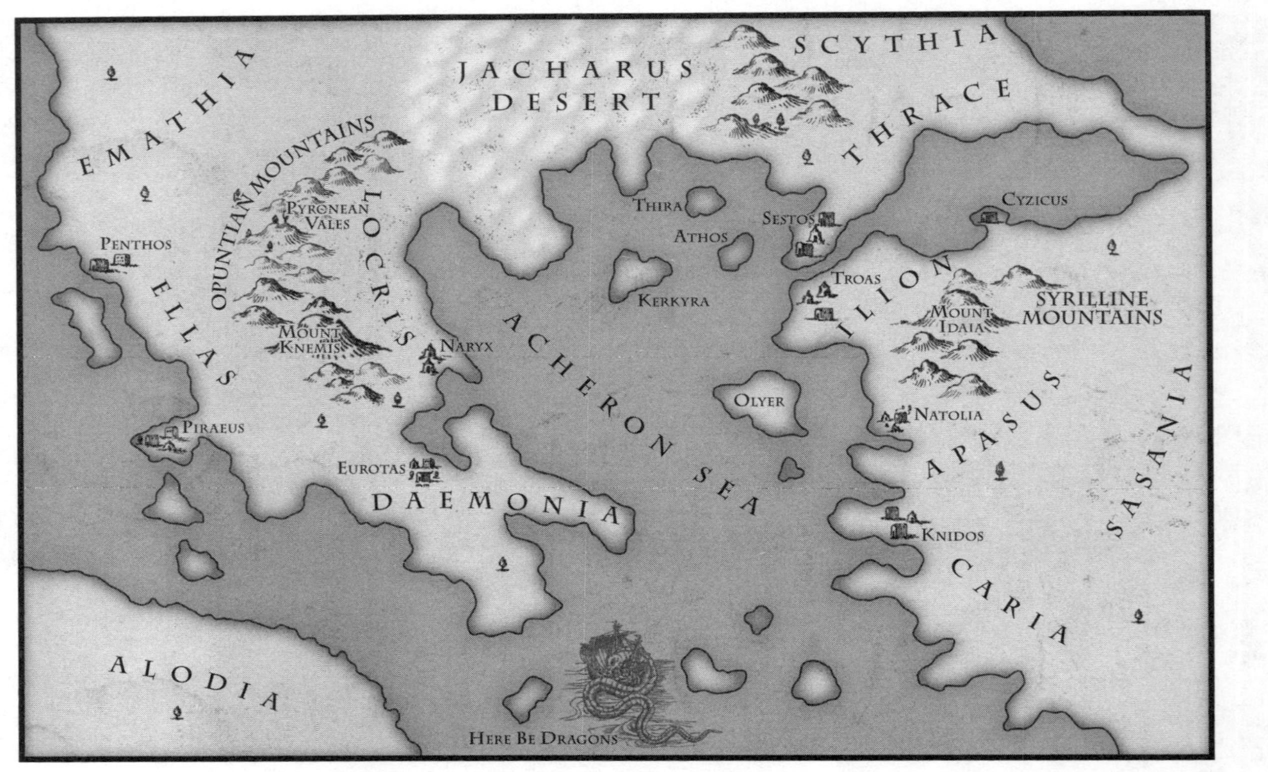
Emathia
Jacharus
Desert
Scythia
Thrace
Opuntian Mountains
Pyronean
Vales
Locris
Penthos
Ellas
Mount
Knemis
Naryx
Piraeus
Eurotas
Daemonia
Acheron Sea
Thira
Athos
Kerkyra
Sestos
Cyzicus
Troas
Ilion
Mount
Idaia
Syrilline
Mountains
Olyer
Natolia
Apasus
Sasania
Knidos
Caria
Alodia
Here Be Dragons

CONTENT WARNING

Please be aware that this book contains some possible triggers and adult themes, including suicidal ideation and suicidal death, disordered eating, discussion of miscarriage and sexual assault, as well as violence, fighting, and death on the page. Some mythical creatures are harmed and killed. And for readers who are fans of my sweet romantic comedies: Please note that this story is much steamier than what I normally write, with open-door love scenes. If you'd like to avoid the spicier scenes in this book, I would recommend skipping over chapters 28, 58, 59, and 62 (while understanding that you will miss some important plot points!).

CHAPTER ONE

Darkness is coming.

The warning from the goddess echoed in my head as I climbed the temple stairs to rejoin my adelphia. I found them standing near the mass grave we had dug to bury our fellow priestesses and acolytes. The image of those women all lying dead on the temple grounds . . .

It was not something I would ever forget.

"How do we go on?" Io asked sadly while sliding her hand into Suri's. "What do we do now?"

After a few moments of heavy silence, Zalira lifted her chin and turned toward us. "We do what women have always done. We swallow down our pain, endure our heartache, ignore our suffering. We rise. We persevere. We carry on. We put one foot in front of the other because we have no other choice."

"We are all that's left," Ahyana said.

There was one other person, but she couldn't help. Our temple battle master, Antiope, had barely survived the slaughter. I didn't know if she would ever wake up. It seemed like she had stayed alive solely to give us a message.

Hammer of Arion.

Was that what had knocked big chunks out of the temple walls? I still wasn't sure whether the hammer was a person or an object.

"We have to avenge these women. Help protect Ilion," Ahyana went on, sounding determined. "It has to be us."

Ahyana was right. This was up to us.

We had to stop Artemisia.

A former fellow acolyte, she had been working for an unknown enemy and somehow managed to wipe out an entire temple of trained warrior women. I kicked at the red dirt beneath my feet. Why did they throw this when they attacked? Would I ever discover what it meant?

The traitorous high priestess had to know who Artemisia was conspiring with. She had refused to say more after our fight, but I intended to question her as soon as I could.

"What were you doing in the temple?" Io asked me.

"I went in to pray. They destroyed the statue of the goddess, broke it into pieces." We prayed to that statue. Had taken our vows in front of it.

Io's free hand went over her mouth as she gasped at the blasphemy. "How could Artemisia do that?"

I suspected that she had done it far too easily. "The statue was covered in a thick layer of gold and that's gone. I'm assuming Artemisia took it."

"Why would she?" Ahyana asked.

"She could pay for troops. Ships. Make sure her army has enough supplies," Zalira said.

Artemisia couldn't have massacred all the people in the weapons quarter and here at the temple alone. She'd had help.

Which could be an issue, as I had begun to suspect that the thousand-year-old high priestess, Lysimache, no longer had the other eye of the goddess.

And that she'd given it to Artemisia.

I didn't want to have to fight my way through an army to get the eye back. But that relic was the only way to remove the curse that Lysimache had put on Locris.

"There's another eye," I said, realizing that I hadn't shared this information with my sisters.

"How do you know that?" Zalira asked.

I explained to them about the voice I'd heard in my head, that of my Daemonian battle master, Demaratus, asking me how many eyes the goddess statue had and how I'd realized that the Ilionian and Locrian statues each had two eye sockets, meaning that there were four eyes of the goddess and not only two, as I had previously assumed. "One of the Locrian eyes was split up and given to life mages. She used the other Locrian eye to curse the land. Theano used one from Ilion to stay alive and strengthen us. Then she destroyed what was left. Which means there's one more Ilionian eye, and we have to get it back."

"Theano was the one that cursed Locris?" Io sounded shocked. Suri's lips compressed into a thin line. She was the only other member of our sisterhood who knew everything that I did, because she'd been with me when I confronted the high priestess.

In the midst of all this chaos, I hadn't yet told the others what I knew, and I felt a bit guilty, as I had recently resolved not to keep any secrets from my adelphia. "Her real name is Lysimache. She was Kysandra's sister."

"The one we read about in books?" Io asked at the same moment that Zalira said, "Kysandra from the Great War? That took place a thousand years ago?"

I nodded. "Lysimache was grinding up and ingesting one of the eyes to keep herself alive, and she put shards of it into the fountain water to make us strong." The high priestess was unaware that I knew she had put those pieces in the fountain, that I'd made the connection after she admitted that she'd used the eye to strengthen the priestesses and acolytes.

She had been surprised when we fought because I was strong enough to beat her. She apparently didn't know that Maia, our mentor, had been sending us the fountain water to protect us.

"Lysimache also wanted me to marry Xander and create a distraction for the city so that Artemisia could carry out her plan." I didn't know what that plan was other than murder and destruction, but I would find out.

"Why did Theano . . . er, Lysimache keep herself alive for so long?" Ahyana wondered.

"She was waiting for the savior. She wanted to stop me from saving Ilion." I felt a bit foolish saying those words. I had told Lysimache that I was the savior, and in the moment I had believed it.

But now, in the light of day . . .

Io believed so fervently that I was the prophesied savior. When she was a little girl, she had made a promise to the goddess to protect the savior—a person who was flame-kissed and bore the mark of the goddess.

I had been in a building full of flames and not been burned while my husband had nearly died. The goddess had changed my hair color to red, like a flame. And her mark was on my shoulder, where Io had sealed a stab wound with Lysimache's official seal.

Arguably, I was the worst possible person to be Ilion's savior. Until recently I would have gladly seen the entire nation burn.

But there were so many innocents in Ilion. And there were people I loved here. My adelphia. My sister, Quynh, who had fallen in love with Thrax, a man I was still attempting to be nice to so that I wouldn't risk my relationship with her. This would be her home, and so I would do what I could to keep it safe.

They aren't the only ones you love, a voice whispered. Xander's face filled my mind and I shook my head in response. That wasn't something I could even allow myself to consider. I knew that we had to work together, rely on one another, so that we could survive what was coming. We were still physically linked—whatever injury happened to one of us happened to the other.

Io had discovered that Xander and I could break the link by consummating our marriage, but I had made vows to the goddess to remain celibate. I had to honor the goddess's laws and abstain from what a life mage had called "pleasures of the flesh" so that I would be able to wield the eye and restore Locris.

My skin heated as I thought back to when Io had drugged her brother with honeyed wine and he had attempted to seduce me—and very nearly succeeded before I realized what she had done.

He was too tempting.

And he currently seemed determined to keep me at arm's length. We hadn't had a chance to truly speak about our relationship since the massacres in Lycia and the temple, and I didn't know where we stood.

Because the last time I had attempted to broach the subject with him, he'd declared that he hadn't meant any of the things he'd said to me while under the honeyed wine's influence. I didn't believe him.

But I wasn't sure what to do about it.

"You will stop Artemisia," Io said, bringing me out of my thoughts. "No matter what you think, you are the savior. You will make her pay with her life for what she's done."

Io's recent thirst for vengeance concerned me. She had always been the strongest acolyte, the one who had worshipped the goddess her whole life. In the past she had always tried to protect life, so it felt very strange to hear her calling for someone's death.

Even if I agreed with her.

"I don't know what's going to happen," I said. "But I do know that we will all face it together."

"And then what?" Io asked. "After we save Ilion and find the eye of the goddess, what will you do?"

"Go back to Locris," I said quickly. "I have to restore it and undo Lysimache's curse. I also promised the goddess that I would reopen her temple and restore worship for her there. Now there's no one else who can help do it. Like Ahyana said, we're all that's left. I have to keep my word if I expect her help."

I was speaking about more than just that promise—I had so many to keep, whether I wanted to or not.

None of my adelphia responded and they all looked crestfallen. Remorse settled deeply into my stomach. I'd been very honest about the fact that I intended to return to my nation. My sisters had to have known that nothing had changed for me. That was still the plan and always would be.

"We should go home," Zalira said.

That word, "home," struck me. Not only because I was thinking about saving Locris but because I remembered how it had felt when my husband had said that word to me.

I will leave a guard to watch over you. Come home when you're done.

This temple had been a home for me, but it never would be again. The palace was a home to me now, something I never would have thought possible. It made me wish for things I knew I couldn't have.

When we reached the front gate, I asked, "Should we lock it up?"

"No," Io said. "Close the gate but don't lock it. I'm going to ask Xander to post a guard here to protect the grounds, and then I'll arrange for someone to keep bringing us the fountain water."

That was a good idea. I had the feeling we were going to need all the strength we could get for the days ahead.

We crossed through the archway and onto the street. Suri closed the gates behind us and I saw that Xander hadn't left just a guard.

He had left what must have been half his army outside the temple walls, to keep us safe.

A warm thrill unfurled in my gut. I knew I shouldn't want his actions to mean something more.

Zalira headed out and we followed, while the soldiers kept their distance behind us.

Io came over to me and tugged on my arm to get me to slow my pace a bit, to put some distance between us and the others. "You have to break the link you have with Xander."

If I died, so would he. "Is this where you again encourage me to consummate my marriage?"

"No."

Her response surprised me. She'd done nothing for the last few weeks but try and get Xander and me to have sex and had repeatedly endeavored to get me to admit that I loved him.

"Everything has changed, Lia," she said. "I am going to find a way to break your physical bond with him. But I don't want the two of you to get any closer." Her voice wobbled while she spoke and I knew that it was hard for her to say this to me.

I didn't understand. "Why?"

"Because of how it will destroy him if you die. Whatever it is that has happened between the two of you, it needs to end. When our mother died . . . he was never the same. I've spent my whole life witnessing what that loss did to him. And if you survive what's coming, you're going back to Locris and Xander will become king here. There is no future for the two of you."

I nodded, ignoring the hot, thick lump in my throat. I told myself for the thousandth time that I wasn't going to die.

"Please don't make this worse for him. No matter what he says or what you think, I know that he loves you. And when Xander loves, he loves completely. This might be unfair of me to ask, but for my sake, please promise me that you won't hurt my brother. Keep your distance from him. Please don't tell him that you love him."

If either Xander or I said those words, it would bind our souls eternally to each other. It had happened to Zalira and Stephanos, and I knew she was in agony over that connection. Loving Stephanos but not being able to be with him because of the vows we'd made to the goddess . . . I understood her pain all too well.

Something Io had apparently intuited even though I'd never admitted it to anyone. Not even myself.

And now I never could.

Because I saw how important this was to her. "I promise that I will do my best not to hurt him."

It felt as if I'd just lost something important.

Her eyes were bright with unshed tears. "Thank you. I do worry that it's too late already. For both of you."

I tried to swallow that lump down and break the tension by attempting to joke with her. "If I really am the savior, then there's no future for me with anyone."

But my jest fell flat.

She only nodded and then quoted the prophecy: "After a trial of the elements, the savior will die, offered up as a worthy sacrifice to the goddess, and in return Ilion will be kept safe."

Her words struck me as hard now as they had back when I'd first heard them. It was the main reason I didn't want to accept that I was the savior.

I didn't want to die.

Not when I had so much to live for.

"Have you had time to consider what a trial of the elements means?" I asked, needing to distract myself.

Io's face crumpled. "I think you've already gone through the first one."

I nearly stumbled over my own feet as I came to an abrupt stop. "What?" I only vaguely noticed that the soldiers behind us also halted, giving Io and me the chance to speak without them overhearing.

"When you ran into that burning home in Lycia to save Xander . . . I think that was your trial of fire."

Blood rushed in my ears as my heart thundered in my chest. Was she right? Had the trials already begun? What would the other ones look like?

And if Io was correct, then I had survived one trial and only had four more to go before I died.

CHAPTER TWO

When we entered the palace, I saw my pregnant maid, Parthenia. She had obviously been waiting for my return. She said, "They want you to go to the council chambers."

I hadn't bathed in days and was hungry and tired but knew I couldn't refuse the request.

When I arrived at the council chambers, the entire room was in an uproar. People were yelling over each other and it looked as if a fight might break out at any moment.

Xander stood in the middle of the room, and the veins in his neck strained as he tried to make himself heard over the din.

"Enough!" Pelias, the self-appointed head of the council of elders, hit the wooden table with the butt of his sword, making all the glassware on it rattle. He was the father of Lykaon, the abusive monster currently betrothed to my sister Kallisto. Xander had told me he suspected that Pelias and Erisa, the former queen and Xander's stepmother, were having an affair.

It made Pelias completely untrustworthy.

He was also the father of Chryseis, a woman I had seen Xander kissing, but I shoved that thought aside. I needed to pay attention to what was going on.

"Only one person should be speaking at a time," Pelias said, putting his sword back into its sheath. "Prince Alexandros?"

I was a bit surprised he allowed Xander to speak first.

"We have been attacked," he said. "We have an enemy who wiped out the entire city of Lycia and left traps there to kill us as well. They killed people in the weapons quarter, stealing everything they could. They slaughtered every priestess and acolyte at the temple. We need to prepare. Ask our allies for help. Send out spies to find out who is trying to destroy us."

Erisa rolled her eyes. "We are not under attack! That is ridiculous and an overexaggeration of what's occurred. What proof do we have that what you say is even true?"

Xander's mouth dropped open, and I couldn't blame him for the shocked reaction. Despite what I had just promised Io, I found myself crossing over to stand next to my husband, sliding my hand into his, trying to offer what support I could. He squeezed my hand and I ignored the tingles that raced up my arm.

"The dead bodies," I said to Erisa. "Like the ones that my sisters and I buried at the temple. That's proof."

"It seems rather convenient that you supposedly buried them without any witnesses who can verify that what you're saying is true," Erisa retorted. "And how would a group of five girls dig a hole big enough to bury that many women so quickly? For all we know, the priestesses are traveling to care for plants or whatever it is that they do."

I exchanged a heavy glance with Xander. I thought about asking him where he'd put Lysimache so that I could bring her here to verify what I was saying, but I saw in his eyes that he and I both arrived at the same conclusion at the same time—she would lie. The high priestess would say whatever she had to in order to keep sowing seeds of discord and doubt.

And I would never allow anyone to dig up the grave at the temple. The thought horrified me. Those women deserved peace and to be reunited with the earth.

Pelias agreed with Erisa, to no one's surprise. "I acknowledge that there was some kind of incident, but that is what happens when we let so many strangers immigrate to our city. They are upset that they aren't full citizens and they attacked the weapons quarter as a protest."

Xander had told me about the people who came in from the country after the harvest season ended and would sometimes cause chaos—stealing, fighting, vandalizing.

It actually sounded like a believable theory, which was not good.

"We have no enemies," Pelias added.

"Locris," I immediately responded.

Pelias narrowed his eyes at me. "We have no enemies who could do us actual harm."

I bristled at his response but he wasn't wrong. Locris wasn't in any position to launch an offensive against Ilion.

"We only have the prince's men saying that the city was attacked," Erisa pointed out.

"You also have the word of the residents of the weapons quarter," Xander snapped back. I put my free hand on his forearm and felt his body relax a bit.

"People are easily bribed to say whatever you'd like them to," she said.

I tried not to scoff. Erisa knew that from personal experience. She had stolen a fortune from Locris to finance her campaign to get her creepy son, Kyros, chosen as king and had been bribing some of the other archons.

A fortune she no longer had, since my husband and I had taken it from her.

"Why would I make this up?" Xander's voice had gone deadly soft in the way that it did when he was beyond furious.

"To use fearmongering to force the council to choose you as king. If we were at war with these imaginary enemies, then you'd argue that we would need your strength and skill to keep us safe. There is no war, and Prince Alexandros would convince you otherwise solely for his own selfish political reasons."

Erisa had obviously practiced her answers—they came to her so quickly and easily and almost sounded believable.

Themis and Heliodora, two of the archons, looked as if they didn't know what to think. Zethus was more interested in his goblet of wine than in the council's proceedings.

Stolos seemed lost in his own thoughts until he said, "I think we should read and consider the reports before we make further decisions. We don't want to needlessly worry everyone in the city before we have all the facts."

"That sounds like an excellent idea," Erisa immediately agreed. "The council shouldn't make any decisions about troops or allocations of funds until we know for sure what is happening. And we certainly can't risk panicking the populace. Perhaps we should do something to distract them. Like a party to honor the prince's birthday."

"My birthday has come and gone," Xander said. "We don't need another party."

"You would deny the people a chance to celebrate you? If we really are in danger of going to war as you insist, this might be their last chance to enjoy themselves. Would you take that from them?" Erisa looked far too pleased with herself.

And I understood why as I looked around the room, which was filled with servants, soldiers, and other nobles. Erisa had just neatly trapped Xander. If he refused her, word would get back to the people that he had denied them the opportunity to have a citywide celebration.

"I will make all the arrangements," his stepmother added. "You'll only have to show up."

Pelias said, "I second Erisa's suggestion. We will utilize this distraction to give us time to find out the truth." He called for a vote and all the other archons agreed with this plan, although Themis and Heliodora seemed hesitant.

Xander didn't say anything. He gripped my hand tightly as he turned around and left the council chambers. I hurried to keep up with him as he always walked too quickly when he was upset.

"There are unburied bodies in the weapons quarter and she wants to throw a party," he said with a growl. "That woman and her ambition are going to get us all killed."

"Do you think she's part of this?" I asked in a low tone, looking around to make certain that we weren't overheard. I hoped not, because a citywide celebration would be the perfect time to attack.

"Not even Erisa can be that foolish. Whoever is coming for us is willing to massacre everyone in their path."

He was taking the stairs two at a time, and it wasn't easy to keep pace. "Perhaps she's the kind of person who would rather rule over nothing than not rule at all."

"Goddess help us if that's true."

We had reached the hallway that led to our room when I said, "We will stop her."

"We?" Xander asked, and I didn't know how to respond. He and I were supposed to be a "we" in this fight and I couldn't think of the right way to tell him that.

He abruptly stopped and I almost smacked into him. "You saved my life," he said.

"What?" His nearness disoriented me and I had to force myself to focus on what he was saying. "When?"

"In Lycia. You ran into a burning house and saved me. My phratry brothers told me."

Oh. We hadn't been alone to speak about it since it had happened. "Io did, too. Her salves and medicines are why you're standing here now."

He studied me with that intense gaze of his that made my knees feel like they were made out of water. "Why did you save me? Were you worried that you would share my fate? Or was there another reason?" His voice was gentle and I thought I heard just the faintest note of vulnerability.

Or maybe that was just my hopeful imagination.

Part of me wanted to joke that I owed him, given how often he'd saved my life. But it was time to be honest. I had to learn how to stop hiding this part of myself from him.

"I was afraid," I confessed.

"Of what?"

I had to lower my gaze. "That you would die. I didn't want that. And not because I thought I would die, too." I was too much of a coward to tell him that his death would have destroyed me.

Too scared to tell him that I cared about him.

Because I knew where it would lead.

One of his fingers went under my chin and lifted my face so that I had to meet his eyes again. My breath caught at his expression, and my heart felt as if it might explode.

"You didn't want me to die? I suppose that's progress," he said in that teasing tone of his that I was far too fond of. "You truly want us to work together?"

"Yes."

Something flashed in his eyes and then he said, "It's what I've wanted from the beginning."

A flash of regret made my skin feel hot. I had been so difficult where he was concerned, holding on to my anger so tightly that I couldn't see past it.

"We have the same end goal," I said weakly, as if that were enough of an explanation.

He nodded. "We will have to do this without the council. They aren't going to be of any help, especially with Erisa and Pelias feeding them misinformation. Which means I'm going to have to pay for everything myself—the armor, weapons, ammunition."

"It's a good thing you can afford it," I said.

He gave me a half smile. "Have you broken into my treasury again?"

"Not lately."

It felt surreal to be standing here with him, having this nice moment. The world was falling down around us, but we could still be us.

The us we used to be.

The us I suspected we could be in the future if things were different.

There was movement on the stairs behind us and I turned to see my adelphia joining us, all bearing different expressions at seeing Xander and me together.

I jerked my hand away and stepped back.

"There you are," Io said in a false cheery tone. "We are going to get cleaned up. We may commandeer your washroom."

Xander nodded and I felt his gaze while Io raised her eyebrows to me, as if to ask why I had been standing so close to her brother and holding his hand when I had just promised her that I would try and keep my distance from him.

He greeted my sisters as they passed by, and I was too embarrassed to do anything but just stand there.

I'd never been very good at staying away from Xander.

How could I keep this promise to Io?

"Lia," he said, moving closer to me, and the blood in my veins seemed to sing with delight from his nearness. He was looking at my lips and they tingled in response. I wanted his kiss more than anything.

I wasn't strong enough to resist him.

Io was going to be so upset with me.

As if my thoughts alone had caused it, the air was rent with Io's wailing the word "No!" and we both sprinted down the hall toward her.

"Gone," she choked out. "They're all gone."

CHAPTER THREE

My adelphia's room had been destroyed. The furniture had been slashed, the bedding torn, books and papers shredded and thrown everywhere. Red dirt covered the floor.

Io was crying about her pets—their cages and enclosures were all smashed.

Suri darted into the room and ran over to Io's bed. She reached beneath it and pulled out Io's ferret, Chara. Io let out a sound of relief and rushed over to hug them both.

"What happened here?" Zalira asked.

None of us knew.

"Someone intended to kill you all," Xander said, practically growling the words. "You are acolytes from the temple and they wanted you dead, too."

When I had volunteered to accompany Xander and his men to Lycia, I had considered not bringing my sisters with me. Whoever ordered this attack hadn't realized that they'd come.

What if I hadn't asked them to go? They would have been here. They could have been . . .

I couldn't allow myself to finish the thought. Suri found a tortoise near a trunk and handed it to Io. I was so profoundly grateful that I had brought my adelphia along and hadn't lost them.

Then I wondered whether the person who had ordered the attack realized that I had gone to Lycia as well.

My heart started to pound loudly in my chest and I ran to my room, throwing the door open.

It was in as much disarray as Io's bedroom. Red dirt and bloodstains on the floor. A fight had happened in here. How many guards had died?

"Luna!" I called and started looking for my lizard. I didn't know what I would do if they had hurt her. I checked under the bed and it was completely clear. I ran behind my torn-up screen and started throwing open chests to search inside.

I didn't see her anywhere.

Xander came into the room.

"I can't find Luna," I told him, my voice shaky.

He crouched down to peer under the bed. "I already looked there," I told him. He didn't immediately straighten up, as if needing to verify for himself that she truly wasn't there.

My tunics and dresses were scattered everywhere and I kept picking them up and tossing them aside while calling for her. Xander went into the washroom to check.

When he came out empty-handed, my panic increased. What if the attackers had killed her?

Then I heard a chittering noise and went completely still.

"Under the bed," Xander said, locating the sound before I could.

I dropped to my knees and saw Luna sitting there, in the middle of the space, blinking expectantly at me. She sneezed and I almost laughed, so relieved that she was all right. I reached for her, my hands shaking. I noticed that there were tiny silver flakes on my skin, as if she had sneezed part of herself off. Strange. I cradled her to my chest.

"Are you all right?" I asked, holding her up so that I could see her face.

She blinked slowly at me.

Yes.

"Where were you?" Both Xander and I had checked under the bed and she hadn't been there. It was like she had just suddenly appeared.

"Are you . . . talking to your lizard?" He asked the question as if I had taken leave of my senses.

"I am."

"Why?"

"Because I think she can talk back. And I understand how that sounds, but it's the truth." It didn't even occur to me to hide this from him, which meant that my instincts where he was concerned were definitely shifting. A couple of weeks ago, I would have kept this information to myself. "I can show you. One blink is yes, two blinks means no."

He came and stood next to me as I asked, "Luna, did men attack our room?"

Yes.

"Maybe she's just blinking," Xander said.

"Then ask her a question that she would say no to."

"Did centaurs also attack you?" He sounded as if he found this entire thing ridiculous.

Luna didn't respond to him. Her eyes stayed open.

I repeated Xander's centaur question and she immediately blinked twice.

No.

"See? She is communicating."

"Or it was a coincidence."

I felt frustration welling up inside me. I wasn't sure why it was so important to me that he believed what I was telling him. I asked Luna, "Does Xander snore?"

Yes.

"I do not!" he protested.

"You do."

"Does Lia snore?" He directed his question to Luna, and again she didn't answer him.

Then I asked her if I snored.

No.

Why would she only answer the questions once I had asked them? "I suppose this means she'll only communicate with me." Or maybe I was the only person she *could* communicate with. That we had some type of bond that I didn't fully understand that allowed us to speak. Xander's phratry brother Rokh could sense her as well when he was in his raven form. What did that mean? This was all so odd.

Nothing in my life seemed to be making much sense lately.

"I've never heard of a lizard that talks by blinking," Xander said, sitting down hard on our bed. He looked exhausted, and I wondered what he had been doing while I was at the temple.

And why he had been surprised by our rooms being destroyed. If he'd come straight back here, he would have seen it. I sat down next to him, still holding Luna close. "Where have you been?"

"The thought of you and your sisters at the temple, doing everything by yourselves . . . I had to do something productive. I've been in the weapons quarter, helping them bury bodies and starting to rebuild what was destroyed."

This was why he should be king. He cared about his people in a way that Erisa never would.

"I only returned to the palace because the council summoned me," he added. Then he put his face in his hands. "So many dead."

"It must have been difficult to have the council doubting and questioning what happened when you saw it all with your own eyes."

He raised his head to look at me. "All of this has been difficult."

That was an understatement. "How could this enemy do so much damage? Didn't anyone hear them or try to stop them?"

"They attacked in the middle of the night. It took the people in the weapons quarter some time to get enough soldiers to help. I'm not sure if anyone even knows what happened in the temple."

The middle of the night? Thrax had been with us. Which meant he hadn't been watching over Quynh. "Where's Quynh?" I asked, feeling completely panicked.

"She's fine. After Thrax locked up your high priestess, he came straight back to the palace and moved your sister to a safe house. He has one of his Thracian half sisters watching over her, and she is the most terrifying woman I have ever met and might actually be a better warrior than Thrax. Anyone who crosses her will meet a swift end, and she is almost as protective of Quynh as Thrax is."

That was a relief. Maybe this would mean I could see my sister more often now that she was out of the palace. I wondered if I'd have to resort to subterfuge. Perhaps I could say I was going to the temple for some reason and then end up at her house.

Which reminded me . . . "Io wants you to post a guard at the temple," I said, not wanting to forget. Even if the ground had been desecrated, I couldn't bear the thought of anyone going in there and making it worse.

"I already gave the orders. Some of the men watching over you stayed behind. I didn't think anyone should be entering the temple."

"We need to get water from the fountain." The words were out of my mouth before I could stop them. I hadn't meant to tell him that because of the implications.

"Why?"

If we were going to work together, he needed to know. "Do you remember when you had me pinned to the floor and I was able to push back against you? It was because the water from the fountain makes us strong like men."

"How?"

"Magic."

He considered this information and I was relieved that he didn't ask for further details. I couldn't tell him about the eye of the goddess.

Stupid girl, do you really think he would try to steal it from you?

I no longer thought he would take it from me out of spite or vindictiveness, but if he thought it would save Ilion? He wouldn't hesitate.

And I didn't know what all the eye could do. It obviously had multiple uses, and maybe it could be wielded like a weapon. I needed it for Locris, even if that was selfish.

I couldn't share the whole truth.

"What happens if a man drinks it?" he asked.

"I don't know."

We sat in silence for a few moments and Luna grew heavy in my arms. I peered down at her and saw that she had gone to sleep. I carried her over to the enclosure Xander had made for her, and she barely fit in it. She had somehow grown again.

I hesitated, not sure what to do now. I reminded myself that Io wanted me to stay away from him, but all I wanted was to go over and sit next to him on our bed, talking and planning for the dark future that was barreling toward us.

So that was what I did.

"We will have to be cautious," he said. For a moment I wasn't sure what he was speaking about—did he mean that he and I would have to be cautious? "We need to be ready. Prepare. I'm going to have my phratry ride out to the surrounding villages and get them to move into the city. They'll be safer behind Troas's walls."

I had always cursed the labyrinth walls but now I was grateful for them. Any sieging army would have an extremely difficult time against them.

Unless they were already inside. Hiding in plain sight, pretending to be Ilionian when they weren't. Like Artemisia. "Do you think there are people still in the city that are working for the enemy?"

His expression somehow turned even grimmer. "I hope not, but we won't have any way of knowing until it's too late."

That was ominous. "And your citizens will be unprepared if they attack again."

He nodded. "People don't want to believe that bad things are coming. They want to hang on to their normal lives and keep living them as they always have. It's easier."

"And more foolish," I said.

"And more foolish," he agreed. "But the people of Troas won't be caught totally unaware again. I ordered the security to be increased and strengthened. I had let it be a bit lax intentionally."

"Why?"

"Because I was hoping to catch Erisa in the act of attacking one of us. But trying to catch her is like trying to capture smoke."

No wonder it had been so easy for me to sneak out of the palace. Xander had used us both as bait. Part of me thought I should be outraged, but I was too tired and too emotionally wrung out to do more than say, "Oh."

"How . . ." His voice trailed off and he looked uncomfortable. It wasn't something I was used to seeing from him. "What happened at the temple?"

We were interrupted by Io shrieking with joy next door, and I assumed another lost pet had been returned to her.

"You might need to keep an eye on your sister," I said. "I'm worried that she's become a little bloodthirsty."

He nudged my knee with his and heat blossomed where his skin touched mine. "Because you're a bad influence." He said it jokingly, but his smile faltered when he saw my face. "What do you mean?"

"Io thinks we should kill whoever did this."

"I don't disagree with her. Why do you?"

Xander needed more of the story so that he could understand. I told him about finding Lysimache and shared her true backstory—that she had used magic to stay alive for a thousand years, waiting to exact her revenge on both Ilion and Locris because of what my ancestor, Ajax, had done to her sister, Kysandra, after the Great War ended.

"Lysimache intended to fight her way out but I didn't let her. I was so furious with her. I wanted to kill her," I said.

He shrugged. "And?"

I liked that he didn't judge me for things like this. That he understood.

"If your sister is right and I really am the savior . . . life is sacred to the goddess. I'm worried that in order to be worthy of her favor, I have to treat life as sacred, too. I knew I couldn't strike Lysimache down in anger and vengeance. I think it might have offended the goddess if I had. But it was a struggle. I stood there, wanting to, my sword raised, and then . . . I heard your voice. Telling me I could choose to be different. It gave me the strength to stop."

I heard him suck in a sharp breath, as if my words deeply affected him.

"We can both choose to be different," I said. I put my hand in his, and after a moment, his warm, strong fingers wrapped around mine. I kept talking, telling him how we'd found Antiope and how she'd said "hammer of Arion," a phrase he was unfamiliar with, and that Artemisia was involved with the people who spread the red dirt. "I remembered that she had a reddish-brown hammer tattoo on her chest like the one we saw on the enemy soldier in Lycia. I only wish I had remembered sooner."

"Why does that name sound familiar?"

"Artemisia?" I asked, and when he nodded, I said, "She was the one I fought the night of the new acolyte race."

"The one who hurt you. I already want to kill her."

That gave me an illicit thrill. I liked it far too much when he sounded deadly on my behalf. "There's a statue of the goddess in the temple, and it was covered in a thick layer of gold. Artemisia stole the gold."

His jaw clenched while he took in this information—I wondered if he was coming to the same conclusion that Zalira had about what Artemisia planned to do with that much wealth.

"Gold alone doesn't explain why she would slaughter everyone at the temple. Or why they came here intending to kill you and your adelphia."

My husband had always been far too clever for his own good. My chest felt impossibly tight as I worried about his reaction to what I was about to tell him. "I think she did it because . . . priestesses and acolytes can do magic."

CHAPTER FOUR

A long silence stretched between us as I waited for Xander's response.

"What?" he finally managed to say.

"My adelphia can do magic."

At that his eyebrows shot up his forehead. "Can you—"

"No," I interrupted him. "Not me. But everyone else can."

He seemed truly astonished. "What—how—what—"

I'd never seen him at a loss for words before. "That life mage apprentice they found passed out, the one you thought I had something to do with? I might have temporarily kidnapped him and forced him to tell me how magic works and then made him drink a potion that caused him to forget and fall asleep."

"I wish I could say I was surprised—"

"But you knew," I finished.

"I knew."

Because he knew me. And not just the pieces I wanted to show the world, the good and kind parts of me. He knew me at my absolute worst. The dark desires and jealousies and anger that I wanted to keep hidden—he had seen them all. I didn't think there was anyone who knew me the way he did.

Why hadn't I realized that before? I swallowed down the emotion I was feeling and instead continued my explanation.

"Priestesses and acolytes connect to an aspect of the goddess. And then when they say her name combined with the aspect, magical things happen. When Io did it for the first time, she used the life mage's words and made every single flower in the courtyard bloom. We're more powerful than the life mages and we don't need their amulets. I think magic was always intended for women."

"Io?" he echoed, and I realized how strange it must be to discover that his sister could wield magic.

"Performing magic drains them just like it does with the life mages. Io passed out and slept for hours before she recovered. Zalira thinks they need to train, and that it will strengthen them."

"You could go to the temple to train. I don't want anyone seeing what your sisters can do."

My sisters being condemned for using magic was a real possibility. The people in Ilion might consider it blasphemy because they had been told their entire lives that only men could do it.

One more thing I needed to question Lysimache about.

"That's a good idea," I said.

"What other powers do they have?" He tilted his head toward the wall we shared with Io's bedroom.

"Ahyana can control pollinators, which was why that cloud of bees appeared when we camped overnight on our way to Lycia. Zalira's always been connected to water and storms, but as far as I know, she hasn't had a chance to try her magic yet. And Suri—when Erisa asked how the five of us could bury the bodies so quickly, it was because Suri made a hole big enough by herself. She finds hidden things and manipulates the earth."

Another long silence. I understood. This was a lot to unload on him all at once.

"Can Artemisia do magic?"

"I don't know." By the goddess, I hoped not. That was the last thing we needed. "I have to assume that Lysimache told her that the women in the temple could potentially wield it." It would explain why Artemisia had gone to the effort of murdering them all, why she risked going to a heavily guarded palace to try and kill me and my adelphia.

That wasn't some grudge—she had wanted to make certain that no one could stand in her way.

"Now the five of you are all that's left."

"Yes. And Antiope, if she wakes up."

He began to absentmindedly rub his thumb against the back of my hand and I tried to ignore the warm tingles shooting up my arm.

"You're being very forthcoming," he said in a quiet tone.

Not entirely. I still hadn't told him about the eye of the goddess. I ignored the pang of guilt I felt and said, "Don't you think we should be?"

"By all means. I'm just a little concerned that you're some kind of shape-shifter and not actually my wife."

I smiled at his joke. "No, it's me."

Our gazes met and my stomach tightened at what I saw. The look in his eyes—it was the same as when he had hovered above me and told me that I would be his undoing. The honeyed wine might have pushed him into saying it, but despite his denial, it felt as honest now as it had then.

He cleared his throat and looked down at our joined hands. "Why is your hand sparkling?"

"Luna sneezed."

"She sneezes shimmering flakes?"

"Apparently." I was glad I wasn't the only one confused by her.

He let out a dramatic sigh. "Such a mess. I should have thrown her out the window the first night we found her."

I was prepared to become indignant on her behalf until I realized that he was joking. "Maybe this is why she won't talk to you."

"Maybe," he agreed. I loved that glimmer in his eyes, the way he half smiled at me.

Now I was the one clearing my throat and changing the subject. "Where is Lysimache?"

"She's in a safe house nearby."

"I need to question her to find out what she knows." I let out an accidental yawn, covering my mouth with my free hand.

He shook his head. "I will take you to her first thing in the morning. You need to rest. We both do."

I thought of the nightmares I'd had last night because I'd been out of his arms and was glad that I wouldn't have to deal with that again now that we were back together.

"Go and use the washroom first," he said.

A bath sounded divine. There was so much dirt under my fingernails from digging that I didn't know if they would ever be clean again. Not to mention the dried-over blood in the places that Lysimache had managed to superficially cut me. I stood up, and I wasn't sure if it was my imagination, but he seemed reluctant to release my hand.

I walked over to the washroom door and turned to see him watching me. A spike of longing pierced my gut, and I was struck with the urge to invite him to join me.

And given the heated, hungry look in his eyes, it felt like he knew exactly what I was thinking.

But he waited. Xander didn't speak, didn't make a move.

He was leaving it to me to act.

The words burned on my tongue, and I was about to say them when I heard Io exclaim, "You found Phoebe!" while Phoebe meowed loudly.

It brought me back to myself. This couldn't happen. I knew better.

He always made me forget. When I was with him, it was as if he were the only thing in the entire universe that mattered.

I went into the washroom, closing the door behind me.

But I didn't lock it.

While I undressed, I allowed myself to fantasize about him coming in here. What he would say, what he would do, the way he would make me feel . . . my skin began to flush in response.

I had just gotten into the water when the door opened. My heart leapt until I saw who it was. Io, Zalira, and Ahyana.

"We need baths, too," Zalira said as she shut the door.

"Where is Suri?" I asked as I reached for a bar of soap.

"She's looking for Priam, one of my mice," Io said. "She seems to think that my birds flew away but that Priam's still in the palace."

I wondered if that was the only reason she hadn't come with them. Suri usually bathed alone, and I assumed that was because she didn't want anyone to see the self-inflicted scars that she kept hidden under the wrappings on her arms.

As my sisters got into the pools, it occurred to me that if I had asked Xander to join me in my bath, and he'd said yes, Io would have found us in here together. She had been our biggest advocate, wanting us to be together, and now she was part of the reason I had to try and stay away from him.

Zalira let out a satisfied sigh and leaned her head against the edge of the pool. Io was talking about her ideas for new potions—she wanted to create a fortification one so that their magic would last longer and had already started planning out what plants she could use to separate my physical link with her brother.

When Io dunked her head into the water to rinse her hair, Ahyana took advantage of the temporary silence to say, "I know this is probably not the appropriate time to mention this, but there are no more temple guards."

She was right. I put a hand over my chest as if that could calm my galloping heartbeat. Zalira exchanged a worried glance with me.

Io lifted her head and pushed her hair out of her face. "And?" she asked, not immediately seeing where Ahyana was going with this like Zalira and I did.

"That means there's no one left to bury any of us alive if we break our vow of celibacy."

The look of panic on Io's face might have been comical in another situation. I decided to put her out of her misery. "I still have to use the eye to save Locris and need the goddess to find me worthy of wielding it. That hasn't changed."

"And you're the savior," she said. "You can't be the savior if you break her laws."

"That thought had occurred to me."

Io's reasons for wanting me to stay away from Xander were sound. Logical, even. It made sense. She didn't want him to be hurt if I left.

Or if I died.

He wasn't the only person who could potentially be harmed if he and I grew closer. I knew how easily my heart could be shattered and ruined. How I could become like my almost sister-in-law, Doria, perpetually waiting for my brother to return from the dead and not able to move on without him. I knew I had the potential to be exactly the same way.

The thought of Xander dying . . . it was almost more than I could bear.

"Have you done anything that might warrant temple guards?" Zalira asked Ahyana, and I was glad she had done it because I would have felt like a hypocrite if I'd been the one to ask.

"Not for lack of trying," Ahyana said in an annoyed tone. "Rokh is usually the one who stops. He says we need to get to know each other better first."

"Ahyana!" Zalira protested.

"I am an adult and can make my own decisions. Whatever happens between Rokh and me is just that—between us. I'm not interested in hearing anyone else's opinions about it." She briefly closed her eyes and exhaled sharply. "I'm sorry. I don't mean to sound harsh, but I love him and we are going to be together when this is all over. And now there's no reason that you can't do the same thing with Stephanos."

Zalira gasped slightly. I knew it was what she wanted more than anything—to be able to be with Stephanos again. To tell him that she loved him, as he had already told her. To completely bind their souls to one another.

Ahyana's face and voice softened. "Zalira, none of us know how much time we have left. Life is too short, and it might be even shorter for us. You should be allowed to love and be loved in return."

I thought I saw a tear go down Zalira's cheek but sensed that she wouldn't want me to call attention to it.

"We should get out," Io announced, apparently coming to the same conclusion that I had. "I think what we all need is a good night's rest."

We climbed out of the pools and dried ourselves off. It was then that I realized that they had brought tunics to change into and I had come into the washroom without one. I stood there awkwardly with my linen draped around me. When they were all dressed, Io said they would see me in the morning and they left, closing the washroom door behind them.

I listened as she spoke briefly to her brother and felt foolish for not asking her to grab me a tunic.

And I suspected that it was because my body had come up with a ludicrous plan to go out into our bedroom in my wet linen. The words Xander had said to me about the first time he'd seen me this way—

You were like the goddess herself emerging from the deeps. If it were not blasphemy, I would have fallen to my knees and worshipped you.

They were seared into my mind.

It was as if my brain simply ceased to function and my body took over on the decision-making, because once I heard the room go quiet, I opened the door and entered our bedroom.

CHAPTER FIVE

Xander jumped to his feet when he saw me and made a sound in the back of his throat that had my toes curling. His eyes devoured me, and I shivered under his gaze, my heart thumping in anticipation.

He walked toward me, and my breath caught.

But my ridiculous plan hadn't worked, as at the last moment he veered left and went into the washroom.

And he locked the door.

I had no right to feel crestfallen.

Nor could I continue to stand here pathetically waiting. I needed to get dressed. I glanced around and saw that probably several maids had come in and cleaned up our room, putting away my things. I was glad they had swept up the red dirt—I didn't like the idea of touching it with my bare feet.

I went over to one of my trunks and found something boring to wear to bed, instead of what I had been considering—the practically see-through nightgown I'd worn the night I was attempting to distract him so that I could sneak out. I shouldn't be trying to provoke him.

A bird cawed in the distance and I wondered if it was Rokh, which made me think about what Ahyana had just admitted. She had said that he held back in their physical interactions because he wanted them to get to know each other better. That told me that he hadn't shared his secret with her yet, that he was a shape-shifter and if he and Ahyana married and had children, their sons would be under the same curse that he was. They would suffer excruciating pain while being compelled to turn into ravens.

I wondered if he was delaying being intimate with her because of his secret.

Rokh wasn't the only one still keeping secrets. As I put my tunic over my head, I thought about how there was still so much I hadn't told Xander. I kept things from him and I suspected that he kept things from me. How could I want our relationship to become deeper when we couldn't even fully trust each other?

I tied my belt loosely, went over to my table, and grabbed my brush. I sat down and began to work it through my wet hair. Part of me didn't want to look at my own reflection because I was disappointed in myself.

Even if I wanted a closer connection with my husband, I knew it was selfish and put so much at risk, not to mention how much it would upset Io. I wanted to be strong. To do what was required of me.

A voice inside me whispered that maybe Ahyana had a point: If I really was fated to die, then I wouldn't be able to save Locris anyway. Wouldn't it be better to have a few days or weeks of happiness with him than not ever having it at all?

I hated how torn I felt. I reminded myself that there wasn't a future here—things would end with us one way or another. The problem was all rational thought fled when he was near.

It had been easier before, when I'd been using anger to drive a wedge between us. I wasn't sure how to hold on to my resolutions without it.

But I was done with being mad all the time, so I would have to find another way.

I decided to begin by making plans for myself. Perhaps if I stayed busy, it would help. Xander had already told me that he would take me to see Lysimache tomorrow. I wanted to be prepared—I would be going into a kind of battle—so I started braiding my hair.

Xander came into the room and I got a brief glimpse of his bare chest in my mirror. I didn't allow myself to look at him and tried to focus on my hair. I'd never been as good at this as Quynh was. And knowing that my husband was mostly naked behind me was not helping me to concentrate.

The strands kept slipping through my fingers and I had to restart an embarrassing number of times.

"Do you need help?" Xander asked, and it startled me. I was usually so aware of where he was and what he was doing—how had I not realized that he'd come to stand directly behind me?

"You know how to braid hair?"

"I do."

Send him away, I told myself. *Tell him you don't need help.* The very last thing I needed was those marvelous fingers of his running through my hair.

Instead of doing the wise thing, I opted, again, for the selfish one. "I do need help. Thank you."

"How many braids?"

"Three, one in the middle and one on each side, and then braid them all together in the back."

I had to stifle a moan when he pressed his fingers against my scalp to separate out strands. He took to his task quickly and I forced myself to pay attention to what he was doing instead of focusing on how amazing it felt. The intimacy of this moment was overwhelming.

He was quick and efficient, which shouldn't have surprised me. His braids were smooth and even and tight against my head.

My husband really was good at everything he did. "How do you know how to do this?" I asked, mostly to distract myself.

"It's very simple and doesn't take much to learn. You just need to practice."

The anger that I'd tried to banish wanted to rise, accompanied by jealousy. That ugly monster inside me wanted to roar and demand that he tell me who else's hair he had braided.

I closed my eyes for a moment and took in a calming breath. I wasn't going to do that anymore. I wouldn't jump to the worst possible conclusion.

If I couldn't master the desire I felt for him, at the very least I could control my anger and stop letting it rule me.

He immediately made me glad that I'd made that choice when he said, "I used to do this for Io. The women from my mother's nation always braided their hair at night, and our mother would do that for Io. After she died Erisa was trying very hard to curry favor with my father and wanted to braid Io's hair. Io would scream and wouldn't allow her to do it. Erisa forbade any of the servants from helping and I was the only one who could do it without risking bodily harm. So I braided her hair every night for years until she could do it herself."

He was only a few years older than Io. I imagined him as a little boy, as I'd seen him in our shared dream, dedicating himself to learning how to braid his sister's hair to comfort her and make her feel loved, and a swelling of warmth filled my heart.

I looked at his reflection. "Erisa did inflict bodily harm on you."

"It's only a scar," he said, his eyes meeting mine in the mirror.

And I thought about how the scar on his face was just one of so many. His life had been full of scars, one after another, piling up on top of each other so that it was a marvel he was still moving forward, still striving.

A lesser man might have crumbled under the weight of it. He was so strong.

I felt guilty that I had inflicted some scars on him as well.

"Tie," he said, and it took me a moment to realize that he'd completed the first braid and needed something to finish it off with. I opened a drawer and pulled out some twine, handing one length of it to him and keeping extra strands for the others.

"Io doesn't do that anymore," I told him. I'd never seen her braid her hair before bed.

"That doesn't surprise me," he said, finishing the first braid and starting on the second. I had to fight off a sigh. How could something be so soothing and stimulating all at the same time? "I think when Io moved to the temple, she put a lot of things from the past behind her. She wanted to start over, have a different life."

And now she was back in the palace, forced to be near the woman who had abused her and having her life threatened on a constant basis because of me. I didn't want her to be in danger. "I'm sorry that she came here for me."

At that he stopped and stared at our shared reflection. "I'm not. Her being here saved her life. If she had been in that temple . . ."

Io would have been killed. Something that had nearly taken out Antiope would have crushed Io first thing.

I saw him swallow hard. "I'm sorry that I accused you of putting Io's life in danger while you were in the temple together. I shouldn't have done that. I shouldn't have blamed you."

My lungs couldn't manage to gather in air. That was something he had said he would never forgive me for, and now here he was apologizing for it. My throat felt too thick and it prevented me from speaking. I nodded.

He went back to braiding and worked in silence. I was too overwhelmed by what he had just said. Should I apologize to him for the things I had wrongly held against him?

I hadn't been wrong about everything I'd accused him of. Dolion, his own phratry brother, had confirmed that Xander had known who I was the moment he had stepped foot in Locris, something he continued to deny.

What would he do if I asked him to just be honest about it? I wasn't angry about it any longer because I knew that had our positions been reversed, I would have done the very same thing.

But this was such a nice moment that I didn't want it ruined. So instead I stayed silent. I handed him the ties when he requested them.

He was combining all three braids when he said, "It's not like you to be so quiet."

"I . . . have a lot on my mind," I said.

"We all do."

The last few days had been nightmarishly horrendous. The atrocities we had seen—they changed everything. Before we had gone to Lycia, I'd planned to tell him that I wanted us to have separate rooms.

Now I didn't want to be apart from him, even if it was unwise.

"All done," he said.

"Thank you." We looked at each other in the mirror and it made the memories of him undressing me in front of my full-length mirror flood into my mind.

I wondered if he was thinking the same thing, if he noticed how my breathing had gone shallow.

"We should go to sleep," he said, and he started his nightly walk around the room, putting out the lights.

I got up and went to my side of the bed and climbed in. My palms were clammy, my heart was racing. I was nervous and didn't know why. We had done this so many times already, but tonight felt different for some reason. He put out the last candle and I felt him get into bed beside me.

He lay there for a little while before he turned and said, "Are you going to . . ."

Taking that as my invitation, I snuggled in closer to him. He put his arms around me, but his hold felt tentative. Usually he was so sure of himself. We had both let our guards down and were in a new, strange place.

One I had promised his sister we wouldn't be in.

Even when we'd been angry, we'd always been drawn to each other, two flames burning so bright and hot that we would leave nothing but ashes in our wake. I put my hand on his bare chest, letting the steady beat of his heart comfort and soothe me.

I still felt strange. This was like it had been in the beginning, when he'd first started holding me while we slept. I remembered how we'd have stilted conversations about our days and everything felt awkward until it didn't.

"I need to learn to ride a horse," I announced, looking up at him.

He turned his head toward me. "Why? Were you planning on fleeing in the middle of the night?"

I smiled at his teasing tone. "No. But I need to learn how."

"Io could show you. Maybe you can practice on your way to the temple to train."

Disappointment made my shoulders drop. I had wanted him to teach me. "What do we do next?"

"Sleep."

"No, I meant what do we do about Ilion being attacked?"

He hesitated before answering. "I thought you planned on seeing my entire nation burned to the ground."

"Not anymore. People I love are here." I regretted the words as soon as I said them, as they made the awkwardness of the moment intensify. He tensed with what I guessed was surprise, and I considered going back over to my own side of the bed and dealing with whatever nightmares might come.

Would he think I was talking about him?

"I'm concerned that none of our spies saw this coming," he said, and I was intensely grateful that he changed the subject. "Rokh has been trying to track them down and hasn't been able to find a single one."

How could his spies have just disappeared? "Do you think Erisa had something to do with them going missing?"

"I wouldn't know who else to blame. I'm going to recruit new spies and have them report directly to Thrax, so that no one else will know their identities or locations. We will also have to gather what allies we can. I'll have to send out riders with messages."

"We don't know what direction the enemy will attack from." Those riders could be heading directly into a trap.

"Which also presents a problem," he agreed. "But if those messengers see an approaching army, they can ride back quickly and warn us."

"And you're planning on bringing in the people outside of Troas."

"Yes. I'm going to send my phratry brothers and members of the army that I know I can trust to every village, town, and city to convince the people to come to Troas so that they can be safe behind the walls."

I remembered how he had said people didn't want to believe the worst was coming, that they wanted to stick their heads in the sand and ignore it. "What if they won't come? If they don't believe your men?"

"I've already thought of that. I'm going to try and use Erisa's party to gather them in."

"Using your stepmother's diversion to your advantage."

I saw the ends of his mouth curl up in a satisfied smile. "Yes. And if that doesn't work, they'll tell them about the attack and that they're not safe out in the open."

"What if they don't listen?"

"I can't force anyone to come. And without the council's support . . ." He let out a frustrated sigh. "If only I were king. Everything would be so different."

He was right. Everything would be different.

Our contract would be ended. He wouldn't have need of me any longer.

Would . . . would that change things between us?

What if he wanted to find a true wife?

CHAPTER SIX

Despite how tired I was, I hadn't slept much the night before. As if I didn't have enough to be anxious about already, now I had to worry about Xander being named king and telling me he needed to find a real wife. I supposed, in the end, it wouldn't matter if he let me stay in the palace or not—my goals would remain the same. Get the eye of the goddess and restore Locris.

And find a way to stop Artemisia.

I didn't have to be sleeping next to him every night to stop her.

When I dropped by my adelphia's room to tell them that I was going to interrogate Lysimache, Io insisted on coming with me. Xander walked both of us down to the stables, with the siblings chatting the whole way. I didn't pay attention to what they were discussing because I couldn't stop thinking about what it would feel like if Xander told me that it was time for our marriage to end.

My stomach churned. The thought of never seeing him again . . . at one time it had been the only thing I wanted, and now it felt like the worst kind of punishment.

When we got to the stables, one of the servants brought out the horse his mother's family had given me as a wedding gift.

At first glance the horse almost looked white, but when I got closer, I saw that it was a goldish/silverish color and its coat and mane seemed to shimmer in the sunlight.

"She's so beautiful," I said.

"Come say hello," Io told me. "Give her a treat and she'll love you forever." She handed me a parsnip and I offered it to the horse. The horse took it quickly and I brushed my hand down her nose.

"Do you like her?" Xander asked.

I couldn't keep the grin off my face. "I can't believe she's mine."

"You'll need to use a stool to help you mount, but today I can just do this." He came over and put his hands on my waist and lifted me up so that I sat on the horse. I felt so many things at once—swoony at how strong he was, lightheaded from being close to him and lifted up so quickly, thrilled that he was touching me. "Swing your leg over."

I did as he asked and was sitting on the horse. The leather saddle was small and a blanket had been folded up on top of it, probably to make me more comfortable.

Xander lifted Io onto her horse and then got onto his own by leaping up quickly. It was one of the most attractive things I'd ever seen. His black horse was massive and powerful, and Xander looked like an angry storm god about to ride off into battle, destroying anyone who dared to stand against him.

"I thought Rokh said that we got a matched set as a gift," I said, ignoring the way my mouth had gone dry.

"We did. But the male is a stallion and has to be kept away from the mares," he said. I was about to ask why and then realized it on my own. It was perhaps a problem that the stallion and I had in common—I should be kept away from Xander.

Maybe it would be a good thing if he told me to go after he was made king.

"When did you get your horse?" Now I was just saying inane things and didn't know what was wrong with me. *I should stay silent.*

"Aides has been with me for the last five years." It was easy to see how much he adored his horse, and for some reason that just made me like him more.

Io was crooning to her own horse and I suddenly realized just how far off the ground I was.

Xander started explaining to me what to do, in a calm, soft voice. He told me how to use the reins and that I shouldn't sit as if I were in a chair, but like I was standing with my legs apart while riding. He told me how to use my legs and the reins to get the horse to go in a different direction or to stop or speed up.

"But we'll start off at a walk today," he said. "Follow me."

Io and Xander rode their horses out, and mine, thankfully, followed behind them. It was an unfamiliar sensation, swaying as the horse walked. It reminded me of being on the *Nikos*, the ship that had brought me and Quynh to Ilion.

I hoped I wouldn't get whatever the horse version of seasick was.

The house was thankfully close by and Xander jumped down and handed his horse's reins to a guard stationed outside the front door. He went over to help Io dismount and then it was my turn. He held out his arms and I swung my right leg over and reached for him.

His hands were at my waist and I crashed into his chest. He held me close as I slid slowly down the hard length of his body. My breathing had gone sharp and irregular and my entire body tingled with delight at being like this with him. His hands tightened around my waist, as if he were trying to draw me even closer, and it caused my heart to pump violently in my chest while bright, fiery sparks lit up my veins.

"You good?" he asked, his voice a rough silk whisper that created unmentionable images in my mind.

I could only nod. I wasn't sure that I would ever be this good again.

Io coughed loudly and I turned to see the mixture of disappointment and concern on her face. I stepped back from Xander and immediately missed his warmth.

"I have some things to do, so I'll see you at the palace later," he said.

Again I could only nod and watch as he got back up on Aides and trotted off.

I walked over to Io, expecting her to scold me. It was somehow worse that she didn't. Thrax was inside the house, waiting for us.

"She's upstairs," he said with a nod of his head. "And don't expect her to be very talkative. She hasn't said a word since we brought her here. She's also been refusing to eat and drink."

Lysimache could go for a long time without eating, but she had to drink something. I didn't want her to die from dehydration before she answered our questions.

"Thank you," I said. "How is Quynh?"

His whole face lit up at her name, and that helped to soften me even more toward him. It was obvious how much he loved my sister. "She's doing well. She and my sister, Basileia, are becoming good friends."

"Xander mentioned something about her being able to protect Quynh."

"She's supposed to take over as chieftain of our clan after my mother dies, and I've never seen her lose a fight. You would like her."

I suspected that I might. I thanked him again and then Io and I went upstairs.

We greeted Stephanos, who stood outside the room. I knew that Xander wanted his phratry to help him gather in citizens outside Troas's walls, and I appreciated the fact that they were here, watching over Lysimache.

Your husband did that for you, that voice inside me whispered. I ignored it while Stephanos had me give him my weapons; Io wasn't carrying any. I made a mental note to tell her to start wearing some. We all needed to be prepared.

"Just a precaution," he said as I handed over my knives and sword.

He couldn't have thought that I would kill her. I was the one trying to keep her alive. Or perhaps they wanted to make sure that Lysimache couldn't steal a weapon from one of us.

Stephanos opened the door and ushered us into the room.

Lysimache had removed her armor and was bandaged in several different places. They had brought a healer for her, and while I would have enjoyed the idea of her suffering, I was glad she wouldn't bleed out anytime soon.

The room was minimal—she had a bed and a table and a chair. A tray of uneaten food sat on the table and she was seated in front of it. I noticed that she hadn't been given any utensils.

"If it isn't the traitor and her little mouse," Lysimache said with a sneer.

Stephanos stood in the doorway and said, "That is Princess Thalia and Princess Iolanthe to you and you will treat them with respect."

Her eyebrows lifted and a smile played at the corners of her mouth. "You hid that very well, didn't you, Io? I suppose that makes us family."

"You aren't the first person in my family who deserves to die," she snapped back, and this served to only amuse the high priestess.

"The little mouse has grown fangs!"

I heard Stephanos muttering something, so I quickly turned around. "We can handle this. Would you wait downstairs? I'll call if I need you."

"Are you sure?"

"Yes. We'll be fine." I wasn't at all worried about my ability to subdue Lysimache if need be.

I was, however, a bit concerned about possibly having to restrain Io.

"Don't worry, Io," Lysimache said after Stephanos had shut the door. "My end is coming soon."

"Yes, I heard you haven't been eating and drinking," I said. "That seems like a pathetic way to die."

The smile slid off her face. "If you wanted to give me a sword, I'd be happy to go out fighting."

"With as weak as you are right now? That would be a short and boring fight."

Her eyes flashed with anger. "What is it that you want?"

"Answers," I said.

"And you think that I'll give them to you?"

"I do. What good is it doing all this plotting and planning if you don't get to tell anyone the details?" I asked. I glanced over at Io. She was vibrating with anger. I took a step to the left to adjust my position so that I was between the two women. Just in case.

Lysimache nodded. "Yes, you should know how you made those plans possible."

She was trying to goad me into anger but I wasn't going to let her do it. "How did you curse Locris?"

"I told you that already. I used the eye of the goddess."

"No," I said with a shake of my head. "What words did you say when you called on the goddess, Dea? What aspect did you use?"

She made a surprised sound, and her mouth turned into a round O. "How do you know any of that?"

"I kidnapped a life mage and got him to talk."

"Again, Princess Thalia, I underestimated you," she said, that amused, mocking smile returning to her face. "I'm happy to tell you. I used the goddess's fury aspect and said 'Dea Erinys,' envisioning the whole land turning to dust."

It was obvious why she didn't have an issue telling me—using that aspect couldn't reverse the curse. Fury led to destruction, not creation.

If the fury aspect was what Lysimache had connected to, then why didn't she wield her magic when she said the words? Or pass out?

"Are you wondering why nothing just happened?" she asked, and it bothered me that she could so easily read my thoughts. "I have been cut off from using the goddess's power since I cursed Locris. I haven't felt or heard her in over a millennium. I imagine it's her way of punishing me."

"And you made sure that no other priestesses and acolytes could tap into that power themselves by taking away their knowledge of how to do so. Destroying the books and changing what was taught in the temple." Letting Artemisia strike them all down so that they wouldn't be able to perform magic against her.

"Fortunately for me, your people had managed to kill or kidnap most of the women who were still at the temple in Troas, so it was easy to begin anew."

"Why go back to the temple? Why not take over as queen and rule?" I asked.

"There's no power in government. All the power is in religion. If you control people's beliefs, you can control them. I only had to wait a generation or two to start changing everything. You let the elders die off, you destroy every book and text about religion, and then you tell the people what to believe and how to worship. It was almost laughable how quick the men were to embrace the idea that the goddess had intended magic only for them, the ridiculous way they treasured their amulets and the fraction of power they could tap into. They called themselves 'life mages' and put themselves into the upper echelons of society even though they could do so little."

"So what's true and what's not?" I asked. "What are the goddess's laws and what did you make up for your own amusement?"

Her mouth twitched as if she was suppressing a smile. "We are done talking, Princess Thalia."

Anger rose up suddenly, viciously. It was a good thing Stephanos had taken my weapons. I briefly considered going downstairs and getting my sword back. I was trying to follow the goddess and respect life, even in people who didn't deserve to have it. I needed her to see me as worthy, to not risk her anger.

If I didn't kill the high priestess, I wondered how mad the goddess would be about me cutting off both of Lysimache's hands instead.

"What will it take to get you to answer our questions?" Io asked. She sounded calm but I recognized that tone. It was the same one her brother had when he was beyond furious.

I wasn't sure why Io had asked. What could we offer the high priestess? I certainly wasn't going to release her. I intended for her to spend the rest of her life locked up.

Lysimache considered Io's question. I expected her to stay silent, so I was surprised when she said, "Water."

"You don't have water?" Io pointed toward the tray, where there were several full cups of it.

"I want water from the fountain at the temple. I miss the taste. City water is foul."

That wasn't why she wanted it. She wanted to keep her strength up. She was going to try and escape. Lysimache still hadn't realized that we knew what that fountain water did.

"We can do that," Io said, and it took everything in me not to intervene. What was she doing? "But first you must drink one of those cups. We can't have you dying of thirst before we can fetch the water for you."

After a few moments the high priestess picked up the cup nearest her and drank the entire thing, showing it to Io when she had finished.

Io took me by the arm and said, "We'll be back tomorrow."

She hurried me out of the room before I could protest and led me down the stairs. Stephanos waited at the bottom. "All finished?"

"For now," Io said. I wanted to question her but thought it would be better to wait until we were alone.

He handed me back my weapons and I thanked him.

"Will you . . . will you tell Zalira that I'm thinking of her?" he asked, and I felt so sad at the pain in his voice.

"I will," I said. I probably shouldn't. It might hurt her to be reminded of how much he loved her.

But if I were in her sandals, I would want to know.

Io and I left the house and retrieved our horses. They didn't have a stool here for us, so we decided to walk the horses back. When we were far enough away that no one would overhear us, I asked her, "What are you doing?"

"Returning to the palace."

"No, why did you agree to Lysimache's demand? She obviously wants to use the water to overpower her guards and break out."

A determined look furrowed her brow. "I'm sure that's her plan. But I need her to drink it because I know how to make her talk."

CHAPTER SEVEN

When we got back to the palace, Io decided to stay behind and work on her potions while the rest of us went to the temple. She promised she would share her scheme to get Lysimache to talk later and that she'd spoken to her brother about having one of his phratry members watch over her so she wouldn't be alone.

The current plan was for us to gather fountain water and to try out Zalira's magic in the gymnasium. I asked my sisters if they wanted to practice riding and take horses there, but none of them needed the practice. They all knew how to ride.

But they humored me and we rode to the temple. While I still didn't care much for horseback riding, it was nice that it took so much less time than walking would have.

Io had asked me earlier what I planned on naming my horse, and I decided on Eos. Like Themis's granddaughter, named after the dawn, because of how she shimmered.

One of the stable hands had attached a small cart to Ahyana's horse. It was filled with empty vases for the water.

When we arrived I was surprised to see a group of women gathered at the gate. We dismounted, which for me was basically falling off the horse, and tied their reins to a nearby column. We made our way through the crowd to the gate and Suri pushed it open.

Realizing that we meant to go in, someone asked, "Who are you?"

"We are acolytes," Zalira said.

A woman stepped forward and asked, "When will we be able to return to the temple and worship? To ask the goddess for her help and her blessings?"

"Not yet," Ahyana said, gently and kindly. "But we hope soon."

"Where are all the other priestesses?" another woman asked. "We have heard so many different things."

"It's a long story," Zalira said. "We will let you know when you can return to the temple to worship."

Some of the women immediately left, while others stayed behind, as if we would change our minds within the next few minutes. I greeted the guards Xander had left to watch over the temple and told them that I was Princess Thalia and we were going to be coming every day to the temple.

"We were already informed," one of the men said to me.

We went into the courtyard and Suri closed the gate behind us.

"You don't think we should tell those women what happened to the servants of the temple?" Ahyana asked.

Zalira shook her head. "Not until it's announced that we're at war. We don't want anyone panicking."

It was exactly what Xander had said to me. I wondered how Zalira knew that. Or had she just come to that same conclusion on her own?

Ahyana and Suri were walking ahead of us, so I took advantage of the opportunity to tell Zalira, "I'm not sure if I should mention this, but I saw Stephanos this morning. He wanted me to tell you that he's thinking of you."

She smiled sadly and put a hand over her heart. "I'm glad you told me. It is so strange to miss and love someone so much and have them close at hand all the time."

"I understand."

"I'm sure you do. How are things with you and your husband?"

She was the only member of my adelphia that I felt like I could be open with about this. "Strange. I want to be close to him, but I'm afraid that once he's made king, he might send me away to find a new wife. And Io is worried about the savior prophecy and that I might die. And if I do live, I'm going back to Locris to reopen the temple there. She's afraid that either way I'll hurt her brother. She thinks he's in love with me. So she made me promise that I would stay away from him and not hurt him."

"Which I'm guessing isn't going so well."

It was scary how Zalira could read me. "Yes. I want him physically, I want him emotionally. Every way that you can want someone, I want him. And it terrifies me. To let someone else have that much power over me . . ."

I didn't want to be consumed.

And I knew that Xander could absolutely have that kind of effect on me.

Zalira let out a short laugh. "I know exactly what you mean."

"I don't know what to do."

"That makes two of us," she said with a sigh. "I keep thinking about what Ahyana said. That the temple guards are dead and so there's not anyone to punish us any longer. But that's not the reason that I've held back. It's because I made that promise to the goddess herself and I can't go back on my word."

That felt like a thunderclap inside my chest. I certainly hadn't wanted to get buried alive, but that was never the main reason why I had refrained—I had to keep my vows so that the goddess would help me restore Locris.

When I didn't say anything, Zalira put her arm around my shoulders. "I'm sorry this is so hard for you."

"And I'm sorry this is so hard for you," I said. "It feels wrong to be worried about my relationship with him when so many terrible things are happening."

"Terrible things are always happening, Lia. In times like this, we need to hold on to the things that bring us joy. The things that make life worth living. We should laugh when we can, love when we can. That's a very human thing to do. Feeling that way doesn't mean you're wrong."

We entered the gymnasium and my gaze darted over to the dais where I had fought Lysimache before I captured her. The wood was still stained with her blood.

Zalira walked into the center of the room and I ignored the shiver that passed through me. It was eerie being back here. This room had once teemed with women training and sparring, and now it was just us, trying to see if we could control magic. We came over to stand in front of her in a semicircle.

"You'll be struck with a surge of power," Ahyana told her older sister. "It feels like burning and freezing at the same time. It will drain you almost instantly and that's when you pass out. Try to hold on for as long as you can."

What if Zalira was like me and couldn't do magic? Would she be disappointed? I knew that I was.

Zalira nodded. She shook her hands and jumped in place three times, like she was preparing to start fighting. She let out a deep breath and then said, "Dea Maimaktes."

A booming clap of thunder shook the entire building and then rain started pouring down hard, like tiny missiles striking the roof. Zalira held on. Ahyana and Io had collapsed by now, but Zalira was toughing it out. Wind shrieked all around us and lightning flashed outside, so big and bright that it turned the sky purple.

She let out a groan of pain and dropped to her knees. "It . . . hurts."

It hurt to do magic? No one else had said that. Maybe because they had passed out before this point.

Zalira lifted her head and I gasped. "Your eyes are green!"

"Why are you all surrounded in white light?" she asked right before she collapsed to the ground.

The storm dissipated immediately, as if it had never been.

We all stood there in shock. Zalira's magic had been so powerful and had lasted for longer than anyone else's. "None of us were watching when Ahyana and Io did magic. Do you think your eyes changed colors, too?" I asked.

"We can find out," Ahyana said.

Before I could tell her not to, she said "Dea Karpophoroi," and a group of leather-winged creatures flew in through one of the upper windows and landed in the rafters.

She made sure to look at us, and her eyes were indeed the same shade of emerald green that I'd seen on Zalira.

"What are those?" I asked, pointing up.

"Bats," Ahyana said through clenched teeth as she dropped to her knees. "I thought about what animal I wanted to come and they did. Zalira's right. This hurts."

"Do you see lights around me and Suri?" I asked.

"Yes." She breathed the word out and then fell next to her sister.

Suri and I exchanged glances. How were we going to get them both back to the palace? We didn't have the room. She raised one eyebrow at me as if to ask—*Now what?*

"We're going to need a bigger cart," I said.

It only took a few hours for Zalira and Ahyana to wake up, and they both felt refreshed and invigorated. I had thought they might sleep longer, given how long they'd kept using the magic, but that didn't seem to be the case.

When we got back to the palace, it was late—we had missed dinner. I was hungry but I was also in a great deal of pain. The others went off in search of food and I stumbled upstairs to my room. I considered checking in on Io, but all I wanted to do was go and lie down. My thighs and buttocks were sore, and my abdomen felt like I'd been punched. I got into my room, patted Luna, and then lay in my bed, not wanting to move. This had to be from riding Eos.

Someone should have told me that riding a horse would hurt. This was worse than the day after my first training session with Demaratus.

Wanting to distract myself, I thought about all that had happened today. Not just the way my adelphia had performed magic, but being back in the gymnasium had made me relive what Lysimache had said to me there. She had repeatedly told me that she and I were the same. That I would have made the same decisions she did.

Her aspect was fury.

If we truly were the same . . . what if that was mine as well?

I was so glad that Maia had made us memorize the list containing the names of the various aspects of the goddess.

"Dea Erinys."

Power slammed into me, filling me with icy heat and fiery cold. I felt connected to everything around me, brimming with an energy that made me think I could do anything. Conquer the world. Vanquish every foe.

And it was all underlined by a throbbing beat of unimaginable anger.

Then the world went black.

"Lia?" I awoke to see Xander leaning over me, looking concerned. "What happened?"

I felt disoriented. "What?"

"Did you get yourself beat up today?" he asked, gesturing toward his legs. "I can feel your pain."

That caused me to become aware again of the throbbing sensation that had been blocked while I'd been unconscious. "I think it's from riding my horse."

Understanding lit up his features. "Some people do get sore after riding for the first time. But you'll get used to it. It's often the same way with sex for women."

He said it so matter-of-factly, but his words made my entire body flush with heat. Almost like I was performing magic again.

This was not something I could think about right now. "I think I have a power."

"What is it?" he asked, interested. He sat down on the bed next to me. I moved into a sitting position.

"Fury."

He blinked a couple of times but didn't respond.

"You're not going to say anything?" I finally asked.

"Were you expecting me to be surprised? It seems about right."

I sighed. "I'm trying to not be vengeful and angry. To choose differently." I didn't want this to be my aspect.

"I understand, but remember that there is such a thing as righteous fury. You can be upset about the evils that people do and use your outrage to protect others. You don't have to shy away from the parts of you that you think are dark. They can help you and drive you just as much as the others."

"I don't even know what it can do." It could apparently curse a nation and turn it into a wasteland, but I didn't know how else to utilize it.

"Fighting," he said, like I was foolish for not immediately realizing it. "Come on. Get your xiphos."

He pulled a dagger out from his belt and I realized that it was the one I'd given him on our wedding day. Why did that make my heart beat faster?

I stood up, ignoring the pain I felt. "I thought we weren't going to fight anymore."

"I'll go easy on you," he said with a grin.

"I'm going to pass out. Like life mages do."

"Oh." He grabbed the pillows from our bed and put them on the floor. "I'll catch you before you hit the ground, but this is just a secondary precaution."

"Are you ready?" I asked.

He nodded, looking excited.

"Dea Erinys."

The power rushed into me again and I was ready for it this time. It was the same power I'd always felt humming in the ground at the temple, just out of reach. Now it was here and I could weaponize it. Use it to destroy.

A part of my brain registered that a white light surrounded his entire body; this was what Zalira and Ahyana had seen. But the rest of me just wanted to fight.

I lunged at Xander and was thrilled by the shock on his face when I nearly cut his chest. I was almost as fast as he was, almost as strong. He blocked me with his dagger and then spun to the left to come at me from that direction, but I was ready. I stopped his advance and went to elbow him in the face but he moved away at the last moment.

Now he wasn't the only one who was goddess-blessed.

He tried to knock my sword loose but I wouldn't permit it. I twisted out of his way, keeping my grip, and then sliced at him from his right side. He again moved at the last moment.

We had broken apart, studying one another, when the pain started. Not the aches I'd been feeling from horseback riding, but sharp, shooting barbs—as if I were repeatedly being stabbed in every part of my body.

I saw the concern in his eyes and heard him say, "Are you all—"

And as promised, he caught me before I hit the ground.

CHAPTER EIGHT

"How long have I been asleep?" I asked when I finally came to.

"A couple of hours," Xander said. He had put me in bed—a pillow under my head and my blanket tucked in around me. I felt very cared for.

"That was unlike anything I've ever seen!" He offered me a glass of water and I eagerly took it and drank. "Not quite punch-a-goose exciting, but that was something. All those times you threatened to kill me and now you could actually do it."

I supposed he was right. That seemed like an odd thing to be grinning about, though. "What good does it do me? I can only keep it up for a short amount of time."

"Like you said, you'll need to practice. Build up your endurance."

"Get used to the pain," I said. At his quizzical expression I explained what it felt like and how there was excruciating pain that would cause me to pass out—that the pain seemed to increase with every moment that I stayed in the magic. He listened intently, hanging on my every word.

It reminded me of what he'd been like in our shared dreams.

"Why is fury one of the aspects of the goddess?" he asked.

I told him the story I'd learned at the temple—that when the goddess discovered her daughter missing, she had searched far and wide for her. When she found out that her son had sold her daughter into marriage with the god of war, she drew out her golden sword and intended to fight the war god. The other gods intervened, attempting to assuage her fury, and she went and hid herself in a cave. She swore that she wouldn't let anything grow until her daughter was returned to her. The goddess's mother finally convinced her to come out of the cave and save the world from the famine they'd been suffering under. She agreed, and a bargain was struck so that her daughter was allowed to join the goddess for certain months during the year. But when she is returned to her husband, the goddess still lets the earth go cold so that nothing will grow.

"It seems to me that her fury got her what she wanted. The return of her daughter," he said after I had finished.

"I suppose it did." I tried to stretch but my thighs were still throbbing.

He seemed to know this, which was most likely due to his own still hurting as well. He glanced down at my legs and said in a light tone, "I would offer to massage them for you, but . . ."

That would be bad. Very, very bad. Not good and amazing. Bad. "I'm fine." I croaked the words out, and the look in his eyes made me think that he knew exactly what I was currently envisioning. The thought of his hands on my thighs made me feel lightheaded.

Or maybe that was the effect of the magic wearing off.

"Did you feel the pain of the magic?" I asked.

"No, I only feel your physical pain."

Interesting. Did that mean the pain wasn't real? If it was in my head, could I somehow fortify myself against it so that I could keep going?

"Now that I know you're safe, I'm going to go take a bath."

Xander stood and took off his tunic in a slow and deliberate way that felt like an invitation. My skin heated in response, my breath stuttered in my chest, and I gripped my blanket with both hands.

But he turned around, went into the washroom, and locked the door. Shutting me out again.

Xander was gone the next morning when I woke up. I felt completely invigorated and excited as I got ready for the day. My physical aches had disappeared. The sleep had been healing, as seemed to be the case after we used magic.

My adelphia were all in their room talking to one another when I entered. They fell silent as I closed the door, perhaps seeing on my face that I had something to tell them.

"I have an aspect," I said. It thrilled me to be able to tell them that. I was so glad that I wasn't powerless.

Ahyana shrieked with glee while Zalira grinned and asked, "What is it?"

"Fury. Which is good for fighting, apparently, and not much else. It was the aspect Lysimache used to destroy Locris with the eye. I tried it out on Xander last night and I could keep up with him!"

Io's smile faltered slightly at that. "Xander knows about the magic? I thought we weren't going to tell anyone."

My mouth dropped slightly. I wasn't sure how to respond to that. Because sharing secrets with my husband was not keeping him at arm's length. It was inviting him into my life.

"It's good that she did," Ahyana said. "We should be able to tell people that we trust."

I knew she was trying to help, but this just seemed to upset Io even more. I noted the dark circles under her eyes and wondered if it was stress or if she hadn't been sleeping well. "Did you get up early this morning?"

Suri folded her arms over her chest in apparent annoyance as Zalira told me, "Io didn't sleep at all. We told her to, but she didn't listen."

"I'm so close!" she said. "I think I figured out a fortification potion so that we can do magic for longer. And since Ahyana told me about the pain, I'm in the process of adding something to dull that."

"Maybe the pain is important," Zalira said in a worried tone. "We might need to know when we reach the end of our limits and not push ourselves too hard. What if we burn out and then never wake up?"

"I'll figure it out," Io said.

Zalira had a point, but I also trusted Io to know what she was doing. "Are we going to see Lysimache this morning?" I asked her.

Io still hadn't told me her plan to get the high priestess to talk, but she was ready to share now. "No, I'm not done. I'm taking a page out of my father's book and we're going to give her the truth serum with the fountain water. The metallic taste of the water will disguise it. I'm trying to figure out a serum that will compel her to speak so that she has to answer your questions. I'm hoping to have it done by tomorrow."

"Shouldn't you take a break?" Ahyana asked while Suri vigorously nodded behind her.

"I'm fine," Io said with a wave of her hand. "I've been taking the fortification potion and it's working well. I don't feel even a little bit tired. And Xander stopped by this morning on his way out and I told him we're not ready to see Lysimache yet. So he thought you might like to visit Quynh."

I would get to see Quynh! There was a knock at their door and my heart lifted as I opened it.

That feeling went away when I saw that it wasn't Xander. It was Rokh.

Which made Ahyana giddy, and she rushed over to hug him. "What are you doing here?"

"Xander asked me to take you and Lia to where Quynh is staying. You and I are seen together so often that no one will question your adelphia sister joining us for a walk," he said, his dark eyes drinking Ahyana in.

Even if I was disappointed that Xander wouldn't be accompanying me, I was so happy that I was going to visit my sister! It had been such a long time since we'd last spoken. I needed to make sure that things were right between us. I had made an effort to be nicer to Thrax. I hoped he had told her.

And that she wouldn't be angry because of how I'd treated him. Though I wouldn't blame her if she was.

Since Ahyana and I were both ready to leave, we headed out. I had to ignore the lovebirds as they kept paying each other compliments and laughing over private jokes.

Perhaps my annoyance was something residual from invoking the fury aspect. Was I going to start being short-tempered and wanting to punch things again? I hoped not. I didn't like how the anger had taken over my life, blocking out everything else.

It seemed like the goddess had a very ironic sense of humor where I was concerned.

I looked down at my hands and thought about what it was like when power coursed through me. I had felt utterly invincible.

When we walked through the palace gates, Ahyana slipped her arm through Rokh's and he was murmuring things in her ear while she giggled. Given what she'd said a few minutes ago, I assumed that she had already told him about her magic. I couldn't imagine her keeping it from him. I wondered if it would make her feel more betrayed when she found out that he had been keeping something from her while she was being open and honest with him.

That led me to thinking about my own relationship and the trust between Xander and me. We weren't quite there yet. We were working on it, and I hoped trust was growing on both sides as we were more vulnerable with each other, but I knew that we still had a very long way to go.

Not like Ahyana and Rokh, who were finishing each other's sentences and looking so deliriously happy that it was a bit painful to be around them.

I wondered if it was hard for Zalira as well.

We arrived at the house, and this one didn't have a guard outside. I remembered when Xander had taken me to Erisa's safe house—he'd said there weren't any guards so as to not draw attention to it. My guess was that Thrax had insisted on it so that no one would guess there was a precious person inside.

"I'll leave you here," Rokh said. "I'm going to walk Ahyana back to the palace, and then I'll return for you."

I nodded and thanked them both for accompanying me, and they left. I knew we had to be careful—Erisa still wanted me dead and there was an army on its way, but after discovering my aspect? I wasn't quite as worried as I had been before.

The door opened slightly and I wasn't sure what to make of it. Had it not been latched properly? I reached for it and then a hand clamped down on my wrist and yanked me inside.

Before I could react, a woman pushed me up against the wall and held a knife to my throat. She was almost as tall as Xander, had red hair and pale skin that was covered in blue tattoos.

"You must be Basileia," I said, not moving so that she wouldn't accidentally slit my throat. That could get both me and Xander killed.

She grinned and dropped her blade, taking a step back. "I am. You must be Lia. I've heard a high amount of nauseatingly good things about you."

Thrax had been right. I did like her. "And I've heard almost nothing about you."

"Doesn't surprise me," she said with a wink. "Thrax and his precious male ego are very, very intimidated by me."

I definitely liked her. "Thank you for protecting Quynh."

She sheathed her blade. "She will soon be my sister, so it is both my honor and my duty. Even if it weren't, I suspect I would still do it. How does someone so tiny have that much fire and spirit?"

I was proud of myself that I didn't tense up when she talked about Quynh becoming her family. It made sense that Quynh and Thrax would get married if they loved each other. I told myself it was a good thing. The more people who could love my sister, the better. She deserved to have that.

Especially if I wasn't going to be around long enough to make sure that she was safe. "She's always been that way."

Basileia nodded. "Stubborn, too. If it were up to me, I would take her back to Thrace. I worry about her safety here, especially without knowing who your enemies are. But she refuses to leave."

"That sounds like my sister." I paused for a moment and then asked a question I'd been dying to have answered for a long time. "What do the blue tattoos mean?"

If she found my question strange, she didn't show it. "Each mark is for an enemy I've killed."

She had more of them than Thrax did.

"More than my brother," she said with a grin, as if she could read my mind.

"How did you come to be in Troas?"

"Our mother wanted me to come check on Thrax, as we hadn't heard from him in a while, and I arrived right before the attacks. I wish I had been staying in the weapons quarter so that I could have helped. By the time I got there, it was over."

I was certain she would have taken out quite a few people, had she been given the chance.

"Thrax was gone," she continued on. "I believe you went with him to Lycia?"

"Yes." Someone else saying the name of that village filled my mind with images of all those people who had been slaughtered.

"When he returned he found Quynh and made sure she was safe. I found him at the palace. He entrusted me with watching over her because he didn't know who else he could trust. He wanted to make sure that your enemies couldn't find her."

I had so many of those, he could have been worried about a variety of different people who might want to hurt Quynh to hurt me. Keeping our familial connection a secret from the rest of the court was probably the only thing that had kept her safe when the attack on the palace happened.

It made me very grateful that Xander had put that in place.

Basileia was looking at me expectantly and it made me feel as if I had to make conversation with her. "Did you travel here alone?"

"Of course. Who would I be afraid of?" she asked with a scoff. I wished that I had even a quarter of her confidence. She sat down in a chair and took out a dagger, which she started to clean. "Quynh is upstairs."

I thanked her and ran up quickly. There were two doors and I stood in the hallway for a few moments. What if she didn't want to see me? Sent me away? I wasn't sure I could deal with that right now. I was desperate to see her and talk to her.

Choosing the door on the right, I opened it and there sat my sister.

My heart swelled as if it would pop, and I promptly burst into tears.

CHAPTER NINE

"Lia!" Quynh rushed over to hug me. "Why are you crying?"

"I'm just so happy that you're safe and that you're here. And that you're willing to see me." I was hiccuping and sobbing at the same time, trying to calm down.

"Of course I want to see you. Why would you think I wouldn't? You are my sister."

I cried harder at that and let her lead me over to a chair to sit. She poured me a drink of water and put it on the small table next to me. Then she got a chair of her own and sat close so that our knees were touching.

When I finally got a hold of myself, I said, "Because I've been awful to Thrax and you love him. I'm sorry."

She gave me the kindest smile and it made me want to start crying again. "Lia, you have nothing to apologize for."

That wasn't true. I understood that it might make things worse between us, but I had to be completely honest with her. "Did he tell you how I tried to attack him when I saw him wearing your bracelet?"

She took me by the hand. "He did. And I understand why you did it."

"You do? Everybody else thought I was overreacting. Including me."

"You dealt with a lot of suffering and trauma from what you went through in the tribute race, and you thought I was dead for weeks. The bracelet was the last piece of me that you had, and it means something special to you that it doesn't to anyone else."

"Yes," I said, relief soothing my soul that she understood.

"Of course you'd have big emotions where the bracelet was concerned."

I had to hug her again. "I thought that was why you didn't want to come and see me."

She pulled back so that she could look me in the eyes. "Because you wanted to attack Thrax? That would make me a hypocrite. Need I remind you that I'm the one who used to bite him?"

That made me laugh, which had been her intent.

"One of the kitchen maids seemed a little suspicious and asked me a lot of strange questions, some of them about you," she said. "I was trying to lay low and stay clear of you so that she wouldn't make the connection. She made me uneasy. I told Thrax about it and he kept an eye on her, but nothing happened. He wrote her off as a nosy gossip. After the attacks on the palace, she disappeared. I think she was one of the spies that were hiding in the city."

It sounded like the attackers had the same plan that Quynh did—infiltrate the palace kitchens to find out information. "Did you ever notice a reddish-brown tattoo of a hammer on her chest?"

"I never saw her with her tunic off. Why?"

I explained to her everything that we had learned so far, including Artemisia's role in it and who Lysimache was. I could tell that she already knew about the massacres in Lycia and the temple; Thrax must have told her.

"I'm so, so sorry for your loss. All those women that you knew and lived with and cared about." The sympathy in Quynh's voice was almost enough to get me to start crying again.

"Honestly, I can't let myself think about it too much," I confessed. "I have to push it out of my mind."

"You've always been good at that. Ignoring and suppressing things you don't want to confront."

She hadn't meant it as a rebuke, but it felt like one. Changing the subject, I told her about the magic my adelphia and I could do and she asked so many questions about how it worked and how it felt.

"I am concerned that mine seems to be anger-based, when I've been trying to not let that emotion rule me." The constant anger was eating away at my soul, destroying me bit by bit. It was exhausting. And I had witnessed what it had done to Lysimache. It had consumed her, and I refused to become like her.

"You'll have to show me your magic sometime," my sister said.

"When I get stronger. Right now I pass out not long after I use it."

We sat in silence for a few moments, and given her expression, I knew what she was going to say next.

"You should tell Xander about the eye."

My guess had been correct. "I can't. I think he would take it so that he could use it to protect Ilion, and I couldn't blame him for that. I would do the same. I *am* doing the same. I need it for Locris." I waited a moment and then asked, "You haven't told Thrax, have you?"

"No," she answered immediately. "I told you that I wouldn't, and I won't until you say it's all right."

"Thank you," I said. I wondered if it was hard for her to keep things from him. I knew I had a difficult time of it with Xander.

"At least you don't flinch every time I say Thrax's name," she said cautiously, as if she knew that we were about to enter dangerous waters.

"I'm trying to be careful and manage my reactions. I'm also afraid of saying the wrong thing and upsetting you."

"Lia, you could never say the wrong thing to me."

"Oh, I think I could," I said.

"No, you couldn't, because we are sisters and that will never change, no matter what either one of us does. There is nothing but love and forgiveness between us and there always will be. I want your honesty. I would never want you to pretend just because you're afraid of how I might react. Even if you hated Thrax, it would never change how much I love you."

"Stop that. I am trying not to cry!" I told her with a half laugh, half sob, tamping down the emotions swelling up inside me. "I have been making an effort where he's concerned."

Her whole face lit up. "I know. He told me. It makes him so happy."

"Why?"

"Because he knows how important you are to me."

That made me feel ashamed, that Thrax had wanted us to be friends for Quynh's sake and I'd been awful to him.

Then she carefully added on, "And he knows how important you are to his brother."

What she'd said earlier was right—I did ignore and suppress things I didn't want to deal with. And I fully intended to do so right now. "What is it you love so much about Thrax?"

She gave me a knowing look, telling me she understood exactly what I was doing, before a silly, lovesick smile settled on her face. "So many things. He is kind and loyal and strong and brave and smart and funny and . . . Sorry, I could go on like that for a while."

I understood the feeling, so I nodded.

"I realized how I felt when he took me into the city. Troas is such a metropolitan center that there are people from all over the world here. There is an entire quarter of people from Goguryeo and neighboring nations. The first time Thrax brought me there . . . it was overwhelming. The smells of the food—it took me back to my parents and my village growing up. I hadn't smelled those spices in so long! And the language! I understood it when the people around me spoke it, and it was like getting a piece of myself back. It was as if Thrax understood how much that would mean to me. He had given me something I never thought I would have again, and that was when I knew that I loved him."

I realized with a twinge of sadness that Quynh was going to be happy in Ilion. Not just because of Thrax, but because of the connection she would have here to people from the land of her birth. That was not something she would ever have in Locris. "Was that before or after you told me he was only your friend?"

Shame filled her eyes. "I'm sorry. I shouldn't have said that. I knew how you felt about him. I was trying to make things easier for you but I should have been honest. I knew that it would hurt you if you discovered that I was falling in love with someone from Ilion."

I thought of how I had cried in Xander's arms when he told me that Thrax and Quynh loved each other and had spoken the words.

"You did tell me to choose a life for myself," she said. "This is the life I choose."

It took me a moment to remember when I'd said that to her. "I was talking about Andronicus." He was the captain of my former regiment and had been courting Quynh before we were chosen for the tribute race.

"Andronicus? I haven't thought of him in so long."

"I thought you were falling for him."

She looked incredulous. "I never felt about Andronicus the way that I feel about Thrax. It's like comparing a single drop of rain to the entire ocean."

I nodded. "I know I shouldn't feel this way because all Thrax has done is love you and take care of you, but there is a part of me that feels like he's taking you away. Like I'm losing you."

Now she took both of my hands in hers. "Lia, I promise you that you are never going to lose me. You're just going to get more people to love."

At that I let out a short bark of laughter. "I'm not sure I'll be able to love Thrax."

"Give him time," she said with a knowing smile. "He will win you over like he did with me."

"Maybe." I wasn't sure I believed it, but I would say it for her benefit. Even if she thought I couldn't say or do anything that would make her turn away from me, I was fairly certain that I could.

"This was always going to be our fate," she said softly. "I was not going to live with our family forever, and neither were you. We were meant to grow up and move away to start families of our own."

I wouldn't. That wasn't my destiny. "You know the prophecy about me being the savior. I'm supposed to die."

She shook her head. "I don't care what some prophecy says. If there's anyone who can circumvent a goddess, it's you. I believe in you."

"Even if I did, war is still coming. People are going to die."

"I know. Thrax is so worried. He's talked multiple times about putting me on a boat back to Locris or letting Basileia take me to Thrace."

"On this topic he and I agree completely." I would be much happier knowing that Quynh was far away from here and not in the path of danger.

My sister got that determined look in her eyes that I knew all too well. "I'm not leaving. I'm going to stay right here. Whatever your fate is, Thrax's fate, mine will be the same."

Perhaps Thrax would be able to find a way to convince her. I just nodded and smiled as if I agreed, but I made a mental note to find him later to privately discuss a possible plan for getting Quynh to safety. Maybe we could give her one of Io's sleeping potions, and by the time she woke up, she'd already be in the middle of the ocean headed for Locris.

This was so strange, me wanting to scheme with Thrax. The world had certainly turned upside down.

"If you are planning on staying here," I said, "then I'm glad you're out of the palace. I will miss you being close by but I will sleep better knowing you're safe and hidden."

The grimace on her face made me think she didn't share in my sentiment.

"Are you enjoying being here?" I asked, wanting to look for good things about her current arrangement in hopes that she wouldn't get upset about it.

"I'm so used to working that it's been strange to not be busy all day. I have plenty of books and I've been cooking and cleaning, which has been strangely comforting. I have a loom to weave on. Basileia is a fun companion and we're enjoying each other's company. I'm not certain how long Thrax wants me to stay here. I'm guessing until Xander is made king and everything's settled."

Not if I had anything to do with it. I wanted her here where she was safe. I did have to make one last attempt to get her to see reason before I possibly stooped to subterfuge. "I actually agree with Thrax and Basileia and think you should go somewhere else. Because it's not just Xander being made king now—it's the battle that's coming."

"I told you, my place is here. With you, my sister . . ." Her voice trailed off as she took her right hand away and placed it over her stomach. "And with Thrax, the father of my baby."

CHAPTER TEN

For a few moments I did not understand the words in the way that Quynh had used them. "What?"

"I think I'm pregnant." She said it tentatively, like I might be upset.

"You think or you know?"

"It's too early to be certain, but I have missed my monthly courses and I never miss that." It was true. Quynh's cycle happened on an exact schedule, while my own was chaotic and unpredictable.

And it only now occurred to me how much that matched our personalities. "Io has a pregnancy test. I could bring it here and use it on you."

She put both of her hands over her stomach. "I don't think I need it."

I was in complete and utter shock. I didn't know what to say, and so without thinking I said, "Our mother is going to kill you. And then Father will kill Thrax."

"We will be married by the time we go to visit Locris. Thracian women do not wait for marriage. Thrax suggested that we should delay, but then I . . . gave him some very compelling and persuasive arguments for why we should not."

I fought off the urge to cover my ears with my hands.

She apparently didn't sense my discomfort with this particular subject, as she kept talking. "I didn't want to wait to show him how much I love him. I've never felt . . . I've never wanted someone so desperately like that."

Unfortunately, I knew exactly what she meant.

"Are you going to get married soon?" I asked.

"No. We're going to wait until . . . everything settles down," she said. While she was talking about the larger things happening right now, I knew she was also doing this because of me. Maybe to see whether I survived what was coming. Once again, Quynh was putting her life on hold for my sake. I didn't want her to do that.

Knowing that I wouldn't be able to change her mind, I instead nodded toward her stomach. "May I?"

"Yes, but you can't feel anything yet," she said with an indulgent smile.

I placed my palms on her and something bizarre happened. I could sense a bright white light inside her, pulsating up into my hands. I felt an overwhelming surge of love. "You *are* pregnant," I breathed.

"How do you know?"

"There's a light inside you that I've only seen when I used magic, but right now I can feel it. A new, strong little life." I had put my hands on Parthenia and this hadn't happened. Why was it different with Quynh and her baby? It was like power was being fed into me. I could feel it swirling around inside my body, as if I could use it.

She put her hands over mine, perhaps hoping she might be able to feel it, too. After a few quiet moments, I removed my hands and the power immediately disconnected, as if being turned off. "What did Thrax think?"

Because I understood that this was how things had changed. We would always be sisters, would always love one another, but someone else was her priority now.

Two someones.

Her eyes were bright. "He's torn between excitement at becoming a father and terror that something will happen to us."

I was feeling the same way.

And selfishly, I was also a little sad. This was Quynh's moment, and I knew that I shouldn't be making it about my thwarted dreams, but I could be happy for her while still disappointed that this would never happen for me.

"I don't want you to take this the wrong way, because I adore our family, but being adopted . . . I have longed my whole life to have someone who looks like me. To see my face reflected back from someone who shares my blood."

My throat felt a bit too tight. "I understand that. And I'm so glad that you'll get to have what you've always wanted."

"You can have this, too." Her voice was so low it was practically a whisper.

"No, I can't. I promised the goddess."

"I don't mean to speak ill of a deity you believe in, but why would she make you miss out on one of the greatest joys in life? Loving and being loved?"

"I'm not missing out on that," I said. "I have you. Our family. My adelphia."

"Romantic love is different. And it should be allowed. You can save Locris and then come back to Ilion and be married to Xander for real."

I remembered the vision that I'd had, where I had been in Locris in the tree courtyard where he and I had first met, and he was cradling my pregnant stomach while kissing me. I could feel the love he had for me.

But that was only a dream.

"I promised the goddess that I would reopen the temple in Locris if she would help me. Now, with all the other priestesses dead . . . it has to be me. One of the last things Maia said was that as long as there was one priestess who believed, the temple would go on."

"Maybe one of your adelphia would want to do it."

My heart lifted momentarily with hope, only to immediately crash back down. Ahyana planned on leaving with Rokh. Io and Zalira would never leave Ilion, and Suri would never leave Io. This was their home.

In the dream I'd had, the goddess had handed the eye to me. I was the one who watched Locris be brought back to life. It was my responsibility. I couldn't hope that one of my sisters would do it for me so that I could flagrantly break my vows.

Not to mention that I didn't know how to use the eye and was worried that I wouldn't receive further messages from the goddess if I did the things I so desperately wanted to do.

"I don't think so," I said. "And even if they did . . . there's no future for Xander and me."

"Why do you say that?"

"As I mentioned earlier, I'm not supposed to survive. Which would certainly put a damper on our relationship."

Ignoring my sarcasm, she responded, "If I had to lay odds on you or on a prophecy, my money would be on you every single time. You're going to live."

There were other factors. "Io made me promise not to hurt Xander. To keep my distance."

A frown marred her features. "Why would you agree? I would think you'd enjoy hurting him. Getting him to fall for you and then leaving him to twist and suffer."

"No, I'd never do that—"

"Aha!" she exclaimed triumphantly while pointing at me. "I knew it! You do love him!"

Her words punched deep into my gut and I almost doubled over in response. "That's not what I'm—"

Quynh seemed determined to not let me finish a sentence. "Thrax told me how you raced to save Xander in Lycia. That you didn't even hesitate."

"Because of the physical link we share." Quynh wanted me to be honest with her and I was lying through my teeth. Which made no sense, because I'd already told Xander why I'd gone in after him.

But if I said it out loud, if I said it to my sister, it would make it all real. And I wasn't prepared to face it.

"That's not true."

I knew it wasn't true, but I wished people would stop saying that he and I had feelings for each other. It was too much, too big, too overwhelming. Too many different things were happening all at once. I needed to keep putting one foot in front of the other and get through what was coming.

Not worrying about silly things like this. I kept up my charade. "I'm a means to an end for him. I'm how he gets to become king."

She let out an exasperated sigh and then said something I couldn't understand before saying, "That was me questioning your intelligence in Thracian. Basileia taught me how to do it. And I understand that Io is your sister, but it wasn't fair for her to ask that of you."

Feeling defensive of my adelphia sister, I said, "I don't want to hurt him, either. He's been through a lot, suffered so much loss."

"So have you," she pointed out. "And unfortunately, getting hurt is the cost of loving people. Not just romantically, but with every kind of love. And it's not a choice that either you or Io get to make for Xander. He gets to decide what he wants and what he's willing to risk."

I didn't want to tell her my fears, but I couldn't help myself. "He's never said anything remotely like that to me."

"Hasn't he?"

"Not as Xander." When he'd been masquerading as Jason, he had made some big declarations. *I pledge to you my whole heart. My entire soul. Every part of my being already belongs to you. Ask for anything and it is yours.* And I had dismissed them as being part of his scheme to trick me. "And not while undrugged. Which, by the way, Io told me you conspired with her to have him drink honeyed wine."

She didn't even look a little ashamed. "I heard that went the way we thought it would—he headed straight for you and tried to seduce you. And sometimes people show you how they feel instead of telling you. Thanks to Thrax, I know how Xander has shown you."

My husband had done things that might be construed that way. Even the night before, when he had braided my hair. My heart raced faster and faster until I had a hard time completely catching my breath. I couldn't let myself believe what she was saying. It couldn't be true.

"Love is supposed to be gentle and sweet," I said. "Understanding. Peaceful. Comforting. Like what Father and Mother have. Or what Haemon and Doria shared." Xander and I were not those things.

"Sometimes," she agreed. "And sometimes love is battles and fires and earthquakes and bloodshed. It can be small and quiet or it can be loud and epic. It doesn't look the same for every couple."

My limbs trembled slightly. This was such a ridiculous reaction to be having. "I feel . . . too raw. Like my nerve endings are frayed and painful."

"That's understandable. You need some time to figure things out."

It wasn't time that I needed. "All I wanted was to heal my nation and lead a quiet life."

"That's not what you were meant to do," she said. "It sounds as if the goddess chose you before you were ever born. But it's up to you to decide. I think you could find a way to make this all work, if that's what you want."

What I wanted didn't matter.

"Maybe you should ask him," she said. "See what he feels, what it is he wants. Then you can make your decision from there."

I truly could not picture myself doing that. Because if he didn't feel the same? The rejection would break my heart.

"I'm going to use the washroom," she said. "I'll be back. I feel like I have to urinate every half hour now."

There was a slight edge of exasperation, but her tone was mostly just joy.

When she left, I heard the front door open downstairs and then Thrax's voice greeting Basileia. I understood that to be my cue to leave. I went downstairs to join Thrax and his sister.

He had his ever-delighted grin on his face. "Lia! I didn't know you were here. I was just with Xander in the weapons quarter and took a break to come home and check on Quynh. I can go if you'd like to keep visiting."

That was thoughtful of him to offer. "I have so much that I need to do. I should be going." I would have loved to sit there all day and talk to Quynh, but I had to learn and practice and fight and prepare. "She's in the washroom right now."

"Something that's become a regular occurrence," Basileia said while twirling a dagger on the table.

I turned toward Thrax. "Can I ask you something?"

"Anything."

"Why do you always look so amused when you see me? It feels like you're laughing at me."

"Not at you, never at you. It's because it gives me endless pleasure watching my stubborn brother, who said he had no room in his life for someone, who after having every woman in Ilion throw themselves at him, finally fall under the thrall of a woman who would torch his palace down around him."

"I wouldn't do that," I protested. Not now, anyway. "I wouldn't let my adelphia or Quynh get hurt."

His eyes twinkled. "Quynh, who no longer lives there, and your sisters. They're the only ones you're concerned with."

Thrax and Quynh really were perfect for each other. "Xander is not under my thrall."

"Disagree."

Everyone spoke as if I had some sort of power over Xander, when it felt the other way around to me.

I decided they were entitled to their opinions, no matter how wrong they might be. "Thrax, you and I are going to be friends. And family."

"We are?"

"Yes. And you are going to treat my sister like the princess that she is and you'll never let her be unhappy. You will love and adore her every day of her life and you will keep her safe."

His face went serious, which was so unlike him. "I swear to you that I will."

"Good. And congratulations on the baby."

Basileia suddenly spoke up. "You should make him kill a boar and bring it to you. It's what the men in my clan do when a man desires to marry a woman—he delivers a boar he's hunted."

Xander had told me all about boar hunting and how dangerous it was. A boar could easily run Thrax through. While that would have appealed to me before, it didn't now. Quynh and the baby needed him. "I wouldn't want him to get gored."

"Why not?" Basileia asked. "A little goring is good for men. Keeps them humble."

"It sounds like *you* might need to be gored," Thrax replied with a laugh.

She pointed her dagger toward him. "It is a good thing I love you, because you are the only person that I allow to tease me. I do not care for it. And my humility is fine. I'm the most humble person I know."

Thrax laughed before turning back to me. "Can I ask what brought this on?"

That was probably a fair question. "When you marry Quynh, which you will, you're going to be my brother."

"Lia," he said with a soft smile, "you're already my sister. You have been since the day you married Xander. I would protect you like I would him. Or Quynh."

That unexpectedly made tears spring to my eyes, which surprised me. I was saved from anyone noticing when Quynh appeared at the top of the stairs. "Thrax!"

Her entire being lit up at seeing him, as if the light I felt inside her were coming out through every pore in her skin. She practically flew down the stairs to his open arms.

"What did I tell you?" he asked while cradling her close. "I don't want you to run down the stairs and fall."

She pulled back so that she could peer up at him. "I am not going to fall, you overprotective oaf. You are not going to wrap me up in linen until the baby comes. You can't make the world stop turning to try and keep us safe."

He lovingly stroked the side of her face. "I will fight the entire world to protect both of you."

This was what I had to protect. Quynh deserved this happiness. I would make sure that she got it by keeping Ilion safe.

"I am drowning in sentiment!" Basilea declared with disgust.

Both Thrax and Quynh laughed, and when they had finished, I said, "I should be going."

Quynh managed to let go of Thrax long enough to come over and hug me. "Be safe. And think about what I said."

I worried that it would be all I thought about. I said goodbye to the others, and Basileia offered to walk me out.

When we got onto the porch, I said, "If you ever get a break and want to spar, come to the palace and find me."

"I think I would squash you like a bug," she said.

"You might be surprised at how well I can hold my own."

She looked at me appraisingly. "Perhaps I will. I wouldn't want my skills to get rusty. You are married to my brother's brother, and now your sister will marry my brother. We are also family."

"We are," I agreed. Quynh had been right. I was going to get more people to love.

And more people I had to keep safe.

I told Basileia goodbye and she went back inside, closing the door. I looked around, expecting to see Rokh waiting for me, but he wasn't here. He was probably off kissing Ahyana somewhere.

Xander wouldn't like me going back to the palace without Rokh to watch over me.

But I didn't want to go home.

Despite feeling sensitive and nervous, I was struck with an overwhelming urge to see my husband. He was the person I wanted to tell about the things I'd just learned.

So I headed off in the opposite direction to find him.

CHAPTER ELEVEN

When I reached the weapons quarter, I felt a bit ridiculous because I wasn't sure how to track Xander down. I started walking and was dismayed by the chaos surrounding me. Buildings had been obliterated by fire, and there were ashes and chunks of stone in the street.

What kind of fire could burn hot enough to destroy brick and cement?

"Lia?"

I turned to see Dolion, who smiled broadly at me. "What are you doing here?" he asked. "Did you come to see me?"

"No, I was looking for Xander."

His face fell slightly, and my heart twinged at the thought that I might have hurt his feelings. I was about to apologize when he said, "The last time I saw him, he was over near the armor smiths. Two blocks north and then three blocks west."

It felt like I should say something to him, but he turned his back on me and walked off. He had offered to be my friend and I worried that I'd been so caught up in my own life that I hadn't been a very good friend to him.

But then he went around a corner, so instead of trying to talk to him, I turned and followed the directions he had given me, darting in between the mess that littered the streets. People were out doing their best to clean up, but I could tell that it would take a long time for the quarter to be restored.

Heat poured out of the various armorer and weaponsmith buildings, accompanied by the sound of hammers banging against metal. I stopped to watch as one man hammered out a shield with flecks of metal flying—smoothing it out, knocking the dents from it, forming it into shape before plunging it back into the fire.

It's what had happened to me since I'd come to Ilion. I was constantly being battered and reshaped by my experiences, forged into something new. Something useful. A shield to safeguard these people, to be wielded in battle. My prejudices and anger being hammered out of me, forging me into a better person.

I wouldn't have chosen it, but I was glad it had happened. All that I'd witnessed, all that I'd lived through and survived, it had changed me. In some ways it had hardened me, but in others I'd been softened. Brave but vulnerable. Strong but gentle. Battle ready but desiring peace.

Softness wasn't a negative thing. It allowed me to be a more compassionate and caring person.

I spotted Xander with a group of men putting up a scaffolding around a column so that it could be mended. He was down here working with his people, helping them. Not back in the palace planning a party. I wished the archons of the council could see this.

He straightened his back and turned his head to the side, as if he sensed something. Then he rotated around and saw me, and the moment his eyes met mine, my heart immediately started thumping.

Would I ever get accustomed to him? Was I forever doomed to heart palpitations because of how handsome he was?

He stalked over to me, his long legs closing the distance quickly.

"There you are!" I said when he was close enough. "Thrax said you were here and—"

"You came alone?" He stopped directly in front of me and crossed his arms over his chest.

"I can protect myself. I'm armed and I have power." I said the last word softly so that no one would be able to overhear.

"A power that lasts for a few moments and then you pass out. Leaving you completely vulnerable."

He didn't need to be so protective. "As you can see, I'm fine. Nothing happened. You are worrying too much."

He waved one of his arms toward the broken buildings behind him. "I don't think I am."

That was probably fair. "I understand. I'll try to be more careful in the future."

His eyebrows shot up his forehead in surprise. "Come over here," he said and walked off, clearly expecting that I would follow. I did, but it slightly annoyed me.

He led me to a makeshift outdoor tavern and pulled out a chair for me. "Sit."

"Why don't you ever ask things nicely?" I did sit but my annoyance was increasing.

"What?" he asked as he took his own seat.

A barmaid approached and Xander said, "Bring us two beers."

She nodded and headed off, and I said, "There's a perfect example. You demand. You give commanding orders. I don't think I've ever heard you say 'please.' I thought princes were supposed to have manners."

"Life would be easier if people would do what I say. I expect to be obeyed."

It did feel like he was trying to provoke me. "I am not obedient."

"I noticed," he said dryly.

"My mother taught me that 'please' is a magic word. That people are more likely to do what you want if you ask politely."

He shook his head. Like I was the ridiculous one.

"You could also ask people what they want before you place an order for them," I said. "I don't like beer. I would prefer wine."

"I think both you and I should steer clear of wine for the time being."

That filled my head with images I did not need in there. I wasn't going to allow myself to get riled up. I tried to imagine why he was being so gruff with me right now. I knew he was upset that I had traveled here alone, which I probably shouldn't have done. The last time he'd warned me about something like this, he'd been shot with a poison dart trying to protect me.

It probably didn't help that things were so awful in this area. These were his people. There had been such a loss of life, so much destruction. It must have been hard on him. "I'm glad you're here helping. This is so terrible."

He ran a hand over his face and let out a tired sigh. "We arrive at places too late. I keep thinking that if we'd been here earlier, we could have stopped them."

By "we" did he mean me and him? Or was he talking about his phratry brothers? "You can't think that way. We'll be there the next time."

"And if we're not?"

"We can only do our best and rely on the goddess for the rest."

The barmaid returned with our drinks, putting them down in front of us. I thanked her and she hurried off to serve another customer. Xander took some coins out of his pouch and put them on the table. Then he took a long drink from his cup.

One of the coins rolled and fell off the edge. I leaned down to pick it up and noticed the red dirt that hadn't been cleared away from the ground yet.

"Do you have any theories about the dirt?" I asked.

"None. Nobody seems to know anything about it." His frustration was evident.

"Well, Lysimache said she spent a lot of time culling books and texts so that no one would figure out what she was doing."

"Maybe after you've finished questioning her, I should take a stab at it," he said before knocking back more of his drink. I pushed my beer over to him in case he wanted more. I didn't think it would be a good idea for him to interrogate Lysimache because he might actually stab her.

"Io is coming up with a potion that will make her talk. She hopes to be done by tomorrow morning."

He made a grunting sound and took my cup to drink. Lysimache had to know about the dirt since she had plotted with Artemisia. Although she had repeatedly told me at the temple that she didn't know who Artemisia had pledged her allegiance to and didn't care, she might have been lying. I supposed we would find out soon.

I would uncover what I could, but I also needed to make sure that I gave as much information to Xander as possible. "There are at least two different groups trying to kill me."

He set my cup down and leaned toward me. "What do you mean?"

"The attack at the temple, the one with Io . . ." I sucked in a deep breath, hoping that he would remember he had apologized for blaming me that Io had gotten hurt. "Those people did not have red dirt. And they were specifically looking for me. The Locrian maiden. They wanted me dead and they nearly succeeded. And the red-dirt attackers are also looking for me."

His honey-colored eyes flickered over to my left shoulder, where I had been stabbed. Then his gaze returned to mine, watching me intently, but he didn't say anything. And that was almost worse—the quiet before the storm.

When he finally spoke it startled me a little. "The red-dirt attackers are after the city as a whole."

While I had told him about the pirates before, I hadn't given him the entire truth. "The pirates on the *Nikos*—that wasn't random or an accident. They had come looking for Quynh and me."

"How do you know?"

"The men that came down into the bottom hold—the ones you killed? They told me. They didn't say who they were or where they'd come from, but they knew that we were Locrian and wanted to take us with them. They tried to present themselves as our liberators, but I could tell something wasn't right."

"Erisa," he said. "We know that she's behind one of those groups, if not both."

"As you said earlier, we have to assume that she's not working with the red-dirt enemies because they do seem intent on killing as many Ilionians as possible." We had already discussed the possibility that she might be involved with that group, but it didn't make sense. She would be left with nothing.

He nodded. "I hope Lysimache has answers as to how the pirates came looking for you specifically, because I can't imagine how they could have known or why they would try to take you."

That was true. How could an enemy we weren't even aware of know who Quynh and I were? "Maybe they hoped to capture us so that Troas would be punished by the goddess for not doing the tribute race."

"Perhaps." Xander was like me in that he also didn't like not having answers. "But how could Erisa have known who you were? That attack at the temple—there was no reason for her to kill some unknown woman from Locris."

"That means she must have known exactly who I was. She was trying to prevent us getting married."

"And what, because you believe that I knew who you were from the beginning, I must have told her?"

"No! Because you never would have shared that with her." I knew that for an absolute fact.

"Do you think someone from Locris betrayed you?" He had that tone that indicated he was going to hunt someone down if I answered yes.

"It's hard to explain to an outsider but the selection is sacred to us. We promise to never reveal the identities of the tributes. I don't think a Locrian would have told her. But the only Ilionian who knew who I was . . ." My mind started racing as I began to put things together.

"Who?"

"The witness." The man sent by the Ilionians to make certain that the Locrian maidens who boarded their ship were the same ones whose names had been drawn. A man who was mute and uneducated so that he couldn't reveal those identities to anyone in Ilion.

"I saw him on the ship and can verify that his tongue is gone," Xander said. "He couldn't have told anyone."

That made me think of Suri. "What if the witness has another way to communicate? That night when we went to the Golden Lamb, I thought I saw the witness there. What if he was following me?"

"Why didn't you say something then?"

"Because I thought I had imagined it and I thought you were just a sailor."

He started drumming his fingers against the table. "So if he's working for Erisa, then somehow he told her that you were my betrothed and she decided to get rid of you before we could be married to stop me from becoming king."

"This might be what you've been looking for. If you can find the witness and prove that he can communicate, you can expose Erisa." I felt genuine hope. This could help him become king.

My excitement was echoed in his expression. "He shouldn't be hard to find. Not with that public of a job."

Xander and I both stood up at the same time and I wanted to celebrate. To hug him, kiss him, do something because we were in this together. And we were finally making some headway.

"I have been looking everywhere for you!" Rokh said as he approached from my left. "You were supposed to wait for me at the safe house. Ahyana wants you to come to the temple to practice your . . . particular skill set."

"Go," Xander said. "Take her to the temple and then come back. I have an assignment for you."

I spoke up. "But I was hoping that we could . . . talk more." I wished Rokh weren't here to witness me being pathetic.

"Practice and we can talk later tonight." He rushed off to start whatever plans he had come up with.

While it wasn't what I had hoped for, I was happy that he hadn't shut me out again.

As I walked off with Rokh, I wondered how my husband would react if I did as Quynh suggested tonight and told him how I felt about him.

I suspected I wouldn't be brave enough to do it.

CHAPTER TWELVE

My sisters were all gathered in the temple gymnasium, and I saw Zalira drink something tinted green.

"What is that?" I asked.

"My fortification potion," Io said. "We're testing it out today. I want to see if we can do magic for longer if we use it." She handed me a full vial, which I put into my pocket. "I've also been thinking about trying to create a potion that might boost our power."

"Something happened today that makes me think there might be a way for us to do that naturally. I saw Quynh and she's pregnant. When I touched her stomach, I could feel that bright white light inside her and I felt power flowing into my hands."

"Were you doing magic?" Ahyana asked.

"No."

"Then how did you feel it?"

"I don't know." Always more questions with very few answers.

"I'm ready," Zalira said. "Dea Maimaktes."

The rain outside was gentle this time. Constant. There weren't any lightning bolts or thunderclaps.

"Her eyes *are* green," Io breathed out. Like she hadn't quite believed that it had happened, even though we'd told her it did. "Like the eye of the goddess is inside us."

"How are you doing?" Ahyana asked.

"Good. The pain is here, but not as intense. I can take it," Zalira said. "I'm trying to maintain control over the rain as well."

"How do you do that?" Io asked.

"I think of it, picture it, and it happens. But I have to concentrate. And ignore the pain."

We stood there quietly so as not to distract her, and I watched as her limbs started to shake. I could see from her expression that the pain was increasing.

"There has to be a way for her to stop besides passing out," I said.

Io nodded. "Maybe you can think and make it end. Like you were just talking about."

Zalira shook her head. "That didn't work."

"If we speak a command to start, couldn't there be one to stop?" Ahyana asked. "What if it's the same phrase?"

"Dea Maimaktes," Zalira said, and the rain ceased while she sagged down to the ground.

I couldn't tell if it had worked or if she reached the end of her endurance. But then Zalira lifted her head and grinned at us.

"That did it!" she exclaimed.

We could turn the magic off and not let it consume us. We could make it stop before it rendered us unconscious. I could see on my adelphia's faces that they felt as relieved as I did.

"My turn," Io said. She took a few steps back from us and drank the fortification potion. "Dea Khloe."

A single green plant began to come up through the seams in the concrete floor, slowly growing and moving toward Io. She shifted her gaze toward us.

"You are all covered in that white light, but Suri's is the strongest," she said.

"They were all the same when I saw it," Ahyana responded with a slight frown.

Io held her hand out to Suri, who quickly came over and took it. Io immediately gasped.

"The pain is gone. I feel invigorated, like I could go on forever. As if she's charging my power."

I saw the grimace on Suri's face. This was taking something out of her, and I wanted to know what it felt like. So I went over and took Io's other hand. She gasped again, and this time instead of feeling the white light entering me, I felt it going out.

Into Io.

Without being told to join in, Zalira and Ahyana came over and held on so that we were all touching.

I could see the white light surrounding Suri and my other sisters. Suri's was exactly the same as the others.

But none of them were as bright as the light I'd seen around Xander.

"It's like my power has increased tenfold," Io said, breathing hard. "Like I could . . ."

The pain had started to set in for me. Suri was trembling but she didn't let go.

Thick roots suddenly shot up through the seams and began wrapping themselves around our ankles.

"Should we be concerned?" Ahyana asked, peering down at her legs.

"No," Io said. "I wanted to see if it would work."

The roots slithered off our legs and began to move along the floor, like snakes.

Zalira dropped out of the circle, already exhausted from having done magic earlier. She sat down hard, pulling air into her lungs.

"I'm going to stop," Io said, her voice shaking. "Dea Khloe."

The roots immediately went still and we all collapsed near each other. I felt drained, like all my energy had been taken from me.

"So we can power one another," Zalira said.

I sucked in a deep breath and held it for a moment before saying, "If we're using magic to fight, if we're powering each other, we wouldn't be able to do magic of our own."

"We would have to figure out a way to stagger it," Io said as she leaned against Suri.

"Does everyone have a light?" Ahyana asked. "Could we touch anyone and it would power us?"

"We should test it."

Ahyana got to her feet. "I'll do it. There are guards outside the gate."

"I'll come with you," I said. It seemed like we were currently the most recovered of the group.

We walked through the temple grounds quickly. It used to feel eerie to do so, as if we were disturbing a grave. But since we had started using the magic . . . it no longer felt that way.

Instead it was like this was a place that could have life in it again because we were using it the way it was meant to be utilized.

When we arrived at the gate, Ahyana quickly called up her aspect. "No lights on any of them," she said, and then uttered the words to turn it off again.

Curious, I quickly did the same. She was right. There weren't any white lights around the guards.

"So it's only specific people who can power us?" she asked.

Our adelphia made sense. We were bound to one another by blood and ceremony and, now, magic. Of course we could help one another.

But why did it happen with Quynh's unborn baby?

And Xander?

When we returned to the palace, I sent for Parthenia. I asked her to take a message to Themis asking if we could resume our meetings at a later date because of how busy I had become. Those get-togethers were for me to teach her and Zalira, Ahyana, and Suri how to read, but Themis didn't want anyone to know what we were actually doing.

I didn't think it would be a problem to delay, as I supposed that she was probably just as preoccupied with the council, trying to figure out their next moves.

"I'll do it right now," Parthenia said. "Do you need anything else?"

She made an oof sound and put a hand over her belly.

"Is the baby kicking again?" I asked. This was my chance to test whether I could sense her baby the same way I could Quynh's.

"Yes. Always."

"May I please feel?"

She nodded. I came over and she showed me where to put my hands. A second later I felt a sharp jab.

But there wasn't any light. No connection. I whispered, "Dea Erinys."

Still nothing. Not on Parthenia, either. Strange. I quickly turned my power off so as to not suddenly pass out in front of my maid.

"It will be your turn soon enough," she said. "I'm sure of it."

I weakly smiled at her. "That would be something."

What it would be was impossible.

I told her that I wouldn't need her again for the rest of the evening.

"I'm going to have a tray sent up for you and your husband," she said. "You've both been so busy lately. I want to make sure you're eating."

I thanked her for her offer and decided that was probably a good idea. She left and promised the food would arrive soon. My eating schedule had become extremely erratic and I needed to keep my strength up. As did Xander. To that end I reached into my pocket to get the fortification potion Io had given me and swallowed it down. I instantly felt less tired.

Deciding that I needed to get cleaned up, I took a quick bath and dressed. I checked on the sleeping Luna. I was away so often now that I didn't get to see her during her awake hours and it made me sad. I missed her.

There was a knock on the door, and it was a kitchen maid with a tray. I let her in and she put it on the table. I thanked her, and when she left, I grabbed a handful of grapes and began eating. I picked up the book Suri had found for me down in Xander's mother's library and started to read.

I found myself flipping back to the story I'd read earlier about the sun god who had cursed the people of Jacharus and turned their lands into a desert. That same line stuck out to me again—

The gods and goddesses quarrel with one another over the hearts of mortals as they draw their strength from those who believe.

I'd been trying to figure out what the hammer of Arion was. I had thought that Arion might be a person or a place. A city? A king?

But what if Arion was a god? Someone at war with the earth goddess? Was that the sun god's name? Were his followers waging war against us to diminish Dea's power because she had rejected him?

Destroying her believers would destroy her strength.

Why wouldn't she stop it from happening?

Maybe this went back to Io's belief that the goddess gave us what we needed and it was up to us to figure out the rest.

The bedroom door opened dramatically and Xander slammed it shut. He came over to the bed and fell down face first and let out a sigh.

"Hard day?" I asked, closing my book.

"Yes." The word was mumbled into the mattress.

"There's food over on the table."

That got him to lift his head to see where I was pointing. "Later," he said. Then he turned onto his side to face me, propping his head up with his bent arm. "How did your training go today?"

I told him the new things we had discovered—being powered by other people with the white light, turning the magic off before it knocked us out, Io's fortification potion.

"Were you able to fight for longer?" he asked.

"I can't use my power on my sisters," I said. "I might hurt one of them."

"You can always practice with me." He stood. "Show me how long you can last."

"Aren't you tired?" I asked. I didn't want him wearing himself out.

"I have incredible stamina." He said those words in a way that made my breath hitch and my toes curl against the bed. "Show me what you can do, wife."

What would he say if I asked him to show me how extensive his stamina was? Nothing good would come of that. I should beg off.

"I just bathed."

He nodded appreciatively. "I can see that."

I glanced down to make sure that my tunic wasn't clinging to me and then realized he probably meant my damp hair. "I'm clean, and you want me to get all sweaty from fighting?"

"Getting sweaty is fun." He was in a flirtatious and playful mood. I wanted both to take advantage of it and to tell him to stop being hot one moment and cold the next because it was infuriating.

His voice dropped an octave lower than normal. "Come on, wife. Let me make you sweat."

CHAPTER THIRTEEN

Now all I could picture were the times when he and I had . . . aggressively kissed and the way he would sweat, which made his skin taste of salt. Something I probably should have found disgusting, but currently the idea of running my tongue along the strong cords of his neck made me lightheaded.

"Fine," I said, standing up, hoping that he couldn't tell how much I wanted to kiss him.

"As always, your enthusiasm is overwhelming," he teased.

"Are you certain you want to do this?" I asked. "Maybe I'll be the one making you sweat."

"Doubtful," he said with a grin. What had gotten into him?

"Swords?"

He took a few steps back and balled up his hands in front of his chest. "No. We'll do hand-to-hand combat. Because you may find yourself in a situation where you're unarmed and need to keep fighting. Ideally the best scenario would be if you're armed and your opponent is not."

I raised my own hands. "I don't know if I could kill an unarmed person. That is so dishonorable." Demaratus had drilled that into me. It was one of the reasons I hadn't killed Lysimache. Not wanting to act out of anger, needing answers, and she was unarmed.

I had seriously considered it, though.

"Honor has its place, and I would argue with your Daemonian battle master that the battlefield is not one of them. Survival is the goal."

It didn't surprise me that Xander knew where I had learned that lesson. "Demaratus would make you run miles if you said something like that to him."

The light in his eyes dimmed slightly. "Promise me that if you have to choose between honor and your life, you will always choose to live."

"I promise," I said, shaking my head. It was such a silly request. "Are you ready?"

"Always."

"Dea Erinys," I said and swung my right fist at him as the power surged through me.

Again, he was lit up like the sun.

He grabbed my arm and twisted me around, pulling my back to his front. "This seems familiar."

What he didn't realize was that he was currently feeding more power into me by touching me. I spun around and dropped, pulling him as I went and tossing him over my head. That caused him to flip over me while I got away.

He started laughing as he got up. "What was that?"

"You gave me more power."

"How?"

"I told you about the light people emit and how we can use it."

"And I do that?" he asked.

"Yes. You do. It's not everyone—Ahyana and I tested it. It's only specific people, and we're not sure why. But you're brighter than anyone else I've seen so far."

"So you touch me and it makes you stronger?"

"Yes."

"Interesting," he said as he took a step toward me.

But I was ready for him. I punched him in the jaw hard enough that his head flew back. I felt the sharp crack of pain in my own jawline.

I was about to apologize for hitting him so hard when I spotted his fist coming around on my left side. I ducked out of the way, something I'd never been able to do with him before.

"You're so fast," he said admiringly.

"Annoying, isn't it?"

He came toward me. "Annoying, fun—same thing." He jabbed out so quickly that he almost got me. I blocked his shot and then pivoted behind him. I jumped onto his back and put my hands on his shoulders, pulling him down with me to the floor. He turned at the last moment to take the brunt of the fall, allowing me to scramble on top of him.

I sat on his chest and pinned his arms down. "I win!"

"Trust me, I don't feel like I've lost at all," he said, his intense and amused gaze taking me in. My hands were flat against his forearms and I could feel power flowing into my palms.

"You're not going to fight back?" I asked.

"Why would I?" The blatant invitation in his eyes had my heart beating violently in my chest as my breathing went shallow and uneven. "Although this hardly seems like a fair fight."

"Aw, does the poor little prince not lose very often?" I teased, trying to tamp down my desire by covering it up with humor.

His eyes twinkled with delight. "I am neither poor nor little."

He was correct on both counts. I was currently sitting on his massively broad chest, which proved his point.

"Do you feel it? As if you're being drained?" I asked, needing to think about something else.

"A bit," he said. "Not very much."

"It wasn't like that for me earlier. Maybe it's because you're goddess-blessed."

Then the pain started.

It was duller than it had been the night before, but it came on suddenly. My arms went slack.

"What is it?" he asked, sliding his hands out from my grasp and resting them on my thighs. "Are you all right?"

"The pain." I swallowed hard. I could manage this.

Xander took both of my hands and put one against his throat, the other on the exposed part of his chest so that I was still touching his skin. He returned his hands to my legs. "What do you need from me?" he asked.

"Talking helps. It distracts me."

"Stay here and touch me and we'll see how long you can bear it," he said. "Who else has the light?"

"Um, my adelphia. You. Quynh's baby."

"I heard about that today," he said carefully. "How did that make you feel? Finding out?"

"I'm happy for her." His skin was so warm. He was slowly moving his hands back and forth, and I was certain he meant for it to be a soothing gesture but all he was doing was causing my skin to heat and prickle in response. "She's going to be the best mother."

"And believe it or not, Thrax will be an excellent father."

I nodded. "But I was also . . ." Another wave of pain. It was starting to increase even with Xander's light.

"What?" he prompted.

"I'm sad that I can never have that. Because of my vows."

"Would you like that for yourself?"

"Yes," I said far too quickly. Not wanting him to read too much into it, I said, "What about you? Have you thought of having a family?"

I was struck with the memory of him telling me he'd give me a dozen children if that was what I wanted, and I pushed it out of my head.

His hands came to a stop. "I'll need to have children to secure the kingdom. But even if I didn't, yes, I think I'd like to be a father."

That caused a pang of sorrow so deep and sharp that it rivaled the pain I felt from the prolonged magic use.

"Keep talking," I said through clenched teeth. "Tell me something I don't know. Something secret."

His expression turned serious. "I dream of you."

"That isn't a secret. I know that."

"No. You talking about Quynh made me remember a dream I've had about you. You are pregnant with my baby. We're in Locris, in that courtyard where we first met. And we're happy."

The air solidified in my lungs. That hadn't been a dream. I'd been awake. There was no way he could have been a part of it.

But I'd never told anyone else about it. "When did you dream this?"

"The day of our wedding."

Now I had to work hard to pull air into my chest. That was exactly when I'd had that vision. How had we shared that?

His expression was guarded, and I couldn't make out what his tone meant as he kept talking. "There are other times that I dream of you walking with the goddess in fields of golden wheat, moving farther and farther away from me. I can't reach you, no matter how hard I try."

I'd had a dream like that as well—trying to get to him and not being able to. What did that mean? "They're just dreams," I said with a lump in my throat. "They don't mean anything."

I could tell that neither one of us believed that. Too many things were happening at once. My traitorous feelings rushed around inside me, exacerbating the pain. I let out a stifled moan.

"Breathe," he said. "In and out. Is there a way for you to take more from me? Would that help?"

I didn't know. I remembered Zalira talking about how she had thought of what she wanted, focused on it. I did that. I concentrated on his light and tried to pull it up into my hands, and then I imagined it spreading into my body and soothing every part that hurt.

"I think it's working," I said. "Tell me if it's too much. I don't want to hurt you."

"You won't," he said. "You are doing so good." He reached up to rest his right palm against my face and I leaned into him, closing my eyes.

He spoke again. "Thank you for sharing with me today. For telling me the things that you did. I know it hasn't been easy for you to trust me." There was a rough quality to his voice that made me open my eyes again.

"You're welcome."

He smiled slightly. "Your eyes are so green right now."

"That's what happens when we do magic. Io said it's like the eye—" I clamped my lips together as an internal alarm sounded. I had just been about to tell him about the eye of the goddess when I had been so careful. What was wrong with me? "Like the goddess is with us and showing it through our eyes."

If he picked up on what I'd just done, he didn't convey it. "I suppose I didn't notice yesterday because your eyes change colors depending on what you're wearing."

They did? I hadn't realized that about myself. Growing up, I hadn't been able to wear different colors, so my clothing had been some shade of beige or gray.

He moved his hand so that he could run his fingers through my hair. "The night of the festival, when you wore that green tunic, your eyes were such a bright green and . . ."

Now he was the one falling silent. This felt like extremely dangerous territory. I held my breath.

"It happens in our dreams, too," he said. "Your eyes are always the shade they are now."

They were? I hadn't known that. Probably because I hadn't spent time looking into mirrors in our dreams.

No, there was the one time in the cavern when I'd stood in front of a large green mirror asking to see my fate. I had seen my family, including my brother, Haemon, and had been focused on them. I hadn't noticed the color of my eyes.

The main thing that dream had wanted to show me was Xander. Telling me that he was my fate. My true reflection. I felt so conflicted. I wanted so badly to just be selfish and give in to my desires.

"What are you thinking?" he asked. How did he always seem to know when I struggled with my attraction toward him?

"There are two terawolves inside me. And they are demanding completely opposite things. Both would consume me if given the chance. They would take over my life, and I'm not sure that I'm ready for either option. I want them but I can't have both."

"You can only choose one." I heard the challenge in his voice.

"I can't. Even if I want to."

"You can," he insisted.

The pain returned and I realized that it was because I was no longer drawing from him. As if I couldn't let him inside any longer. I had to keep us apart.

"It hurts," I said. And I wasn't just talking about the pain from the magic. "I don't know how long I can hold on."

"You don't have to. You can let go. I have you," he said as he sat up, keeping me in his lap. I wrapped my arms around his neck while he held me against his chest.

"Xander . . . I . . ." There was so much I wanted to say to him.

But I couldn't.

"I know, Lia." His words were so soft that I didn't know if he had actually spoken them or if I'd only imagined them.

Instead of asking I took the coward's way out. I didn't turn the magic off and let it overwhelm me into oblivion.

CHAPTER FOURTEEN

My plan worked. When I woke up the next morning, I was in our bed but Xander was already gone. I had managed to avoid a conversation that probably would have destroyed all my good intentions.

I got ready for my day and went next door to Io's room. Ahyana was braiding Zalira's hair while Io read a book. When she saw me she held up a vial. "I've done it. The truth serum mixed with a compulsion element. Not only will Lysimache tell the truth, but she won't be able to stay quiet and refuse to answer. It should work immediately and she's going to confess every vile and horrible thing that she's done."

Furious Io was an unsettling thing. She poured it into a small vase filled with what I presumed was the fountain water.

"Where's Suri?" I asked.

"She's checking on Antiope," Zalira told me. My stomach twisted with guilt. I needed to go visit her.

"How do you know it works?" I asked as I took the vase from Io.

"We tested it on Ahyana this morning," Io responded.

"And let's just say that she was a little too forthcoming, and we now know far too much about what she and Rokh have been up to," Zalira added, sounding a bit disturbed.

Ahyana gave me a mischievous grin to let me know that she hadn't minded in the least.

There was movement near the open door and I turned to see Xander walking by, heading to our room. My heart began to pound at just the sight of him.

"I've also been working on a formulation to break the physical link," Io said. "Here. Drink this."

I put down the vase she'd handed me earlier and did as she requested. I drank the bitter concoction down, struggling to not throw it back up. "That's awful."

"Taste wasn't my primary concern. Give me your hand."

I held it out and she swiped the end of a dagger across it, drawing blood. I hissed slightly and heard a loud "Ow!" coming from next door.

"It didn't work." She sounded so disappointed.

"Wouldn't Xander have to drink it, too?" I asked.

"You're right!" She shook her head, as if to help herself think more clearly. "I'll go do that now."

When she left I turned to Ahyana and Zalira. "She doesn't seem like herself."

"She didn't sleep last night, either," Zalira informed me. "She's using her fortification potions to stay up all night."

"That can't be good for her." I grunted as I felt the moment when Io dragged her dagger against Xander's palm. "It didn't work!" I called out. I went over to her worktable to grab a length of linen to wrap my hand up.

When she came back into her room, I said to Io, "You have to sleep."

"I will. After I figure this out." She went through her handwritten notes on the table and started muttering to herself.

"No, Io. Now."

"She's right," Zalira said, while Ahyana nodded. "You are going to wear yourself out."

"There's just so much I need to do . . ."

I put my hand over hers. "It can all wait."

"But I wanted to go with you to interrogate Lysimache."

Ahyana and Zalira looked as concerned as I felt. I didn't want her to come with me. "I don't think that's the best idea. You haven't slept in two days. That means you're not the most reliable person to interrogate an evil woman with. I'm worried that you might try to choke her to death."

"I've imagined it," Io admitted wearily as she sat down.

"That's what worries me," I said, crouching next to her so we could still be eye level. "I want you to remember who you are. You're the acolyte of the goddess who is studying as a healer because you want to help save people."

"Maybe the best way to save people is to kill those responsible for putting them in danger."

"This isn't you," I reminded her. "Don't get away from who you are, because we all love you just as you are. We will take care of this for you. We will stop Artemisia, and Lysimache is going to answer our questions. You've made sure of it."

Io nodded. "I want you to ask her about Daphne."

"Daphne?" Io's former mentor had died suddenly not too long ago.

"When she died, Lysimache got sick at the same time. I think she's responsible somehow."

"I'll ask her," I promised, although I feared the outcome if the high priestess had killed Daphne. I might not be able to stop Io from doing something drastic. She had been so close to Daphne.

"You need to remember that Lysimache was a princess, probably in a court similar to mine. She's used to trickery and maneuvering," Io said. "Start off by asking her easy questions. Things she wouldn't mind answering, or things she would be happy to brag about because she thinks she's so clever. Then build up to the more serious ones—where the eye is, who Artemisia is pledged to. You don't want her to realize that she's being compelled. Let her think she's answering because she wants to."

"Why would that matter? What could she do if she figured it out?" I asked.

"Attack you."

"I'd take her easily."

"She could cover her ears and yell loudly so that she can't hear you. Or beat her head against a stone wall to knock herself out. My point is, she's been alive for a very long time. She would come up with something. We have this one chance. Once she realizes what we've done, she'll go back to refusing to drink any water."

Maybe I could get one of Xander's phratry brothers to hold her down and pour water down her throat. But then she'd probably force herself to vomit it up.

Io was correct. We had this one opportunity to get it right. Lysimache was too wily to let us trick her a second time.

Zalira stood. "I'll go with Lia, and Ahyana can stay here to make certain that Io sleeps and that she's safe."

Ahyana nodded to show she agreed with the plan.

"Fine," Io said. "I'll sleep if you promise you'll tell me everything that happens."

"Agreed," I said.

Io lay down in her bed and then took a vial with a dark green liquid that I knew was her sleeping potion. Within a few moments she was fast asleep.

"Potions to stay awake, potions to sleep," Ahyana said with a shake of her head. "Could they create some kind of dependency? Should we be worried?"

"I don't know," I admitted. "And I'm afraid that if we ask her about it, she'll just lie."

"We could always trick her into taking some of the truth serum," Zalira suggested.

"Zalira!" I protested with a laugh, and she gave me her dazzling grin in return. I grabbed the vase Io had prepared for Lysimache. "We should go."

I didn't want to delay my chance to finally get answers to questions I'd had for so long.

Zalira and I rode side by side on our way to the house where they kept Lysimache. I felt like I was getting better at horseback riding, but I wasn't as good as the others. I focused on what I wanted to ask the high priestess, trying to come up with a mental list.

"When we get to the safe house, I'm going to let you question her alone," Zalira announced, interrupting my thoughts. "I'll stay downstairs."

"Why?"

"Because based on what you've told me and what I've seen, Lysimache has some kind of connection to you. Like you're an opponent she plans on defeating. If you're the only one talking to her, I think she'll feel like she's outsmarting you and it might make her more prone to answer."

I considered what Zalira said and it did seem possible. "How are you always so insightful?"

"When you live on the streets like I had to, you start to understand what it is people want and what they'll best respond to. Sometimes I can read people the way you read books." She didn't mention that time of her life very often, and I was glad she felt like she could share with me.

"You can read me? What is it I want?"

"I know what you want," she said. But then she didn't continue with her thought, leaving me waiting.

When I couldn't take it any longer and was about to ask her to explain herself, she said, "I hope you know that I'm loyal to you."

"Of course," I responded. That wasn't something I would ever doubt.

"And because of that, I want to hate him on your behalf. But I like your husband," she confessed.

Since she understood my situation so well, it was easier to be honest with her. "I'll tell you a secret. I like him, too." That was the closest I'd ever come to admitting to all the contrary feelings I had about Xander.

"Oh, we all know."

That made my heart freeze in my chest. "Do you think he knows?"

"He's an intelligent man, so I'm thinking yes."

Out of all my sisters, Zalira had always been the most straightforward, the one to say exactly what was on her mind. And I didn't know how to deal with her guess.

"Then why doesn't he say something? Or do something?" I asked.

"You have given him no indication that you want him."

She was probably right about that, too. "I can't want him."

"Even if you can't, you still do." She sighed. "With everything happening, maybe giving in to those wants and severing the link is the best choice."

Her words hit with the precision of an arrow.

And she didn't help by adding, "And maybe Ahyana had a point. If this is the end, maybe we should be allowed to enjoy ourselves before it happens."

"Do you really think that?"

"I might think it, but I won't ever act on it," she said with a note of sadness.

Letting out a deep breath, I said, "I wish I had your strength."

"I don't have to share a bed every night with Stephanos. Nor do I have to pretend to be in love with him for the sake of the court. Our situations are not the same. It is much easier for me. I can mostly avoid him."

Whereas I could not. And the more time I spent with my husband, especially when he was the way he'd been last night . . . I suspected that my feelings grew with every encounter.

But I still wasn't sure whether those feelings were reciprocated. "I wouldn't even know how to go about any of this even if I could act on it."

"I'm probably the last person you should ask. I'm obviously no good at it, either. You have a bunch of virgins leading other virgins and none of us know what we're doing," she said, and I nodded. She wasn't wrong.

We rode in silence the rest of the way while I considered everything she had said. Was that why Xander had been so playful last night? Because he sensed that my feelings had changed, that I cared about him? Was he responding to it? He had been so caring and supportive and helpful, and I needed him cold. I needed him angry and distant, putting walls between us.

When we arrived at the house, Thrax opened the door with a smile as we tied up our horses.

"We weren't expecting visitors," he said. I hadn't told Xander I was coming here, even though he'd been right next door in our room. I wasn't ready to face him yet.

"I hope it's all right that we're here," I said.

"Of course! Come in." He ushered us inside.

"How is Quynh?" I asked.

Another grin. "Loved, adored, and being treated like the princess that she is."

"Good."

"I'm assuming that you plan on questioning your prisoner?" he asked.

"Yes," I said.

"Then I'll need your weapons before you go upstairs." I set down the vase I'd brought and took off my weapons. As I handed them over, he said, "The last time I asked for your weapons, I thought you were going to stab me."

That was when Xander and I'd had our marriage negotiations.

"I did consider it," I told him, and he laughed as he took my xiphos and put it on the table.

He turned toward Zalira with an outstretched hand.

"I'm going to stay down here, if that's all right," she said.

"Perfect. Maybe you can tell me the secret to winning Lia over."

"Be the crown prince of Ilion," she said and then laughed, while he joined in. I hoped my cheeks weren't turning red out of embarrassment.

Thrax offered her a seat and I picked up the vase and headed upstairs, steeling myself for what I was about to do.

Dolion was keeping guard outside the top door. “Lia!”

“How are you?” I asked.

“A little bored,” he admitted with a smile. “But I’m happy to see you.”

“I’m glad to see you, too.” I nodded toward the door. “Is it all right if I go in?”

“Yes. What have you brought?”

“It’s water from the temple. Lysimache said she prefers the taste and I thought it might get her to open up.” I *knew* it was going to get her to open up.

He quickly looked in the vase and then nodded. “Be careful. I’m here if you need any help.”

“I’ll be fine,” I said.

Dolion opened the door and I readied myself and went inside to face Lysimache.

CHAPTER FIFTEEN

"I thought you were coming yesterday," Lysimache said as I entered the room.

"It may surprise you to know that I'm very busy, especially with an army on their way to invade us."

She was again seated at her table with an untouched tray of fresh food. I set down the vase next to the tray and then backed away. I didn't want to be within arm's reach of her.

Dolion left the door slightly ajar so he could hear me if I called for help.

The high priestess reached for the vase and poured herself a drink. She downed the entire cup and I saw the look of smug satisfaction that temporarily crossed her features, as if she had fooled me.

"Shall we begin?" she asked.

"You're going to answer my questions?"

"I said I would and I'm a woman of my word." In a horrible way that was true. She had said she would avenge her sister and destroy two nations, and she'd kept herself alive for more than a thousand years to make certain that it was done.

"Should we start at the beginning?" I prompted.

She stayed silent for a moment before she spoke. "It was my brother who did this. His obsession with Menelaia is why the Great War happened. He stole her from her husband, brought her back to Troas, and risked the anger of everyone around him, including the goddess who protected marriage. Before he died I told him that I would make certain no one ever remembered his name, but they would never forget what he had done."

I was tempted to ask for his name, but that was only for my own curiosity. It would be a foolish thing to do because it would definitely tip my hand that she was being compelled. "During the war, why didn't you use magic to fight your enemies?"

"Our high priestess forbade it. She limited our access to magic because she didn't want us using it at all. She thought that the glory and power of it belonged solely to the goddess and we shouldn't try to take it for ourselves." She sounded both furious and disgusted. "I practiced in secret. Kysandra refused—she wanted to be obedient to what the high priestess ordered. If she had only practiced with me . . ."

The pain and regret in her voice were real. I told myself to not be affected.

"We could have saved our city," she said. "But one woman's opinion stopped that from happening. It's why I knew my plan would work. That I could control everything once I took over the temple."

Lysimache poured herself another cup and drank the entire thing again. Making herself strong. And dosing herself with Io's mixture.

"When the army began to hammer away at the main gate, I tried to get Kysandra to hide with me in the temple because I incorrectly assumed the goddess would keep us safe. My sister refused. She had seen the Achaeans using the secret tunnels under the palace to gain access and knew they would attack from that position as well. She went to warn our father, to tell him to flood the lower levels to stop them, but he wouldn't listen. What did a woman know about warfare?"

I had questions but thought it better to just let her speak. I would let her talk until she ran out of words.

"In the lower level of the temple, there is a room behind the statue where priestesses can hide. Kysandra tried to reach me there but she wasn't fast enough. Ajax, prince of Locris, came and raped her in front of me, next to the statue of the goddess, then dragged my sister out of the temple."

I couldn't stop my jaw from dropping. The blasphemy was terrible enough, but I hadn't known that she'd witnessed her sister's assault. That was horrific.

Her voice trembled slightly. "I was pregnant and I had just lost my son and husband. I was determined to keep my baby so that she could someday rule Ilion. I knew that if I went to my sister and tried to help her, I would meet the same fate. I wasn't strong enough. I didn't know how to fight. So I watched and bore silent witness to every scream of pain, every entreaty she made to the goddess that was ignored, every plea with your ancestor to stop raping her, and I could do nothing."

All I could think about was what I would have done if it had been Quynh. Kallisto. My adelphia. What would I have done in Lysimache's position?

She added, "Kysandra was good and kind and loving. She didn't deserve what happened to her."

What would I do to men who harmed my loved ones? I had been ready to kill Thrax just for wearing Quynh's bracelet. What would I have done if someone had assaulted her?

I could easily imagine myself lying in wait for a thousand years if it meant that I could destroy the people who had hurt and killed my sisters.

Lysimache had taken such great pleasure in pointing out how similar she and I were when we had fought, and much as I didn't want to believe it, I was starting to.

We had the same aspect.

And there was a version of me that could make the same decisions she did, taking revenge on everyone who had hurt my loved ones, destroying the places that had caused my sisters pain and death.

"Are you thinking how you might understand what I've done?" she asked with a knowing smirk. "That I'm not the villain you imagined me to be?"

The fact that she could intuit what I was ruminating on bothered me as well.

She cocked her head to the side. "Do you know what it's like to devote years of your life to a goddess who ignored you when you begged for her intervention?"

Maia had taught me the answer to this. "The gods are not allowed to directly interfere with our lives. They can't stop evil things from happening. We all have the ability to choose for ourselves."

"That's convenient," she snapped.

"It's not," I disagreed. "Perhaps our lives would be easier if the gods could make all our decisions for us and we didn't have to struggle and suffer and make mistakes. But we wouldn't learn anything."

"Quite the philosopher," she said sarcastically. "If that's true, it didn't stop the goddess from taking Ajax's life."

That had happened. The goddess had opened the earth under him and smothered him to death. "Then why didn't she stop you?"

"After Ajax died I no longer felt her. As if she had vanished completely."

"But you still tapped into her power when you destroyed Locris."

"That was the last time," she admitted. "I didn't need her magic to help me take over Ilion. I was their princess, the last remaining priestess, and they followed me without question. My younger cousin was only five years old, and as his regent, I was able to start changing everything, to bend this nation to my will."

"Why would you hurt Ilion? These were your people." Locris, I understood. But here?

"The weakness of my brother, of the men of this nation, the way they abandoned us to save their own hides, leaving us behind. They hid in the outskirts and mountains while women were taken as concubines to their enemies and their children made slaves." She practically spit the words out.

There was somewhere else the men of Ilion had gone—I remembered hearing about it but couldn't recall the details.

"And I wanted all the goddess's believers dead. I wanted her power gone. That meant Ilion also needed to be destroyed."

Just like I'd read in my book. "Then why not destroy the temple? Remove her worship entirely? It's what you did in Locris."

"I considered it. But after ruining your nation, I had to make sure that my changes would be permanent. I went to the oracle in Phocis, and she made the prophecy about the savior who would rise up and undo everything I had put into place."

"How did you expect to find the savior?"

"That was easy enough," she said. "I took away women's rights and education and said they were inferior, which, again, the men of Ilion were eager to agree to. Women who wanted a different kind of life, who wouldn't accept the new status quo, they would join the temple. I knew the savior would be among them."

"So . . . you've hurt Ilionian women for over a thousand years to make sure you found the savior?"

"It worked, didn't it? I also had to be certain that the savior couldn't access magic by eliminating the knowledge of how to do it. I kept some rituals, reinstituted old ones that other priestesses had done away with, and created some new ones. Although I hadn't ever considered that the savior would come from Locris." She narrowed her eyes at me. "I still have a hard time believing that you're her."

I pulled down the left shoulder on my tunic to show her the mark of the goddess.

Her eyes widened slightly before her expression of superiority and disdain returned. "I should have slit your throat the first night you arrived."

"Yes, you should have. Because I'm what you feared. I am going to undo everything you've done."

Lysimache shot me a look of such pure hatred that I could feel the chill of it seeping into my bones.

"Why did you write the prophecy down? Why did you share it?" I asked. Wouldn't it have been in her best interest to hide it? Io had found it in a book from her mother's library.

"I wanted the savior to know that she was going to die, that all her efforts would be in vain."

How was I supposed to respond to that? I had spent so much time worrying about this very thing, and she'd shared it to make sure that I would suffer. That chill inside me grew.

"And it gave the people something to look forward to and distracted them from what else was going on. Whenever there were hard times, they pressed forward because they foolishly thought they were going to be saved."

She had kept it from Locris. Because she didn't want us to hope. "Why didn't you just destroy Locris outright? You had the ability to wipe us out at any time." They had the wealth, population, control of the blockade.

"That would have been too good for you. Locris deserved to suffer slowly. I preferred giving them a death by a thousand cuts. Every time the economy crashed, every time a tariff was raised, when sickness overtook the entire capital city, I was there. It's why I instituted the tribute race. Every year I got to put Locrians through incredible pain."

"You created the race?" It was such a cornerstone of what little belief Locris had left that it felt unreal that this was something else Lysimache had manipulated.

"Oh, yes. Terror campaigns are highly effective. A cowering populace is easier to harm."

Thousands of Locrian maidens. She was responsible for all their deaths. For the grief of their families and friends. "Why would you hurt innocent women?"

"Why should Locris get to keep their daughters and sisters when mine had been taken from me?" Her vehement voice unsettled me.

"And think of all the Ilionian men that I told to hunt them down. Their souls will be forever tainted because they murdered those 'innocent women.'"

Despite the fact that I knew this was real because she could only speak truth to me, I still had a hard time accepting it. "But we suffered from a plague because we stopped sending maidens."

"The plague was an infected sailor that I sent to your shores. It was the oracle in Phocis who said that you had to reinstitute the race, wasn't it? The same oracle that I paid a large bribe to and said that if any Locrians came to her for help, she was to tell them to keep sending maidens for the tribute race, no matter what."

"All their deaths are on your head," I said, still shocked. She had planned so many steps ahead.

"Have I upset you, Princess Thalia?" she asked in a mocking tone.

"You are pure evil." There was no other way to describe her and her actions.

"What I am is effective. I win, daughter of Ajax."

She wouldn't win. I wouldn't allow it. And at least now there would never be another Locrian maiden hunted in the streets of Troas. Quynh and I were the last ones because Lysimache could no longer convince these people with her lies. The tradition would be stopped.

Io had been right. The high priestess was more than eager to brag about her brilliant schemes. I needed her to keep talking, even if everything she said sickened me and made my stomach turn over. "How did you manage to stay in charge of the temple for so long? Didn't any of the priestesses notice that you were always the high priestess?"

She gave me a conspiratorial smile, as if we were two neighbors gossiping. She was actually enjoying this. "It was easier than you might imagine. It was why the high priestess always wore a veil. I would choose my replacement, someone on the younger side who resembled me in height and had a similar voice, and announce it to the temple. I would say that once she became high priestess, she had to take a vow of silence for a year to honor the goddess. By which point everyone would have forgotten my replacement's voice and mine. Then I would kill her, take her place as the 'new' high priestess while the 'old' high priestess suddenly died from some illness. I would bury them with a veil on, and no one knew."

"How did no one ever figure it out?" My adelphia and I had already begun to suspect that there was something strange about her long before we discovered her true identity.

"People generally believe what you tell them. And if anyone ever did suspect, well, they met an untimely end through an accident. Like Daphne."

I hadn't even had to ask her. She was volunteering information. "What happened with Daphne?"

"She served me a drink that had poison in it. One that she drank herself in order to lower my defenses. She was willing to sacrifice herself to make sure that I didn't suspect her scheme, which I have to give her credit for. It was clever. And it would have worked. But I had been ingesting the eye of the goddess for so long that I was able to survive the encounter. Daphne did not."

How could she treat this so matter-of-factly?

"I had planned your accident, as well," she said. "You were going to cut your own wrists because of how much you missed your family. But before I could put it into motion, Daphne knocked me out of commission, and then the prince came for you."

I couldn't stop my gasp, which made her laugh.

"You said you made the women of the temple strong." I didn't indicate that I knew how she'd done it and I realized that I was skirting close to the edge, but I had to understand. "Why would you bother when they were all expendable to you? Nothing but a means to an end?"

"Every general needs an obedient army. Even if I didn't care about them, I wouldn't want them to be raped. No woman deserves that. They should be strong and know how to fight. That was important to me. You would judge me for that?"

"I judge you for all of this," I said.

"Why? As I told you, you're just like me. You are also willing to do whatever it takes to reach your end goal. You would use people, discard them if they no longer served you. You would do anything you had to in order to achieve what you want. Am I wrong?"

I suspected that she wasn't, but I refused to give her the satisfaction. "And now you've condemned everyone in this nation to death because you are petty and small."

She opened her mouth and nothing came out. She pursed her lips together in confusion and then said, "What have you given me?"

My pulse started to pound. "What do you mean?"

"I was going to lie to you about my motives but I can't. You gave me a truth serum," she said with a laugh. "I'm not sure it was necessary, as I'm mostly willing to tell you what you want to know. And again you make my point that we are alike. I've done that so many times myself. Drugging someone to get what you want no matter who you hurt. You would have made a fine heir, Princess Thalia. Perhaps I might have been able to sway you to my cause and get you to work with me if Artemisia hadn't put her plan into motion."

I would never have been her heir or her acolyte or anything else. No matter what she said, we were *not* alike. I had to tamp my anger down and stay calm.

She seemed to sense my internal struggle.

"How does your husband deal with your fury and desire for vengeance?" she asked, again as if we were old friends catching up. "With your total disdain for rules, your willingness to do whatever is necessary to get what you want? You must be making his life miserable. Has he kept his promise to me? He seems like the honorable type. The sort who would keep his word."

What was she getting at?

"Have you had sex with the prince?"

CHAPTER SIXTEEN

Her question surprised me so much that I couldn't formulate a response.

"I would guess you haven't," Lysimache said. "And if he hasn't bedded you, then you're physically connected. His pain is yours. Someone only has to kill one of you to get to the other, and my guess is that will happen sooner rather than later."

Of course she would know about my physical link with Xander. Another reason she'd been willing to let the wedding go through instead of killing me outright as she had planned. She had gambled that someone else would do the job for her. I glanced down at my bandaged hand. "I'll go home and have sex with him today."

This seemed to amuse her. "And break your vow? I know you think you can save Locris. Do you really think you can access the goddess's power if you do not do what you promised her?"

My worst fear laid bare. I did my best to not react.

She added, "He doesn't trust you. He never will. You don't know the royal family. I'm certain he keeps things from you."

Why was she saying this? How had she figured out that Xander had become a weak spot for me? Enough. It was time to get at the bigger questions.

"Where is Artemisia really from? Who is she working for?"

"As I've already told you, I don't know."

It seemed she really didn't care who destroyed Ilion and Locris, only that it was done. "Why didn't you go with her?"

"When I initially consulted with the oracle, I asked her how I could stay alive to defeat the savior. She told me that I could ingest the eye in micro amounts, but that by doing so, I would never be able to leave Ilion again or else I would instantly die. I must be connected to the lands where the goddess's power lies. It's become my prison."

Which was another reason why she hated Ilion so much. "You told Artemisia to kill everyone in the temple because they all had the potential to tap into their goddess aspects and could have stopped her."

"Yes, and it's why they went looking for the rest of you in the palace. If I'd known that you five had already figured the magic out, I would have paid for assassins myself."

"Where is the final eye of the goddess?"

"I gave it to Artemisia." If she was surprised that I'd figured out there was another eye, despite her implying at the temple that she had destroyed the last one, she didn't show it.

"And where is she now?"

"I don't know."

It was incomprehensible to me that she hadn't asked Artemisia any questions about her background at all. "Why did you give her the eye? Why not just destroy it like you did with the other one?"

"Because it has power and she can use it."

"And in exchange she will obliterate Ilion and Locris off the map for you."

Lysimache nodded.

A thought occurred to me as I remembered the prophecy. What if the eye was the greatest weapon? It was worth asking about. "What is the greatest weapon that I'm supposed to wield?" I asked.

"I know it's part of the prophecy, but I don't know what it is. I would assume the eye."

If that was true, then I didn't currently have a way to use it to protect Ilion. "What is the red dirt?"

"I don't know," she said with a sigh, as if she were bored.

"What is the hammer of Arion?"

At that she frowned. "I'm not sure, but if I had to wager a guess, I would say the weapon Artemisia was using."

Now we were making progress. "What or who is Arion?"

"The son of the goddess." Her eyes went wide. "What have you done? Why do I have to answer? What is this?"

I had known it was only a matter of time until she realized what I had done. I pressed forward. "Who worships Arion?"

"Many . . . many people do," she said with a groan. "Why am I being forced to say things that I don't want to? This isn't how truth serum works!"

"Why does Arion want to attack Dea's believers?"

"Because he hates his mother and wants to destroy her!" The words were just above a whisper, as if she were trying desperately to contain them. She jumped to her feet and took the tray of food and threw it against the wall.

"What rules and laws did you change at the temple?" I asked.

Her words were coming out a garbled mess as she fought against the compulsion. Was the fountain water giving her the strength to resist?

"Get away from Lia!"

I had been so focused on the high priestess that I hadn't realized Dolion had entered the room. He positioned himself between us, as if he meant to protect me.

"Did priestesses used to marry?" I demanded.

"Yes!" she shrieked, pulling on her hair like the pain would prevent her from answering.

"Who changed it?"

She tried to clamp her lips shut. "Many . . . many high priestesses changed things!"

I realized that she was avoiding the question and speaking in generalities. I needed her to be more specific. "What changed with priestesses marrying? How did it change? And when? Why was it altered? Tell me why!"

Lysimache fought every word that escaped her lips. "Be-because . . . couldn't risk . . . them . . ."

The high priestess started to scream while she reached for Dolion's belt and yanked out his short sword. She kicked him in the chest and knocked him against the far wall.

She's going to kill me.

Adrenaline surged as I prepared for her to leap at me. I heard Thrax and Zalira coming up the stairs. They must have heard the chaos. I was about to call on my aspect when the high priestess suddenly stopped screaming.

Because she lifted Dolion's blade and, with a malicious smile, drew the sword against her own throat, cutting her vocal cords.

Blood streamed from her neck as she collapsed to the floor.

"No!" I tore a strip of cloth from the bottom of my tunic and ran over to her, putting pressure on the wound. "You do not die," I said. "We are not done!"

She managed to smile at me, blood staining her teeth.

Her words from earlier echoed in my head.

I win, daughter of Ajax.

"What happened?" Thrax asked. Dolion explained it to him, but I was focused on stopping the bleeding.

Lysimache made a gurgling sound, and it sounded as if she was choking on her own blood. Drowning in it.

The cut was too deep. She wouldn't survive.

I put my face over hers, making certain that she was looking into my eyes. "When you face the goddess, she is going to give you exactly what you deserve," I promised her.

The high priestess's expression changed at my words to one of horror, and then she was gone—her mouth wide, her eyes glassy and open.

I should have brought Xander with me. He could have stopped her before she was able to kill herself. What had she been about to say?

What would have been so important that she would take her own life rather than be forced to answer?

Zalira's hand rested on my shoulder. "She's gone."

I was still holding the ripped part of my tunic against Lysimache's throat. I stood and turned toward Dolion.

"Why did you do that?" I asked angrily. "Why would you come in here armed?"

"You had a weapon with you?" Thrax demanded.

"I thought she was going to hurt Lia," Dolion said, sounding annoyed. Because we were upset with him? He turned toward me. "You were in danger and I just acted. I was trying to protect you!"

"I can protect myself," I told him. His interference had cost me the rest of my answers.

"You know that no one is allowed to bring any kind of weapon into this room!" Thrax said.

Dolion's tone shifted to one of regret. "I should have known better. I'm sorry. I was worried about Lia."

"I understand." Thrax clasped his phratry brother on the shoulder. "It was an honest mistake."

Zalira asked me, "Are you all right?"

"I should have let Io come. She might have been able to save her."

"You can't think that way," she said. "First, with the way she's been lately, I'm not sure Io would have even tried. And second, no one could have saved Lysimache. She made sure of that."

Zalira was right. The high priestess had bled out too quickly.

I had come so close and didn't get all the answers I needed. I felt disconnected from myself, my mind hazy, as if I couldn't think straight. I had to get out of this house. I turned and went down the stairs, grabbed my weapons, opened the front door, and started walking toward the palace.

I was vaguely aware of Zalira trailing behind me with the horses, but I was in some kind of a daze. I didn't hear or see anything else. I kept replaying the moment when Lysimache had killed herself over in my head. If I'd just been a moment faster. If I had only realized what she'd been about to do, I could have stopped her.

I relied entirely on muscle memory to lead me back to my room.

At some point Zalira must have handed off the horses to one of the guards, as she hadn't gone to the stables and was right behind me.

When I opened my bedroom door, she said, "Do you need anything?"

To sleep for a hundred years? So that when I awoke, this would all be over? "No."

She nodded toward her room. "I was able to hear your entire conversation with Lysimache. I'll tell the others everything that happened."

"Thank you. I just want to . . ." I wanted to curl up in a ball and pretend like none of this was happening. To shut out the entire world and have it all disappear.

"Go rest," she said, and I saw the concern in her eyes.

I went into my room and closed the door. I headed straight for the bed and got under the blankets, pulling them over my head. I wished I could sleep. Instead I lay there and continued to repeatedly run my final encounter with Lysimache through my head. Seeing the expression on her face just before she died. I lost track of time, staying in that moment.

My stomach grumbled. I was hungry. And thirsty. But I didn't want to move.

"Lia?"

Xander had come into our room and slammed the door behind him. I stayed under the blankets.

He sat next to me on the bed. "Are you all right?"

"No."

"I heard about Lysimache. Thrax found me and I came straight here." He sounded so concerned that I started to cry.

"Don't do that," he said as he tugged the blankets down from my face. "You know it destroys me when you cry."

I swallowed down what I was feeling, determined to stay in control. I couldn't weep and fall apart in his arms. Once I managed to get it to stop, I said, "At least this time there's no one for you to slay. The person responsible is already dead."

He wiped away the tears on my cheeks and then glanced at my hands. "I hope you strangled her to death."

"This wasn't from me trying to kill her. I was trying to save her," I said, holding my hands aloft. Her blood had dried on my skin.

"Why?"

"Because I had more questions. She killed herself before I could finish. So she wouldn't have to answer." I exhaled loudly, willing myself to not start sobbing. I had been so close, but in the end she'd taken her secrets with her. "Will you promise me something?"

"Anything."

"I want you to burn her body. I don't want her to be reunited with the earth. She deserves to suffer and wander as a shade for the rest of time, never knowing peace."

If he was alarmed about the anger in my voice, he didn't show it. "I promise. I will personally make sure it's done."

"Thank you."

"Do you want to tell me what happened?" he asked carefully, averting his gaze.

As if he expected me to shut him out.

That would have been the wisest choice. Not the easiest, but the one that would keep me on the right path.

I didn't do that. I told him nearly everything that I had learned, leaving out mentions of the eye of the goddess. I included what she'd said about him and our relationship. "Lysimache said that you keep things from me. Do you?"

"Yes." His answer was immediate. "But they're not things you need to know."

My heart lurched. I had absolutely no right to feel hurt, because I was doing the same to him. Had just deliberately made that very choice a few minutes ago.

And the things I kept from him . . . he probably should've known them.

My reaction made no sense. I was being a hypocrite.

He studied me and my pulse began to beat erratically. Because he looked like he knew exactly what I was thinking.

"I'm glad she's gone," he finally said.

"So am I."

We lapsed into silence, and I found myself blurting out words. "You saved my life and you didn't even know it." I could at least give him this. Let him know that despite all my anger at what he'd done, I was sitting here because he had forced me into marriage.

"What do you mean? Because every time I've saved you so far, I've definitely known it." That teasing lilt was back and my stomach fluttered in response.

"It's not my fault everyone wants me dead," I said miserably.

"No, it's not," he agreed.

"Lysimache planned on killing me while I was at the temple. She was going to make it look self-inflicted because of my homesickness. I was so angry with you for blackmailing me into marrying you, and it's the reason I'm still alive."

He watched me, his expression guarded.

"And if I'd told you no, if we'd all been at the temple when Artemisia attacked . . ." The lump in my throat refused to let me keep speaking.

"Don't think about that," he said.

"How can I not when I literally have Lysimache's blood on my hands? All that she has taken from me, all that she has made certain to keep away from me in the future . . . I can think of nothing else."

"Like what?"

You. She made sure I could never have you. Lysimache had put all this in motion by cursing Locris. She had put me in this position where I couldn't have the life I wanted because I had to remain worthy to undo her evil actions.

"None of it matters," I said, defeated. "Because I'm just like her and I'm going to meet the same end and there's nothing either one of us can do to stop it."

CHAPTER SEVENTEEN

"Why would you say that?" Xander asked, surprised.

"That she and I are the same? When she and I fought at the temple, she repeatedly told me that we were. That I was vengeful, angry, petty, and every other bad thing just like her. It was one of the reasons I didn't strike her down. I was afraid that doing so would make it true."

"It's not true." He let out a deep breath. "If she were not already dead, I would kill her for making you cry and for causing you to doubt yourself."

I shook my head. He didn't understand. "We have the same aspect of the goddess. Fury. And she could tell what I was thinking."

"That doesn't mean anything. As I've told you, you have an expressive face. Sometimes you are easy to read. Regardless, you wouldn't do what Lysimache did."

I admitted out loud the thing that I'd kept entirely to myself. "But I would want to."

"Wanting and doing are two different things. Actions speak to your character, not your thoughts. We all have thoughts we can't control, desires for things we cannot have, but we don't act on them. Life is choices. What we choose and do is what matters."

"I understood her," I whispered, scared to be sharing something so dark and ugly. "I understood the decisions she made. She even told me that she should have made me her heir. She thought that I would have joined her if she'd asked."

"Did you allow a temple full of priestesses to be murdered?" he demanded.

"No."

"Lia, look at me." When I raised my face to his, he said, "I know you don't have much reason to trust me. But believe me when I tell you this—you are *nothing* like Lysimache."

The rough conviction in his voice made tears form in my eyes.

"And I promise you now that if you become an evil monster bent on the destruction of two nations, I'll run you through myself." He had switched from seriousness to teasing me.

As if he could sense that I needed his lightheartedness. That it was the only thing keeping me from slipping under.

"You would never," I said.

"No, I wouldn't," he agreed. "If she claimed you as her heir, then you can go and take the temple treasury for your own. That could certainly help with the war effort."

"Io said all the treasure is covered in fire dragon's blood, so we'd have to find a way to remove it."

"Another vault you've broken into? And you brought my sister? Why am I not surprised?" he said with a smile.

That got me to smile in return. Xander had become my sheltered port in the storm. The world could rage around us, but here together, just the two of us, we could talk and tease and ignore how everything else was falling apart.

"Stay here. I'll be right back," he said.

He left and I missed him. He had only gone into the washroom but I wanted to follow him. To stay close to him. I needed his strength.

I was grateful when he returned quickly. He had a damp washcloth in one hand and a bar of soap in the other. He sat down next to me again.

"Sit up." He helped me into a sitting position. "Your hands are not the only place where there's blood."

I thought that he would hand me the washcloth, but he began to clean my face himself. My breath hitched when the warm cloth made contact with my skin. He was being so careful and gentle. I closed my eyes, overwhelmed with sensations and feelings.

"Last night you told me you could control your magic. Why didn't you turn it off?" His face was so close to mine that his words washed over me.

"I let it go too far," I said. I wasn't talking about the magic. I was talking about him.

He rubbed soap into one corner of the cloth to clean and then used another end to rinse it away. "There," he said. "Finished." He then turned his attention to my hands and began to clean those as well.

I didn't know what to do with this brutal warrior who was so carefully and sweetly washing me.

Xander had nearly finished with both of my hands when I whispered, "You scare me."

That made him pause. "Why?"

Because of what you make me feel.

I couldn't say that to him. Would he see it in my face? Would he understand?

"You scare me, too," he admitted quietly. He finished with my hands and let the washcloth and soap drop to the ground. He kept my hands out in front of me, running his fingers over mine. He touched me like I was delicate and precious and might shatter at any moment.

Then he lifted my right hand to his lips. I was about to ask him what he was doing when he pressed a kiss to one knuckle, then the next, down the line. He turned my hand over, and my breathing went shallow as he gently kissed the pad of each finger, one after another. Then a kiss on my palm, moving down to my wrist, where my pulse throbbed.

And every time his lips made contact with another spot on my skin, it was like he was sending me secret messages.

I'm here.

I understand.

I'm with you.

You are not alone.

I care about you.

His sister had been so insistent that he loved me.

What if he did?

If this was love, then it was the kind that made my bones ache and my soul burn. Fire and flood and earthquakes, just like Quynh had said.

He placed my hand against the side of his face and closed his eyes, as if he wanted nothing more than for me to touch him.

So I did.

I used both of my hands to trace the outline of his face, to run down the bridge of his nose, along his strong jawline, over his cheekbones, along his eyelids.

My fingers glided over his warm, smooth lips. I saw the knot in his throat bob, as if he were swallowing hard.

His eyes opened again and I gasped at what I saw there. I recognized the desire. The hunger. I had seen them many times before.

But now there was something else that made me tremble.

Tenderness. Warmth.

He looked at me like I was the only thing in the whole world that mattered to him.

A heaviness pressed into me as we gazed at each other. Something was different. Things had shifted in a way I didn't fully comprehend. I ached for him. I wanted him to make me feel whole again.

As if he sensed my need, he took my hands and placed them around his neck. I felt his hesitation as he put his hands on my waist, pulling me into his lap as he had last night. Like he expected me to shove him away. To tell him to stop.

I needed his strength, his sureness. When I pressed myself against him, he gave it to me. His arms hugged me to him so tightly.

"You are a good person." He said the words against the side of my head and I closed my eyes. "I know who you are. All will be well."

I let my face fall against his neck. I wanted to believe him. To sink into his arms and block everything else out. Let him be my true husband and partner. To allow myself to rely on him, to let him fight off everyone and everything that would hurt me.

In that moment, I knew he would, if I only asked.

It had become so natural to me to seek comfort in his arms. He stroked my spine, slowly up and down, meaning to soothe.

Not to inflame.

But it still happened.

I drew my head back so that I could see his beautiful eyes. "Xander, what are we?" I asked.

Confusion briefly marred his features. "Husband and wife."

"No, what *are* we?"

"I . . ." He didn't have an answer.

At least not one with words.

His expression turned guarded and unsure for a moment, showing me his vulnerability, before he leaned forward and rubbed his nose against mine. As he had so many times before in our shared dreams.

I melted from it.

Then he tilted his head so that his lips were just above mine, our breath intermingling while I waited in a crazed anticipation.

His mouth finally landed on mine, soft as butterfly wings. His kiss was slow, every movement intentional in a way that no other kiss between us had ever been.

So deliberate. So undemanding. So careful.

So tender.

Somehow he had captured my entire soul with this kiss.

"What is that?" I whispered.

"This is called kissing," he said with a soft smile before returning his lips to mine.

When he and I had first met, he had kissed me this way. Gently and sweetly. I had demanded that he kiss me passionately. I had dismissed his soft kisses as less than.

What a fool I had been!

This was still like slipping into a warm bath, but a warm bath that caused me to feel safe and protected and made every inch of my body demand more. Emotions swirled behind his kisses, enveloping me. As if they'd always been there, hiding behind the anger, behind the passion we had used to disguise them.

There had been a connection between us from the beginning, no matter how hard I'd tried to fight it.

I clung to his powerful shoulders, his biceps, the parts of his body that promised they would protect me. Shelter me from every enemy. Keep out the storm.

His kiss was devastatingly sensual, poignant, light as air. He moved his lips against mine as if to prove that there was a universe of sensation I had never experienced before and he was determined to show it to me.

I sagged into his kiss. Surrendering. Wholeheartedly giving myself to him, willing to be swept up in this.

He kissed me as if I were precious. Cherished. It made my heart swell and soar to the point that I was worried I might stop breathing.

Then he began to slowly lower me back against the bed. I went more than willingly, arching up against him so that our connection wouldn't be broken. But he did take his lips from mine when I lay flat, and I nearly whimpered.

"Why are you kissing me like this?" I asked, feeling dazed.

"Not every fire needs to be ignited quickly. They can also be built slowly." His voice was low and ruined and every one of his words felt like falling sparks against my skin, singeing me.

"But why?" I marveled at my ability to speak.

He froze in place, his eyes locked on mine. "You know why."

I wanted him to say the words. I wanted to say the words to him.

Neither thing could happen.

His mouth returned to mine, and at least his kiss was completely honest. There were no lies there, no deceptions, no manipulations.

Just us.

He worshipped me with his lips, touched me with a burning reverence that made all the blood in my body throb fast and molten. I didn't understand how a kiss could be so devastatingly tender and overwhelmingly passionate at the same time.

"Wife." He somehow managed to make the word both gentle and possessive.

"Husband," I sighed back. His lips whispered along my throat, and I lifted my chin to give him better access, arching up into him. My stomach knotted with pleasure. I wanted more. I needed to feed the fire that begged to be set free, to burn and consume everything in its path.

To kiss him in a way that felt more familiar and less scary.

I pulled his face back to mine and tried to kiss him, to show him how I was feeling, but he held himself just out of reach.

"No," he said, kissing my forehead so tenderly that I thought I might cry. "This isn't that."

My mind was numb and buzzing at the same time, and it was like I couldn't understand anything that was happening. Why had he stopped me?

"Don't be afraid," he murmured against my lips. "I feel it, too."

He was in no hurry. He didn't deepen the kiss. Instead it was like he was trying to convey something to me, only it was in a language I didn't speak.

Then I realized that this was for me. He wasn't pursuing his own desires—he wanted to show me this. How it could be.

He kissed me with a dreamy, delicate thoroughness that unleashed a cascade of exquisite sensations inside me. His long, slow kiss broke me apart, flooding me with warmth, and I combusted, turning into smoke. Ethereal, intangible. Floating away. Our edges blurred together in this slow intimacy and I couldn't stop trembling.

This was what I had wanted—to pretend bad things weren't happening. To shut out everyone and everything. Only Xander and his kisses could make the whole world disappear.

He lifted his head slightly and gazed at me again.

"How does this make you feel?" he asked.

"Good."

"No, my little princess. How do you feel?" He took my hand and placed it against his chest so that I could feel his heartbeat. Steady, strong. It reminded me of when Suri had done it . . . as a way to express her feelings to me.

How did I feel? I felt cherished. Adored.

Loved.

It was Lysimache's taunt that filled my head. *Do you really think you can access the goddess's power if you do not do what you promised her?*

My heart beat violently and erratically. It was suddenly too much. I couldn't do this. I couldn't risk everything just for this moment. I wouldn't let Locris be utterly destroyed.

Not Ilion, either.

"I can't. We can't. I have to go." I shoved against him, and he moved slightly so that I could dart out from underneath him. I bounded across the bed and scrambled for the door, running out into the hallway.

CHAPTER EIGHTEEN

It felt like I had ripped my own skin off and left it behind. My nerves were raw and exposed, and for the rest of my life, I would never forget the look on his face when I told him we couldn't. The betrayal, the disappointment.

The hurt.

My body ached so badly for him that I nearly went back. I wanted him more than almost anything else. He was the one who had just told me that it was fine to feel desire for things we couldn't have so long as we didn't act on it.

But we had acted on it.

Had my words somehow caused this? I was the one who had told Lysimache that I would go home and have sex with my husband. As if I had spoken it into existence.

That woman was haunting me. I thought of how she had stopped caring about other people because it had brought her too much suffering and grief. She had closed herself off to everyone.

Would I do the same?

Didn't I have to? How was I supposed to keep my vows when Xander kissed me like that? Wasn't turning off my emotions the only solution?

Tears blinded me and I ran into someone.

"Lia? Are you all right?" It was Dolion.

I shook my head, not trusting myself to speak. He led me into a small sitting room. I had come down to the main floor and not even realized it.

"What happened?" he asked as he closed the door. "Did someone hurt you?"

Again, I shook my head. No one had hurt me.

Except me.

I went over to the table and chairs and sat down, running my hand along the edge of the table to give myself extra leverage because I wasn't sure that I could control all my limbs properly.

"Ow!" I said when a small piece of wood went into my finger. I held it up. Did Xander feel this?

This was what he had done. He had embedded himself deep in my skin, a painful, constant reminder that no matter what else I was doing or thinking of, he was there.

"Let me help you with that," Dolion said. He took out a small knife and used the tip of it to dig the splinter out of my finger. It hurt but not as bad as what had just occurred in my bedroom. A few seconds later it was over, the piece of wood gone, but my finger still throbbed.

"I'm sorry about what happened today with Lysimache," he said. The polite thing to do would be to acknowledge what he was saying and forgive him. But I was still too upset about today's events. I didn't have it in me to be benevolent.

He moved his chair close to mine so that we were nearly touching, which surprised me. "Lia, it is so hard for me to see you this way. There have been so many times when I have witnessed how unhappy you are and it tears me apart."

What? My pulse spiked. This didn't sound like ordinary concern. It almost sounded . . . romantic. This was not the way he should speak to me. "You're saying this because you are my friend." I needed to make certain that line was there.

Then Dolion reached for my hands. I was so shocked that I didn't immediately pull away as I should have. "I would be more than a friend to you if you would let me."

I yanked my hands from his. "I am married. To your phratry brother."

"It's not a real marriage." I remembered the day after our wedding, when Xander had told me that his brothers all knew the truth of our relationship. "He doesn't make you happy. I could make you happy."

"You don't know what you're saying," I protested. I didn't feel that way about Dolion. At all.

"I heard your conversation with the high priestess. I know that you have to remain celibate. I would honor that. I would respect your vows. My intentions toward you are pure." Was he implying that Xander's weren't? What had Xander told his brothers?

He leaned toward me and I jumped out of my chair. He stood slowly, his gaze never leaving my face. "I would take care of you. Erase your sadness, wipe away all your tears. Treat you the way you should be treated."

"Dolion, no." I didn't know what else to say.

Something that looked like anger briefly flashed in his eyes. "You would let him use you to get what he wants. You're a means to an end for him."

"At one point I believed that, but now—"

"Now what?" he interrupted me. "He's seduced you into trusting him?"

The Lia from a few weeks ago would have believed everything that he was saying. But too much had changed.

His shoulders dropped. "I'm sorry. I don't know what I'm doing. It was just . . . when I heard your conversation and you told Lysimache that you were going to go home and have sex with Xander, I thought that I had run out of time to tell you how I felt. To let you know that you don't have to stay with him. We could run away from all of this."

If he thought that I would leave Quynh, my adelphia, Ilion, with everything that was going on, he couldn't possibly love me.

Because he didn't know me at all.

My grandmother had taught me how to let down a suitor kindly, and I tried to remember her words. "Dolion, while I appreciate that you—"

Before I could react, his mouth was on mine, kissing me. Revulsion filled the back of my throat. This was so wrong. I quickly put my hands on his chest and shoved him away. I wiped my lips with the back of my hand, as if I could erase it. "Do not ever do that again."

"Don't lie to yourself out of some kind of misplaced loyalty. You enjoyed that."

Nothing could have been further from the truth.

Dolion was not the man I had thought he was.

This made me look at everything that had happened between us through a different lens. Like when he had brought me flowers. I had thought it was a nice, friendly gesture, but it had been because he had feelings for me.

I remembered how jealous Xander had been that night when he found Dolion and me together. And nothing had even happened. What would he do if I told him about this?

He might actually attack Dolion. And I didn't want their relationship to be destroyed. They were still phratry brothers.

"I am not going to tell Xander," I said. It was not for Dolion's benefit, but because I didn't want it to hurt my husband. "Whatever friendship you and I had is over. I don't want you to speak to me or come anywhere near me."

He stared at me and said bitterly, "I shouldn't be surprised. This is what you do. Destroy the hearts of the people around you, oblivious to the pain you cause."

He wrenched the door open and left while I stood there, unsure of what to do next. Would he tell Xander? I couldn't imagine that he would, but if he did . . . would Xander believe that I had nothing to do with it? That Dolion had kissed me and I had immediately put a stop to it?

I couldn't stay in this room. I exited and went right, toward the main library. That felt like a safe place to go. No one except me ever went in there.

Maybe if I could hide here the rest of the day, nothing else bad would happen.

I tried reading but I couldn't concentrate. So instead I sat there with a book open in front of me and stared out the window. I thought about my life and how wrong everything was and how I didn't know what to do to fix it.

Hours and hours passed while I sat and stared and pondered.

"There you are!" It had started to grow dark when Io and Suri came into the library.

"How did you find me?"

Suri smiled to let me know that she had been responsible.

"And why are you awake?" I asked Io. "You took a potion. I thought you were going to sleep for a long time."

"I've slept long enough. The dose I took this morning was a small one so that I could get back to work. After Zalira told us what happened with Lysimache, Suri and I went to my mother's library to search for answers."

Io didn't know this, but I supposed that it was now technically my library, since Xander had gifted it to me. Back when she was trying to convince me to love her brother, she would have seen his gesture as romantic, which was why I hadn't told her. Now I worried that it might hurt her that he'd given it to me instead of her. And that she would be upset about the potential implications.

"We tried to look up information about people who worship Arion but couldn't find anything. And Suri couldn't sense any books about his hammer. I do remember Maia mentioning something about god-weapons, weapons forged and used by the gods in their battles with one another, but that information doesn't seem to be in the library, either."

"Perhaps Lysimache was able to destroy those books."

"We did find one book that spoke about Arion and his hatred for his mother," Io said. "He is close to his father, the sun god, and despises his mother for rejecting his father. It also said that he always thought his sister, with her celestial powers, was their mother's favorite, while he was bound to the earth and metal. He blamed and resented his mother for restricting his gifts. It's why he sold his sister into marriage, to punish both the mother and daughter."

"That . . . sounds incredibly petty. You would think gods would be above such things," I said. "Lysimache said Arion wanted to destroy the goddess. Do you remember that line I read to you from the book Suri found for me? It said the gods bickered over mortals because they draw their strength from their believers."

"So if Arion wanted to destroy his mother, he would have to kill everyone who believes in her to weaken her."

I nodded. "I can't imagine that it would be easy to destroy an immortal goddess. If he could eliminate where she draws her strength from . . ."

We sat there quietly for a few moments, absorbing this information. "Again, I understand why the goddess doesn't want us to have children," Io said with a shudder. "Can you imagine what it must feel like to have your own son hate you so much?"

With what I'd felt from the goddess in my dreams, I didn't understand. She was so loving and kind. Why would Arion want to end her?

"When is the last time you ate?" Io asked me, and my stomach grumbled in response. She laughed and said, "Come to my room and we'll feed you."

I felt a bit anxious about leaving the library, not knowing if we might run into Dolion. Fortunately, neither Io nor Suri seemed to pick up on my discomfort as I trailed behind them.

Io was discussing the potion she'd been working on to break the physical link between Xander and me. "I feel like I have the right ingredients. It's just the ratios that aren't correct."

"Maybe you'd be able to figure it out if you slept," I said. Suri nodded, agreeing with my point. "We've already seen that lack of sleep makes you stabbier."

Io ignored my last comment. "When I take the fortification potion, if I'm not using magic, it lasts for so long. Sleeping takes up a ridiculous amount of time. I'm getting so much done without distractions. Like I've already ordered all our dresses for Erisa's party."

I did not care about that party. I wondered if we could skip it. I didn't want to feed into Erisa's delusions.

There were more important things to worry about.

We got back to Io's room and Suri cocked her head toward the door.

"You're going to find Zalira and Ahyana?" Io asked, and Suri nodded. Once she had gone, I decided this was as good a time as any to ask Io for help. I only hoped that she would say yes.

Taking in a deep breath, I said, "Io? I need to ask you for a favor."

CHAPTER NINETEEN

"What?" Io's expression had turned wary. It was very unlike her. She was usually the first person to volunteer to help.

Then I realized why she had reacted that way. She thought I was going to ask her for a favor about her brother.

Like asking her to retract her request that I stay away from him.

"If something happens to me, I need you to promise to do what you can to get the eye of the goddess and then use it to restore Locris. You don't have to stay, just save it."

Her face softened. "Of course I would do that for you."

"I don't know the right words or what aspect to use but I know you would be able to figure it out." If anyone had the right kind of magic to fix Locris, it was Io.

"I promise that I will," she said.

That was a relief. I thanked her. I hoped it would be possible for either her or me to save Locris, but there were so many obstacles in our way. "What if Artemisia destroys the eye?"

"I don't think that she would," Io said. "She'll be looking for a way to use it. She knows it has power, and she will utilize every weapon at her disposal to annihilate us. I'm sure Lysimache never told her that it could restore your nation. Why would she? She wanted Artemisia to wield it against us."

The only reason that Artemisia would move against Locris was because of Lysimache. Locris didn't have enough believers to power the goddess, so she would attack solely because of Lysimache's personal need for vengeance.

The rest of my adelphia entered the room. Suri closed the door so that we could sit and talk. Io handed me a bowl of dates and nuts and I snacked on them as everyone took their spots.

Io told them what we had figured out about Arion and how his followers were most likely planning to attack his mother's believers to weaken her.

"Could we invoke him?" Ahyana asked. "Call on him since we have his name? Use him somehow?"

"I can't imagine that would work," Io said. "We are followers of his mother. He has no power over us or to give us. For all we know, his abilities might counteract our own because they're enemies."

"There's so much we believed that is turning out not to be what we thought," Zalira said. "It's scary how one person could trick so many people. It still baffles me that Lysimache made up the tribute race and convinced everyone that it was the goddess's will."

It was something I couldn't think about too much—all those lives needlessly lost, all those grieving Locrian families. "It also wrecks my theory that the red-dirt pirates came after Quynh and me in order to offend the goddess. She wouldn't have been upset if the Locrian maidens had been taken from the race."

Zalira shook her head. "The pirates wouldn't have known that. Your entire nation thought you were doing the goddess's will—why would it be different anywhere else? No one knew about Lysimache's lies. So that might still be why they tried to abduct you."

That was true.

"Speaking of things that Lysimache made up," Ahyana said, "I was hoping you could tell us a bit more about what happened at the end of your interrogation. Not the part where she died, but what exactly she said. Zalira could only remember the gist."

I didn't think I'd ever forget—it was like every word of that conversation had been permanently seared into my soul as some kind of curse.

"At first she told me that she'd kept some rituals, reinstituted old ones that had been done away with, and created new ones."

"But we don't know which thing we follow is which," Ahyana said in frustration.

It was easy to guess which particular rule she was concerned about. "I asked her what laws and rules she had changed, but she was resisting answering and didn't say anything coherent. I specifically asked about priestesses marrying in the past, which she confirmed and seemed to indicate that the rules around it had been changed by different high priestesses, including her. When I asked her why, she fought not to answer, and what came out was, 'Because couldn't risk them,' and then she slit her own throat so she wouldn't have to answer."

Ahyana frowned. "So Lysimache was willing to tell you every other part of her evil plan, but when it came to priestesses getting married, she killed herself rather than discuss it? That seems significant to me."

She was right. It did mean something.

"Which way did it get changed?" Io asked. "Is marriage allowed and Lysimache undid it, or was it not allowed and she instituted it and then took it away again?"

Lysimache had mentioned the high priestess who had forbidden them from using magic. We didn't know who had made changes over the centuries or for what purpose. What was true and what had been tampered with.

"Maybe she changed her mind about it every few hundred years to hurt people," Zalira offered.

"I can see Lysimache doing that—telling women they could marry when it went against the goddess's law just to condemn them in the next life," I said.

"If it was allowed," Ahyana said, "and Lysimache stopped it, then that means the celibacy vow is fake and shouldn't be followed."

There wasn't anyone in this room who wanted that to be true more than I did. "Lysimache specifically talked to me about my relationship with Xander. She said that if I broke my vow, I couldn't use the goddess's power."

"Did she know at that point that you'd given her a truth serum?" Io asked.

"Yes."

Io looked troubled. "What exactly did she say?"

"She said, 'And break your vow? I know you think you can save Locris. Do you really think you can access the goddess's power if you do not do what you promised her?'"

"I was afraid of that," Io said with a sigh.

"What?" Ahyana demanded.

"Not that I want to encourage anyone here, but it is possible with the serum to say something that isn't a lie and sounds like the truth without it actually being true. Lysimache asked questions. She didn't give answers or definitive statements. She let Lia's imagination do the work."

I dropped the date I'd been holding. By the goddess, how had I not realized that before? What did that mean?

Io added, "Someone like Lysimache, who told you that she'd used truth serums many times before, would know how to circumvent it."

Ahyana instantly stood and after a moment sat back down.

"What was that?" her sister asked.

"I was going to go find Rokh, but I just remembered that he's on a mission for Xander," she replied.

My first thought was, *What mission?* My second was that if Rokh had been in the palace, Ahyana would have found him and broken her vow. It seemed she had decided the celibacy vow wasn't real, but I couldn't take that risk by leaping to the same conclusion. I didn't know what was true and what wasn't. I'd made that promise to the goddess, and I had to hold to it if I expected her help.

"What did the high priestesses risk by priestesses being married?" Zalira asked, and no one responded.

"There's no way to even guess," Io said. "It could be a million different things."

And now we would never know because Lysimache was gone.

"I wish I had a second aspect," Ahyana said. "One that could bring the goddess down here so that we could ask her our questions."

That reminded me of something I hadn't told my sisters yet. "Xander mentioned something strange to me last night. He said that my eyes turn green in our shared dreams. That it looks the same as when I do magic."

More silence from the group.

"Do Xander's eyes turn green in your dreams?" Io asked.

"No." He always looked like himself. I was the one with changing hair lengths and different-colored eyes.

"Then that means that you're using the goddess's power. I would think that if it were due to the goddess creating the dreams, you'd both be affected, and so both of your eyes would turn green. The fact that it only happens to you . . . you're behind the dreams."

That couldn't have been true. "That would mean I have two aspects. That's not possible." It was something Maia had emphasized to us repeatedly—that we could connect with only one aspect of the goddess. Fury and controlling dreams? Those were two different aspects.

The only person I could ask about it, Lysimache, had eliminated herself as a possible resource.

"And I've never used the words," I said. "I've never called on the goddess before dreaming."

"Maybe because you're the savior, it happens naturally. You don't need to call on her," Io replied.

"Are you saying there's two kinds of magic?"

"There might be thousands," Io said. "We don't know."

I thought of Rokh and his shape-shifting. How the women in his family could control the sex of their babies. I hadn't heard of anything similar in Ilion. There were obviously other types of magic in the world—I just hadn't realized that we'd be dealing with that personally.

"When did the dreams start?" Zalira asked.

I thought back. "On the *Nikos*. That was the first time." I had dreamed of Xander. Or Jason, the name I called him back then.

Was he tied into this somehow? Was he responsible for me gaining this ability? I'd always felt a connection to him. Was this part of it?

"You should try it tonight," Io said. "Use the aspect and see if you can control what happens."

To a degree, I already had. There had been the night when I had started to dream of when Haemon left Locris. Xander had already seen some of my most vulnerable moments, and I hadn't wanted him to witness that one as well. I had verbally complained that my dreams were always about my life and not about Xander's.

And then the dream had shifted and changed and I saw him as a little boy, when he'd found his mother's body after she killed herself.

Did this mean I was also responsible for the nightmares that had been plaguing me for the last few weeks? Had I somehow sent the message to Xander that he needed to hold me so that I wouldn't have them? As if my subconscious were manifesting my desire to be close to him?

If that was true . . . I would owe him another apology.

"What is the dream aspect again?" I asked, not sure if I remembered it correctly.

"Nyctipolus. Night walking," Zalira said.

I had interpreted that aspect literally. When the goddess had searched for her missing daughter, the sun god had removed himself so that she wouldn't have any light. She had carried a torch and walked through the endless night looking for her. It had never occurred to me that it might be speaking about dreaming. But that was true—in a sense, I had been night walking.

And night talking and night fighting and night kissing.

"I'll try it," I said. It still seemed unbelievable to me.

"You had better hope we can have more than one aspect," Io said. "Because if we don't, you won't have a way to save Locris."

She was right. I had been operating under the belief that the magic of the eye of the goddess would work without an aspect. That its power was independent of all this. But Lysimache had said she'd used her aspect to destroy, which meant that I'd need an aspect to create. My fury aspect wouldn't restore anything. It wasn't meant to.

"I can worry about that later," I said. Although fixing Locris was my priority, too many other things had to happen first.

Namely, getting the eye back from Artemisia. "If Artemisia is carrying a god-weapon, how are we supposed to stand up against that?" I asked.

"It seems to me that the only way would be to have a god-weapon of our own," Ahyana observed.

"The savior is supposed to wield the greatest weapon," Io mused. "It can't be the eye because Artemisia has it. And I can't imagine how you'd get it back from her if she has Arion's hammer."

Zalira leaned back against the wall. "The goddess had a god-weapon. Her golden sword."

Maia had spoken about that particular sword on multiple occasions, including during my induction ceremony at the temple. She had said that the goddess had used it, cutting her hand and letting her blood spill upon the earth to create all life.

"Maybe it's in the temple vault," I said.

Suri shook her head.

No.

We'd never specifically looked for that item, but considering what it was, I couldn't blame her for being certain. I guessed something like that would wield a great deal of magic and power. She wouldn't have been able to miss it. It would have stood out.

"And not in the palace vault either, I'm assuming," I said.

No.

"The palace vault!" Io jumped up and ran over to her bookshelf. "I completely forgot about this."

She pulled out a scroll. It was the one Suri had found for me in the palace treasury. It had been labeled "the greatest weapon," but the scroll was blank. Io had tried various methods to get it to reveal its secrets, but nothing had ever worked.

That was also before we had magic.

She took it over to the table and used full cups of water to weigh down the edges, rolling it out smooth. "It's a puzzle," she said. "We just have to solve it."

I noticed her hands were trembling. Had she been eating and drinking? "Are you all right?" I asked.

"I'm fine," she said, waving me off. "I think if we all work together on this, we'll get it. Maybe we could all take a fortification potion tonight and stay up? I'm sure we'll solve it quickly. Or Suri could use her power to find the secret of how it works!"

Suri shot Io an apologetic look, indicating that her aspect wouldn't work in this situation.

I wondered why. Perhaps because the information the scroll had wasn't lost. Or what if it was protected by some kind of enchantment?

"Maybe we should call it a night," Zalira said, sounding as worried as I felt. "Get some rest."

"You should all stop worrying," Io said. "I told you I'm fine. Perhaps we need to do more research. Go down to my mother's library and have Suri search to see if there's an answer about the key to unlocking this scroll. We can just—"

She had been reaching for a book on the far end of her table but accidentally knocked over one of the glasses of water holding the papyrus in place.

It soaked the scroll.

"Oh no!" Io said, her hands going to her cheeks. "I didn't mean to do that! That was so . . ."

Her voice trailed off as we all witnessed the same thing.

The papyrus soaked the water up and lines began to form on the scroll in front of us.

CHAPTER TWENTY

None of the lines connected. They were just randomly dispersed across the scroll. It made no sense.

"What just happened?" Ahyana asked.

Io started muttering to herself. "The savior, greatest weapon, a trial of the elements . . . that's it!"

She rushed forward toward the scroll and Suri put her hand out, as if to stop her from getting too close, but she brushed past.

Io sucked in a deep breath and then blew as hard as she could on the scroll.

More lines appeared.

"We need the elements to unlock it!" she exclaimed.

"I have dirt!" I said. I ran into my room and opened my trunk to get my pot of Locrian soil. I brought it back into Io's room and placed a handful of it on the scroll.

But nothing happened. The dirt remained on top of the scroll and no new lines appeared.

"Why wouldn't that work?" Zalira asked.

I racked my brain until I came up with, "Maybe because this is from Locris? Lysimache cursed it, so it won't work on the scroll."

Suri ran out of the room, and without her saying so, I knew she was going to grab dirt from the courtyard. That would be the closest place. Io picked up the scroll and let the Locrian dirt fall to the ground before placing the papyrus back on the table.

"We need fire!" Ahyana said, rushing over to where the flint and tinder were kept. She brought them back over.

"What if the scroll catches fire and gets destroyed?" Zalira asked. That was a valid point.

"We have to have faith," Io said. She took the flint and tinder and went over to the fireplace and sparked an ember onto a long piece of bark, which immediately caught fire. Io brought it back over to the scroll, laying the bark on top of it.

Everyone held their breath and watched. The scroll sucked in the fire until it was gone. The papyrus didn't burn.

More lines appeared.

Suri returned then with a handful of dirt and dropped it on top. The scroll accepted this dirt, and it dissolved into the papyrus.

Even more lines.

"Is that writing in the bottom left corner?" Zalira asked, getting closer. If they were words, they were unintelligible. What if they were written in a language we couldn't read?

It was impossible to tell what the scroll was trying to convey. The lines needed to be completed. We were missing an element.

"We need aether," Io said sadly. The fifth element. "Where are we supposed to get that?"

"I'd bet if Lia told Xander to go pull her down a star, he'd find a way to do it." Ahyana was teasing, probably in an attempt to lighten the mood, as I was sure we'd all come to the same conclusion.

We had no access to aether. We couldn't get our answer from the scroll.

Her words also had the unintended side effect of making me remember Xander asking, "Would you also like me to fetch the sun and put it on a chain so that you can wear it around your neck?" when we had been negotiating the terms of our marriage.

Then he'd given me a sun pendant. And I remembered the way he had caressed me with that necklace, and it put all sorts of unbidden images from that night into my mind.

I tried to shove them out. This wasn't the time.

But now that my husband was in my head, I again started thinking about the dreams and how I might be responsible for them. Could my dreams help me find solutions? If it was the goddess's magic, I had spoken to her in my dreams before. What if I tried to focus on getting an answer?

"Is there a substitute for aether we could use?" Zalira asked.

Io shook her head. "Not that I can think of. And it can't be created, either. It's an element, a base material. We have to get something that has it in order to complete the scroll."

She sat down dejectedly in a chair, putting her head in her hands. We had been so close but it wasn't enough.

"We'll figure it out," I said, leaning down to hug Io.

I hoped that was true.

It was well past midnight before Xander came to bed. He looked surprised to see me sitting up, waiting for him. My heart pounded furiously in my chest, bruising my rib cage.

"Why are you still awake?" he asked as he closed the door. He tended to do it more quietly at night.

"I was waiting for you." Could he hear how loud my heartbeat was? Could he see my pulse throbbing in my neck? I was so nervous to talk to him.

"It's late, wife. I want to go to sleep."

"Please. Just a few minutes."

He hesitated, as if making up his mind, and then he nodded. He took off the cloak he'd been wearing and let it drop to the floor. I wondered where he had gone, what he'd been doing.

But I knew now was not the time to ask.

Xander sat down on our bed, leaving a great deal of space between us, unlike earlier, when he'd sat so close that we were touching.

I wasn't sure how to begin. Should I apologize for fleeing this morning? Explain why I had panicked? Help him to understand what I'd been thinking?

That wasn't really what he and I did. We didn't sit down and discuss things rationally. We threw out accusations and threats and fought.

I wanted more than that. I wanted to work with him, not against him.

"Earlier today . . ." I started and then immediately stopped, wringing my hands together. Why was I so scared? Why was this so hard?

After another few beats he spoke. "I shared what you told me about the hammer of Arion with the palace's scholars and historians. I'm hopeful that they'll find something."

"Lysimache bragged about destroying books. I'm not sure they'll come up with anything useful. Io and Suri checked your mother's library and there wasn't any information about it there, either."

"Your library," he absentmindedly corrected me while rubbing the back of his neck.

"My library," I said, ignoring the warmth currently spreading through my chest.

More silence until he asked, "Why did you run away from me this morning?"

"Because . . . because nothing has changed."

I couldn't tell what he was thinking. His passive expression gave nothing away. "Everything has changed. The high priestess is dead. My contract with her is null and void."

Oh. I hadn't considered that. He had promised to keep me a maiden, and he had promised that to Theano.

"And there are no more temple guards," he added. It made me wonder if Ahyana had told that to Rokh, who had passed it along to Xander. "No one will bury you alive."

Despite his calm demeanor, I heard the tone in his voice that made me think he was holding himself back. There was longing, even if it was faint.

“My vow wasn’t to the high priestess,” I reminded him. “I made my vow to the goddess. I . . . I can’t.”

A dark mischief lit up his eyes. “I promise not to tell her.”

“That’s not how this works. She will know.”

“What do you think she would do to you?”

“In order to be able to wield magic, I have to abstain from ‘pleasures of the flesh.’”

“Who told you that?”

“The life mage apprentice that I briefly held against his will. He said that in order for the magic to work, the life mages had to avoid ‘pleasures of the flesh.’” I felt foolish saying the phrase again.

“That’s a shame. Pleasures of the flesh are the best kind.”

I think he meant to tease, but it came across rough and full of desire and my body responded. My stomach went molten; my skin felt feverish, desperate for his touch; my lungs no longer functioned. I had to swallow it all down, push it aside.

When I finally got my voice working again, it was shaking. “It’s not just the magic. It’s the fact that I’m supposed to be the savior. I don’t know what I’m meant to do, but I do know that I have to remain in favor with the goddess by obeying her rules.”

“Do you really believe that you’re the savior?”

Part of me wanted to laugh. “I don’t know what to believe. Can you imagine a worse person for that position?”

“I can think of no one better,” he said quietly. Oh, that was like a direct hit to my heart. He was tugging on my emotions again and that was too dangerous. It would be easier if I kept this about our physicality.

I wished this nervousness would abate. “I know that we have always had this.”

“This?”

I gestured between us. “This physical attraction. We have always wanted each other, even when we were furious. So maybe this isn’t fair of me, but I want us to be . . . us. The way we were in our dreams. Being able to talk and laugh. We have been friends and I would like that again." We had also been doing many other pleasurable things to one another in those dreams, and I hoped he wouldn't bring that up.

This seemed foolish. I reminded myself that, just a few hours ago, I had wanted his disdain and anger because they helped to create a chasm that made things easier for me on the attraction front.

But I needed him in my life in some form. I knew we were meant to work together. There was a reason he'd been in my dreams for so long.

A reason why when I first met him, it was like remembering someone I had forgotten.

"I told you," he said, and his heated voice skated over my skin. "Whatever you want, you have only to ask and I will do it."

All the air in the room left and I couldn't breathe. When he'd said that before, we'd been mostly naked and he had been using his mouth to do the most—

He suddenly stood and went into the washroom.

I decided to take this opportunity to teach my body how to move oxygen in and out of my lungs again, and to calm myself down. I couldn't ask him to be my friend and then immediately turn around and pounce on him.

When he came back out, my heart lifted at seeing him. He walked over to the bed, looking down at me. He reached for a pillow and a blanket and put them on the floor.

A sick taste filled my mouth as I watched him settle in. My racing heartbeat was no longer from desire but from fear. He had told me once that he would never sleep on the floor. That if I wanted to be away from him, I was welcome to do so—but he never would.

Now he was.

I should let this happen. Get distance. Let the divide between us grow wider.

But I didn't want to keep being caught in the same endless cycle.

"Are you angry with me?" I asked.

He was in the midst of arranging the blanket over him when he stopped to look at me. "I'm not trying to punish you, wife. I'm . . . doing what I promised Io. Protecting you. Even from me."

I didn't want that. I wanted to be close to him. Even if that wasn't fair to either one of us.

"I trust you," I said softly. I knew that he could control himself. Much better than I could.

He made a sound at the back of his throat and then lay down. "I think it's better if we stay apart."

My legs were trembling, but I managed to scoot to the edge and walk over to him. I knelt down. "I don't. I want to be with you."

It was one of the most honest and scary things I'd ever said to him, and I felt completely exposed. Vulnerable. Like I had crawled out on the highest limb of a tree and walked to the edge.

Would he pull me to him or let me fall? I waited. He could turn on his side and ignore me and I would leave him alone. Or if he told me to go, I would.

"Please," I said.

He held his arms out and reached for me. I cuddled up next to him while he put the blanket over both of us. The floor was cold and hard but I didn't care. I wanted to be close to him.

No, it wasn't just want. I *needed* it. At some point I had started to need him, and while the thought terrified me, this time it wasn't enough to make me leave his arms.

CHAPTER TWENTY-ONE

His breath quickly evened out and stirred the hair along my forehead. I felt his heartbeat beneath my hand and tried to remind myself that I had promised Io not to do this.

Her request should have meant more to me. She was my adelphia sister and I loved her, and I had given her my word to try not to hurt her brother. I thought of Quynh saying what Io had done was unfair, that it should be up to me and Xander to choose what we wanted.

The problem was that I didn't usually think of Io when I was with him. Keeping my oaths was important to me. I did want to keep my word to her, but I couldn't hang on to it. The only thing driving me where he was concerned was the vow.

If it were not for that . . .

I sighed. I shouldn't let myself get caught up in what might have been, because those things never would be.

Since I couldn't keep away from Xander, at the very least I could test out Io's theory that I had two aspects.

"Dea Nyctipolus," I said. "Let me see what I need to see."

"Have a seat, stupid girl." Demaratus sat on a crumbling stone fence. We were staring at an open field covered in broken weapons and dead bodies. Carts and trees had burned, leaving a haze of smoke behind. The air reeked of blood and decay.

"What happened here?" I asked.

"War." He lifted his wineskin to his mouth and took a long drink. He offered it to me but I remembered all too well that Daemonian wine tasted like vinegar and shook my head.

"When you talked about battles, this isn't what I pictured. You made it sound glorious and exciting. This is just death. Destruction. Loss."

"That's all war is. Two great flames racing toward one another, consuming everything in their path until all that's left is a curse of ashes."

"Then why do it?"

"Do you know the secret of happiness?" he asked. He must have been drunk. It was the only reason he would speak this much.

"Terrible wine?"

He shook his head. "The secret of happiness is freedom. And the secret of freedom is courage. We fight to stop those who would take our freedom and our lives from us."

"War is coming for me," I said. I explained to him what was happening, what I was up against, the prophecy. He took it all in and didn't ask any questions or interject. "Erisa, the former queen, is telling everyone that nothing is happening. The council won't prepare for a possible invasion."

"Truth is usually the first casualty of war," he observed.

"I'm not sure I can do any of this. Be the savior. Why me? I'm not a hero."

"You can be. Heroes aren't braver than anyone else. They're just braver for a few minutes longer."

"The odds against me are overwhelming. I don't think I'm going to survive this," I confessed.

"It's from the greatest dangers that the greatest glories are won."

"You are waxing very poetic," I said.

He held up his wineskin as an explanation.

I smiled. "You know, I don't hear you as often in my head as I used to."

Demaratus frowned. "Why were you hearing me in your head in the first place?"

"I don't know. You're the person always questioning me and helping me figure things out. Like when we trained together."

"Stupid girl, I'm not in your head."

"You are now. This is my dream."

"Maybe you're in my head," he countered.

"I don't think you'd enjoy that very much."

"I would not," he agreed.

That made me laugh, and then I sighed. "I miss seeing you. I'm very grateful for everything you've taught me. It's why I'm still here."

"I am an excellent teacher."

"Yes, you are. I wish you were here in Ilion to help with this fight. I was going to send you a letter about it, but you never respond. No one in my family responds."

"I've never received a letter from you."

The battlefield in front of us cleared—everything disappearing instantly. I heard growls and watched as terawolves suddenly appeared at the far end of the field, coming out from the tree line.

"Finally, a worthy opponent," Demaratus said. He put his wineskin down and pulled out his sword.

"You're going to fight them?" I asked. He didn't know what he was signing up for.

He pointed at the largest wolf in front. "There's something the ancients used to do. They would decide their wars with one-on-one combat between two great warriors. But since we don't do that anymore, concentrate on taking out their leader. If that one falls, the others will scatter."

They were a pack; I doubted that was true. "I hate terawolves."

He gave me a half smile. "Battles are won because you love who is behind you more than you hate who waits in front of you. It's why you'll win your war."

Then he let out a roar as he ran into the empty field. The terawolves barreled toward him. I reached for my xiphos, ready to help.

I woke up to my face pressed against the cold floor. Xander had gone and I was freezing. I climbed up into our bed and covered myself with blankets so that I could warm up again.

Then I realized that my husband hadn't left—I could hear him in the washroom. I liked having him nearby. I tucked the blankets in around me while I thought about my dream.

Why was that what I needed to see? While I had been glad to spend time with Demaratus again, it didn't answer my questions.

Stupid girl, are you sure?

Shock slammed into me. I sat straight up and threw off the covers. I ran next door and woke everyone up, which I felt bad about because of how much Io needed her rest.

"Terawolves!" I exclaimed.

"Where?" Ahyana grumbled at me.

"No, terawolves are part aether dragon. If we could capture one . . ."

Io's eyes went wide. "Then we'd have the last element!"

"Your husband is never going to let you go out and hunt terawolves," Zalira pointed out. He was annoyingly overprotective. And he'd become more so ever since we'd discovered our physical link.

"We have magic. It will be different this time." If I had to sneak out, then I would. This was too important.

"How did you think of this?" Io asked.

"I invoked the night-walking aspect and spoke to my former battle master, and terawolves appeared. Before I fell asleep I asked to see what I needed to, and the terawolves are the answer to our problem! And I think that this means that I can control the dreams; I'll have to work on it. But the dream magic doesn't feel anything like when I call on fury.

What the rest of you feel when you do magic. This . . . just happened. It didn't cost me anything. I wasn't in pain, I didn't have to turn it off."

Again we were in a position where even though we had more answers, the questions continued to pile up.

We all heard Xander moving around next door.

"I thought he was going out with his phratry brothers today," Ahyana said. She would be the one who best knew their schedule. I wondered if Rokh had returned yet.

Thinking of the phratry brought Dolion back into my mind, and I tried not to shudder. I considered telling my sisters about him and what he had done, but I wanted to pretend the entire thing away. If I didn't speak of it, I wouldn't have to relive it.

I also didn't want to get mired down in what I should have done differently. I knew it wasn't my fault, but that wouldn't stop me from questioning whether I had played some role in it.

And I wouldn't allow his poor decisions to make me doubt myself.

"I'm going to go get dressed," I said to my sisters.

"Do you want us to help you get ready later?" Io asked as she got out of her bed.

"For what?"

"The party my stepmother insists on throwing."

Already? That had come together quickly. I supposed it made sense—it needed to be near Xander's birthday. "I can call for Parthenia."

Io nodded and I promised to see them all later. I went back to my own room. Xander sat at his desk, writing. It reminded me of what Demaratus had said in the dream about not receiving a letter from me.

I didn't want to interrupt him, but I had to ask. "Why haven't I heard from my family?"

He stopped moving his lead across the papyrus, frozen in place.

"I have sent them a lot of letters, but I haven't heard back from them." There had been so many other things going on that I hadn't realized it earlier.

Xander exhaled and then got up. He walked over to one of his trunks, opened it, and began emptying out the contents. I followed and saw him push a lever to reveal a false bottom.

He handed me a stack of my letters.

All unsent.

I could only stare down at them in shock. My parents hadn't heard from me at all.

My first instinct was to let the anger currently simmering in my veins explode into life. I had been suppressing so many different emotions lately that they were more than eager to funnel themselves into rage and unleash on him.

And I could fight him now. I could so easily call up my fury aspect and then . . .

But I refused to get locked into that spiral again. I did my best to stay calm. He could have had a good reason. *I should let him explain.* "Why did you do this?"

He seemed surprised. Had he been expecting my rage? "Despite the fact that you tried to hide it, your misery was evident in your letters. I was afraid of two things—the first, that if Erisa saw them, she would use it against us, and the second, that your parents would get on the first ship and come here."

Xander had told me previously that there were all sorts of spies in the palace who went through the letters sent out. He was right that Erisa would have seen them and I understood why he couldn't risk that, given how hard we had been pretending to be in love and happy for the court.

"Why couldn't my parents have come?" A sharp pang of homesickness pierced my heart. I would have loved to see them.

"I wouldn't have been able to hide who they were and their relationship to you, as I did for Quynh. Erisa would have found a way to hurt them or take their lives. Being in Locris is the only thing keeping them safe."

He had told me that he'd written to them and advised them that both Quynh and I were alive, so they at least knew that. I might have even seen their reaction to finding out. I had always dismissed that as just another dream, but with my night-walking skill . . . what if it had been real and I'd witnessed it? Had I actually seen my parents?

Would I be able to do it again?

I shook my head. That wasn't the point right now. I chose to believe him, to not be upset about what he had done. I understood why he had made that choice. "You did this for me."

His eyebrows lifted even higher. "I did."

"Thank you. For protecting them and for protecting me."

He stood there, as if he didn't know what to do next. He seemed to be at a total loss. A few beats later, he finally said, "This is not how I thought this conversation would go. I thought there would be more stabbing attempts involved."

That made me smile. "I can always grab my xiphos if you'd like me to try."

"I wouldn't mind seeing it."

Now it was my turn to be stunned. He'd never indicated that he was interested in my weapon before. I went over to our bed, to where I'd left it under my pillow. I brought it back to where he stood.

"May I?" he asked. It was the first time in a long time he'd asked for something instead of demanding it.

I spun my sword around so that he could take the handle. "I'm surprised you offered me the non-pointed end first," he said wryly.

He held my xiphos aloft, looking at it in the sunlight as he turned it one way and then the other. He lowered it and ran his fingers along the edges, careful not to cut himself while testing their sharpness.

"It is a finely crafted weapon," he said, handing it back to me the same way I'd given it to him. "Wielded by a great warrior."

Tears sprang into the corners of my eyes. Why did that mean more to me than every other compliment he'd ever given me?

I had to clear my throat before I could speak. "A great enough warrior that you wouldn't mind if I went hunting for a terawolf?"

"You're not hunting for a terawolf."

"Why not?"

I had rendered him momentarily speechless so many times in this conversation and did so again. He finally collected himself enough to say, "Are you serious? Why don't I want you to go looking for supernatural creatures that are, based on what you've told me, still hunting you? That have venom in their fangs and can turn invisible at will?"

"When you put it that way, you make it sound . . ." *Entirely unreasonable.* I couldn't tell him about the scroll. Not until I knew what it contained. "But what if I really, really needed to?"

"There is no reason for you to—" He sounded as if he might have been on the edge of getting angry and he pulled himself back, much as I had done myself earlier. His tone was much calmer when he said, "Wife, I would tie you to that bed before I'd let you do something so dangerous."

The night of his birthday, he had told me what delicious things he would do to me if I were tied up, and I had to draw in a shaky breath. I put my hand over my heart, as if that would stop it from galloping.

And he noticed.

I saw his eyes darken, saw the knot in his throat bob, his jaw clench. A heavy and weighted silence stretched between us. He leaned forward as if he wanted to be closer, and then right when I thought he would reach for me, he took several steps back.

"No terawolves," he said as he sat back down at his desk.

Even though I'd promised myself that I was going to try and be more honest with him, I was going to have to allow one small lie of omission.

Because I would absolutely be headed out to catch a terawolf as soon as possible.

CHAPTER TWENTY-TWO

I spent most of the day training with my sisters, practicing the magic using Io's fortification potions. We could last for longer, and now that we knew how to stop using our aspects, we didn't have to worry about passing out.

Late afternoon I sat at the table in my room, reading one of the books Suri had chosen for me. I skimmed the pages, hoping something might stand out.

Luna basked on the table in a fading ray of sunlight. She was nearly the same size as Io's cat and slept constantly. I had moved her over to the table, thinking she might enjoy the warmth. I had never realized that animals grew so quickly.

She woke suddenly and yawned as she stretched. Her eyes slowly blinked open, and when she saw me, it almost looked like she was smiling.

"Did you enjoy your nap?" I asked her.

Yes.

One moment I was looking at her and the next she was gone.

Vanished.

Startled, I stood up. My heart thudded hard in my chest. I touched the spot where she'd been resting. Not there.

So she hadn't turned invisible.

Twenty seconds later she reappeared in the same spot.

"Where did you go?" I asked her, feeling bewildered. "What were you doing?"

She studied me for a moment before opening her two front paws. She was holding a mouse.

It squeaked and got free from her grasp, jumping off the table. Luna chased after it until she caught it and . . . ate it. It made me feel slightly nauseous.

"Don't ever let Io see you do that," I told her as she happily crunched on her prey. It looked as if it might be time to upgrade Luna's food to bigger game.

After she'd finished with her meal, she shook her head and sneezed. Silver flakes flew out from her body. "You have to stop making a mess or Xander is going to toss you out the window," I said.

No.

I wasn't sure if she was saying no to not making a mess or to him tossing her. Maybe both. She crawled up into her enclosure. Xander had removed the interior ramps and shelves and it was now just a big wooden box with some bedding on the bottom, which seemed to make her very happy.

My maid, Parthenia, entered the room. "Were you just talking to yourself?" she asked.

For a moment I wondered which answer would make me seem less like I was descending into madness. I settled on the one that didn't have me conversing with a lizard. "Yes. I was."

"I have your dress," she said, holding it out so that I could see it. It was a deep, dark purple. Purple dye was ridiculously expensive and they had used so much to make it this shade.

"It's so beautiful!" I breathed. I reached out to touch it, and the silk was so light that it felt as delicate as a spiderweb. "Io has excellent taste."

"She does," Parthenia agreed with a smile. "Go and bathe and then I'll help you get ready."

The last thing I wanted to do was go to this party. I had other more pressing concerns, such as figuring out how to sneak out of the palace without my extremely observant husband realizing it. I hurried through everything, my mind racing as I tried to think of a way to go to the woods south of Troas.

I would also have to formulate a plan on how to actually catch and kill a terawolf.

Parthenia told me about a silly argument she'd had with her husband the previous night, and I only half listened as she helped me dress. She got out the black pearl necklace that Xander had gifted me at our wedding. She had acquired a new hair ornament for me, a silver comb with black pearls along the edges, which she used to draw my hair back from my face while leaving the rest of it hanging down my back. I turned my head slightly to see the comb in my mirror. It almost looked like a tiara.

Then she handed me a ring that had three black pearls on it, and I put it on my right hand. I still wore my Chalcidian steel ring on my left. I glanced down at my wedding ring—it seemed to pale in comparison to the other jewelry I had on.

But it was the only one attached to the vein that ran to my heart.

Xander greeted us when he entered the room, carrying a length of purple cloth over his arm. I guessed that Io had made us match again. He headed into the washroom while Parthenia finished. She asked if I needed her to return tonight to help me undress, but I had watched her carefully as she had twisted and turned the fabric so that it hung the way she wanted it to. I could undo it myself. I told her to enjoy the city celebration with her husband.

"I hope he's ready to apologize to you," I said.

She smiled. "I'm sure he will be. He is fond of romantic gestures." She put a hand on her swollen belly and wished me a good night and then left.

I found myself envying her again for what she had.

Up until the moment when my own husband walked out of the washroom. I shakily stood up. That shade of purple on him—it had the effect of making his hair somehow even darker while his eyes practically glowed golden.

Like a terawolf's, a mischievous voice inside me whispered. *He would happily devour you if you only asked.*

I waved my hand toward him. "It's . . . very purple."

Very purple? Had I actually just told him that his tunic was very purple?

"Io did it on purpose. She wanted us to make a statement. Only royals wear this color. We're supposed to remind everyone who should be the next king and queen of Ilion."

My breathing hitched as regret darkened my soul. Even when he was named king, I would never be his queen.

He walked over to me, wearing that charming smile of his, and I nearly collapsed at the sight of it. So, so handsome.

"Do you know how many soldiers I could feed with that dress?" he asked playfully.

"We can sell it," I immediately offered.

"No! I was only teasing. It's beautiful. You're . . . it's beautiful."

Feeling a bit uncomfortable, I started babbling about the dress. "The stitching is not as elaborate as some others I've had. Like . . ." I tried to think of one with more stitching, but my mind had gone blank because he'd moved closer.

"My wedding dress!" I practically shouted the words because the blood rushing in my ears made it hard to hear myself. "That one was very, very intricate."

That dress had also made me initially disbelieve his story that he hadn't known who I was from the beginning. It had been blue and gold—my family's colors. There was no way he could have had a dress created with that much embroidery unless he had known for weeks that—

"Did you like the dress you wore when we were wed?"

I loved it. It had been the one good thing that had happened to me that day. "It's still one of the most beautiful things I've ever worn."

"I'm glad. The dress was my mother's."

It was as if he had stepped back and let an arrow fly directly to my heart. I couldn't catch my breath—I was shocked and then delighted and confused and wanted to swoon and . . .

He had let me wear his mother's dress.

Xander had hated me, been so furious with me, but he'd let me wear his mother's dress.

I knew what she had meant to him, so I understood what kind of gesture that had been. "But it was in Locris's colors."

"My mother's nation has the same colors. That was one of the reasons why I thought you might like . . ." He trailed off, leaving so much unspoken.

By the goddess I was going to kiss this man until we both forgot how to breathe.

As if he could read my desire for him, he foolishly came closer and reached for my hand. I sighed when his warm fingers enveloped mine. "I misspoke earlier. About your dress."

"So you don't think it's beautiful?"

"This may not be the wisest choice, but what I meant to say, what I should have said, is that *you're* beautiful."

It probably would have been better for our situation for him to have kept that information to himself, but I was so glad he'd said it.

Especially because the only other time he had called me beautiful had been when he was drugged. "You haven't been drinking any honeyed wine, have you?"

Merriment made his eyes glow even more. "No, I stay away from all wine now. I'm giving you my true thoughts."

Oh.

"But the morning after . . ." I didn't have to clarify which one I meant—I could see from his expression that he knew. "You said you didn't mean anything you said to me on your birthday. That it had all been due to the wine."

He looked down at our joined hands and then rubbed his thumb along the delicate skin of my wrist. My pulse leapt up to meet him there, keeping an unsustainable rhythm.

"I have a lot of regrets, Lia. And the lies that I told you that morning outside the council chambers, in an attempt to protect myself, are among them."

Part of me exulted in the fact that I had been right—I'd known he was lying—while the rest of me panicked at the desires I was having. How they urged me to go lock our door and let him slowly take this beautiful dress off me.

"When you said that, it made me feel like . . . you didn't want me." I knew I was playing with fire. Pleading to be burned. No, not just burned. Incinerated. Completely consumed.

His eyes dropped to my lips and they tingled in response. "I've already told you—then, now, I always want you."

The confidence, the honesty, the raw desire in his deep voice threatened to overwhelm me. My vision blurred, my limbs quivered, and molten fire erupted in my gut.

Io called to us from her room, saying that we should head down to the party. Her voice startled me and I realized that I'd been swaying toward him, ready for his kiss. I shakily pulled my hand away from him. She would have been upset if she had just seen how we were looking at each other, heard the things we were saying.

What I had considered begging him to do to me.

"We should go," I said, averting my gaze. I walked out into the hallway and greeted my adelphia, ignoring my racing heartbeat. We all gushed over each other's dresses, but in my mind, I was still back in my bedroom with Xander, where he was leading me over to our mirror to have a redo of his birthday.

Only this time both of us would be clearheaded.

He came into the hallway and told everyone good evening, but his gaze was on me the entire time.

We all started to walk toward the dining hall.

"I can't believe how quickly this came together," Ahyana said. She was almost skipping her way down the stairs and it made me think that Rokh must have returned from his secret mission.

"Erisa does move quickly," Xander said. "She has made sure she's getting all the credit for this celebration while spending my money on it."

"She wants everyone in Troas to think she's a good mother and cares for the princes of Ilion," Io muttered. "While in reality, if she could unhinge her jaw, she would probably swallow her offspring whole."

Xander walked alongside me. The backs of his fingers kept brushing against mine. There was no pattern—I never knew if his skin would touch mine from one moment to the next and waited in breathless anticipation for each time it did. Every single brush sent shivers up my arm.

When we arrived at the dining hall, the party was in full swing. It seemed very much like the party we'd had to celebrate Xander's birthday a few days ago.

"We should all separate and find an archon to speak to," Io said. "We still need to get Xander named king."

She put her hand on my arm, as if she intended to take me with her.

Xander stepped in between us. I shivered at the heated promise in his eyes. "Not yet. Right now, I am going to dance with my wife."

CHAPTER TWENTY-THREE

Xander took me by the hand and led me to where the others were dancing.

The people around us wanted to greet him and wish him a good birthday, again. While he acknowledged everyone who spoke to him, he only had eyes for me, and it was exhilarating.

When we came to a stop, I said, "I don't remember you saying, 'Lia, will you *please* come and dance with me?'"

"I don't have to ask because you are the one who promised to be obedient in our wedding contract."

"Why did you say yes to everything I asked of you then?" It was something I had wondered about. Io had thought it was because her brother was such a reasonable person, something I still disagreed with.

"Because it wasn't very much, and I knew that I would be requiring something a great deal more difficult in return. Pretending to be affectionate with someone you hate isn't easy," he said.

"You should know."

He paused before he finally answered, "Yes, I do know, wife."

I quickly glanced around and saw that all eyes were on us. I leaned in so that only he would hear me. "I don't know Ilionian dances. We don't dance like this in Locris. I don't want them all laughing at me."

"They will think it's endearing that your dashing, charming husband is teaching you because of how much he cares about you." He reached for my hand. "Only look at me," he said. As if I weren't already. He explained that there were collective circle dances done by all the dancers holding hands, line dances with specific steps, and then partner dances, like the one we were doing now.

"It's called the Ballos. It's an upbeat and celebratory dance meant to mimic a marriage. Attraction, flirtation, courtship, pursuit, refusal, and then it ends in surrender." He showed me the four small, basic steps and how we would move around one another. Sometimes he would twirl me in place.

"And like marriage," he said, "there is an intimacy and a vulnerability in not knowing the steps but figuring them out together."

The tiny bumps on my skin multiplied. Did he know the effect his words had on me?

"Eyes up," he said. "Don't watch your feet. Heavy eye contact is an important part of this dance."

I looked around at the other couples and he was right. Instead of watching us, they were gazing into one another's eyes. But staring into Xander's beautiful eyes . . . I didn't know if I was strong enough to endure it.

"Or if that doesn't work for you, think of dancing being like fighting. It's about footwork and paying attention to your opponent."

The longer we danced, the easier it became. "Do you have any other analogies for what dancing is like?"

"Only one more . . ." he said as his hand went around my waist to bring me closer to him. "An activity that has two people focused on each other, touching constantly, moving their bodies in harmony . . . but it wouldn't be appropriate to mention in a public place like this one."

I knew exactly what he meant, and it caused me to stumble over my own feet. Thankfully he caught me, but that meant I was now pressed up against him with all the images he'd just painted running through my mind. His gaze again dropped to my lips and I was about to push up on my toes and kiss him when we were interrupted.

"Forgive the intrusion, but Prince Alexandros, may I speak with you privately?" Stolos, one of the archons on the council, waited for Xander's response.

"Certainly." He somehow managed to get me back on my feet while he moved away. "I will find you later," he promised. "We can finish our dance."

My neck felt like it was on fire. I reached up to make sure that I was not actually burning. Finish our dance?

It was supposed to end in surrender.

Yield to me.

Couples twirled around me as I stood on the dance floor watching Stolos and Xander walk away.

"Lia!" Io called, waving me over. I didn't quite feel in control of my body yet, so I was relieved when I managed to walk to her without tripping over my own feet again.

"Zethus is in listening to the bard," she said. "We should go try to talk to him."

Speaking to Zethus felt like a waste of time. He was an archon devoted solely to his own hedonistic pleasures and seemed to vote whichever way the wind blew. His only allegiance was to himself.

But I would welcome the opportunity to get away from the dancing and focus on something else besides my husband and how he made me feel.

Io and Suri walked with me to a smaller antechamber where the bard was performing. I realized that I recognized him—it was the same one I had seen in the Golden Lamb, the night I had sneaked out of the temple with Xander.

The bard was singing a song about other nations that Ilion had faced in battles. I hoped I had already missed the Locrian portion.

"He's over there," Io said, and I heard the disgust in her voice. Zethus was, once again, being inappropriate with a young hetaera. I was so glad Io had escaped a possible betrothal to him by joining the temple. “We should wait until the bard is done before we try approaching Zethus.”

I still thought it was pointless but stayed to humor her and because I needed the distraction.

We sat down with the other people who were all listening intently to the bard, something Zethus was not doing.

I forced myself to pay attention to the bard singing instead of thinking about dancing with Xander. The bard spoke of fighting with Thrace, with the Sasanians. I wondered how many times Ilion had gone to war.

The bard moved on to the Carians and sang:

> “The men have fled and gone
> The others work and toil
> The Carians, now rich,
> Rule upon iron soil.”

Iron soil? I tried to picture it. Did that mean that it was a silvery-gray? Like steel? That couldn’t be right. I thought of what rust looked like on iron, and my heart began to drum inside my chest. “Io, what color is iron soil?”

“Red,” she whispered in shock, apparently having come to the same conclusion that I had.

The Carians. We were fighting the Carians.

My grandmother had been right. All the answers I needed were in books, scrolls, poems, and songs.

I tried to remember what the bard had said at the inn near the docks all those weeks ago, when he had told stories about the Carians. After being defeated in the Great War, many Ilionian men had abandoned their nation and gone elsewhere. Some of them went south to Caria to seek refuge, but they were turned away. Those Ilionians tunneled their way into the city and slaughtered the men. They forced the women to marry them and bear their children, which upset the goddess.

The Carians did not share the men's belief in the goddess and the Ilionians missed their homes, so after ten years, the Ilionians abandoned their new families and went back to Troas, making the walls higher and thicker and creating the labyrinth so that no one could ever defeat them again.

The way they had treated the Carian women was why men were not allowed on the temple grounds. All Ilionian men had to take on the punishment and shame of what their ancestors had done.

But the bard had also said that Caria had been wiped out within a single decade and was only spoken of in song. Something wasn't adding up.

I grew more and more impatient as I waited for the bard to finish. There were many more verses about other nations, places I didn't recognize, and then he finally ended his song. I took the opportunity to push through the crowd so that I could speak with him.

"You did a wonderful job," I told him.

The bard beamed at me. "Thank you!"

"You sang about the Carians . . . I thought their nation had been destroyed."

"That is what the songs say."

Supposedly Troas had been utterly ruined after the Great War, and yet Ilion had found a way to rebuild and come back stronger than ever, putting a blockade on Locris and slowly starving us to death.

Why couldn't Caria have done the same?

It wouldn't have surprised me if the reason the songs said Caria had been ruined was because the men of Ilion had thought that, without them, the nation must have fallen apart.

And no one had ever bothered to check.

"What's important about their iron soil?" I asked the bard.

He seemed delighted to have someone so interested in his stories. "The songs of long ago say that the Carians would stand on their dirt when they fought. That their god would give them supernatural strength so long as their feet stayed in contact with it. It's why they didn't attack other nations—they had to be standing on their own soil to win."

It sounded similar to what we could do when performing magic—if we touched someone with a white light, it powered us. Their soil seemed to do the same.

But their dirt hadn't worked for them when the Ilionians had attacked. I wondered why.

And the Carians had apparently decided that they no longer had to stay home to fight. They had come up with a way to distribute the dirt to bring their fight to others.

"Which god do the Carians worship? Is it Arion?" I asked.

The bard looked alarmed and made a motion with his fingers and then spit on the ground. "We do not speak his name, but yes, he is the god of the Carians."

I was about to ask why we knew Arion's name but not the goddess's until I remembered that it was Lysimache's doing. She had done her best to remove the goddess's name so that no priestess could call on her power again.

She wouldn't have cared if Ilionians knew the Carians' god's name.

Maybe Io's theory about Arion's power being in opposition to his mother's was correct. What if the Ilionians had done something to disrupt the dirt from working?

I asked the bard that question but he only shrugged. "That has been lost to us. We don't know why the Ilionian men were successful, other than the goddess willed it."

That seemed doubtful to me, considering she had put into place the rule that men were no longer allowed into her temple because of their actions in Caria.

Or had Lysimache been the reason behind that, too? She had been furious with the men abandoning them after the war and removing their ability to worship the goddess. That must have been a terrible blow.

"Thank you," I told the bard. "You've been extremely helpful."

The scholars and historians hadn't known this information, but a storyteller had. This bard might have just saved all of Ilion.

Now we could prepare. Now we would know where to send scouts and spies. We could get ready.

I made my way back over to Io and Suri and filled them in on what the bard had told me. "You need to go find Zalira and Ahyana. Tell them what we learned. I'm going to go tell Xander, and then we should all meet up to figure out our next move."

Suri nodded and led Io out of the room.

The Carians worshipped an earth god with dominion over metals. It made sense that his symbol would be a hammer. Did every Carian have a reddish-brown tattoo of a hammer on their chest? We had seen one on a dead soldier, and Artemisia also bore it.

How far was Caria from here? When would their armies arrive? Would they come by land or by sea? The Carians had come after me on the *Nikos,* so they obviously had some kind of navy.

When I entered the dining hall, I spotted Stolos and Xander deep in conversation. I was sure that whatever they were discussing was important, but this was more pressing.

I had begun to walk toward them when an extremely large man suddenly stepped out in front of me and I nearly ran into him. I was about to apologize when I looked up into his face and froze.

It was the man who had tried to kill me in the temple.

CHAPTER TWENTY-FOUR

"Pardon me," the man said as he moved around me. My heart finally started to beat again when he was several feet away.

I was back in the high priestess's office at the temple with that man sitting on top of me, trying to stab me in the throat, and I was doing everything in my power to keep him from killing me by moving his blade to my left shoulder. I found myself rubbing my shoulder, my limbs trembling.

How was this possible? I practically ran to Xander, desperate to talk to him. I slid my hand into his and squeezed, not wanting to make a scene in front of Stolos.

My husband had an easy smile when he turned to look at me, and it fell off his face.

"Excuse us, Stolos. I need to speak with my wife immediately."

He led me out onto the patio, where we could be alone. "What happened? You look as if you've seen a shade."

"I might have," I said, my heart still pounding far too quickly. "Do you see the man over there, the very tall one with the dark brown tunic?"

"Yes."

"That was the man who stabbed me in the temple."

"Are you certain?"

"About the man who did this?" I pointed at my shoulder. "It's not a face I will ever forget."

"But he's dead. Io killed him. That man is living and breathing, so he can't be the one who hurt you."

"Identical twins?" I offered. It was the only explanation.

He nodded. We both watched as he walked over to Erisa and then took up a position behind her. Like he was a bodyguard.

"Antiope said that the assassins in the temple bore no insignias or had any indication who they served. They were meant to be anonymous," I said.

"Because they work for my stepmother and had been sent there specifically to find you. She didn't want to risk me finding out." He pulled out his broadsword.

I put my hands on top of his. "What are you doing?"

"I'm going to go kill him," he said through clenched teeth. "If I can't kill the man who hurt you, then the least I can do is take it out on his brother, who looks just like him."

When had I become the voice of reason and the advocate for not murdering? "You have to stop trying to kill people that could testify against Erisa and help make you king."

"He'll lie."

"Then use Io's truth serum with the compulsion. He'll have to tell the truth and won't be able to keep anything from you. Just make sure he doesn't have any access to weapons. And tie him up so that he can't do damage to himself."

A lesson I had learned the hard way.

"I still want to slit his throat," he said.

"If he works for your stepmother and you kill him, then she'll retaliate and go after your men. More people will die."

"That's usually how civil wars work."

Something Demaratus had once taught me came into my head. "Any throne taken by the shedding of blood will require blood spilled again to keep it."

"I am fine with that. I'll kill her, too."

"Xander," I said gently. "Stop. We will find another way."

For a moment he gripped his sword even tighter, but then he relented and finally put it back into its sheath. I let out a little sigh of relief that the party wasn't about to become a bloodbath.

"If he works for Erisa, we still don't know how she knew who I was," I said. We had theorized that the witness had been involved, but we weren't certain. I heard a bird call and looked up to see a raven fly overhead. It landed behind a column and then Rokh came out from behind it.

He was uncharacteristically grim as he walked to us. As if he knew what we'd been discussing, he said, "I did as requested and followed the witness from the tribute selection. His home was filled with books and I watched to make certain—I saw him both reading and writing."

"Bring him here. We'll give him the truth serum, too," Xander responded.

Would that even work with someone who couldn't speak?

"I'm afraid that won't be possible. I just found him dead and came straight here to tell you."

"Dead? By his own hand?" Xander asked.

Rokh shook his head. "Not unless he was flexible enough to stab himself in the back of his own skull."

Whoever had done that must have been exceptionally strong.

"How did she know that you and Dolion were watching him?" Xander asked.

"I don't know," Rokh said. "We were so careful."

"It's not as if she still has an extensive spy network," Xander said in frustration, his hand again going to his sword. "We eliminated her funds when we emptied out her safe house."

"Perhaps Pelias is funding it," Rokh countered.

The two men fell silent, considering.

I was trying to work out exactly how this had all happened. "So Erisa knew that your betrothed was chosen as one of the Locrian maidens from the beginning. And that one of the maidens survived, but she wouldn't have known which one."

"It's not as if your high priestess would have shared the name of which maiden lived within the city," Xander said.

Yes, she'd been too busy plotting how to kill me. "The witness was at the Golden Lamb and saw me, so he knew that I was the one who had finished the race. He told Erisa that Princess Thalia lived, and then she sent the assassins to kill me at the temple to stop you and me from getting married."

I had known Erisa was evil, but this . . . I wanted to stab her myself.

While I was picturing doing that, Xander filled Rokh in on everything that had occurred that evening, pointing out the tall man working for the former queen.

Then a terrifying thought came into my mind.

"By the goddess," I said, my heart racing in alarm. "What about Quynh? The witness would have known that she's my sister. What if he came to the palace and saw her and told Erisa who she really was?"

"Quynh is safe. She's no longer in the palace. No harm will come to her." Now my husband was the one soothing me.

A short horn blast sounded and Xander swore.

"What is that?" I asked.

"You and I have to go out on the balcony overlooking the outer courtyard and wave to all the citizens who are out celebrating my birthday."

No one had mentioned that to me. Another thing that seemed totally inconsequential, given what was happening.

"It's important that you go," Rokh said. "Not only to give the people what they want, but so that when Thrax and I kidnap Erisa's man, you'll have an alibi."

Rokh went into the dining hall, presumably to find Thrax.

"This way," Xander said. He led me back to the front hall and took me up a staircase that I hadn't used before at the southern end of the hall. It led out to a large balcony, and when we stepped out, the sound of cheering was deafening.

I couldn't even begin to guess how many people waited below to celebrate their prince. He smiled and raised both of his arms in greeting and somehow the sound became louder. They were thrilled to see him.

Someone called out, "Princess Thalia!" and I waved and got my own set of cheers.

The crowd began singing a song I wasn't familiar with.

"We just stand here and wave while they sing?" I leaned in to ask him.

"Yes. Not every part of this job is assassination attempts and defying death. Some of it is a bit boring."

"I could stand a little boring," I admitted and kept waving.

One song ended and a new one started. "They really love you," I said.

"I've got men down there distributing gold. That helps," he said with a wink that made my knees hollow out.

"You should be their king," I said. And he would be if his father had bothered to tell anyone that he had never had sex with Erisa. "Why didn't your father tell the council that Kyros wasn't his son?"

"I've thought about that," he said. "Perhaps he was embarrassed about being cuckolded. He was a very proud man, and he only told me about Kyros because he was drunk. I don't think he would have wanted to admit it to anyone else."

His father's pride might possibly cost his son the kingship. I didn't understand that.

Because your pride never stopped you from doing anything, that sarcastic voice of mine whispered. I ignored it.

"There was a story that my father used to tell me," he said, "about a hero named Demophon. He was the son of a king and had to be smuggled out of the city because the king's enemies wanted to kill him. The king told the queen that he had buried his sword under a massive boulder until Demophon was ready to return and claim his rightful place as heir. If Demophon was strong enough and determined enough, if he was truly worthy, he would figure out how to move the boulder and become king. I think my father wanted me to have to fight for my place as he had to. To prove that I was worthy of it."

"There's no one more worthy," I told him.

He went silent as he studied me. "Thank you."

I smiled shyly back at him and then turned to keep waving.

"Two worthy people with a vow between them, keeping them apart," he said.

I had to ignore the way my heart leapt at his implication. "It isn't just the vow I have to worry about. I'm prophesied to die."

He dropped his hands. "What?"

It seemed that Io had truly kept her promise to me that she wouldn't share anything with her brother unless I told her it was all right. I had thought for sure she would have shared the entire prophecy with him.

"We found a more complete version of the prophecy in one of your mother's books, and Lysimache confirmed that it was correct. It said the savior of Ilion is fated to die. I'm supposed to wield the greatest weapon, endure a trial of the elements, and then die as a sacrifice to the goddess, which will save Ilion."

His mouth dropped slightly and I saw so many emotions flitter across his face. Fear. Anguish. Concern. He looked as if this information devastated him.

I watched as he squared his shoulders, his expression resolute. "That proves you're not the savior, then."

"How so?"

"Because I would never let you die," he said seriously.

That warm, loving feeling burned inside my chest again. That wasn't hyperbole. Xander wouldn't let me die if he could help it. I tried to make light of it. "Well, yes, because then you'd die, too."

"That's not why, Lia."

I couldn't let this happen. Couldn't let these feelings come out. I had to pretend as if I didn't understand what he was saying. "If I were gone, then you could marry Chryseis and get her father's vote on the council."

That had not come out quite as lighthearted as I had meant it to. Probably because I was still peeved about him kissing her, even if he had explained why he'd done it.

He gave me a knowing look, as if he understood exactly what I was doing, but played along. He said in a teasing tone, "Perhaps I've been soured on marriage."

I was going to elbow him until I remembered the thousands of people beneath us who probably wouldn't take kindly to it.

Xander's face turned serious. "I already have a wife, and I do not want a different one."

I had to put my hand over my heart, as if that could stop the way he made me feel.

The song ended and someone started chanting, "Prince Alexandros!" The crowd quickly took up the cheer, and they called his name over and over.

Then it transformed into "King Alexandros!"

"All this adoration is going to swell your head," I said.

He was pensive for a moment. "I belong to everyone and no one. Having this kind of adoration but still . . . by myself."

"What about your phratry?"

"I love my brothers. But I will be their king. There will always be a disconnect there. A way in which I have to be separate and apart. The only person I could ever really be close to is . . ." His voice trailed off.

A wife.

He could only be close to a wife, to a woman who was his true partner. Someone he could confide in, somewhere that he could lay his weary head at the end of his day. The way my parents did for each other. How Doria and Haemon had been for one another.

I longed for it, too. Even now there were parts of myself that I kept private and secret from my adelphia. From Quynh, too. I wanted a companion who would know and love all of me. Who would appreciate the good things about me and wouldn't turn away from the bad. Someone I could tell everything to, who would accept me completely.

The prophecy had increased my sense of loneliness. Just like Xander had to be separate and apart from those he loved, so did I. My fate was not their fate.

He looked down at the people, who were still calling for him to be their king. He put his hands on the railing and rested his weight there. "Surrounded by people who love me and yet . . ."

"And yet?" I prompted.

"I think this is the most alone I've ever felt."

It was like he'd gutted me. *Goddess help me.* I put my hand on top of his. "You're not alone."

He turned his gaze toward me. "Neither are you."

Not able to help myself, I leaned over and kissed him softly, oblivious to the wild cheers of the crowd.

A loud explosion rent the air and we jerked apart.

Two seconds later there was another explosion.

The people in the courtyard started screaming and running.

"That came from the docks." Xander turned and darted inside and I followed.

CHAPTER TWENTY-FIVE

Xander barked out instructions to the soldiers, who were milling about, unsure of what to do. I followed him to our bedroom, where he started putting on armor and gathering weapons.

I went to change out of my own clothes and get ready.

"What are you doing?" he asked.

"Going with you."

"No. You can't come," he said as he slipped two daggers into his belt.

"I can help you," I said. "That metallic smell in the air—it's the same as when that house exploded in Lycia. Which means the Carians are behind this."

"What?"

I realized that I'd been so busy earlier telling him about the man who worked for Erisa that I hadn't shared what I'd learned from the bard. "I will explain later, but the Carians are the ones attacking us. If they stand on their red dirt, it gives them power from their god."

"All the more reason for you to stay here," he said.

"No, I want to be there so that I can—"

"Wife, this will be easier for me if I don't have to worry about you getting hurt."

"Fine," I said. This was part of choosing differently. He would worry about me. I understood his concern.

He looked as surprised as I felt. "Promise me you won't go to the docks."

"I promise. So long as you promise that you'll be careful and come back to me."

He crossed over to me and was about to pull me in his arms when Dolion and Stephanos entered the room.

"I promise," Xander said before kissing me quickly on my forehead.

The three men left and I headed out into the hallway to find my adelphia, but they were walking toward me from the opposite end. We all went into Io's room.

"We've caught Zalira and Ahyana up on everything," Io said.

I nodded. Smoke and that metallic scent hung heavy in the air around us. People were still screaming and crying outside.

"We have to help," I said. "I told Xander I wouldn't go to the docks, but we have to do something. I can't just sit here."

Ahyana stood near the window, looking out. "What if the attack is another distraction?"

I hadn't even considered that. "We should go make sure the main gates are shut. We'll start with the southern one. I'm going to go get changed."

When I went back to my room, I realized I hadn't even asked my sisters if they wanted to come—I had just assumed that they would. We were a fighting unit, a true sisterhood.

I dressed more quickly than I ever had before, loading myself up with weapons. Thankfully my sisters had done the same—they were waiting for me in the hall and all wore a similar determined look.

We ran through the palace, which was in total chaos. Nobles were fleeing for the safety of their homes, and there was a confusion of chariots and horses outside, all tangled up in each other.

I had to shove my way through the crowd. When we got past the palace grounds, the citizens were every bit as frightened as the nobles had been. No one knew what to do or what was happening.

After we had checked on all of the gates, I would suggest to my sisters that we help direct people to safety. Try to calm the panic.

Zalira led us to the southern entrance, where the gate was partially open. It would only allow one person through at a time. Which meant that a Carian soldier could enter and throw it open for the others.

I was about to yell at the guards to close it when a long howl sounded. Then another. And another.

Terawolves.

And they were headed toward Troas.

"They're coming here!" I said.

"Maybe they're being drawn by the smell and the screams," Zalira said.

The reason didn't matter. Stopping them did. I was not going to allow them to attack Xander and his men, who were outside the walls. Not when I could do something about it.

"This is our chance," Io said. "We can prevent them from hurting anyone else and get what we need for the scroll."

I hadn't even been thinking about the scroll.

It didn't matter. We needed a plan, even if I was terrible at them. "Follow me," I said, leading my adelphia outside the gate. A lone soldier called out to us, but I ignored him.

We ran to the edge of the thick forest. "Suri, I need a deep pit here." I took a branch so that I could show her where it should be located and how long it should be. "After you make it, cover it with brush. That's how we'll stop the terawolves."

The howling came closer.

"Io, stay here with Suri and be a lookout. If the wolves come and you aren't done, run back into the city and have them close the gate," I said.

"What are you three going to do?" Io asked.

I exchanged glances with Zalira and Ahyana. "We're going to draw the wolves here and trap them."

Suri raised her eyebrows at me as if to ask how.

"Io said once the terawolves have selected their prey they never stop hunting. I'm going to go out there and make sure they know we're here."

The panicked look on Io's face wasn't enough to deter me. If those terawolves got any closer . . . they could harm so many people. Everyone at the docks would be at risk.

"Which way?" I asked Suri. She closed her eyes for a moment and then pointed southeast. We ran off in that direction.

We had been running for around ten minutes when Zalira came to a stop. "There. I see them." The wolves were coming this way and seemed spread out.

"For the trap to work, we need them closer together," I said. How long did we have before they turned invisible and we could no longer see them?

"I have an idea," Zalira said. "Dea Maimaktes."

A bolt of lightning crashed down southwest of us, and then another bolt equidistant in the opposite direction.

She turned off her aspect. "That should drive them straight down the middle."

"I can help with that, too," Ahyana said. "Dea Karpophoroi."

High-pitched shrieks filled the air. Zalira went over and put her hand on Ahyana's arm to help, to give her more strength.

"The bats can see them," Ahyana said, slightly out of breath. "They're herding them this way. No, wait, they're invisible now."

"Let's give them something to follow." I took out my xiphos and cut my hand as Ahyana shut off her power.

We turned and ran back toward where we had left Suri and Io. My blood dripped from my hand along the ground. I heard the moment when the terawolves caught wind of it. The howls and snarls increased. They sounded close.

Too close.

I felt the air around me shift, as if one of them were leaping at me.

"Dea Erinys!" I turned and used my ability to grab the invisible wolf by the throat and throw him hard against a tree trunk. He turned visible and collapsed to the ground with a whimper. My adelphia sisters wisely kept running and I hurried to keep up with them, shutting off my power. I had to conserve my energy.

I should have taken a fortification potion.

When we got closer to the city, I noticed that there was now only one path. Io had used her abilities to create vine nets between the trees so that the terawolves would have to follow us straight to the trap.

Suri knelt on the ground, tired, and waited with Io next to the city wall. I saw when Io's eyes went wide. I risked a glance behind me.

There were a dozen terawolves, with their golden eyes and terrible growls. All visible. My heart leapt up into my throat.

"Right!" I yelled to Zalira and Ahyana, and they pivoted at the last moment, barely missing the trap themselves. Suri had made it longer than we'd anticipated. We ran alongside the trap and I stopped at the middle, praying that this would work. That the terawolves wouldn't notice what we had done.

"Come and get me!" I shouted.

All the wolves barreled toward me and I stood with my sword in hand, waiting. My whole body pulsed with adrenaline and fear. Zalira and Ahyana stayed by my side with their weapons out.

I held my ground as they raced closer, even though my instinct was to flee.

One moment they were there and the next they were gone as the ground collapsed beneath their giant paws.

The trap had worked.

I had to draw in several big breaths and wait for my heart to stop thundering before I let myself glance over the edge.

The pit was not only deep, but somehow Suri had managed to add rock spikes at the bottom.

Every terawolf was dead.

The three of us were breathing hard as we stared down at them. We were quickly joined by Suri and Io.

"I was off making those nets and had no idea that you did this," she said to Suri. "Those spikes? That's amazing."

Suri ducked her head, as if embarrassed.

How had she managed it? I was about to ask her, but the stinging in my hand drew my attention. I needed to clean and bandage the cut.

"Your husband's going to notice that," Zalira said.

I was sure he would. I wondered how many marks and bruises I would have on me before the night was through.

"How are we going to get one out?" Ahyana asked, and none of us had an answer. I probably should have thought about that.

All the hairs on the back of my neck suddenly stood up.

"Down!" I screamed. My sisters all dropped to the ground.

The terawolf that I'd thrown into a tree earlier came straight for me, leaping over the trap, teeth bared, mouth open.

"Dea Erinys!"

It slammed into me, its foul breath right above my face. It kept snapping at me with its teeth. I used my left forearm against its throat to keep it away. The impact had caused me to drop my xiphos, but I reached for a knife in my belt.

"Lia!" Io screamed.

I plunged the knife up through the beast's jaw. I kept stabbing until it collapsed on top of me, dead.

I lay there for a second, being crushed, until I shoved the terawolf off. I released my aspect as my sisters gathered around me.

"I'm fine," I said. "At least now we don't have to go down into the pit to grab one."

Io hugged me fiercely and the rest followed.

"Can I get up now?" I asked, and they laughed, sounding relieved.

Zalira helped me to my feet and I noticed that the terawolf had four swords in its back. While I'd been attacking it from the front, my adelphia had been stabbing its other side.

After everyone had retrieved their weapons, Io asked, "How are we going to transport that thing?"

Suri went and found a sturdy stick and used the length of rope she had at her waist to tie the terawolf's paws to the stick. Zalira and I, being the tallest, carried the stick on our shoulders with the beast hanging down between us. It wasn't easy but it worked.

The soldiers at the gate gaped silently at us as we approached.

"You just killed all those monsters," one of them said in an awed voice.

"Can you please help us transport this back to the palace?" I asked. Several guards volunteered and the captain directed the others to return to the posts and make sure the gate was shut. I wondered where he had been earlier.

The guards took the load from us and my shoulder ached with relief. Normally we would have been able to carry it ourselves, but using the magic had wiped us out. Tired and bedraggled, we made our way to the palace. The screaming had stopped and people were no longer running through the streets. Many had returned to their homes, while others had gathered in groups and spoke in hushed tones. Everyone stared as we passed by.

I heard a cawing above us and Kunguru came down and landed on Ahyana's shoulder. He cawed again, flew up into the air in the direction of the palace, and came back to Ahyana, still calling out.

She turned toward me, her expression serious. "Something is wrong at the palace."

CHAPTER TWENTY-SIX

When we reached the palace, Kunguru flew inside and we followed. He landed directly in front of the council chambers, where the doors were shut. I pushed against them.

Locked.

I wouldn't be able to climb up to the roof here and break in. But there was something else I could do. "Dea Erinys."

As the power surged into me, I took a few steps back and then threw my shoulder against the doors, as hard as I could. I felt the doors give way.

"What is the meaning of this?" Pelias demanded as we entered the room.

I shut off my aspect and then turned to the guards who had carried the terawolf for us. "You can drop that. Go and locate Prince Alexandros and tell him he's needed."

The only people in the room were the archons and Erisa. There were no other guards, no nobles listening to the proceedings. Kunguru landed on my shoulder, and I whispered, "Find Xander. Bring him here immediately."

He cawed and flew off. Something nefarious was happening. "Why were the doors locked?" I asked.

Themis seemed surprised. "The doors were locked? We weren't told that."

"It was a safety precaution," Pelias practically sputtered, as if scrambling for an explanation.

Heliodora stood. "What is that?"

"A terawolf," I said. "We fought it outside the city's walls. We killed the rest of its pack. What is this secret meeting about?"

"It isn't secret," Pelias scoffed, his confidence quickly returning. "And you're not entitled to know what it's about because you are not a voting member of the council."

Xander hadn't said anything about whether I could stab Pelias. I let my fingers rest on the handle of my xiphos, but I didn't unsheathe it.

"Erisa called for a meeting to discuss tonight's events," Themis told me. I was glad I had befriended her. "She seems to think this is some kind of show or manipulation orchestrated by your husband. To trick us into thinking that Ilion is being threatened."

"You can't possibly believe that," I said, aghast. Xander would never. I gestured toward the terawolf. "You are being threatened."

"And we're to take your word for it?" Erisa sneered.

"That, and the creature that hasn't been seen for hundreds of years that is dead at my feet." I hoped my eyes were conveying the message that I would gladly add her to the pile of things killed to save Ilion.

Erisa glowered at me. "Lies."

"I suppose that's an easy assertion to make when you're here cowering behind the palace walls and not out at the docks helping like Prince Alexandros is," I heatedly responded. Perhaps it was because I'd called on my fury aspect so many times this evening, but hatred and rage for this woman boiled through my blood.

No one in this room could stop me. I could run over and slit her throat before anyone could even react.

I heard yells and other noises, and they got louder, as if headed toward us. Relief engulfed me when I saw Xander striding in.

He dragged a dead body in each hand. He took them directly to the council table and the archons all recoiled.

"These are Carian soldiers," he announced as he dropped them. "They have a tattoo of a hammer on their chests, indicating their allegiance. I have brought them as proof. They have rebuilt their nation and are coming to destroy all of Ilion. You can no longer put your head in the sand and wish this away. Or believe the lies that my father's second wife has told you."

Erisa was not intimidated by him, even though she should have been. "Why are you bothering to pretend like you need the council's approval for anything? We know about how you have been bringing noncitizens into the city."

"Those are Ilionian people. I don't care if they're from Troas. They deserve protection and safety."

"You should care," she countered. "Where do we put them? What do they eat? Have you even bothered to think about the practicalities?"

"We have more than enough. We can share."

Neither Zethus nor Pelias seemed to like Xander's response, and none of the council members spoke.

"Tonight is proof that we have enemies intent on destroying us," he continued. "A choice must be made. You either follow someone who doesn't know what's happening in her own city or you elect me as king and let me protect Ilion—"

"He is the worst choice," Erisa interjected.

"I am everything the council wants!" he roared back. "My father's trueborn son, married and stable, willing and able to lead this fight."

This seemed to be the opening Erisa had been waiting for. "You want this council to believe that your marriage is a happy one? That you and your bride love each other?"

My breath caught. What did she know?

"They hate one another," Erisa said. "Letting Alexandros become king could very well bring us to the brink of war with Locris because of how he treats his wife."

I wanted to say that was ridiculous, because even if we did despise one another, Locris did not have the means to launch any kind of fight on my behalf.

"That is not what I have witnessed," Stolos said.

"Nor I," said Themis as she nodded at me.

"The entire city just watched them kiss." Heliodora sounded slightly confused. I walked over to Xander and put my hand in his. His long, warm fingers wrapped tightly around mine.

Our relationship seemed to be something that actually interested Zethus. He said, "The guards have spoken about the noises they've heard coming out of their bedroom."

Xander had told me once that his guards weren't gossips, and I had to guess that he had told them to spread that information.

For this very moment.

"We have all seen them together," Pelias said. "The matron reported that she saw the blood on their wedding sheets." It didn't seem to bring him any joy to contradict Erisa.

"Those bloodstains could have come from anything! A false marriage cannot produce the heir that Ilion needs!" Erisa seemed to sense that she was losing ground.

And I was ready to push her over the edge to make sure Xander was named king.

I put a hand over my womb and smiled serenely. "This marriage is true and I am pregnant."

My husband tensed slightly next to me, and I saw a mixture of expressions on the council members' faces—from Erisa's hatred to Themis's excitement.

"Congrat—"

"No!" Erisa cut Themis off. "That isn't possible!"

Did she have proof? Or was this merely a guess? The desperate flails of a drowning woman?

"I can prove it," Io said. "The healers have a potion that indicates whether a woman is pregnant. I can bring it here and prove that Princess Thalia is indeed carrying the heir of Ilion."

"Go," Stolos said, and she turned to run out of the room. Suri got Ahyana to help her with the terawolf, and I supposed they meant to carry it back to their room for the scroll.

Zalira stayed right behind me, her hands near her waist so that she could quickly grab her sword if need be.

Xander leaned down to brush his lips across my left ear in what probably looked like a caress. "What are you doing?"

"What I promised," I whispered back. "Getting you the throne of Ilion."

The room stayed silent as we waited for Io. I had no idea what she had planned but I trusted her. Thankfully, she didn't take long to return, and she brought Parthenia with her. Suri and Ahyana were a step behind.

Io demonstrated the potion for the council, much as she had with us. When she took Parthenia's blood and added it to the mixture, it turned blue. Io asked Heliodora if she could use her blood to show what it did for a woman who wasn't pregnant and the liquid stayed clear.

"Now Princess Thalia," she said. She came over and drew my blood and I watched as she used a different drop from the one she'd taken from me—the council couldn't see her sleight of hand as she switched them.

The liquid turned a bright blue. "There! You see?" she said triumphantly. "Princess Thalia is pregnant!"

The former queen went apoplectic. "None of that means anything! I don't trust Iolanthe!"

"You are questioning a princess of royal blood?" Xander asked with a raised eyebrow, and Erisa immediately stopped. That wasn't a path she could go down. She was totally reliant on her son's "royal blood" to make him king.

Even though she knew that Kyros was not the child of her late husband.

She wanted to use her lie to get her son on the throne, so I would use my lie to keep him off it.

"If tonight was an attack by some unknown enemy," Erisa said, "then it's happened before. Where was your great leader when people in the weapons quarter were killed?"

"Investigating the attack in Lycia while you sat here, on the council, and failed to notice the enemy at our doorstep," Xander said quietly, and I saw the moment when Erisa realized her miscalculation.

She couldn't paint him as an ineffective leader when she had been in a similar position of power, and the city had been attacked under her watch.

"How long until the main Carian army reaches Troas?" Stolos asked. I saw the panic on Erisa's face. The council seemed to be accepting reality and not listening to her alternate theories.

"We don't know," Xander admitted. "Something happened to our spy network and we have been left in the dark, without information. It will depend on where they're coming from. They might be marching on us already, or they might still be preparing before they come here. I can tell you that they're not within three days' travel—that's the latest reports I've received."

"If the army is not close, then what was the purpose in attacking the docks?" Zethus asked, surprising me.

"They're causing fear," Xander said. "It was an extremely small force. They ruined some ships, burned down a couple of buildings, but the fight was over before it began."

It made me think of how Lysimache had talked about using terror to make a populace cower. It was what she had done to Locris.

Xander continued his explanation. "But we don't know when or if they'll strike again. It will unnerve and unsettle the people. Which is why you need a strong leader in place. The citizens will feel less afraid when they know that we're making certain to protect them to the best of our abilities. And not wasting our time and money throwing unnecessary celebrations."

Erisa opened her mouth to speak, but Stolos interrupted. "Perhaps we should try to reach out to the Carians. Should we not be a people of peace?"

"While it is admirable to desire peace, our enemy has already declared war against us," Xander said. "People of peace are not safe unless you have people of action at your side. We have the goddess-given right to defend ourselves and those we love from harm."

Erisa seized on the door Stolos had opened. "If we are truly under attack, then we should try to sue for peace. We do not need to go to war."

"That is ironic, coming from you." Thrax entered the room with the man I'd identified at the party. His wrists were tied together.

To her credit, Erisa didn't seem ruffled. "How dare you speak to me that way!"

Thrax nudged the man. "Tell them what you told me ten minutes ago."

"My name is Diocles. I work for Erisa. My twin brother and I, along with many others, were hired to kill the Locrian maiden while she was at the temple. We did not succeed and I barely escaped with my life. Erisa also hired assassins to attack the princess in her rooms here at the palace, trying to kill her. The queen was attempting to destroy the marriage of Princess Thalia and Prince Alexandros." His voice was dull and pained, as if he didn't want to say the words.

"You cannot believe such blatant lies!" Erisa screamed, banging her hands against the table.

"What were you doing when I caught you?" Thrax asked.

"I was on my way to deliver a message to the attackers at the docks for the queen. Saying that if they would kill Prince Alexandros, she would open the city gates to them."

"What has he offered you?" Erisa demanded. "Obviously the prince and his men are now bribing people to lie on their behalf!"

"Diocles was given a truth serum laced with a compulsion element that forces him to answer. He cannot lie and he cannot stay quiet," Xander said. "Io can verify the validity of the serum, as she is the one who created it."

Io nodded. "We have used it on others and it works perfectly."

"I invite the council to interrogate him further, if you would like," Xander offered.

"The prince is desperate and will say and do anything to get his way!" The former queen looked as if she were about to go mad. I'd never seen her so disheveled before.

"Erisa is right. I am desperate," Xander said. "Because war is here. We have to stop behaving as if everything is fine when it's not. We can no longer pretend it away with parties and bribes or hide it behind assassination attempts. It all needs to stop. Now is the time to decide. Be people of action. Who do you want leading you? Choose me as king and let's save our city."

CHAPTER TWENTY-SEVEN

My husband was magnificent. I felt actual chills as he spoke. If I hadn't wanted him before, this would have changed everything for me. I felt proud to stand next to him.

"Tonight the citizens were calling for him to be their king," Heliodora said. "I move that we make our official vote now, and my vote is for Prince Alexandros."

"I second the motion," Themis said.

Pelias, who looked extremely uncomfortable, took over the vote. "Erisa?"

Defiant, she said, "I vote for Prince Kyros. I will be his regent until he comes of age."

Stolos and Themis both voted for Xander.

"Zethus?"

"I vote for Prince Alexandros." While it surprised me, it seemed that Zethus didn't want to die. He was probably worried it would disrupt his drinking and harassing hetaerae.

That was it. Those were all the votes Xander needed. Four council members had voted for him, and there were only two votes left, one of them being his.

And he voted for himself.

Pelias still had his vote, but it was too late. This was happening and couldn't be undone. Something he seemed to realize. "My vote is for Prince Alexandros."

Erisa was so stunned she couldn't speak.

"I am grateful for your votes, and I accept," Xander said. "Guards, take Erisa. She and Kyros are to be confined to their rooms and not let out without my permission."

His stepmother screamed and protested, but the guards did as their king commanded and dragged her out.

"You did it," I said to Xander, putting my arms around his neck so that I could hug him.

"We did it," he said, gripping me tightly.

"Let's go to the throne room and officially crown you," Themis said, which caused him to take a step back from me. She walked over to a locked cabinet and put in a key, opening it. She pulled out a gold-plated crown of laurel leaves.

I briefly wondered why it was not down in the vault. I supposed that when Erisa had organized her secret meeting to take over, she had brought it upstairs to the council's chambers.

We went as a group to the throne room. I'd never been in here before. I supposed it made sense—there wasn't a king, so there wasn't any reason to enter. It was a smaller room, a fraction of the size of the dining hall.

A throne sat at the top of a dais, with multiple steps leading up to it.

"The high priestess usually crowns the new king," Heliodora said worriedly to Themis. I wondered how many new kings of Ilion Lysimache had crowned.

"My wife can do it," Xander said. He walked up the steps and sat on his throne. Looking regal and deadly and dashing and a thousand other things that made my stomach flutter.

Themis handed me the crown and gestured toward the dais. I walked up the stairs, aware that everyone was watching. "I'm not a high priestess," I told him. "Io should do it. She's an Ilionian princess."

"So are you."

Oh. I supposed in a way that was true.

My father had told me once that, in other lands, coronations were elaborate affairs, with flowery speeches and long rituals. But in Locris, as in Ilion, it was as simple as placing the crown on the person's head.

Which I did carefully, trying to act with grace. The same crown his father and grandfather had worn. This was a monumental moment, and I wanted it to have the gravitas it deserved.

It fit him perfectly.

"Long live King Alexandros!" Heliodora called out, and the other council members cheered as well.

Including Pelias, who did it while also looking even more miserable than he had earlier.

"Thank you," Xander said. "My first act as king will be to put together a plan for the upcoming war. I would like the council to meet to decide the best ways to prepare our citizens and channel funding into creating weapons and armor. We will need to help house and feed the Ilionians arriving from different villages and cities to make certain that they're provided for. The citizen army will also need to be called up for battle."

"It will be done," Stolos promised.

"My second act will be to break the betrothal between Lykaon, son of Pelias, and Princess Kallisto of Locris."

He had remembered his promise. I gripped the back of his throne so that I wouldn't throw myself at him to thank him. He had just saved my older sister from a monster.

Pelias was outraged. "You have no right, no authority to—"

"I have every right," Xander interrupted him. "And the only authority. I am your king."

"There are penalties, fines that the Locrian royals will have to pay!"

"That is only if they break the contract, and they have not. I did. If you feel you are owed compensation, write a request and I will consider it," Xander said.

Pelias looked as if he wanted to continue arguing, but seemed to quickly realize that there was nothing he could do.

Xander looked at the others and said, “I would like for the council to meet immediately to begin work on a plan of action. And for the throne room to be cleared so that I may have a moment alone with my wife.”

Him becoming king had changed everything. The council no longer had any sway over him. They were now subject to him and his decisions.

The power had shifted.

And power looked good on him.

Everyone who had gathered to bear witness to Xander’s coronation filed out of the room. Io was the last to go, and I saw the look of concern on her face. It made my heart twinge but it wasn’t enough to get me to excuse myself and leave.

I wanted to be here with him.

When Io shut the door behind her, he said, “Why did you break your promise to me?”

It took me a moment to figure out what he was talking about. “The terawolf?”

“Yes,” he angrily confirmed. When he’d asked to be alone with me, I hadn’t known what to expect, but it hadn’t been him being mad about the terawolf.

“I didn’t go to the docks, so I didn’t break my promise.”

“You knew that I meant for you to stay in the palace!”

“I . . .” I couldn’t lie about this. “I did know that. I’m sorry. But I had to help. And the terawolves were headed for the docks. I was afraid they would hurt people.”

He was quiet for a long moment. “You wanted to help Ilionians?”

I nodded. “And you.”

His anger quickly receded. He tried to be stern. “No more hunting terawolves.”

“We won’t. I think we killed them all.”

"You what?"

I quickly told him the story, and despite him being upset that I'd left the safety of the palace, I saw the admiration and respect in his eyes. It completely thrilled me.

And he didn't yell at me for involving Io in it.

Progress.

But it also caused me to move away from him, putting some distance between us, because seeing him on his throne with his crown was doing something inexplicable to me. He exuded authority and a masculine energy that made me weak-kneed.

"You finally have everything you wanted," I said.

"Not everything."

I wanted his words to be about me, but I couldn't be that self-centered. There were probably many other things that he was speaking about. I wouldn't allow myself to ask him to clarify and instead found a more neutral topic to speak about.

"I think Pelias regrets voting for you. He wanted two thrones for his children and now he will get none," I said.

Xander's gaze followed me as I slowly walked around the room. "His vote wouldn't have mattered either way. But it was politically smarter of him to throw his lot in with mine."

I went around a column, tracing it with my hand. "It also backfired spectacularly for Erisa."

"Yes, I don't think that was what she thought would happen."

"She tried to organize a secret council meeting to get them to vote for Kyros before you could return. I'm glad that you arrived as quickly as you did," I said.

"I was already on my way back when Rokh found me. Then I sent him off to retrieve Thrax and the prisoner."

"Speaking of . . . now that you have proof, what are you going to do with Erisa?"

He watched me like a bird of prey, aware of my every movement. I found his attention intoxicating.

"Honestly, I'm not sure. Exile seems like the best option. But I'm not going to cast her out of the city with an army on the way."

I went slowly around another column while looking at him over my shoulder. "Perhaps you should. Let her run into Artemisia. Maybe they would take each other out."

He smiled, the first I'd seen since he'd dragged in those Carian soldiers. "That would be convenient."

It seemed like he enjoyed watching me. Despite the fact that nothing could happen, I found myself wishing that I knew how to be beguiling.

"Where will your queen's throne go?" I asked. There was only one throne in the room.

"When my father was alive, Erisa had a chair down on the bottom step."

I glanced at where he pointed. That must have infuriated her. "And what will you do?"

"Depends on the queen." His eyes darkened. "If you were my queen, I would have them build your throne next to mine. We would rule as equals. Make the changes that Ilion needs, together."

"You would do that?" My heart beat so fast I worried it might give out.

"Yes."

But I couldn't be his queen. Even if I survived everything to come, him being made king put an end to any hope of a relationship between us. He was now their ruler. He would never be able to leave Ilion.

And I couldn't stay. I had to return to Locris when this was all over.

"Are you going to send me away?" I asked. I wasn't able to make eye contact and hoped he couldn't hear the worry and fear that I was feeling.

"Why do you think I'd send you away?"

It aggravated me when he did that. Answered my question with a question. I looked at him as I said, "You're the king. Our contract has ended."

A smile played at the edges of his mouth. "Does this mean I'm going to have to assign a bodyguard to Thrax?"

"No. Because Quynh would kill me. And she'd do it slowly and make sure I suffered."

He laughed and I wanted to sigh. I loved that sound.

"Why would I ever send you away?" he asked. "Who else would I talk to about murdering my beloved brother? And what kind of king would I be if I kicked my pregnant queen out of the palace?"

When he called me his queen . . . I had to stop for a moment to absorb that. I was as much his queen as I was pregnant.

But oh, I wanted to believe.

"You could go home if you wanted." He made his offer carefully, his tone neutral.

"You would let me go?" Why did that feel disappointing?

"If that was your wish. I offered that to you in the beginning."

He was talking about when I'd first joined the temple. On more than one occasion, he had told me that if I wanted it, he would help me get on a boat back to Locris.

Why would he have done that if he knew who I was?

"And before you start in on me, I didn't know who you were at the time." It was uncanny how well he could read me, how he always seemed to know what I was thinking.

Dolion had already told me that wasn't true, and I had believed him. But with his recent confession to me . . . what if Dolion was the one who had been lying? Because of the feelings he had for me? I had so easily accepted his words as truth.

What if I had made a grave mistake?

"If I had known your true identity, I would have marched you off the *Nikos* when we landed and made you marry me then. I never would have let you be in that kind of danger."

"It doesn't matter," I said. Because it didn't. "I would have done the same thing if our positions were reversed."

"Meaning what?"

"Meaning that if I had to seduce you to secure the throne of my country and save my people, I would have done it."

"Oh?" He raised a single eyebrow at me. "And how would that have gone?"

"What?"

"You seducing me."

How was it possible to feel aroused and embarrassed at the same time? "I assume it would be incredibly easy."

"You do?"

I nodded, hoping my cheeks hadn't turned pink. "Yes. I think all I'd have to do is remove my clothing and I would get my way."

His eyes sparkled in the low light. "I think I might be a harder sell than that."

My pulse pounded at his challenge.

I didn't understand all the rules of this game, but I knew I wanted to play.

CHAPTER TWENTY-EIGHT

"I've never tried to seduce a king before," I said, hoping he couldn't hear how my voice wobbled.

"You haven't tried to seduce anyone before."

Xander was right. And it was why I felt a bit foolish.

"Are you certain I can't just take off my clothes? You told me no man alive could resist me when I was naked."

His eyes lit up with interest. "I wouldn't advise it. Anyone could walk in. And I wouldn't want my third act as king to be murdering the man who saw you that way."

His words infused me, giving me strength. Challenging me. I never could back down from a challenge. I started disarming myself. It wouldn't be a successful attempt if I accidentally stabbed him.

"What are you doing?" he asked.

"Removing my weapons."

"You possess others," he said, his gaze hotly raking over my body. "Ones you cannot discard."

"I am how the goddess made me. You can't blame me for that."

"I don't. I praise her for it. Hurry."

The shivers had already started and we weren't even touching yet. "Be patient," I scolded him.

"You have no idea how patient I am." His words were heavy and thick with desire, and I again had to worry about my ability to stay upright.

"Take off your weapons," I told him in a soft voice. I felt awkward. I was no seductress.

But he watched me like I was the most enchanting thing he'd ever seen. "Should I be worried?"

"About?"

"Our contract is ended, and as I recall, you did swear that you would kill me. Perhaps you disarm me now to carry through with your promise." The mischievous smile on his face let me know that he was teasing.

"You are perfectly safe."

He shook his head. "You have that look where I can't tell if you're planning on kissing me or stabbing me."

"Maybe I haven't decided yet."

That smile turned into a grin as he continued to take off knives and daggers and dropped them onto the floor. "You've both kissed me and stabbed me before, so you should know which one you want more."

"I've never stabbed you," I said.

"I still have the scar on my throat."

"That was your fault," I reminded him. "You pushed against my blade."

"So that I could kiss you. Of your options, I know which one I prefer." He held his hands out to show me that he was weapon-free.

Summoning all the courage I possessed, I moved closer to him. His gaze felt weighted, like he was touching me.

Then he did touch me, as if he couldn't help himself. He reached out and ran his fingers along the length of my hair. "You never did tell me how you got your long hair back."

"I woke up the day of our wedding and it was like this," I said. "I don't know how to explain it. Io thought it was a sign."

"A sign of what?"

That we were meant to be together. I couldn't tell him that. "She thought the goddess was blessing our marriage."

His expression shifted, as if considering my words. I didn't want to talk about signs or anything like that. I just wanted to be with him.

Grateful that I wore one of my training tunics, I climbed up into his lap and straddled him.

Heat coursed through me when we made contact, my soft and warm places against his hard ones. Xander hissed a curse as I settled. His hands went to my hips, his fingers digging into my curves.

I took him by the wrists and placed his hands back on the arms of the throne. "You're not allowed to touch me," I said in a breathy voice. "I'm the one seducing you."

This was an entirely necessary precaution, as I knew how easily he could make me forget myself. I felt like a novice being handed a finely honed weapon. I was more likely to cut myself than I was him.

"If you touch me," I said, "that means that I win."

He liked my challenge. I could see it in his eyes.

I tried to think of what to do next, the things that he had liked in the past. He seemed to have liked everything.

So perhaps I should be doing the things that I liked. His eyes were hooded and his pupils were so large, they looked like two deep pools that I could happily drown in. I reached up to the pin at his right shoulder and undid it.

"What did I just tell you about the possibility of being interrupted?" He sounded both amused and aroused.

The idea that we might be caught made it seem more exciting and strengthened my boldness. I leaned forward and pressed my lips to the base of his neck as I pushed the top of his tunic to one side. His breath caught, and he made a soft groan at the back of his throat that I both felt and heard.

I continued to softly kiss along his exposed skin, loving the warmth and feel of it. The way his muscles would tense and pulse everywhere that my lips touched him.

"How is my seduction attempt going?" I asked.

"Passable." His judgment might have wounded me, but I could hear the strain in his voice, as if it took everything in him to hold back.

"Passable?" I repeated. "That won't do."

I heard his breathing, each inhale and exhale coming quicker than the one before. "You always have to be the best, don't you, my little princess?"

It drove me wild when he called me that, but I did my best not to react. The roaring of blood in my ears made it almost impossible for me to think or speak for a few moments. "I suppose I'll have to redouble my efforts."

I began to kiss and taste his skin, reveling in the tautness of his muscles as he strained to hold still. I could tell that all he wanted was to reach out and grab me. But he was too competitive to do so. I sat up and studied him, watching the different emotions flitting through his eyes, how his mouth tensed as he drank me in.

"How does this make you feel?" I asked, putting my hand over his chest so his thundering heartbeat could move against my palm. My own beat just as hard and just as fast.

"I'm indifferent." He could barely get the lie out.

I smiled. "Yes, I can feel your heated indifference against me." I canted my hips and he made a strangled noise that sounded as if I had ripped it from his chest.

I was not unaffected. Threads of pleasure wound their way through me and I trembled, my skin feverishly prickling with need. But I held still.

"Do that again," he ordered, his pretense of being unaffected completely dropped.

"I didn't hear you say 'please,'" I taunted him. This felt like when I had discovered I could do magic. I wanted to wield it, play with it, test my limits. It was exhilarating.

What could I do?

I ran my fingertips lightly along the ridges and planes of his torso. I let out a little sigh. "I do so enjoy your chest."

"The feeling is entirely mutual," he said, and his desperate tone caused crackling pleasure to race along my veins. His eyes roved over my body and the muscles in his jaw clenched when I reached up to run a finger along my own collarbone.

"I am so soft," I breathed. "As I recall, you like how soft I am. You like many things about me."

He didn't respond. Given the look on his face, I wasn't sure he could.

I returned my hand to his chest. "I like how it feels when my bare skin is against yours."

No response. Just his ragged, broken breathing.

I thought of the night of his birthday, what his words of desire had done to me. He had given me those words. I had never done the same.

Would mine have a similar effect on him?

Longing curled and twisted low in my gut, and it gave me the nerve to continue. To be honest with him, even if it was entirely foolish. "I owe you an apology."

He hadn't been expecting that. "You owe me an apology for so many things you'll have to be more specific," he teased.

"I think I control the dreams. And the nightmares. I didn't realize it until recently, but it seems that they come from me."

"You didn't have to resort to dreams if you wanted me. You only had to ask. And climb into my lap," he said, looking down at where my body pressed against his.

"The dreams started on the *Nikos*," I said, rocking against him once, twice, before stopping. "I wanted you to be with me. To feel what I was feeling, to touch me the way that I longed to touch you."

"You're finally admitting that you want me?"

"I do want you," I said. "Then, now, I always want you."

His eyes darkened. "Are you saying these things to win your game?"

I shook my head. "I'm saying them because they're true."

His pulse beat so hard at the base of his throat that I could see it. I leaned forward to kiss it quickly before continuing.

"I've never told you how safe you make me feel. How all day long I wait for the moment that I get to lie in your arms because I know nothing will happen to me so long as you're there."

The knot in his neck bobbed slowly.

"I haven't admitted how I've become an oath-breaker. I'm not going to kill Thrax. I'm not going to kill you. But I can hardly hang on to my vows when you kiss me. And worse, I'm not sure that I want to."

"Don't tell me that," he pleaded with a groan.

I continued my exploration of his torso. I didn't think I would ever tire of doing so. "You told me once that you could satisfy my curiosity. But there is so much I'm curious about."

"Such as?" His heated voice was thick in his throat.

"What it will feel like when you're inside me, and how I ache when I think about it."

He growled in a way that completely thrilled me, his eyes turning hazy and unfocused. He gripped the arms of his throne so tightly that his knuckles went white.

"Have you imagined that?" I asked innocently.

"Many, many times. Can I touch you now?"

"Not if you want to win," I said, despite the fact that my stomach quivered and desire beat through my superheated blood. "You've done so many amazing things to me, and I think constantly about how to return the favor. How I could use my mouth on you to—"

He groaned and swore and then his lips were on mine, his arms around me. At first I gloried in the fact that I had won, and then I gloried that he was touching me.

He slid his tongue into my mouth and I moaned in response. Complete and total bliss. I melted against him as he turned my blood into liquid sun. Burning and bright and more than I could take.

I instinctually moved against him because of the unbelievable pleasure it gave me, and the promise of what was to come next. He let out a ragged groan of approval.

Especially once I realized that the faster I went, the better it felt.

"So beautiful," he murmured in a raspy voice. "So good. So, so good."

Pressure built, accompanied by shooting stars and heated sparks that twisted and swirled inside me. So many parts of me ached in a way I didn't completely understand. His kisses kept pace with me, twining his tongue with mine over and over again.

The hardest part of this was that it didn't feel wrong. It never had. It had always felt fated, as if the goddess herself had decreed our relationship.

I needed more of whatever this was. Molten fire radiated through me until I felt like I might burst. Somehow I knew that there was an ecstasy waiting for me, I just had to reach it.

"Lia . . ." His frayed words were against my lips. "I'm going to—"

His body arched, drawn taut, and he shuddered as he roared my name.

CHAPTER TWENTY-NINE

"What was that?" I asked as he collapsed back into his throne, panting. My heart still beat arrhythmically, pulsing with unfulfilled yearning and frustration.

"I climaxed," he said, his voice gravelly and shaking. At my bewildered expression, he added, "You brought me to completion."

"Oh." I was confused. "I thought that could only happen inside of me."

He reached up to stroke the side of my face. "There is so much you don't know."

Show me.

I had to bite the words back. I might have just done something very bad. Something that couldn't be undone.

He looked wrung out. Exhausted. Despite my fear of having potentially, accidentally broken my vow, all I could think about was that I had done this to him. I had brought the mightiest man in Ilion to his knees. A sense of power surged inside me, a feminine pride exulting in the fact that I could make him this way. I pinned his tunic closed for him, as he seemed unable to move.

I couldn't help but smile. "I suppose that means I win."

He laughed. "Wife, you may claim all the victories you'd like. I should probably feel embarrassed, as this hasn't happened to me in years, but all I feel is . . ."

Not able to stave off my curiosity, I asked, "What does it feel like?"

"There are no words to describe it adequately. It is euphoric. The most incredible pleasure you could possibly imagine," he said.

Pleasure . . . that I wasn't allowed to give.

I couldn't ignore that nagging voice in my head reminding me that I might have made a grave mistake.

The smile dropped off his face. "What's wrong?"

"Pleasures of the flesh," I told him. Maybe it wouldn't count because I hadn't intended to bring him to completion. Hadn't known that I could.

Would the goddess hold this against me?

"You didn't know," he said, echoing my own thoughts.

"But if it happened again . . ." I wanted it again. Wanted it for him, wanted it for myself.

His expression sobered even further. "So we can't."

"I'm sorry," I said, feeling the tears welling up in my eyes.

His eyes were so soft. "I'm the one who should be apologizing. I knew better. I should have stopped it."

He crushed me to his chest and I held on tightly. I should give him up. He was king now. We had no further need for pretense. We could have separate rooms. I could stay away from him.

But this was where I wanted to be.

"Stand up," he said. "Try the magic."

I felt foolish for not having thought of it earlier. Fear and apprehension squeezed my heart as I said, "Dea Erinys."

The hot-and-cold rush of the magic filled me. "It's here," I said with relief.

And somehow the glow around him had turned an even brighter white.

"I'm glad," he said. But his smile didn't reach his eyes.

I turned the aspect off and was about to ask him what was troubling him when the doors flew open.

Lykaon strode into the room with half a dozen of his personal soldiers.

"What do you think you're doing?" Xander demanded, getting to his feet.

"I am here to demand satisfaction," Lykaon said, drawing his sword. "You have cost me a kingship. What right do you have to terminate my betrothal contract?"

"I am king of Ilion." Xander sounded like wrath incarnate. "And after having made your acquaintance, my wife requested that you not be allowed on the same continent as her sister. I was happy to agree."

Lykaon looked at me, and I waited for that moment when recognition would fill his eyes.

It didn't happen.

He had no idea who I was.

How many women had he hit?

"So you mean to be the sort of king who lets a woman rule a ruler and command a commander," Lykaon said with a sneer.

Angry, I picked my xiphos up off the ground and took it from its sheath. "You want satisfaction? You can fight me. For what you did to me, to my maid, and what you would have done to my sister."

"Do you want your wife to die?" Lykaon asked Xander incredulously. "You would let her fight your battles?"

"It's not my battle." Xander looked genuinely amused. "You think you're going to beat her? This is going to be fun."

"Your husband must not care very much about you," Lykaon said.

"He's not concerned because he knows I'm going to win," I said, lifting my sword.

At that Lykaon laughed.

"You don't remember me, do you?" I asked as I paced toward him, my xiphos still ready.

"Should I?"

"That is your queen." Xander snarled the words, and I had to smile.

I told Lykaon, "When you went to Locris, I found you beating my maid, Hippolyta. And when I tried to stop you, you backhanded me."

He shrugged. "I don't know why you think I'd remember that."

Because it happened so often? I'd had enough. I swung at him and he looked shocked as he brought his own sword up to stop me. I hit him much harder than he'd been anticipating, and he had to take a step back to absorb the blow.

"Not so amusing now, is it?" I asked before I lunged forward.

Lykaon was not the warrior he apparently fancied himself to be. He could barely hold me off as I pressed forward relentlessly. His reflexes were poor, and he had no idea how to create cover to protect himself from me.

He was a spoiled nobleman's son with battle masters who had probably let him win so as to not risk his or his father's anger.

Giving him an overinflated sense of superiority.

"Why are you moving so slow?" Xander asked me. He was leaning against a column with his arms folded across his chest.

"Not all of us are goddess-blessed," I said. Lykaon was such a poor sword fighter that I didn't even need to call up my power. I could beat him on my own.

"I'm hungry," my husband told me. "Quit toying with him and finish this."

Lykaon mistakenly thought that my husband had distracted me and tried to strike at me. I blocked him with my xiphos, and then with my left hand, I punched him so hard in the face that his nose began to bleed.

He stumbled backward, in shock. He reached up to touch the blood and said, "Did you see what she did? Don't just stand there! Get her!"

His soldiers pulled out their weapons, and my husband turned toward them to calmly say, "I will kill anyone who interferes."

Lykaon's men stayed put.

I forced Lykaon to reengage with me. "Is this why you hit women? Because you're so pathetic?"

"Be silent!" he screamed at me as I began to rain down blows on him.

It was laughable that he thought he could tell me what to do. "What was it you said to me in Locris? You told me to learn my place and obey my betters. I am giving the same advice to you now."

I knocked his sword out of his hand, and it went flying across the room. I whirled around Lykaon to kick him in the back of his legs so that he dropped to his knees. I grabbed his hair and held my xiphos to his throat, letting the edge pierce his skin.

"Don't kill me," he pleaded. "Please, I don't want to die."

I gripped his hair tighter and yanked his head back so that he cried out. "The only reason I'm letting you live, worm, is so that for the rest of your pathetic life you'll remember that you were bested by a woman. And if I ever hear of you hurting another woman, I will find you and cut off all the protruding parts of your body."

I released his hair and stepped back. "Your soldiers witnessed this. They will tell others. Soon everyone in Troas will know."

"Get out," Xander said. "And do not darken the doors of my palace ever again."

Lykaon scrambled to his feet and his soldiers followed after him.

Xander came up behind me and turned me toward him. He kissed me so thoroughly and completely that I stopped breathing and became lightheaded.

He put his forehead against mine. "That was . . . arousing."

"You enjoy watching me beat people up?"

"I find it immensely entertaining when I'm not on the other end of your little sword," he said.

"That's not how I remember it. I recall you very much liking it."

"You're right." He kissed me quickly on the forehead before releasing me. "I shouldn't kiss you like that."

No, he probably shouldn't.

But that was all I wanted, to melt into his arms and his kiss.

"What will your sister do now?" he asked me.

I folded my arms against my chest to stop myself from reaching for him. "Themis mentioned her youngest son being a possible candidate as a prince consort. I'd like to meet him. But as long as he's not Lykaon, I think it could work."

Xander nodded. "I need to go meet with Thrax to set up guard placement throughout the city. I'll probably need to talk to him about putting a guard to watch Pelias's house. I don't trust him or his son."

I was sure I hadn't helped matters by beating Lykaon. "Right now?"

"First I need to clean up and change," he said in a way that made me think I should have understood what he was hinting at, but I didn't.

We walked back to our room in a comfortable silence until the moment when I realized that I shouldn't go into our room with him. We both needed a chance to cool down.

"I'm going to check on my adelphia," I said.

"You don't want to help me bathe and undress?" he teased, and I knew my cheeks had to be an extremely bright shade of pink.

"That should probably be a solo activity," I said.

"You have no idea how many times it has been," he said with a wink before entering our room. Another thing I didn't understand, but the heat of it still flustered me.

His flirtatious invitations would be the death of me. Maybe I should tell him he couldn't do that, either.

I opened Io's door and the smell of the dead terawolf had me covering my nose and mouth with my hand.

"Terrible, isn't it?" Ahyana said.

"Yes. Did it work?" I asked.

Io sat at the table in front of the scroll, looking dejected. "No."

My stomach sank like an anchor. I had been so hopeful.

"We've tried everything. We used blood. Some of its fur. Its toenails. I even scraped its horns, but nothing." Io held up her hand to show me the silver sparkles from the horn still attached to her palm. "The scroll hasn't changed."

"Maybe it has to be alive," I said.

"I can't imagine that would make a difference," Io said sadly.

"The scroll did reject the Locrian dirt and would only work with Ilionian soil," Ahyana pointed out.

"Yes, but I don't think terawolves have enough aether for it to work. Aether was created by the tears of the goddess's daughter when she was parted from her mother. How could there be enough of that in a creature special to her brother? The only aether part of the terawolves seems to be their ability to turn invisible," Io said.

That made me think about Luna, and how I'd briefly thought she had turned invisible. "Did I tell you all that Luna disappeared?"

They all turned slowly to stare at me. As if I had taken leave of my senses.

"She reappeared a few moments later," I added. "What?"

"That's not normal," Zalira told me.

"I just assumed that animals here did that." I had no frame of reference to know differently.

Io stood up and headed out the door. She nearly slammed into her brother, who was leaving. He had gotten ready quickly. She put her hands out to stop from running into him and he quickly grabbed her to keep her from falling forward. He glanced down.

"Have you been holding my wife's lizard?" he asked his sister.

"No. This happened from the terawolf."

"So now we have two things in the palace making this mess?" He raised one eyebrow at me, sharing a heated moment from our inside joke, and then he left.

"What did he mean?" Io asked.

"There have been a couple of times when Luna has sneezed and she gets silvery sparkles everywhere. It annoys him."

Then it was as if we all shared a single brain and came to the same conclusion at the same time. I raced into my room, over to Luna's enclosure.

And saw that there were two long, furled wings protruding from the bumps in her back.

CHAPTER THIRTY

"Luna has wings?" I delicately lifted one and opened it a bit at the end. Definitely wings.

"She has gotten so big so quickly," Io said, sounding awed.

Another thing that apparently wasn't typical and I didn't know.

I picked Luna up and her body stayed limp. She looked as if she were dead, but I knew she wasn't. "She does this when she's sleeping heavily," I told them as I put her back down. "What kind of lizard has wings?"

"No kind," Zalira said, her eyes wide.

"There are only four types of creatures that I know of that can fly," Ahyana told me. "Insects, birds, bats, and dragons."

"You think Luna's a dragon?" I asked. "She doesn't really look like one."

"Maybe dragons are like frogs or butterflies, where they start out as a tadpole or caterpillar and become something else," Ahyana said.

"Is she an air dragon?" Io asked as she ran her fingertip along Luna's back. "They're the only ones with wings."

"She's the wrong color," Zalira said. "Although I've only seen drawings."

Part of me hoped Luna wouldn't change colors. I loved her silver skin. "We were all thinking the same thing earlier. That Luna has aether. Which must make her an aether dragon." Because dragons connected to a specific element. The other dragons wouldn't have aether.

"They were thought to not even exist," Io whispered, shocked. "I've never seen a drawing of one. And there's so little information about dragons that I can't even think of anyone who might know."

More lost knowledge.

There was a way to test whether Luna had aether.

Picking Luna up again, I took her into Io's room to the scroll. I brushed against her sides and sparkles fell from her body onto the papyrus. They dissolved into the scroll.

And it made the rest of the lines form.

The scroll was complete. It was a map.

A heavy silence fell on us as we all stood there, staring at it.

Uncertain of what to do next.

Io read out loud the writing at the bottom of the page.

"When Asteria was stolen, not to be found
In agony Dea hid her face
In a cave where no man or beast may enter
Let the flame-kissed savior who is worthy
Pass the tests of the goddesses
To claim the greatest weapon"

"It has to be her golden sword," Io mused. "The one she used to create the world."

"Asteria?" Ahyana asked.

"That has to be the goddess's daughter," Zalira said.

Suri pointed at the map. The cave was located in Mount Idaia in the Syrilline Mountains, east of Troas.

"How far from here is that?" I asked.

No one knew. It looked close on the map.

Ahyana traced the path that the scroll had created for us. "We have to go and get that sword. Then you'll have a god-weapon to use against Artemisia."

"Me?" I asked.

"None of the rest of us are the flame-kissed savior," she said with a smile.

"This is the worst possible time. We're about to be invaded," I said.

Zalira folded her arms. "Or it's the best possible time. I think we're going to need that sword."

Io looked crestfallen.

I put my hand on her shoulder. "What's wrong?"

"Although I knew we would find it, part of me didn't want to locate the greatest weapon. Because the prophecy can't come true without it."

My heart lurched sideways. She was right. If we stayed put and didn't look for the sword, then I couldn't wield it.

Which meant the rest of the prophecy might not happen.

But Artemisia was coming. I needed to be able to stop her. And the greatest weapon might be the only way that I could do so.

My sisters all looked so sad, but this was not the time to wallow. "What should we do next?" I asked.

Io pulled out a piece of papyrus so that we could start making lists of what we would need for this trip.

And I worried about how I was going to convince my husband to let us go.

I lay on the ground in an unfamiliar place. I was trying to catch my breath, but the wind had been knocked out of me. My entire body ached.

Artemisia strode toward me, carrying a war hammer that was bigger than her head.

My fury aspect was quickly fading and I struggled to keep my eyes open. I was going to pass out. I tried to turn it off but it didn't work. Something was interfering with my magic.

My heart beat faster the closer Artemisia got to me. I felt my sword in my hand but I was too weak to lift it. What was happening?

"Now you die, Locrian."

She raised her hammer over her head and brought it down at me.

I gasped loudly as I sat straight up in my bed. I felt disoriented—how had I gotten here? The last thing I remembered was being in Io's room making plans.

Xander's side of the bed was still warm. My heart caught at the idea of him finding me asleep in his sister's room and bringing me back here. Holding me while I slept.

Had I given myself a nightmare? It hadn't felt like one. Instead it had felt like a vision of the future.

A dark harbinger of things to come.

This had been different. It had felt so real. Like this was fated. It was going to happen.

I would die.

My heart pounded in my chest, and I tried to swallow down the silvery taste of fear in my mouth. If Artemisia killed me, Xander would also die. I couldn't let that happen.

Io thought she was close with her formulation to separate our connection but it hadn't been successful yet.

There was only one other way to break the link.

If my fate was to die, I wouldn't be able to save Locris. I would need one of my sisters to do it.

I wouldn't let Xander share my fate. I refused. Ilion desperately needed him. He didn't have an heir. If he died, the council would have no other recourse but to select Kyros as king, which would make Erisa his regent.

The prophecy said that my death would save Ilion. Xander was the answer. He would defeat Caria. He would protect both Ilion and Locris. The goddess had blessed him with supernatural strength and fighting skill for a reason. He was necessary for this war.

I was not.

If my final battle was with Artemisia, I hoped that I would do enough damage to send her to the underworld before she ended my life.

I had to protect him. I had to keep him safe.

I didn't want to ruminate about my potential death any longer. I forced myself to think about last night and the things I had discussed with my adelphia after we'd unlocked the scroll. What could an aether dragon do when she was actually awake, which seemed so infrequent these days? I told them how Luna slept so deeply and seemed to grow even bigger after.

Ahyana had been concerned about us entering the cave, as it sounded forbidden, but Io had said, "We are neither men nor beasts. We should be fine."

I hoped she was correct.

We had also talked about the tests of the goddesses. Did that mean Dea and Asteria? Or were there others that we would have to worry about? What would happen if we didn't pass the tests and couldn't get the weapon?

I kept my personal concerns to myself. One phrase from the scroll kept repeating in my mind.

The flame-kissed savior who is worthy.

It felt as if it were being spelled out for me yet again: I had to be worthy to enter the cave, pass the tests, and claim the weapon.

And if I survived, I still needed to save Locris with the eye. Which also required me to remain worthy.

I knew that I needed the constant reminders. Because when I was in the moment with Xander, he was all I cared about.

Would last night keep me out of the cave? Perhaps the "pleasures of the flesh" only applied to receiving, not giving. I hadn't reached completion—did that make a difference?

Or was I still permitted to wield magic because it had been accidental? Would it be different now that I knew where it could lead? Would I be held accountable if I made that choice again?

This was not something I could discuss with my adelphia. Zalira and Ahyana would be understanding and might even be helpful, but Io would be devastated and Suri would take her side, as she always did.

It wouldn't help anything if I told them. It would only make things worse.

I got up and quickly got ready for the day. I had wanted to leave for the mountains this morning, but Io had said that she needed time to create extra potions for the trip.

Which also gave me another day to try and figure out how to persuade Xander into agreeing to let me go.

I heard my sisters talking next door and went over to see what they were doing. Io worked on her potions and serums while Suri sharpened her daggers and Zalira studied the map.

"What happened to the terawolf?" I asked. I was glad it was gone.

"Xander removed it," Io said.

Ahyana entered the room then, looking a bit down.

"Where are you coming back from?" I asked her.

"To say goodbye to Rokh. Your husband sent him out on yet another secret mission," she said. "I don't understand why it's always him that has to go."

"Because Xander trusts him," I said. And because Rokh could shape-shift into a raven and fly to places faster than a horse could.

"I found out how far away the mountain range is from here," Ahyana said as she sat down on her bed. "It's thirty miles. On horseback, that's a day there and back. And just to make you aware, Xander seemed suspicious when I asked about it."

That wasn't a surprise. He always seemed to know when I was up to something.

"I also wanted to mention that something interesting happened," she said. "I used my aspect briefly and saw the white light on Rokh but not on Xander or anyone else around him."

That made Io stop what she was working on. "Just Rokh?"

Ahyana nodded. "Do you think that means we see the light on people we love? I can't think of another explanation as to why we see it on each other and then on people like Rokh . . ."

Io turned toward me. "And Xander."

My heart clawed its way up into my throat so that I couldn't breathe. I didn't love Xander. I liked him. I cared about him. I wanted to be with him all the time and sometimes missed him even when he was next to me. I didn't want him to die.

But that didn't mean love.

Did it?

I was extremely grateful that I hadn't been hearing Demaratus in my head lately because I was afraid of what he would have said about this situation.

Even if some part of me felt that way, I couldn't let it be true.

"That seems like a beautiful metaphor," Ahyana said wistfully. "The people we love power us."

It would explain why Quynh's baby had lit up for me. I already loved that little one and was sure I would love it a hundred times more when it was born.

"You love Rokh?" Zalira said. "Have you said the words?"

Before, Zalira's concern for her sister had been more along the lines of the temple guards finding out and fatally punishing Ahyana, but with that possibility removed, it felt like Zalira was more concerned about her sister not getting hurt as she had.

"Not yet. I have wanted to say them, but it feels . . . wrong. Like I need to wait. I'm not sure why. It's like part of him is holding back." I was fairly certain Rokh hadn't said them because he still hadn't told her the truth yet. She would be able to sense where he was when he did. She might notice how quickly he was moving as he flew. I didn't know how far the connection stretched, but at some point he probably flew beyond it.

Ahyana would have questions that he didn't seem ready to answer.

Io's gaze had remained fixed on me. "You can see Xander's light. Lia, you promised me."

Her accusation wounded me. "I'm not trying to hurt him. I'm as surprised as anyone else that I see a light around him."

"You are the only one who is surprised," Ahyana playfully corrected me, apparently not bothered by Io's distress.

Unlike Suri, who looked like she was ready to cut my throat.

I decided now was not the time to mention that Xander's light had grown even brighter than before.

"You will hurt him," Io said. "There is no way around this. He will be destroyed."

And I didn't know what to say. I didn't want to harm Xander.

But a part of me was afraid that Io was right and he and I were destined to destroy one another's hearts.

CHAPTER THIRTY-ONE

We spent the rest of the day preparing. Practicing our magic, working on moving past our previous limits. Io took charge of the food and supplies we would need for the trip. She didn't speak much to anyone, which was so unlike her. It made me feel guilty. As if I'd disappointed her when I hadn't meant to.

I didn't dwell on it, though. Because all day long my mind kept recalling the dream I'd had of myself about to die at Artemisia's hands. Reliving over and over the moment when that massive hammer had been about to flatten me.

Part of me felt scared, as if I were being shown exactly how I would die, but the rest of me was terrified about what would happen to Xander. I refused to let him join me in death.

If Ahyana's theory was correct and we saw the light around people we loved . . . then the magic seemed to believe that I loved Xander.

Was I willing to possibly forfeit retrieving the greatest weapon in order to save my husband?

I was afraid that I was. Afraid that these feelings I refused to name were driving me to protect him in any way that I could.

I was willing to put everything aside, risk my own worthiness, to make sure that he lived. He was part of the prophecy. He had to survive. So I would make sure that he did.

And it surprised me how calm I felt about making that decision.

When he finally returned to our room, it was late. I could see on his face how tired he was. And that he was upset.

"What happened?" I asked.

"I reached out to my mother's brother today to ask for his assistance with the war."

"In Olyer?" I asked. When he nodded I said, "How could they help? You said they were a poor nation."

"They *were* a poor nation. When my father paid his bride price, my grandfather took the money and a page out of Ilion's books. He built ships and a blockade in the straits between the mainland and their island. Going around Olyer takes extra time—heading through the straits is safer and faster. People are willing to pay to pass. It has made them very wealthy. That's why they sent us the horses for our wedding. To show off how rich they have become."

"Rich because of your father," I said. Olyer's success only existed because of Ilion.

He took a letter from his belt and handed it to me. He sat down next to me on the bed. "I sent Rokh with a message to my uncle, asking for him to send men and ships. And to block the Carians if they mean to sail along the coast. This was his response."

I opened the letter—it was extremely short.

> *King Alexandros,*
>
> *I do not address you as "nephew" because you are nothing to me. I have not been a part of your life for a reason. My sister loathed your father. He made her life miserable and she ended it just to escape him. She loved another but your father was too selfish to let her go and be happy. I would never help the son of the man who did that.*
>
> *—King Pausanias*

My mouth dropped open. I had to read through it again to make certain that I had understood it correctly. How could this man treat his own family this way?

"Olyer would be easy for the Carians to reach. He might be in danger as well," I said, trying to keep the anger out of my voice.

Xander didn't seem mad. Just resigned. "If they come by land, the Carians will have to pass through Apasus first. Perhaps they will call for aid."

"Do you think the Apatians will fight?"

"I'm not sure if the Carians will attack. But the Apatians are the ones who were in the best position to witness how Caria was growing. We are supposed to be allies but they never passed that information along."

"Perhaps they didn't want to get involved," I said.

He nodded. "Possibly. And they might be paying for that decision now. And if the Carians are attacking, that might affect when they arrive at Troas. Which makes last night's attack make even less sense. Why send a small force like that? I understand why they hit the weapons quarter and eliminated the priestesses, but I don't understand what was essentially a pointless skirmish."

"If you were in their position, why would you do it?"

He frowned slightly, considering. "As I've said, in part to cause fear. The citizens never know when or where another strike will happen. But there's part of me that thinks it was meant to be a distraction. But a distraction from what?"

I had no idea why the Carians might want to create a distraction. "They couldn't have picked a better time. Attacking the docks while the citizens were relaxed and celebrating. It's made me wonder if that means that there are still Carians here in the city. Hiding in plain sight."

"I've considered that repeatedly since last night," he said. "How else would they have known? There must be people here feeding them information. Using messenger birds."

Tomorrow I would talk to Ahyana about that. Maybe she could direct all the birds away from Troas to make sure that no more messages could go out.

But that might also hinder whatever Xander was doing.

"There's a Daemonian outpost in Olyer. Rokh tried to approach them to ask if they would join our fight, but they refused to speak to him in Common. Do you know any Daemonian?" he asked.

"Only swear words."

"That might actually help," he said with a tired smile. He leaned forward, as if he intended to kiss me.

Then he seemed to realize what he was about to do and straightened up. "Did I tell you I interrogated a life mage?"

"You did?"

"I gave him truth serum."

"You can't just do that," I said.

"I can. I'm his king. He is subject to me."

"Or you could have asked him nicely and I'm sure he would have told you whatever you wanted to know. What did you ask him?"

"I asked him about your pleasures-of-the-flesh situation. He verified that you had to abstain in order to do magic."

Why did I feel disappointed? I knew it was the truth.

"What if he's wrong?" Xander asked me carefully.

If the life mage was wrong . . . I would have wasted a lot of time that I could have spent naked with my husband. "I don't think he is."

Because I didn't know what the actual rules were, and what Lysimache and other high priestesses had tampered with, there was no way for me to be sure.

I supposed it didn't matter now. I had made up my mind to break our physical link the only way I knew how.

But I wasn't sure how to go about it. My seduction attempt last night had been successful. This was entirely different, though.

"The life mage repeatedly told me women couldn't do magic. Which I know for a fact isn't true," he said. "Which made me think his information might not be accurate."

"I think magic was always intended for women."

"You might be right, considering what happened at training today. I needed to work out some . . . aggression. I drank your fountain water."

He had? "What happened?"

"It made me so fast and strong that Thrax couldn't keep up with me at all. There wasn't anyone I could fight."

I wanted to laugh. He actually sounded disappointed. I might have created a monster. "So should we distribute it to everyone in Troas? Make all the soldiers strong?"

"It won't work. I gave some to Thrax and Stephanos and they both got violently ill. They threw it all up. They're fine now."

"Why can you drink it?"

"Maybe because I'm goddess-blessed."

If the magic had been intended for women, it made sense that it wouldn't work on most men.

But my husband was not most men.

"Perhaps we should spar to test it out. You with the fountain water against me with my aspect," I said. That would be an easy way to get physical with him and let one thing lead to another.

"A different night, maybe. I'm too tired."

Luna snorted in her sleep, and it reminded me of all the things I hadn't told Xander about what my adelphia and I had discovered. That I needed him to not be his usual overprotective self and let me go look for the greatest weapon.

"Do you remember when you thought I had broken into your treasury?" I asked.

His eyes narrowed. "Yes. Why? Did you do it again?"

"No." I tried not to sound indignant. "But I did do it back then."

He briefly looked triumphant that I had admitted to it but he didn't interrupt me.

"Suri went with me and I asked her for what I was supposed to find in there. I thought you were keeping something from me. She found a scroll labeled 'the greatest weapon.' It was blank. And we tried to figure out how to make it reveal its secrets. We stumbled on how to solve it by accident." I explained how Io had spilled water on it and how we added each of the elements until there was only one left.

"Aether," he correctly surmised. "And that's why you brought the terawolf back. Because they're supposed to be part aether dragon."

He was so clever. "Yes. But it didn't work. Until we realized that we already had an aether dragon."

His eyes went wide. "You've been keeping an aether dragon from me?"

"No, you know her. Luna."

Silence. Then: "Are you telling me your lizard is an aether dragon?"

"Aren't you glad you didn't toss her out the window?"

"Now I think I definitely should," he said. "We don't know anything about aether dragons. What they can do. How big she's going to get. She won't fit in the palace at the rate she's growing. And she is growing so fast. I thought you were doing some kind of magic on her to make her get bigger."

"It's her own magic. I think it happens while she sleeps."

He craned his neck to look at her. "Are those wings on her back?" he asked incredulously.

"I think so."

"So now she's going to fly and spread her silver mess everywhere."

"It's actually aether that's falling off her," I said, and he smiled as he shook his head.

"What is the greatest weapon?" he asked.

I hesitated for a moment. This wasn't something I wanted getting out. But I knew I could trust him.

"Io thinks it might be the goddess's golden sword that she used to create life. If it is, then we would have a god-weapon to use against Artemisia's. The cave where it's located is in Mount Idaia. We want to leave tomorrow to find out what's there."

He surprised me with his response. He nodded and said, "Obviously I'm going with you."

"You were just crowned king," I reminded him. "You can't go, and we have to."

"If you have to, then so do I."

No, he had to stay here and rule. Get Troas prepared. "What if Erisa makes some kind of move while you're gone? Or Pelias?"

"She's locked in her rooms. And I'm not concerned about Pelias. I'll leave Thrax here to keep an eye on things for me."

"What will you tell the council?"

He shrugged. "I'll tell them I'm going to meet with some delegation in person. The Thracians or the Apatians."

That would give him the excuse he needed, but this mission had to be kept secret. "I need to ask a favor of you. Could you please not tell your phratry brothers what we're looking for?"

"I don't lie to them," he immediately responded.

"I'm not asking you to lie. But tell them something vague. Like we're looking for something that might help with the war. We don't even know if this weapon is there. What if somebody else removed it a long time ago? I don't want word to get out, especially if we fail."

And I didn't want word reaching Artemisia. I wanted her surprised when we fought.

"My brothers are trustworthy," he insisted.

Dolion wasn't. It was on the tip of my tongue to tell him but I didn't. I didn't want to create a schism in their brotherhood. "Would you please do this for me?"

He had told me that I only had to ask and he would do it. "Fine. I won't tell them. But won't they see what you get when we're all in the cave?"

I hadn't told him about the writing on the scroll. I explained what it said about the worthy savior and that no man or beast could enter the cave. I half expected him to lodge another objection that he wouldn't let us go in there without him, but to my surprise he didn't.

Instead he yawned. "I'm going to take a bath. We can talk more about this tomorrow."

He got up and went into the washroom.

And he didn't lock the door.

Presenting me with the perfect opportunity to finally consummate our marriage.

CHAPTER THIRTY-TWO

My heart pounded frantically in my chest as I waited. One minute, two. Enough time for him to disrobe and climb into the pool. With my decision made, I wasn't scared or nervous.

Just excited.

I opened the washroom door as quietly as I could. His back was to me and I saw his shoulders tighten.

He knew I was there.

My breathing quickened as I walked over to him and picked up a sponge. It was already damp, so I rubbed some soap onto it. When I made contact with his back, his hand went around my wrist. His touch burned, as if he'd set fire to me.

"What are you doing?" he asked.

"Scrubbing your back. Isn't that what maidens in Ilion are supposed to do?"

"Wife . . ." He sounded weary. But he released my arm and leaned forward slightly. Permitting me to touch him.

I admired his strong back for a moment too long before I began to rub the sponge in slow, rhythmic circles. I saw the tension go out of him, the way he relaxed under my ministrations. But my desire intensified with each pass, and whatever tension he had rid himself of seemed to find its way to me.

I hated the sponge that kept me from touching him with my fingers. I did an overly thorough job until too much time had passed. I was going to rub his skin raw if I kept going. If I wanted things to move forward, I'd have to do something else. I put the sponge into the water and used it to rinse him.

When I'd finished and put the sponge down, he said, "Thank you."

"You're welcome."

I quickly took off my tunic and then unwrapped my undergarments. He didn't move. If he was aware of what I was doing, he didn't indicate it.

Quynh had once worried about what I'd do around naked Ilionians. I was sure that neither one of us could have ever predicted I'd do this.

I stepped into the pool. His eyes had been closed, but as soon as I was up to my neck in the water, they flew open.

"Why are you naked?" he demanded.

"Because I don't bathe with my clothes on," I said, echoing the words he had said to me the night he'd invited me into his bath. I should have done it then. "You told me once that if I joined you in the pool, you would satisfy my curiosity. That I could look at you as much as I wanted, touch you, so long as I afforded you the same privilege."

His face was unreadable.

"Privilege granted," I told him in a voice that sounded too breathy and desperate to my own ears.

"I don't understand what's happening," he said.

That made me smile. "I'm not being subtle."

When he didn't react, didn't pull me into his arms, I started to doubt myself. After what we had shared last night, it hadn't occurred to me that he might not want this. I reached my hand out toward him and he moved clear of me, causing water to splash out of the pool.

"I thought you couldn't resist me when I'm naked. But you are," I said.

"Barely," he said through clenched teeth. "It's why I lock that door."

Another thrill ran through me. "But you didn't lock it tonight."

"That wasn't an invitation."

"It feels like one," I said.

He closed his eyes briefly. "Goddess give me strength."

I moved toward him, slowly this time. "The goddess gave you me."

Xander held his hand up. "I swore to my sister that I would keep you safe from me."

"I'm not in danger from you," I said with a smile, lacing my fingers through his.

"You are in the worst kind of danger from me." There was a dark roughness in his voice that excited me. "I would ruin every vow you've ever made at the first opportunity with no regard for anything else."

That sent shivers of delight through me. Excellent. We had the same end goal. I moved even closer. He stayed still. Perhaps he'd decided it was undignified to run from me.

Or he was going to give in.

"We have done this dance before," he said.

"Yes, but we've never finished all the steps. We always leave while the music is still playing. Let's stay to the end."

"Your vows," he reminded me.

I leaned forward to kiss one of his fingers. "Aren't you the one who always calls me an oath-breaker? That night of the festival, you told me vows were made to be broken."

"Because I wanted you to break yours. Being with you makes me forget everything else, including things that are important to me. It was another reason I had to send you away—not only because I knew you'd regret it, but so would I, for being the one who convinced you to go against your word."

"I won't regret this. I want to."

He swallowed, hard. "Lust is not enough of a reason to go against your vow. And I won't do to you what my father—" He suddenly stopped and then pulled his hand away.

It wasn't just lust for me. I didn't know how to tell him that, though. Would he even believe me? I was fairly set on making this happen, and he would be right not to trust my word. I suspected I would resort to lying to get what I wanted.

"I want the real reason," he said. "Tell me why you're doing this after we agreed that we couldn't."

His gaze had been so careful the whole time I'd been in the pool. He kept it on my face, not letting it slip down.

Unfortunately, I couldn't manage to do the same. He was so glorious it made me want to weep. "I don't want you to die."

"I don't want me to die, either," he said. "And I suppose it means we're making headway if you're no longer salivating over my impending death."

No, I had new things to salivate over.

And if I wanted to be pressed against any of it, I had to tell him the truth. "The physical link between us . . . there is a way to break it. Io found it in a medical text. If we have sex, it destroys the link."

"Why didn't you tell me earlier?" He didn't sound upset. His question was more probing, as if he already knew the answer.

"I've already told you, because the trust between us hasn't been strong and—"

"No," he cut me off. "That's not why. You didn't tell me because you thought I would use that as an excuse to bed you. And that wasn't how you wanted things to be between us."

My heart had kept up a strong and slightly fast rhythm since I'd entered the pool, but his words made it beat twice as fast. I couldn't deny what he was saying.

"You wanted it to be a choice." Again, his words were far too precise and accurate. "Our choice."

Then he surprised me by reaching for me. He pulled me to his chest and I was giddy to be touching him like this. So, so close, and he felt incredible. It had been far too long since we'd last done this. Skin on skin. I wanted to slide sensuously against him, feel that delicious friction again.

His lips hovered just above mine, not touching. I tingled with anticipation and longing.

"We can't," he said. "We won't."

"You don't understand," I told him. "I have seen a vision of my death. I'm going to die. And I can't bear the thought of you dying because we're connected. Ilion needs you. I—"

I stopped myself before I finished that sentence. I couldn't tell him how much I needed him. How important he'd become to me. It was a step too far.

"When I make you my wife in more than just name," he said as he tucked a strand of hair behind my ear, "it won't be because of an excuse. We will both be choosing it. Along with everything that means."

I wasn't getting through to him, and I didn't know how to tell him how I felt without making even more of a fool of myself. I mentally floundered until I settled on, "Everything in my life leads me to you."

"Why do you think that is?" He pulled his head back so that we could look into each other's eyes.

"I don't know."

"That's a lie," he said softly. "You do know. You've always known."

This was too much. I wanted us to have sex to destroy our physical link. That was all this was about. Putting an end to something that meant if one of us died, so would the other.

It could not be about feelings or anything else.

"I won't settle for a shadow of you. Of us. You just told me that you had to be worthy to enter the goddess's cave. I won't be responsible for you breaking your vow," he said.

Desperation rose up inside me, like a surging wave. "We have to destroy the link."

"Io will find a way." He rested his forehead against mine and then exhaled deeply. "You make it so hard to remember myself."

"Then don't. Let's forget everything." I put my hands on his chest, wondering if he would move me away. His hands went to my wrists, as if he intended to take them off but couldn't bring himself to do it. Heat seemed to flow up into my palms, coursing through me.

I wanted him so much it was hard to think straight.

"Not like this," he said gently.

"But"—I glanced down—"you want me."

"As I've already told you, I want more than just your body. I would have your mind, your heart, and your soul as well. I will not accept less, no matter how much I want you."

My desire was now tinged with shock at his words. When he'd said those words to me in front of the full-length mirror the night of his birthday, I had thought he was being manipulative. That he'd said them in an attempt to woo me into bed.

He had meant them?

And if he had, did that mean . . . that he was willing to give those things to me?

What would he say if I asked for them?

Feelings churned inside me, scattering my thoughts, and I felt like I could choke on my confusion.

"You should go before I lose what little self-control I still have," he said, holding my hands in his.

"This is not at all how I thought this would go," I confessed.

"I know." He kissed me sweetly on the forehead. "Go to bed."

It took me longer to move away from him than it should have. My body wanted to fight every movement that pulled me from him.

And if he had averted his gaze before, he did not do so now. I felt his eyes on me as I climbed out of the pool and wrapped myself in a linen. I had to summon what little dignity I still retained to walk across the washroom and exit through the door, closing it behind me.

I collapsed against it. My stomach roiled with nausea and feverish chills racked my limbs.

And I knew that my husband was the only medicine that could cure my current ills.

I dismissed every foolish scheme my mind concocted—waiting naked for him in our bed. Wearing my gauzy nightdress to tempt him. Rejoining him in his bath.

He had said he didn't want it to happen this way . . . *not like this.*

Unfortunately, this was all I had. There wasn't a different future for us. But I needed to respect his wishes. I would expect him to back off if I told him no.

I dressed quickly and got into bed. There was little chance of me falling asleep before he joined me.

Thankfully, I didn't have to wait long. He came out dressed and walked toward me, his hair still damp. My heart thumped loudly as I wondered what he would do next. He gestured toward the floor. "I should probably sleep here tonight."

I sighed. "Please don't. We have to get up early tomorrow, and if you sleep there, then so will I, and I don't want to sleep on the floor. You wouldn't want me to get a poor night's sleep, would you?"

"You'll be sleeping outside on the ground soon enough."

"But tonight we don't have to," I said as I held out my hand to him.

"I see. You're trying to lure me with your feminine wiles," he teased as he walked toward me.

"I'll use whatever I have if it means I don't have to sleep on the floor."

When he reached the bed, he said, "Will my virtue be safe with you?"

"Yes," I said, sighing at his silliness. "I'll behave."

I let my hand drop and pulled the blanket back so that he could join me. After a moment's hesitation, he did so.

"Turn over," he said. I did, and he pulled me to him, my back to his front.

"Isn't this so much better than the floor?" I asked.

"You're such a princess," he said into the top of my head.

"Thank you."

"That wasn't a compliment."

"Close enough," I said. I thought of how we might have always been this way with each other—teasing, fun, soft—if our circumstances had been different.

He held me so tight that I almost couldn't breathe, but I didn't say anything. I wanted this. I had so many more things to ask and talk about but I held still, not willing to break the spell of this moment.

"You know that I wouldn't let you die," he said. "If I had to fight the god of death to bring you back, I would."

Tears suddenly welled in my eyes while a glowing warmth spread through me. "I know."

I also knew that despite what he thought, not even Xander could stop a prophecy from being fulfilled.

CHAPTER THIRTY-THREE

I was in a cavern, swimming at the top of a long, dark tunnel. A gate closed above me, trapping me in the tunnel while water rushed up and out all around me. I could barely keep my face above the water, struggling to breathe. I put my hands on the metal bars but didn't push. I accepted my fate.

Something waited for me at the bottom of this shaft, and I knew I had to reach it. It didn't stop the terror I felt.

Down, down, down I went. Feeling like the walls were closing in on me, no light, my lungs aching and begging me to return to the surface so that I could breathe.

But I couldn't do that. I had to keep going.

The water crushed me, my head became hazy, dizzy, and my limbs shook, but I kept swimming. Kept going.

I felt like I was about to burst. I couldn't help it. I struggled and fought, but I opened my mouth to call for help and the water rushed in.

"I won't let you drown." I woke up to Xander pulling me into his arms. "You must have rolled away from me. You won't drown."

He had me flush against him, his arms holding me tight. I sighed happily, letting the nightmare recede so that I could enjoy where I currently was.

"I like this better without clothes," I told him.

"So do I."

There was a knock at our door and I heard Io calling out my name.

"Oh no," I said. I moved myself forcefully away from him, back over to my side of the bed.

"What are you doing?" He sounded both confused and amused. "My sister has both seen and heard us doing worse."

"I told Io that I would stay away from you."

"Why?"

"She's afraid that I'm going to hurt you. Because if I survive—"

He interrupted me to say, "*When* you survive."

"*When* I survive," I said, just to placate him, "then I have to return to Locris and stay there."

"What?" This was apparently new information for him.

"I promised the goddess that I would reinstitute her worship and reopen the temple in Locris."

He looked down. "Does it have to be you?"

I couldn't tell him everything about my dream where the goddess had given me the eye, but I could share enough. "I saw it. In a dream. I am the one who is supposed to save Locris. The responsibility is mine."

He nodded and his jaw clenched briefly before his gaze returned to mine. His expression went neutral, disguising whatever he was actually feeling. "That has always been the plan, hasn't it? It's what you've said from the beginning. Our contract ends and you return to Locris."

"Yes. And Io thinks . . ." I couldn't tell him what exactly his sister was worried about. He and I steered clear of saying anything about our feelings.

"I can take care of myself," he said.

"I know. And I don't want to hurt her, either."

"You know that I can hear your mumbling voices, right?" Io called out. "I know you're awake!"

"Come in!" I said as I moved to the edge of the bed to stand up.

Io entered the room with an eager smile. She had Luna with her, and Luna ran around in circles, frisky and excited. Her wings were fully out, and they looked strong and sturdy.

She bounded over to me, and to my astonishment, she used her wings to fly up and land on the bed.

"You clever girl!" I said as I sat down next to her. She looked immensely pleased with herself.

"She's been practicing all morning," Io said fondly. "She can fly short distances. She suddenly appeared in my room and tried to eat Priam. I told her that we do not eat my pets. She disappeared and came back with some blood on her mouth, so I'm assuming she found something else."

I saw Io try to suppress her shudder.

"Are you an aether dragon?" I asked Luna.

Yes.

Not that I needed the confirmation, but it was nice to have. "She says yes," I told the others.

"I still think the blinking is a coincidence," Xander said as he sat up in bed, rubbing his face.

"She's talking," I insisted.

"Luna's the reason I have this new formulation to break your link," Io said. She handed each of us a vial. "I knew I was missing something but I wasn't sure what. But given that aether and dragons are so important to the goddess, I started thinking that if fire dragon's blood burns and poisons, what would an aether dragon do? My instinct is that it heals. So I added aether to the mixture."

Xander held his vial up. "You put dragon dandruff in this?"

"Just drink it," Io said.

I put it to my lips and swallowed it down. "It burns," I told her.

"Hopefully that means it's working." When Xander had finished his, she said, "Let's test it."

He took out the dagger he kept in the drawer of his side table. He cut his left palm and I braced myself for the impact.

But it never came.

"You did it!" I said. But there was no excitement behind my exclamation. It felt as if I had lost something. A special connection that I'd once had with him.

And now it was gone.

"Good," he said gruffly. Would he miss our link, too? "We should get ready. We need to leave immediately."

Io came over to hug me and I could feel her relief in her embrace. Now she wouldn't have to worry about one of us dying and the other meeting the same fate. She hurried out of the room and promised she would meet us in the courtyard in a few minutes with the rest of our adelphia.

She closed the door behind her.

"I've sent a note to the council that I'm heading out to meet with a Thracian contingent," he said. "Which isn't necessary, because Thrax has already sent a message to his people and they're on their way."

"There's no need for pretense with the council. You don't have to come now," I pointed out. "Io broke the link. You don't have to watch over me and make sure that I don't die, because now you're safe."

He stared at me for several heartbeats before saying, "Wife, I know that you are dangerously smart, but sometimes you say things that make me question it."

Then he went into the washroom, slamming the door.

I was trying to avoid our feelings, and by doing so, all I seemed to do was upset him.

Luna pressed her front paws against my chest, as if to get my attention. I stroked her favorite spot, just behind her ears. She made a purring sound like a cat and I smiled.

"I'm leaving," I told her. "I'll be back in a few days. You need to stay here."

No.

"Luna, it's too dangerous. You can't come."

Yes.

She disappeared and immediately reappeared at the foot of the bed, watching me defiantly.

She had made her point. "I couldn't stop you even if I wanted to, could I?"

No.

Stubborn tiny beast. I got up to get dressed. As I stood behind my screen and changed, I thought about how I had been ready to have sex with Xander last night in order to break the bond.

Not knowing that Io had figured out a way to do so with a potion.

How would I have felt? If we had gone through with it and then discovered that we hadn't needed to?

I wasn't sure that I would have regretted it, and that was a problem.

The trip to the Syrilline Mountains was surprisingly uneventful. Xander had left Thrax in Troas, bringing Rokh, Dolion, Stephanos, and my adelphia. I wished that Dolion had been the one selected to stay behind but didn't say as much. He avoided me, refused to make eye contact. I wondered if anyone else would notice.

We initially headed north, as if to meet up with the Thracians, and then turned east. In case we were being watched. I wanted to ask Xander if he worried about leaving Thrax in the city while we went on a mission to meet his people. It would seem like he should be the obvious person to bring along. What if Pelias questioned why he wasn't here?

But I knew that he would want to stay with Quynh and the baby, and he was captain of the guard. He was in a position to issue orders and commands if necessary, more so than the rest of the phratry.

Once we turned toward the mountain range, Ahyana asked what would happen if we ran into the Carian army.

"There's no chance of that," Rokh told her. "They're in the south. They'd be fools to come up this far north and east of Troas. The terrain on the other side of the mountains is particularly treacherous to traverse."

Xander had muttered to himself when he saw that Luna was coming with me but he didn't try to stop it or complain out loud. She practiced her flying, leaping off my horse's back and then flapping around until she tired. I held out my arm for her to land on and she was careful with her tiny claws so that she wouldn't hurt me.

Night was falling when we arrived at the base of the mountains. We all set up camp—Zalira and Ahyana focused on building the fire while Suri, Io, and I helped the men construct the tents.

After the tents were up, we ate a quick dinner, during which I discovered that Luna liked cooked meat as much as she did fresh. She curled up next to the fire and went to sleep.

When we finished eating, Xander asked Rokh and Dolion to scout the perimeter to make certain we were safe and Stephanos to take the first watch.

But instead of looking out for potential enemies, Stephanos only had eyes for Zalira. I could see that she was torn—she wanted to go and talk with him but was worried about how being close to him might hurt them both.

I completely understood.

It was why I ducked into one of the tents. I hadn't been able to stop watching Xander, thinking about everything he had said and done over the last couple of days. I usually felt like I was in the dark where he was concerned, but it had somehow gotten worse. It was better to put a cloth wall between us so that I wouldn't keep staring.

The flap at the front of the tent lifted, and as if I'd summoned him, Xander entered the tent with his bag.

"You didn't eat very much earlier," he said, sitting down across from me.

"My stomach is unsettled." There was a lot going on.

"Here." He reached into his bag and pulled out a cloth-covered bundle, handing it to me.

I took it, but before I opened it, I already knew what it was.

Pasteli.

He had packed that for me.

It should have made me happy but instead it was like tiny knives pierced my heart. It was such a thoughtful gesture, but we . . . couldn't be that way.

The openness we'd shared last night felt like it was gone. His expression was guarded again. Because he needed to pull back, too?

We had admitted we wanted each other.

And I had to think that a man who claimed he wanted all of me—body, heart, mind, and soul—had feelings beyond just caring for me. He was trying to protect his heart the same way I was.

"I wanted to speak to you," he said. "If something happens to me, I've left instructions with Thrax that you are to be made queen regnant."

That meant I would rule, and rule alone. "What?"

"You were right. The only way things in Ilion will change is for them to change at the highest levels. More council members should be women. And the queen of Ilion should be of equal status with the king. Not beneath him, but beside him."

His words managed to both thrill and depress me at the same time. "But I'm leaving."

"If I'm gone, would you consider staying on?"

I didn't think I'd be able to stay in Ilion if something happened to him.

"I think Ilion needs you," he added. "Someone who sees things the way that you do."

Did *he* need me? That was the question burning on my tongue, but instead I asked, "Why are you making arrangements for something that's not going to happen?"

"In case you hadn't noticed, people keep trying to kill us. They may succeed at some point. I'm preparing for the worst."

I nodded, ignoring the dark emotions his words brought up. He wasn't allowed to die. "And if something happens to me, will you—"

"I'll make certain Quynh is taken care of. And your adelphia."

Not able to help myself, I put my hand in his. I needed to touch him. He knew me so well. "I'm not sure Troas would be happy about me being their queen. They might have some negative things to say about it."

"I will kill anyone who speaks against you," he promised.

"Then you would have a very full schedule of shedding blood."

We both smiled and fell into a comfortable silence.

"Eat," he reminded me. "You need to keep your strength up."

With my free hand I broke a piece of pasteli in half. I offered one to him. Something flashed in his eyes and then he took it. "Thank you."

"You're welcome." I picked up my half and began to eat. It didn't affect me the way it normally did. It was still good, but the way that he was speaking, as if we were approaching the end . . . it made the pasteli not nearly as delicious.

Perhaps this was the time to get some answers.

"If I ask you something," I said as my pulse raced, "will you be completely honest with me?"

CHAPTER THIRTY-FOUR

"That is, if you can be honest without a truth serum," I teased, trying to lighten the current mood.

It didn't work. "I wasn't compelled when I had the truth serum. I didn't tell you anything I didn't want you to know."

My stomach was in free fall, my heart beating erratically. "That night you told me about your parents, what happened to your mother. Why would you share such personal stories about yourself with me?"

"I know how important it is to you to understand things. To know what drives people." He finished off the rest of his pasteli. "What is it that you want to ask me?"

"Why did you take Quynh? Why did you let me suffer and grieve for her and not tell me?" My voice broke at the end of my question.

"I didn't tell you that I had her because it would have revealed who I really was and I needed that to stay secret. If I'd told you I had her, you would have known I wasn't a sailor. It wouldn't have taken you long to figure out who I was. I had to adopt the Jason identity so that I could move freely without question while investigating my stepmother. I couldn't risk anyone finding out that Jason and Prince Alexandros were the same person."

But that connection had been made public when he'd come to the temple to retrieve me. He had revealed himself to the entire city. He could no longer go out as Jason once he showed himself in front of everyone with his scar.

"And I am truly sorry for the pain you felt," he said, sounding remorseful. "I suppose I didn't worry too much about your grief because I knew she was alive. It eased my guilty conscience. That, and I intended to reunite you with her."

"What?" That was the first time he'd ever said that.

"I asked you several times if you wanted to return to Locris. If you had ever said yes, I would have put you and Quynh on a ship together and sent you both home."

It was true—every time I had seen him in person before I knew he was the prince, he had asked if I wanted to go back to Locris. I believed that he would have let me go.

Which meant he hadn't taken my sister to blackmail me into marrying him as I'd always thought. My adrenaline spiked and I let out a deep, shuddering breath. "But why did you take her?"

He hung his head. "I did that for you. I knew it would destroy you if something happened to her. I took her to keep her safe. As I said, I intended to reunite you when you were ready to go back. But you insisted on staying."

There was a flash of white, and for a moment I couldn't see or hear. This was what Quynh and Thrax had guessed—that Xander hadn't taken her out of malice or to use her against me, but because of how he felt about me. He hadn't wanted my heart to be broken.

I had been such a fool. I shouldn't have kept things from him. I should have trusted him from the beginning. I'd been so caught up in my own feelings and problems and had let us go through anger and fighting and mistrust because I couldn't see what had been right in front of me the whole time.

We could have avoided all that pain and misery.

There was so much I had to tell him. I didn't know where to start. There was one thing I had to show him, in case he didn't already know.

"Stay here. I'll be right back," I said. I stood and darted out of the tent, going over to the fire. I picked up a medium-size branch and brought it back into the tent.

His eyes questioned me as I sat down in front of him. I put my hand into the flame and he swore and grabbed my wrist to pull it clear of the fire.

"I'm fine," I told him.

Xander turned my hand over, checking it on both sides repeatedly. "How is this possible?"

"Part of the prophecy of being flame-kissed. I don't burn. It was why I pulled you out of that house in Lycia without getting hurt myself."

"I just assumed that Io had fixed you up the same way she had with me," he said, the awe evident in his voice. He released my hand and grabbed the branch, taking it back out to the fire and then returning to me.

Why hadn't his brothers told him? Maybe they hadn't realized. They'd been focused on him. Perhaps they had thought I hadn't been close to the flames. Or they believed, like Xander did, that Io had healed me.

"I don't understand why you can't be burned," he said as he retook his spot in front of me. "For what purpose?"

"Like so many other things, I don't know." My nerves felt frayed as I tried to think of how to approach the thing I most needed to tell him.

What he had suspected from the very beginning.

My hands trembled, and I tried to disguise it by putting them under my legs but quickly realized that would bring even more attention to my nervousness.

He would soon notice if he hadn't already.

"There's a reason why I have to abstain from sex," I said.

"So you can do magic," he said with a nod. "I understand why you would choose that over other things."

"That's not the choice I'm making." I was not picking being able to do magic over him. "I am choosing Locris over . . . other things."

His eyebrows knit together in confusion.

This had been my closest-held secret since I'd arrived in Ilion. "If there was an object of great power that I needed to save Locris, would you take it from me?"

"Why would I do that?" He sounded incredulous.

"During our marriage negotiation, you said that whatever I had planned, you would put a stop to it." That threat had been in the back of my mind every day since.

He frowned. "I said I would put a stop to it if it would harm me, my family, or Ilion."

"It wouldn't," I reassured him.

"Then why would you think I would take it from you?"

"I . . . I don't know." I had let my fears, doubts, and worries control me, right along with my anger.

He took both of my hands in his, holding them between us. "You are not my enemy, Lia. You never have been."

One last fear to put to rest. "What if it could be used as a weapon? If taking it meant you could save Ilion?"

"From my understanding, you're supposed to do that," he said with a half smile. "So I'd never do anything to hinder you."

I pulled in a deep breath to fortify myself. "You were right about why I came to Ilion, why I entered the tribute race. I was looking for something. The eye of the goddess."

Telling him was actually a relief, as if a giant boulder had been lifted from my chest and I could breathe again. Now he knew almost everything.

"Like what the life mages wear?"

I nodded. "There were two eyes in Locris in the statue of the goddess. One was taken and split up and given to life mages. The other was used by Lysimache to curse Locris so that nothing would grow."

"Then Ilion should also have two eyes," he quickly surmised.

"Yes. Lysimache used one to keep herself alive for a thousand years and put pieces of it into the fountain water to make us strong. When we found her at the temple, she had destroyed what was left of it. But there's still one eye out there, and Lysimache gave it to Artemisia. I can use it to fix Locris and remove the curse."

"How?"

"I'm not exactly clear on that point yet, but I hope I'll figure it out. And if I can't"—because I had died—"Io said she would try and restore it for me."

"And you have to stay worthy to wield the eye," he said.

"That's what I keep being told," I said. I desperately wished it could be different. "It's why I told you I feel like there's two terawolves inside me. The things that I want and the things that I have to do—my responsibilities and duties to the goddess."

"Oh." He looked surprised. "When you said that, I thought you were talking about being torn between me and your other man."

"What other man?"

"The Locrian man that you love."

For twenty seconds I had no idea what he was talking about. I didn't love anyone else.

Then it came rushing back to me. The way I had told him at the end of our marriage negotiations that I loved someone in Locris.

He asked, "Do you remember the dream you had, when you were in a large cave with a pool of water, and one of the walls was a giant mirror?"

"You were there?" I asked in surprise.

"I was at the top of the cave, calling down to you, but you didn't hear me. I watched what you were doing. I heard the voice asking what you wanted. And you said you wanted to see your fate. I couldn't see in the mirror—I could only see you."

Why had he been in the dream? Had I done that? Or was that the goddess?

"You said that you were seeing people that you loved. And you said the name of the man. Haemon." Xander's expression was flat but I knew what that meant. That he was hiding his reaction.

I had hurt him.

"Haemon was my brother," I said. "I did see people that I loved in that mirror. My family, my adelphia, and I didn't understand what the message was."

"Your brother? Haemon is the one who died?" he clarified.

"Yes." Had I really never said Haemon's name to him at any time since we'd met? I couldn't remember.

"Did you see . . ."

I waited for a few beats, but he apparently didn't intend to finish his sentence. Was he wondering if I had seen him? The voice had told me that I would see my fate, my true reflection, in the water.

And it had been Xander that I saw.

What a mess I had made. When we had been in his house during the negotiations, he'd wondered how I could have done the things I had with him while loving someone else and I'd callously told him, "You were there. He wasn't."

Then I remembered all the other times he had brought up this other man. It had bothered him. He'd been jealous. It had been a nonissue for me because it wasn't real and I frequently forgot about it.

Maybe this was one of the reasons why he had kissed Chryseis. To have me feel a bit of what he must have been feeling because of a lie I had told him.

I squeezed his hands tightly. "When I told you that I loved someone in Locris, I was talking about Demaratus."

His face went blank as he tried to place the name. "The Daemonian whose hand you cut off?"

"I didn't cut off . . ." When he'd seen Demaratus in our shared dream, Xander had assumed I'd cut off his hand. But that didn't matter. "Demaratus is Daemonian, yes, and he was my battle master."

He looked utterly confused. "I suppose that makes a certain kind of sense. You do love fighting. But he's much too old for you."

"No, I'm not in love with Demaratus. I love him as my mentor and friend. I lied and pretended like I was in love with him to upset you. I wanted to knock down your arrogance and ego. And because I wanted to hold on to my pride. I wanted to hurt you."

"You always have been an excellent shot," he said wryly. Silence stretched between us as he turned my hands over so that they were palms up and ran his thumbs along them. "All this time we were both acting out of pride and spite."

"It was why you kissed her, wasn't it? Why you wanted me to see? You thought I loved someone else and you were showing me that you didn't care about me."

He nodded and stayed quiet.

"You wanted to hurt me the way that I had hurt you," I said, finally understanding what that whole thing had been about.

"And because I refused to be like my father," he said.

Now I was the one confused. What did his father have to do with any of this?

CHAPTER THIRTY-FIVE

"Getting that letter from my uncle reminded me of how much pain my father caused my mother. She loved another and he didn't care. And because of you, for the first time in my life, I finally understood him. I thought you had another man in your heart but it didn't stop me from wanting you," he confessed.

I knew what his father had done to his mother, and not once had this thought entered my mind—that Xander was afraid he was behaving like his father.

He looked down at our joined hands. "I tried to be respectful of you and your feelings. There were times when I didn't care but then I would have to remember myself. I refuse to live his life. To hurt someone that way, as my mother had been. I couldn't allow myself to care about someone who couldn't care about me."

So many things were starting to make sense—why he'd held back, why he had put up walls between us, why he had done things that he knew would upset me. It wasn't just to protect himself. It was because he cared enough about me that he wouldn't let me have his mother's life, forced to be married to him when he thought I loved someone else.

There was also the pain of having a mother who wouldn't love him because he was his father's son. What had it done to Xander to give her all his love and not ever have it returned?

He was afraid. I was sure he'd never admit that out loud, but that scared boy was still inside him, the one who had been rejected over and over again by the woman who was supposed to have loved him most.

I was sure that wasn't the only thing that concerned him. He had told me more than once that he was no one's second choice. He had been worried that he would spend his life pining after a woman who would never return his feelings. Who settled for him because she had no other option.

Because he was there and the other man wasn't.

How had I not realized this earlier?

"I have seen what relationships do to the men in my family. My father. My ancestor destroyed all of Ilion in a war because of his obsession with a woman he couldn't let go of," he said.

And Xander had refused to be those men, even if part of him had wanted to.

"I knew that you were looking for something. You were always reading and studying. I thought to give you my mother's library to help you and as some misguided attempt to win you over. Then I realized what I was doing. I was literally giving you the same books my father had given to my mother in an effort to gain her love, and I realized how terrible and pathetic my gesture was."

"No!" I wouldn't let him taint that. "It wasn't terrible or pathetic. I can't tell you what it meant to me."

He raised his gaze to mine and I saw what looked like hope in his eyes. "When you lay with me on the floor all night, even though you hated it—that being with me mattered more than your own comfort . . . I thought that maybe I had pushed him out of your heart."

"There was never anyone else there," I told him. "Only—"

The tent flap flew open and Io and Suri walked in. I tried to pull my hands away from Xander but he held on to me tightly.

He wanted his sister to see.

She put on a happy face, but I noted the concern in her eyes. "It's so late. We need to go to bed." Her words were pointed at him, wanting him to leave.

For a moment I thought he might ask me to go with him so that we could continue talking, but instead he nodded. He leaned over to kiss me on my cheek, his warm lips making my skin light up.

"Sleep well," he said.

Zalira and Ahyana entered the tent then, and I was grateful for the reprieve. It would mean I wouldn't be alone with Io and Suri. I didn't want to talk about what had just happened. It was private and for just Xander and me. I already knew Io's concerns. I didn't need to hear them again.

He stood up and scooted past Ahyana and Zalira. When he got to the tent opening, he turned toward me and said, "Don't have nightmares."

"I won't," I said.

Xander nodded and left. Zalira asked Io a question and everyone got into their bedrolls, preparing to fall asleep while they chatted.

I didn't think I'd have a nightmare. Instead I was worried that I would spend the night dreaming about what might have been between me and him if not for the world falling apart around us.

Thankfully, I had a dreamless sleep. When I got up I saw that I was the only one awake in our tent. I headed out to relieve myself. Dolion was on watch and so I went in the opposite direction.

You should tell Xander what happened with Dolion, a voice whispered inside me, but I immediately shook that feeling off. It would only create more chaos. Especially now that I knew my husband cared about me.

He was a jealous man and things would not end well.

I found a giant tree that hid me from view. After I finished I stood back up, rearranging my tunic. I saw that there was a red string tied to the lowest branch of the tree. Rokh had mentioned that people often hunted in the mountains to catch the biggest game. Perhaps they had left themselves some kind of marker.

When I got back to the camp, Suri came up to me and pulled me over to a giant stone. She cupped her hands together and put them against the rock.

"The cave?" I guessed.

Yes.

Then she pressed her hand to her chest and closed her eyes.

"You feel where it is?"

Yes.

"Then I'll tell Xander to let you lead," I said, and she nodded.

Rokh was busy passing out clothing and shoes. They were in the Sasanian style—what he called "shirts" and "pants." They were long, to our ankles and wrists, and would go under our tunics. And we each had a pair of boots to put on.

"The higher we climb, the colder it will get," he told me by way of explanation. "We have a heavy cloak for everyone as well. If we need them."

The terrain would be too hard for the horses, so we tied them to a tree, where Stephanos left them plenty of food and water. We would get them once we headed back to Troas.

When everyone was ready, the camp put away, and we had on our bags, I went over to Xander. I strangely felt a bit shy around him, which was ridiculous. "Suri says she can feel where the cave is."

"Then we should let her guide us," he said.

Luna suddenly appeared next to my feet. "You should stay here with the horses," I said to her.

No.

"It's supposed to be cold up there. Do aether dragons get cold?"

She gave me an imperious look.

No.

I pressed my lips together so that I wouldn't laugh. I had apparently insulted her honor in some way. We set out and Luna made certain to trot alongside me. Like she was my own special guard dog. I wondered who she thought she could fight besides field mice.

There was a sort of trail leading up, but it was difficult. I was grateful for the training that we had all done because I couldn't imagine how much harder it would have been without that. We were on a steep incline, and there were several times that we walked along ledges in the mountainside with a sheer drop on one side.

"Are you doing all right?" I asked Xander. I knew heights were his biggest fear.

"Fine," he said, keeping his eyes on the ground.

"It's high."

"I'm very aware."

His paying attention to his surroundings curbed any attempt to have a conversation. Not that we could have, with everyone around us. The things that he and I still needed to say—I thought those should be said in private.

The problem was that the silence gave me far too much time to think about my husband and what might happen now that we had cleared up so many misunderstandings. I felt like a fool for not having tried to talk things out with him earlier but knew that if he'd tried, I wouldn't have believed him.

I had been so angry that I would have assumed he was trying to trick or manipulate me for some nefarious reason.

We had both needed to change and grow to be in the place we were now, and I was grateful that we had.

We stopped several times to eat, drink, and rest. As the sun began its descent from the apex of the sky, I asked Suri, "Do you know how much farther we have to go?"

She held up four fingers and then put three of them back down.

"Three-quarters of the way there?" I asked.

Yes.

I had a strange mixture of fear and anticipation. I didn't know what the tests would be or if we would even be able to pass them. What if something happened to us in that cave? No one would be able to come in after us. There wouldn't be any kind of rescue. Everything would be solely on our shoulders.

I also thought about what we would do if the weapon wasn't there. What if this entire thing was nothing more than a fool's errand?

We resumed heading up the mountain, and Rokh had been right. It was definitely colder up here. When I asked what kinds of trees were surrounding us, Io told me they were called pine. I liked the way they smelled—the air seemed fresh and clean and it energized me.

Luna disappeared and I stopped. I turned around and called her name. She had been sticking so closely to me that it made me think something had happened to her. I supposed it was possible she just wanted to go off and hunt, but I walked away from the group, still looking for her and calling her name.

Something didn't feel right.

I put my hand over my stomach, which had started to flip nervously. I stepped over a large pool of water and noticed that the trees around me seemed to be tilting to the right. Odd.

Then I noticed some strange cracks on the ground near my feet.

Xander was up in the front of the group, near Suri. He cupped one of his hands to his mouth and yelled back, "What are you doing?"

"I'm trying to find—"

The earth opened up beneath me and I fell straight down.

CHAPTER THIRTY-SIX

I immediately pulled my xiphos out and slammed it into the dirt next to me. I just kept falling, my sword feeling as if it were cutting through air. There was no way for me to gain purchase. My heart tried to escape out of my throat while icy terror took hold of my chest, making it so I couldn't breathe.

Then my xiphos struck the top of a giant rock and I came to such a hard stop that I worried my arm might come out of its socket. I let out a grunt of pain as I hit the stone. Dirt continued to fall all around me, like rain during a terrible storm. I could barely see as it showered down on top of me.

Was this how I would die? Wasn't this what the goddess had done to Ajax? Opened the earth beneath him and swallowed him whole?

The hysterical thought occurred to me that I hadn't broken my vow but was going to be buried alive anyway.

I heard everyone yelling my name, but the falling dirt was louder. I couldn't make out what they were saying, what they were doing. I put my hand over my eyes, shading them so that I could see better.

It was then I realized the dirt was closing in on me. The hole was filling up and I would be caught in the middle of it and crushed.

I would drown in dirt.

Someone had thrown down a rope, and I reached for it but missed. I tried very hard not to panic as the dirt compressed against my ankles. I felt the level rise, up to my calves. The soil was heavy against me, pulling down on my legs. My shoulder screamed out in pain, as I tried to hold on.

I forced myself to focus and ignore my spiking adrenaline when they swung the rope to me again. This time I was able to grab it. Someone had made a loop at the end and I put it underneath my left arm as I was still holding on to my sword with my right.

The loop closed around my neck and under my left armpit, and I sent a prayer to the goddess to help me survive this. It was excruciating being pulled up, the rope burning and biting my skin.

But it certainly beat the alternative.

I kept my grip on my xiphos and yanked it out of the wall. I wouldn't leave it behind.

They pulled me up quickly and I landed on the ground when I reached the top. I had just cleared the hole when the entire thing collapsed in on itself.

Xander pulled me into his arms and held on to me so tightly that I worried he would break my ribs.

"I can't breathe," I told him.

He only slightly lessened his grip and then spoke his words against my cheek. "Is this how you plan on killing me? Scaring me to death?"

"I didn't do it on purpose," I said. His heart beat so rapidly against my chest—thumping as hard and fast as my own.

"Are you hurt?" he demanded.

"Some aches and bruises but I'm fine."

I felt my sisters' hands on me, as if wanting to be reassured that I was still alive and whole.

Xander wouldn't release me for a long time, and I finally had to push against him because I could feel everyone watching us.

When he let go, Io was there with a potion. "Drink this. You need to be restored. You have to be at full strength when we enter the cave."

I saw the expression on my husband's face. He was going to propose that we turn around and leave. I shook my head at him and he pressed his mouth into a thin line, but he nodded.

We had to go on.

I drank all of Io's potion and then Suri tapped on my arm. Her eyes were wide and panicked.

"What's wrong?" I asked.

She held her palms out in front of her and then looked down at them and back at me, shaking her head. Then she put her hands flat against the earth, again shaking her head.

"You tried to use your magic to help Lia and it didn't work?" Io asked.

Yes.

"Why wouldn't it work?" Ahyana asked.

My first thought was that Suri might have done something to break her vow, but I immediately dismissed it. As far as I knew, she didn't have feelings for anyone.

"Because it was the trial of earth," Io said miserably, and her words made my blood flash cold. "That's why Suri couldn't interfere with her magic."

"It's a coincidence," Xander insisted.

I was afraid Io was right. First the trial of fire, and now this. The second trial.

Which meant I had three more until I died.

My husband insisted on holding my hand the rest of the way. It felt like it was partly to reassure himself that I was safe, physically next to him, and because if something else happened to me, he would be right there to share in my fate.

And while I was glad to have him close, I didn't want something to happen to him.

Luna still hadn't reappeared and it worried me. Where had she gone?

We came to a large chasm with a rickety wooden bridge spanning the distance. Suri pointed, and on the other side we saw a cave entrance.

This was it. We had made it.

Now we just had to cross the Bridge of Death to reach our goal.

Stephanos stepped forward and held on to the rope railing and used one foot to put some of his weight on the bridge. When it held, he put on his other foot and stood. "I think it can support us," he said.

Xander took the rope he'd used to save me and tied it to the end of an arrow. He handed it to Dolion. "Hit that tree right there next to the cave entrance, as deep as it can go."

Dolion did as asked and embedded the arrow into the tree.

"Rokh, I need you to go over and tie the rope off. We'll tie this end around everyone as they cross as a safety measure."

I saw the panic on Rokh's face and the confusion on my sisters'.

Especially Ahyana's.

Did Xander not know that Ahyana had no idea what Rokh was?

"I'm so sorry," Rokh said to Ahyana. "I promise to explain everything." Then he cried out in pain and turned himself into Kunguru and flew across the expanse.

I heard Ahyana's gasp and saw the shock on all my adelphia's faces.

And unfortunately, Ahyana witnessed the lack of surprise on mine. "Did you know?" she asked me.

My stomach turned over. This was not going to be an enjoyable conversation. "Yes, but let me explain."

Rokh tied off the rope, tugging it tight around the tree trunk. "It's done," he said.

And it was as if he were standing right next to us and speaking.

"The curved rocks around us reflect the sound," Xander said. "We can talk to one another across this chasm without having to yell."

I'd never witnessed anything like it before. And he was right, it was almost like we were standing in an open-air dome. How had I not noticed how the rocks were formed?

Probably because that horrible bridge had snatched up most of my attention.

Stephanos and Dolion had taken another rope and tied it to a thick tree on our side so that there was a rope in place for our trip back across.

"I'm going first," Xander said, which didn't surprise me. I couldn't imagine that it was going to be very easy for him. I had gone over to the lip of the ledge and couldn't see the bottom of the chasm. It was an extremely steep drop.

He took the rope attached to the far side and tied it around his waist. I saw the way his hands trembled slightly, but I was certain I was the only one who would notice.

Then he stepped out onto the bridge and I stopped breathing.

It held.

He walked across slowly and the bridge swayed a bit back and forth. Not too bad, but it didn't seem pleasant.

When he reached the other side, I saw the way his shoulders dropped, as if he were relieved.

His safety allowed my heart to resume a normal rhythm. He undid his rope and handed it to Rokh, who turned into a raven again to fly the end of the rope back over for the next person.

Stephanos took the rope and tied it around his waist and stepped out onto the bridge next.

Rokh transformed back into himself and made the mistake of trying to talk to Ahyana.

"How could you not tell me about this?" she demanded. "You've been lying to me this whole time!"

"Not lying," he said. "Just not telling you everything."

Even I knew that was the worst possible thing he could have said.

"I planned to give up everything for you, Rokh! I was willing to run away with you, leave my sisters behind, and this is how you repay my trust? My commitment? Why wouldn't you tell me about this?"

"Ahyana, I wanted to tell you. I did. But I was scared that it would change how you felt about me."

"Why would it do that?" she asked. "Do you really have so little faith in me?"

I kept my face turned away from them, but given our current acoustics, everyone could hear everything. I was sure Rokh would have preferred to have this conversation someplace private, but that wasn't an option.

Rokh explained about the curse, about what would happen if he and Ahyana had sons. That they would be forced to transform and suffer each time they did it.

Xander tied the end of the rope to a rock and threw it in Dolion's direction. It landed right next to his feet and he grabbed the rope, taking it off the rock. He then tied the rope around his waist so that he could cross next.

As he went onto the bridge, Rokh said miserably to Ahyana, "I didn't think you would want to marry me when you found out."

And while I didn't want to intrude, I couldn't help but turn and look at them. His pain was palpable, and my heart went out to him.

Then Ahyana drew back her hand and punched him in the face.

"Ow, Ahyana!" he exclaimed, his hand going to his jaw where she had hit him.

I was as shocked as Rokh. That was not the kind of thing that I would have expected Ahyana to do.

Maybe I was being a bad influence on her.

"Go to the other side," she told him. "I don't want to talk to you right now."

He hesitated a moment, as if he needed to say more, but he cried out in pain and turned back into a raven.

And he stayed in that form.

After Dolion had crossed, Rokh brought the rope back and gave it to Io. I was concerned about her going on the bridge, but she had that determined look on her face that meant she would do this no matter what.

Suri walked with her to the bridge's entrance and then watched as Io stepped out.

"All this time he was Kunguru," Ahyana said, shaking her head. Zalira stood next to her sister, offering her silent support. "How long did you know, Lia?"

"Not very long. And it's only because I caught him shifting. I told him that he had to tell you, that you would take it better coming from him than me. I honestly thought he would confess immediately. I'm sorry I didn't say anything."

"It wasn't your place," she said. "You were right, it should have come from him. He should have trusted me the way that I trusted him. I told him everything. I didn't hold anything back. I told him about the magic before you told Xander because I didn't want to keep things from Rokh. And he kept this monumental secret from me."

Rokh brought the rope to Suri, and I knew he could hear every word.

"What if we only have daughters? Did he ever think about that? And even if we had sons, who knows what might happen? He obviously loves being a raven, considering how often he is one. Maybe our sons would feel the same! Or maybe we won't be able to have children. Neither one of us knows what the future might hold!"

Sensing that she needed to unload her feelings, I stayed quiet and nodded.

"This is why he's been holding back in our relationship," she said. "Because he wasn't being honest with me."

I nodded again, as that was the conclusion I'd also come to.

"And this is why Kunguru didn't check on you when you first went to the palace," Ahyana said.

"To be fair, he was nice and helpful to me as Rokh," I said but immediately fell silent when I saw the look of annoyance on her face.

Suri had made it across and Rokh returned the rope, bringing it to me. I handed it to Zalira.

As Zalira made her way across the bridge, Ahyana suddenly put her hands on her cheeks. “I can’t believe I hit him. I shouldn’t have done that.”

“I’ve tried to stab my husband multiple times, so you’ll get no judgment from me,” I told her.

At that Xander turned to smile at me, and I grinned back at him.

I wasn’t surprised that Ahyana was already feeling regretful. She had a temper that would flare up and burn brightly, but then it would dissipate just as quickly. I’d always admired her ability to let go of things so fast.

Rokh again brought the rope to me and I gave it to Ahyana. I wanted to make sure all my adelphia were safely on the other side before I went. She tied the rope to her waist and made her way across. She was so graceful that the bridge barely moved and she crossed quickly.

For the final time, Rokh flew the rope over. He turned back into his human form.

“Do you think she’ll ever forgive me?” He sounded so wounded. It was his own foolish fault for not telling her, but I couldn’t help but feel sorry for him.

“For Ahyana, anger is like a cloud passing in front of the sun. She will get over it, probably after you’ve groveled extensively. And after you’ve bought her some pretty things to help with your apology,” I said, and he smiled sadly.

“I would give her the world if she would let me.” He shifted back and flew across the chasm.

I tied the rope around my waist, pulling on it to make certain it was secure. I walked over to the bridge and hesitated before stepping out. The drop was so far down.

“Are you going to cross sometime today?” Xander asked.

“Be quiet,” I told him. He of all people should understand why this was hard. I held on tightly to the rope railing and stepped out onto the first plank. The bridge swayed and it made my stomach lurch. I had to close my eyes for a moment against the sensation.

"I didn't know you were afraid of heights," he commented.

"I'm not afraid of heights. I'm afraid of dying." Was he trying to distract me? It wasn't working.

There was a high-pitched shriek that for a moment I worried was coming from me, but it was wind rushing through the chasm.

The bridge started to sway harder.

"You need to go faster," Xander said, sounding worried.

"I swear to the goddess if you tell me to hurry because you're hungry, I will stab you when I get over there." I took another step forward, trying to fight off the queasiness I felt.

"You can do whatever you'd like to me so long as you make it over here safely."

His words were what made me realize how precarious my situation had become.

The wind suddenly surrounded me, pushing from every direction until I felt like I might suffocate. I dropped down to my knees, still holding on tightly to the sides as the bridge started swinging back and forth, hard.

"Lia, you have to keep moving!"

Nodding, I tried to do what Xander said.

But then the safety rope slipped off my waist and fell down into the chasm.

CHAPTER THIRTY-SEVEN

"How did that rope come off the tree?" Xander yelled at someone. I didn't understand how it had come loose from my waist. I had used the double knot Demaratus had taught me. It shouldn't have slipped off like it had.

The howling wind became louder, echoes bouncing off the rocks around us. It felt like I was in the middle of a hurricane, being violently swung from one side to the other as the air screamed at me from every direction.

"Rokh, can you fly a rope out?"

I looked up to see him try, but every time he attempted to lift off, he was thrown back.

"Dolion, shoot a rope to her!"

"I'll hit the plank just in front of her," he said, tying a rope to an arrow and then letting it fly.

But as soon as it reached the chasm, the wind tossed the arrow aside.

"I'm going to get her," Xander said, and I saw Stephanos grab him.

"You can't! The weight will be too much!"

At that Xander dropped to his hands and knees. "Lia, look at me."

I was trying but the bridge's swinging made it impossible to keep my gaze on his. "I can't!"

"You can. Keep moving. And as soon as you get close enough, I'll grab you. I promise."

Part of me wanted to stay put but I couldn't. With these winds, at some point the ropes on this bridge would snap, and I would plummet to my death.

Things couldn't end this way.

I wouldn't let them.

My hair whipped around me as I started to crawl forward. My heart was in my throat as I grabbed the ropes that held each plank in place and used them to propel myself forward, scooting along the wood. My legs were getting scraped up but I didn't care.

"That's it, keep going." Xander tried to sound calm, but I heard the panic and desperation at the edge of his voice. "You're doing it. Almost there."

Somehow the wind got stronger and the ropes cried out in protest, as if they would burst apart at any moment.

"Just a little bit farther," he encouraged me.

All I could do was edge forward, keeping my head down and moving inch by inch until . . .

I felt his hands on my back, grabbing my tunic and hauling me to him. I was so relieved to be with him I nearly wept. I threw my arms around his neck and held on.

"You're safe, you're safe," he murmured to me over and over.

He was who I'd crawled toward.

Not the cave with the greatest weapon.

Not my adelphia.

Xander.

The winds immediately ceased and the chasm went silent.

"What was that?" Stephanos asked, alarmed.

"The trial of air," Io said.

It was difficult to argue with her. If the other trials all happened this quickly . . .

"Stop almost dying," Xander ordered me.

"Lia, will you *please* stop almost dying?" I teased, but he didn't smile back.

"You can't joke now. I have never felt so helpless. I can't watch you die."

Now I was the one comforting him, telling him that things would be all right, that I was safe, that he didn't have to worry.

And I didn't truly mean any of them. The winds had felt like a portent of things to come.

When he finally released me, we decided to eat and drink something before my sisters and I went into the cave.

"Maybe we should camp here and you could try to enter it in the morning," Xander said.

I knew that he wanted to delay me possibly putting myself in danger again. None of us knew what was in the cave.

And he wouldn't be able to follow me there. He would have to wait, without knowing whether we were safe.

"We have to go," I told him. If the trials were going to keep happening so close together, I was running out of time.

"I know you do," he said, putting his forehead against mine. "I wish I could come with you."

"We'll be all right," I said, and I prayed to the goddess that it would be true. I turned to my sisters. "Shall we?"

As I started to walk away, he grabbed my hand and tugged me back to him so that he could kiss me. It was sweet and delicious and overwhelming, and it made my toes curl.

And it had a message.

Come back to me.

"Do not die in the cave," he said when he reluctantly pulled his lips from mine.

"I won't."

He walked with me to the mouth of the cave. I had to tug my hand away. "I'll be back," I promised.

"You had better. I don't care what the scroll says. I will come in there after you."

My adelphia and I walked into the darkness. The bioluminescence I had seen when I'd first crossed the ocean somehow also covered the cave walls and ceiling and suddenly flickered to life when we entered.

I took out my xiphos. Just in case. We walked down a short hallway, and at the end of it, there was a thick wall. I pushed against it. It didn't budge.

The walls on either side of us were also thick and immovable.

"There's a sign," Ahyana said, pointing up toward the top of the cave. "What does it say?"

"Be ye worthy to enter here," Io read out loud.

"That's not at all ominous," Zalira muttered.

"But how do we enter?" I asked. There had to be some trick I was missing. I thought of the secret passageways in the palace in Troas. Was there a seam to indicate a door? A lever we could pull to create an opening?

What if there was nothing here? Would our quest be over before it began?

As I ran my hand over the cool wall, I felt an indent. As I outlined it with my fingers, I realized that it was a handprint.

I told my sisters what I had found, and then Ahyana said, "Here's another one."

"I've got one!" Zalira said.

"There's five," Io told me.

Of course. One for each of us.

This had never been intended for the savior alone. I had to have my adelphia with me. It wouldn't have worked otherwise.

"Let's put our hands on them and see what happens," I said. Because we didn't know what we were dealing with, part of me was afraid that we would spring a trap, like the rocks suddenly growing up around our wrists and holding us in place while some beast came and attacked us.

"On three," I said. We lined up and I counted. "One, two, three."

We each put a hand against the print in front of us at the same time, and there was a terrible sound of rocks grinding and rending.

I jumped back, seeing my sisters do the same.

The wall in front of us pulled apart, revealing a staircase, also lit by the same bioluminescence.

The stairs had been hewn from marble and looked as if they'd never been used.

I went first so that I could take the brunt of whatever might be waiting below. We walked in silence and I strained to listen, to hear if there was something waiting for us.

Io whispered, "Which goddesses do you think have created tests?"

I shushed her. I didn't want to think about that—I needed to be ready for whatever was coming. I also really hoped that the trial of water and trial of aether weren't in this cave.

At the base of the stairs, there was a door with a sign:

Bravery

I spoke the word for my sisters who couldn't read.

"That can't be good," Io said. "A trial or test that's going to require us to show our bravery."

Like being sucked into the earth or nearly tossed into a ravine hadn't been trial enough of my bravery.

"Ready?" I asked.

The others nodded and I opened the door. There was a large room, but it was completely dark. We walked in and I kept my sword out.

"Do you see anything?" Ahyana said.

When we were all inside, the door slammed itself shut. I felt Zalira moving next to me and heard her grunt.

"The door is locked. I can't get it open," she said.

That had been our only source of light.

"We should have brought a torch with us," Io said.

A light flickered at the far end of the room. A tiny spark.

"Is anyone there?" I called out.

The flame floated in the air. It turned into two flames. Then four. And eight. It kept doubling and doubling.

"I've got a bad feeling about this," Zalira said.

The flames combined to form a giant wall of flame, filling all the space in front of us.

"Lia can go through it, and then we'll see what happens," Ahyana said.

"Did we all just see the same thing?" I asked. "That is not a normal fire. What if it's a magic fire that can burn me?"

"Magic fire? That doesn't make sense," Zalira said.

"None of this makes any sense," I told her.

Ahyana took a step back. "It feels like a real fire."

She was right. The room had become exceedingly hot. Almost like we were standing in an oven.

"Could you call a storm down here?" I asked Zalira. "Put the fire out?"

"Let me try. Dea Maimaktes." She waited and then shook her head. "Nothing's happening."

"I know which story this is!" Io said, and we all turned toward her. "Maia told me this tale once where Dea thanked human hosts for taking her in and sheltering her by putting their infant son in a fire."

"What?" Ahyana asked.

"She was trying to burn away his mortality, but his parents snatched him from the fire and he didn't become immortal. She was angry and told them that he had been worthy of immortality but their fear had kept him from it."

"So you think we have to go into the fire?" I asked incredulously.

"We're worthy, we're brave, so we have to believe that no harm will come to us and pass through," Io said confidently.

"We can't go back the way we came," Ahyana pointed out. "It seems like we only have one option."

Zalira nodded. "I suppose if we burn, Io has salves."

"I do," Io confirmed.

Suri pointed at the fire and then drew her hand toward herself.

She was right. The flame wall was creeping toward us.

Soon we wouldn't have a choice. With every moment that passed, the heat became more intense. "We either go through it or we let it burn us slowly," I said. "Together?"

"Together," Ahyana said.

We all took each other's hands.

"Go!" I yelled.

CHAPTER THIRTY-EIGHT

Running into a wall of fire went against every instinct I possessed.

Be brave, I told myself.

When we reached the flames, they immediately engulfed us, the heat unbearable and excruciating. I heard my sisters calling out in pain, but we pressed forward.

And I ran into the far wall, beyond the fire.

I turned to look at my adelphia and none of them had been burned. We had felt the fire, but it hadn't harmed us.

"Are we immortal now?" Ahyana asked with a short laugh.

The fire suddenly disappeared and the bioluminescence turned on. The room filled with a high-pitched, otherworldly laughter.

"What is that?" I asked.

"If I had to guess, I would say the goddess of mischief," Zalira said. "She's an Alodian goddess. Our father used to tell us stories about her. She enjoys illusions and tricks."

Ahyana shook her head. "That didn't feel like an illusion."

The fact that none of us had burned meant that it hadn't been an actual fire.

"If this was her test, then we should expect everything past this point to be real," Io said. "I don't think there will be any other illusions."

"Is there a goddess of cute baby animals and rainbows?" I asked.

"If there was, she'd probably send both to attack us," Zalira responded.

A door suddenly appeared in the wall where we all stood. It opened. We walked through it into another short hallway that led to yet another door.

The sign on this one said:

VIGILANCE

Io read it out loud and I pulled out my xiphos. I put my hand on the door handle to open it. "Are we ready?"

The others also got their weapons out and nodded.

It was a room the same size as the one we had just left. It was lit up and we could see everything. Long, thick stalactites hung overhead.

And in front of us was a field of sickly yellow flowers. Their blooms were pointed up, almost like a triangle.

Io uttered a curse so foul that Ahyana gasped.

"What is it?" I asked, alarmed at her reaction.

"Manticore's teeth." Io spit the words out. "If we step on or brush against their petals, they will release a deadly poison that will kill all of us in seconds."

Zalira looked as dazed as I felt. "How do you know what kind of flower it is?"

"Daphne joined the temple because her younger sister was killed by manticore's teeth. She wanted to learn all that she could about plants and flowers to help others. It's the first thing she taught us—what flora could kill us."

The door slammed shut behind us, and I supposed it was locked like the other one. The only way out was through, just like before.

"What goddess would set this as a test?" Ahyana asked.

"The goddess of poison, maybe?" Io offered. "Combining her power with Dea's?"

"Can't you do anything?" I asked Io. Plants were her specialty.

"I'll try. Dea Khloe." She held her hands up and closed her eyes.

But just like with Zalira, nothing happened.

"I can't feel the magic," she said.

Had we been cut off from it? That seemed unfair.

"We'll have to be careful. I'll go first," Zalira said. I was about to say that I would do it, but she turned to me and said, "You bring up the rear."

"Take off your tunics," Io told us as she shrugged hers over her head. "We can't risk something accidentally hitting one of the flowers."

Our clothes brushing against them would make them release their poison? It sounded as if they were highly sensitive. We took our tunics off, putting them into our bags. It left us in the pants and shirts Rokh had given us, which thankfully were tight.

"If we stand here long enough, do you think the flowers will start coming toward us?" Ahyana mused with an attempt at levity, but I suspected they probably would.

I had nightmarish images in my head of the flowers stepping out of the ground and walking over to us on legs made out of roots.

"Here I go. Step where I step," Zalira said as she walked into the field. I held my breath as she placed her right foot down carefully and then did the same with her left.

Ahyana went behind her, followed by Suri, Io, and then me. I could see Io trembling in front of me but she soldiered on.

We all fell silent as we concentrated on putting one foot in front of the other. I could only imagine the kind of stress Zalira was under, as she was responsible for making sure that we all passed through safely.

Sweat dripped down my back as I watched Io and then put my foot in the spots hers had just vacated.

Zalira was nearly to the end when Io suddenly froze in front of me.

Petrified that she'd accidentally knocked into a flower, I said, "What's wrong?"

"I have to sneeze!"

If she sneezed . . . there was no way she could keep it from hitting the flowers. "You have to hold it in."

"I'm trying!" I heard the fear in her voice. I reached forward and put my hand on her shoulder. Her body twitched as if she was about to sneeze, but she convulsed slightly as she kept her sneeze internal.

I sighed with relief.

"Are you good?" Zalira asked.

"We're good. Keep going," I told her.

My whole body ached from the tension of trying to do everything perfectly. My breathing became more labored, sounding overly harsh in my ears.

"I'm through!" Zalira called.

That meant we were close. Just a few more steps.

"The door appeared," she told us. Both Ahyana and Suri had cleared the field, and Io was two steps away.

I saw Zalira open the door. When she did so, one of the stalactites by the entrance fell from the ceiling and crashed into the ground. I looked up to see them all swaying above us.

A bitter, silvery taste filled my mouth as fear chilled my bones. Those stalactites were going to fall on top of us and kill us.

"Run!" I yelled. Suri grabbed Io and she jumped to the edge of the field. I did my best to carefully but quickly pick my way through the remaining flowers, terrified that I would accidentally hit one.

A stalactite landed a few feet behind me, and the air suddenly had a sickly smell to it.

The poison!

I reached the edge of the field and broke into a full sprint for the door. My sisters were all in the hallway beyond, and as soon as I crossed the threshold, Zalira slammed the door shut.

We were all breathing hard, waiting to see what would happen. Would the poison come through the seams around the door?

But a moment later the door locked and a new one appeared on the other end of the hall.

"We made it," Ahyana said.

"And we managed to outrun the poison," Io said.

"Maybe we should keep moving to make sure," I said. I liked the idea of putting several more doors between us and the poison-flower room.

Io went down the hall first and read the sign on the door.

WISDOM

"Do you think we'll have to make some sort of wise choice?" Ahyana asked.

Zalira shrugged. "Maybe we'll be tested on our knowledge. Like what we learned at the temple."

Or maybe "Wisdom" was the name of a three-headed monster who waited on the other side of the door.

Io opened the door and walked in.

Another large room. And in the middle were two large statues, approximately twelve feet tall, facing one another. They had been hewn out of the earth itself—they were a contiguous part of the stone surrounding them.

"What are those?" Zalira asked.

"Sphinxes," Io said. "The head and chest of a woman, the body of a lion, wings of an eagle, and a tail like a snake. The gods use them as guardians. They are special to the goddess of wisdom."

"What happens if we walk between them?" I asked. Because this felt like a trap.

"Maybe we can climb over their bodies and avoid the pathway," Ahyana said.

That idea had some merit. Because the idea of walking forward and being caught in the middle of the two statues, their gazes fixed on us, felt wrong.

The door behind us slammed shut and locked.

I couldn't fight off the shiver that danced down my spine. "I suppose that means we've started this test."

Not knowing what else to do, I took out my sword. It wouldn't do me much good against rock, but it made me feel better to be holding it.

I walked farther into the room, keeping my eye on both statues.

What if they weren't the test? They might be a distraction. I scanned the room and kept moving forward.

Were we supposed to show our wisdom by choosing our path? I didn't understand what to do.

All I could do was keep walking, closer and closer to the statues.

The sound of rocks churning and groaning surrounded us, much as we'd heard when we'd very first entered the cave. Was a door opening somewhere?

My heart slammed against my ribs when I realized the sound was coming from the statue on the right.

It turned its stone head to look at us, its golden eyes glowing. It blinked and I took a step back.

By the goddess.

Then the sphinx opened its mouth to speak, and its voice was ancient and rough, as if it had been created from deep in the earth. "Dea's savior, I have been waiting for you."

CHAPTER THIRTY-NINE

I didn't know whether it was a good thing or a bad one that the sphinx knew who I was. My instincts urged me to flee from this giant predator, who in addition to her tail, also had fangs like a snake.

Something Io had failed to mention.

Was I supposed to answer?

Breath rasped out of my chest, rendering me unable to speak.

The sphinx didn't seem to notice. "I have five riddles for the five acolytes of the earth goddess. Each must be answered correctly. If you give the wrong answer, my sister, The Devourer, will awaken."

I looked at the statue on the left. Its eyes were closed, but I assumed that was who the sphinx was talking about.

Anything called The Devourer had to be horrifyingly bad.

Which the sphinx confirmed by saying, "She has a fondness for human flesh and hasn't fed in many millennia."

I had to swallow down the knot of fear that had formed in my larynx.

"You will be given one minute to answer each riddle. If you have no answer by then, it will be considered wrong and you will perish," the sphinx said.

Couldn't anything about this place be easy?

"My first riddle is this: What is it that you ought to keep after you have given it to someone else?"

My mind had gone completely blank. All I could think about was that a giant rock-monster statue was going to eat us if we couldn't answer riddles.

"Love?" Ahyana whispered, and I shook my head. That didn't seem right.

Zalira kept her voice low, too. "What about money?"

"It's your word," Io said, making eye contact with me. "You ought to keep your word after you have given it to someone else."

She was answering the question, but she also meant it as a rebuke to me. I sensed that it was the correct response.

"Dea's savior, you will speak for your adelphia," the sphinx instructed.

"Your word," I said, my heart beating wildly. What if it was wrong?

"Correct." Was it my imagination or did the sphinx seem disappointed? "In the form of a fork or a sheet, I hit the ground. And if you wait a heartbeat, you can hear my roaring sound. What am I?"

"Lightning," Zalira immediately told me. "It can be in a fork or a sheet, hits the ground, and the thunder after is the roaring sound."

"Are you sure?" I asked.

"Absolutely. I feel it."

Trusting my sister, I gave the sphinx "lightning" as the answer.

"Correct. Found by the wise, lost by the weak, broken, not damaged, carried, never touched, sweet, not tasted, unique, but universal. What am I?"

Could I ask her to repeat what she'd just said? There had been so much. The riddles seemed to be getting harder.

"I have no idea," Io said, looking panicked.

Ahyana's hands went to her sword hilt. "Neither do I."

I was fairly certain we would not be able to fight our way out of this if The Devourer elected to eat us.

That didn't mean I wouldn't try.

Suri tapped on my arm. She put her hand against her throat and then raised it up. She opened her mouth and made her fingers wiggle, as if something were coming out of it.

"Your voice?" I asked.

Yes.

"What if that's not right?" Zalira asked.

"You will give me your answer," the sphinx instructed.

We had nothing else but Suri's guess. "A voice," I said as I moved my feet into a fighting stance.

The sphinx paused. "Correct."

"Thank the goddess," Io said with a sigh, and it was a sentiment that we all shared.

"For our ambrosia we were blessed by Dea with a sting of death, though our might, to some, is jest, we have quelled the dragon's breath. What are we?"

"What could quell a dragon's breath?" I asked.

Everyone went silent.

"Maybe it doesn't mean an actual dragon. There is a flower called dragon's breath," Io offered.

"And 'ambrosia' is another word for nectar or honey. Sting of death? Flowers? The sphinx is talking about bees." Ahyana's eyes shone with excitement.

"What is your answer?" the sphinx asked.

"Bees," I said.

Another long pause that made me feel like my heart would give out. "Correct."

Four questions down. I thought of the fact that each one had seemed to be specific in some way to one of my sisters. Suri, who didn't speak; Io, who was upset about my word not being kept; Zalira and Ahyana with their aspects.

That meant the next question was for me.

What if I didn't know the answer?

"I shine brightest in the dark. Though I'm there I can't be seen. To possess me costs you nothing, and without me you'll lose everything. What am I?"

"Air?" Zalira offered.

"That doesn't shine in the dark," Ahyana said.

"If it's cold, you can see your breath. Air doesn't cost anything and you'd lose everything without it," her sister countered.

Io began to fidget. "Maybe it's light. It shines bright in the dark."

"Or fire," Ahyana added.

I looked to Suri and she shrugged at me, the worry evident on her face.

This was about something that had to do with me.

Goddess help me, I silently prayed.

Xander's face filled my mind. And the memory was from last night, when we had been talking in the tent. When he realized that I didn't love someone else, that I had adored the present he had given me, when I had cuddled up next to him on the floor even though I hated sleeping there, what I had seen in his eyes before we had been interrupted.

"You're almost out of time," the sphinx said, and the edges of her mouth curled up into a feral grin, her fangs showing.

We heard a rumbling, rock-groaning sound from her sister, as if The Devourer intended to wake. Golden light started to appear from the slits in her eyelids.

"Lia! What do we do?" Io shrieked.

"Hope," I told the sphinx, my heart beating as loudly as thunder in my chest. "The answer is hope."

The sounds of rocks moving immediately stopped, and the golden light went out of The Devourer's eyes.

I nearly fell to my knees in relief. We had done it.

Io hugged me fiercely and the others joined in.

"That is correct. You may pass," the sphinx told us.

I walked out in front of the sphinx first and stood there, waiting for my sisters to go by. When they were safely at the other end of the room, I would join them. I needed to stay here to make sure that nothing happened. For all I knew the sphinx might be a liar. I wasn't going to take that chance.

The door appeared on the far wall, indicating that we could leave. I had started to head toward my sisters when the sphinx spoke again. "Dea's savior."

I came to a stop.

"You have many," she said.

"I have many what?"

"I do not answer questions; I only ask them." She closed her eyes and went back to sleep.

Hurrying across the room, I joined my adelphia, and we went through the door.

We went into the hallway and I thought about my riddle. There had been a message there for me. Because in a way, I had given up hope. I expected to die. I was planning for it, figuring out contingencies for how to help the people I loved after I was gone.

I needed to have hope again. To think that I could survive and find a way to make things work out.

As the sphinx had said, I would lose everything without it.

"What do you think the sphinx meant?" Zalira asked me. "When she said you have 'many.'"

"The first thing I thought of was that I had many people that I love who love me, but that can't be it. I already know that. She was saying it as if it were something I wasn't aware of."

"Perception," Io called out from the other end of the hallway, reading the sign.

"I want to say it can't be as bad as the others, but I feel like that would be tempting fate," I said as we joined her.

Io opened the door and we all went inside. There was a long table filled with different types of treasure. We walked over to the table and saw another sign.

CHOOSE THE GODDESS'S GREATEST TREASURE AND PLACE IT ON THE ALTAR.

I turned to see that there was a stone altar near the far wall.

Ahyana sighed. "I want to ask what will happen if we pick the wrong one, but I think we already know. Certain death."

"Which one do we choose?" Zalira asked as she started to walk the length of the table. "How do we perceive what's right?"

"Suri? Are you sensing anything?" I asked.

She shook her head. I had hoped her magic might be the one that actually worked since we were in the earth right now, but I supposed that would have been too easy.

I started looking at what was laid out on the table. There were elaborately decorated swords that had jewels in their hilts and blades made of the purest and brightest steel. I saw Zalira grab one.

Ahyana reached for a golden bird automaton that tweeted and flapped its wings when she picked it up. I could hear the gears whirring and clicking.

"I think this is aether," Io said, holding up a vial of silver sparkles. "This comes from her daughter. This must be the goddess's greatest treasure."

"Maybe." I wasn't sure, though. There were so many different kinds of valuables laid out—some that were entirely unfamiliar to me. Where had they come from?

Something glinted at the far end of the table from underneath a cloth and it caught my attention. I went down to see what it was, and when I lifted the cloth, I gasped.

It was the eye of the goddess.

Here.

"Look!" I called out.

"Is that the eye of the goddess?" Io asked.

"It can't be," Zalira said. "Artemisia had the only one left."

"But what if there's another eye? For all we know, the goddess made a thousand eyes. This might be one that she kept in this cave." For me.

This might be the greatest weapon.

And it would help me restore Locris.

"It's obvious that this is her greatest treasure," I told the others and began to walk toward the altar.

Zalira grabbed me by the arm and made me stop. "Hold on, what if you aren't right?"

"Why wouldn't I be right?"

"Because despite what you think, you don't know everything," she snapped back at me. "Did you even see what I have in my hands? It's a golden sword. What if this is Dea's golden sword?"

"That's not her sword," I said. Zalira was behaving so foolishly right now.

"You don't know that. What if it is? And what if we made the mistake of leaving it behind and got kicked out of this room and couldn't go back and get it?"

"If you'd actually been paying attention, you would see that this is the fourth room and everything has been about fives. Of course there's going to be a fifth room, and that's where the actual greatest weapon will be!" I shouted back.

"The bird automaton is representative of the life the goddess created. This must be her most prized possession," Ahyana said.

"That's not what the sign says," Io told her. "It's her greatest treasure, not her most prized possession."

"How do we know that? We're just supposed to take your word for it?" Ahyana retorted.

"You wouldn't have to if you knew how to read!" Io yelled.

"It's the eye of the goddess and I'm putting it on the altar and taking it with us," I told them.

Zalira again got in my way. "Why do you think you get to make all the decisions?"

"Because I'm your queen. Move aside!"

She pointed the golden sword at me. "Stop telling us what to do!"

The four of us started yelling at each other and reaching for our own weapons. None of them were going to order me around when I so clearly had the eye of the goddess and—

"STOP!"

We all turned to see Suri staring at us, her chest heaving.

"Stop," she repeated.

CHAPTER FORTY

Suri's voice was unfamiliar, raspy.

But the shock of her speaking was enough to get us to stop arguing.

"This is a trap by the goddess of discord," she said. "There's something on those objects you've picked up that is making you fight each other. The longer you hold on to them, the worse it will get."

"How do you know that?" Io asked.

"We need to leave this room before those feelings start up again," Suri said, ignoring Io's question. It was so strange to see her mouth moving and words coming out. "You didn't pick the right one, either."

She went over to the table and grabbed a sheaf of barley. I hadn't even noticed it. Suri walked across the room to the altar. "This is the goddess's greatest treasure."

I was about to tell her to stop when she dropped the barley onto the altar. The top of the altar slid open to accept the offering and closed again.

Oh no. My heart beat uncontrollably. Had she picked the wrong one and now we were going to be trapped here forever?

Or were we going to have to fight our way out of this room?

What would the goddess of discord send to kill us?

But the door appeared, indicating that we had passed.

The gem in my hand turned to dust, and I looked up to see the same thing happening with the items my sisters were holding.

"Out now," Suri commanded.

I shook the dust from my hand and did as she said. I was too surprised by her talking to do anything else but obey.

Once we were all in the hallway, Suri closed the door and we heard it lock. She took her tunic from her pack and used it to wipe the dust off our hands.

"You could talk the whole time?" Ahyana asked.

Suri nodded.

Zalira asked the question we all had. "Why have you not spoken before?"

"Because I was afraid that if I did, I would start screaming and never stop."

That made the rest of us fall silent as she continued to wipe off our hands. Her words broke my heart. I hoped that someday she would be able to tell us what had been so terrible that she was scared to even speak.

Sensing that Suri might not be in a place where she would be willing to share details, Io instead repeated what she'd asked her earlier. "How did you know what was happening?"

"The owners of the orphanage I grew up in worshipped the goddess of discord. I know what to look for," she said quietly, her voice still raspy.

I'd initially thought it sounded that way because she hadn't spoken in so long, but now I wondered if someone at the orphanage had injured her and permanently damaged her voice.

"I can't believe the things we just said to each other," I said to my adelphia. "I'm so sorry. I didn't mean any of it."

Zalira nodded. "Neither did I. I felt irrationally angry. I was ready to fight everyone."

We all apologized to one another. What had happened in that room reminded me of how I'd felt when I'd let anger and vengeance control me. I had behaved in ways I didn't recognize, said things I didn't mean.

The discord room had been a good reminder of what I had to remember going forward. To master my emotions, as Demaratus had taught me time and time again.

I could no longer afford to let them master me.

A door appeared at the end of the hallway.

I sighed. "I hope this is the last room."

"Or there might be five tests, and then the greatest weapon is in a room beyond that one," Ahyana pointed out.

"There's only one way to find out," Io said. She walked to the door and read the final sign. "Worthy."

"I almost don't want to open it," Zalira confessed, and I understood completely.

But there was no other option. We couldn't go back. We had to move forward, no matter what it might bring.

Io opened the door and we stepped into a room lit up by the bioluminescence. The door shut and locked behind us. In the center of the room, there was a squat stone, about two feet tall, that looked like a seat. Were we supposed to sit there?

Over on the left side of the room, I saw a round boulder that looked to be about five feet tall. And in the right corner . . .

"A staircase!" Ahyana exclaimed and ran toward it. I was about to tell her to stop, but instead I followed her.

The stairs were made of the same marble as the steps at the beginning of the cave, but these went in a straight line to a landing before veering left. Ahyana went up to the top. A few seconds later she returned, using the long steel handrail attached to the wall.

"There's no way out," she said.

Zalira tried to reassure her sister. "I'm sure once we finish the next task, a door will open."

"What is the task?" Io asked.

"Let's search the room," Ahyana suggested. "Maybe there's something we're missing. Like a secret door that will lead us to the greatest weapon."

Everyone spread out and began running their hands along the walls, just as we had at the cave entrance, hoping to find some sort of trick that would help us know what to do next.

Zalira started feeling along the cavern floor. It looked like solid rock, but I supposed a hidden trapdoor could be just as likely as one in a wall.

"The sign said 'worthy,' and if this is the last room, then the greatest weapon is in here. 'Let the flame-kissed savior who is worthy pass the tests of the goddesses to claim the greatest weapon . . .'" I was thinking out loud because something was nagging at the back of my mind.

Something I was missing.

The word "worthy" kept echoing in my head.

I went over to the large, circular boulder and ran my hand along the surface. It was dense granite, immovable. I couldn't even guess how much it would weigh. Or what kind of strength a person would need to possess in order to roll this out of the—

"Demophon!" I said, the name returning to me in a rush.

Io's eyes went wide. "Yes! My father constantly told Xander and me that story!"

"Who?" Zalira asked as she stood up.

"There was a king who buried his sword under a huge boulder and said that when his son, Demophon, was ready and truly worthy, he would move the rock, claim the sword, and become the new king," Io explained.

Truly worthy.

"We don't have a Demophon here," Ahyana said.

"No, we have me." And I knew what to do. "Come over here and help me pry this railing off the wall."

My adelphia got onto the stairs and did as I asked. The screws holding the railing were rusted out and easy to break off with our swords.

But the handrail—it had to be Chalcidian steel, considering how bright and strong it was. I guessed that it was about eight feet long. That seemed like it would work.

"Lia, what are you doing?" Io asked.

"You're the one always telling me that the goddess has given us everything that we need and we have to figure it out on our own. Can you take the railing over to the large boulder?"

While my sisters carried that, I ran to the center of the room and grabbed the smaller rock, lifting it easily. It was sturdy and solid, and would do the trick. I placed it right next to the large boulder and then took the railing from my adelphia.

"I suppose I didn't technically figure this out on my own," I told them. "Archimedes did. My father used to quote him all the time: 'Give me a lever long enough and a fulcrum on which to place it, and I shall move the world.'"

They helped me put the railing into the right position, wedged between the large boulder and the smaller one.

"Now we apply force by pulling down here to take advantage of the leverage." I showed them the end of the railing farthest from the boulder. "The lever will act as a force multiplier. Come help me!"

All five of us grabbed the top of the bar and pulled with all our might.

"It's working!" Ahyana said.

The boulder was definitely starting to move. "Keep going!"

It went a few inches, and I told them to stop so that I could move the smaller rock close again and readjust the railing. We did this several more times, painstakingly slow, but groaning and heaving with all our might, bit by bit, we did it.

When the boulder was moved, it revealed a circular patch of dirt. I got on my hands and knees and started digging. Vibrations rumbled against my hands, and it reminded me so much of my first day in the temple, when I had been digging in the garden with Io as she taught me how to plant flowers.

I had felt a great pool of power, just out of reach.

And now I felt it even more strongly.

My fingers brushed against something hard. I brushed the dirt away to see the hilt of a weapon that gleamed a bright gold. I assumed it was a sword. My chest felt so light, my mouth gone dry.

Dea's sword. This was Dea's golden sword.

The greatest weapon.

"Is that . . ." Io didn't finish her sentence, sounding every bit as exhilarated as I felt.

My heart beat so quickly it felt like it might float away. I dug around the sword until the hilt was totally visible. I grabbed on to it and yanked it out of the dirt.

It came easily, but I was knocked over once it exited the earth because it was taller than I was. I lay there on the floor, hanging on to it.

Everyone stared at me.

"How are you supposed to wield that?" Ahyana asked. "I don't even think Xander could use it. It's too big."

In my dreams the goddess had always been so tall. I hadn't realized that it was a literal depiction of what she looked like.

So I had come all this way and endured all that I had for a weapon I couldn't even use?

I pushed down the bitter taste in my mouth and got to my feet. There had to be a way to use it. "Maybe there's an aspect that—"

The sword suddenly shrank as I held it, adjusting until it was the right size for me. Not much bigger than my xiphos. It even looked like my xiphos—a cross guard at the bottom and a leaf-shaped blade.

Like it had been meant just for me.

"Did everyone else just see that?" Ahyana whispered.

Zalira nodded. "Yes."

"Good. I was worried I was hallucinating."

I understood Ahyana's concern because I was feeling the same thing. It was like the sword had . . . shape-shifted, for lack of a better description.

"Is it real gold?" Io asked me. It looked as if she wanted to touch it but was afraid to.

I did a couple of swings to test the weight. Easy to maneuver. This wasn't gold.

"No. Gold is soft and malleable and heavy. Weapons made out of gold would bend or deform during battle. This is some other kind of metal I've never seen before." An alloy? A metal found only among the gods?

Whatever this was, it was sturdy. Strong. It shone so brightly. I inspected the edges, and despite being buried in dirt for thousands of years, it was so sharp I accidentally nicked one of my fingers on it.

I finally understood what I had been feeling in the ground.

It had been this sword, calling to me.

"There's writing on the blade," I told the others. I held it up so that I could see it better. "Dea."

I turned it over to see the word on the other side and spoke it. "Nikos."

The sword became engulfed in fire.

CHAPTER FORTY-ONE

"Whoa!" Io yelped. Suri quickly pulled her away from me.

I nearly dropped the sword out of shock but managed to hold on. The flames were intense, but they didn't hurt. My hand wasn't burning.

"Uh, I was going to ask you if I could hold it, but I have changed my mind," Ahyana said as she backed up slowly.

"How did you access your magic?" Zalira asked me.

"This isn't like my fury aspect. It's more like my night-walking one. It doesn't wear me out. I don't have to turn it off," I said.

"Could you, though?" Ahyana asked.

"Dea Nikos." The flames stopped and the metal was once again cool to the touch. The sword was inscribed with the goddess's name and the ancient word for victory.

The fact that the ship I'd come to Ilion on was called *Nikos* made it seem like an ironic joke that the goddess had had at my expense.

Zalira went to stand by her sister. "Did we know it catches on fire?"

"We don't know anything about it," Io said. "This is why you have to be flame-kissed, Lia. So you could wield the weapon and not be burned."

The earth suddenly rumbled beneath our feet. We all held still, waiting, and it happened again. Louder this time. Coming from behind us.

Back near the entrance to the room, an entire piece of the cavern floor suddenly disappeared, crashing down.

"Time to go," I said.

We all ran to the stairs, went up the steps, came to the landing, and turned . . . but there was no door for us to get out. I put the goddess's sword into my pack so that I'd have my hands free.

"But we got the sword!" Ahyana said. "I don't understand."

I pushed against the rock ceiling, but it wasn't budging.

Suri elbowed her way to the front. She closed her eyes and said, "Dea Chthonia."

The rocks above us shook and made a grinding noise. I didn't understand why her magic was working now and I didn't care. I put my hand on Suri's arm. The rest of the adelphia did the same so that we were all powering her.

"It's enchanted," she said. "I can't get it open."

"You can do it," Io said. "I believe in you."

Suri nodded, groaning in pain as she somehow managed to tear the rocks apart, reforming them so that there was a hole large enough for us to escape through. Suri fell forward as she turned off her aspect. That had taken so much out of her.

"Dea Erinys," I said. "Io! Go!"

I practically threw her up through the hole to safety. Zalira was next, and she was able to help pull people up as I pushed them to her. Suri was so exhausted that we had a hard time getting her on the ledge above.

"Lia!" Zalira offered me her hand and I jumped. Ahyana grabbed my other arm and they both pulled.

I had just gotten clear when the stairs fell apart, going down so far that we couldn't see the bottom.

We all lay on the ground, breathing hard. Suri had passed out completely.

"Fortification potion," I said to Io. She handed it to me and I drank it so that I could keep my strength up.

The one good thing was that we weren't lost. We were standing on a mountainside, and from our vantage point, we could see the men on the ledge. I picked Suri up and carried her over my shoulder. We all began to walk down, making our way along what I presumed was the top of the cave.

Rokh flew overhead and he spotted us, flying down to tell the others that we were coming.

When we got to the cave entrance, I started handing people down to Xander. He took them quickly and then reached for me.

I turned off my aspect and fell into his arms. He held me tightly, speaking into my neck. "We felt that earthquake and I thought . . ."

He had thought the worst.

"You were gone for hours," he said.

We were? It had felt like half an hour, if that. "I'm back now."

He held me like he wasn't ever going to let me go again. And I adored the way that felt.

"Were you successful?" he asked as he released me.

I already missed his arms around me. "Yes. We got the sword. I want to show you but not out here. I'll wait until we're alone. Or until we get home."

"Home?" He echoed the word, and there was a strain in his voice. I understood why.

It also surprised me that I had said it. But it was the truth. Being with him in the palace—that had become my home.

"Did you get your book?" I heard Stephanos ask Zalira. She glanced at me, and I felt a twinge of guilt that I'd asked Xander and my adelphia to lie about what we'd truly been after.

"We got everything we needed," she told him.

I could see how much he wanted to embrace her, to assure himself that she was whole.

And how much she wanted that, too.

Rokh tried to speak to Ahyana, but she told him she wasn't ready yet. She apologized for punching him and then said that she needed some time. He nodded but looked absolutely miserable.

"Has Luna come back yet?" I asked Xander.

"Your lizard has not made an appearance," he told me.

Where was she? What was she doing? Why had she been gone for so long?

And what if she wasn't coming back? What if she had discovered that she liked being out in the wild instead of inside the palace?

Or maybe her whole purpose had been to help us solve the scroll by giving us aether, and now that we had retrieved the greatest weapon . . . perhaps the goddess had decided I no longer needed Luna.

I hoped not. I would really miss her.

"We should cross back as soon as possible," Rokh said to the group. It was nearly twilight—it would be dark soon. I wanted to get away from this chasm. We needed to set up camp somewhere that we wouldn't have to worry about another freak windstorm.

"What about Suri?" Ahyana asked.

"I'll get her to wake up," Io said. "I've got some spirit of hartshorn with me. It smells terrible, so I think it'll work."

"Some of the ropes snapped during the winds earlier," Xander told me. "We've been reinforcing the bridge while you were gone."

The tension in his voice was obvious. He was worried about me crossing again.

"You do not go last this time," he demanded. "You follow right after me. We have two ropes tied to the far tree as additional safety precautions."

I looked across the chasm and saw that it was just as he'd said—there were now two ropes tied to a large tree on the opposite side. Xander walked over to the ropes and picked them up. "I'm going first, you go second. And Stephanos is going to tie your knots this time."

It was much easier to deal with his imperious tone now that I understood it was coming from a place of fear and concern.

"I'm going to be all right," I assured him.

"After what happened with Lia last time, let me go first," Dolion said to Xander with a smile. "Ilion can afford to lose me. You're more valuable than I am."

Xander shook his head. "I'm the heaviest, so I should be the one to go first, to test it out and make sure that it holds."

"You don't always have to do everything yourself. You can let others help carry the burden," Dolion said.

As much as I disliked Dolion, he was right. Xander did take too much on himself. It was something he and I had discussed before.

In large part because I had the tendency to do the same thing myself.

"Fine," my husband responded. "You can go. But I don't like it."

"You never do," Dolion said cheerfully as he clasped Xander on the shoulder. Dolion tied the ropes around his waist and I went over to check on Suri.

"The spirit of hartshorn didn't work," Io said, sounding concerned. "She's still passed out."

Suri had expended a great deal of magic to help us escape from the cave. "She's strong. She'll wake up soon. If we have to wait until she does, we will."

Io nodded. "It feels unreal that she can speak. That she actually talked to us. Like it was some waking dream I had that's over now."

What had stood out most to me was that Suri had spoken her aspect out loud. Which made me think she had always done magic by talking, just like the rest of us.

And that we must have been far enough away when she did it in the past that we hadn't overheard.

"Do you think she'll keep talking to us?" Io asked me.

"I don't know."

It wouldn't have surprised me if Suri elected to stay silent. She had only spoken because she'd absolutely had to, so that she could stop us from making a deadly mistake.

Dolion had crossed the bridge and Rokh flew over to retrieve both safety ropes and bring them back to Xander.

Xander quickly tied them around his waist and turned back to look at me. "You're next."

"I know."

When he stepped out onto the bridge, I walked away from the others. I had to watch and make sure that he was safe.

He crossed so slowly that it was driving me a bit mad. He wanted to test every plank, every rope. He was ignoring his own fear to make sure that the bridge was safe. It felt unnecessary to me, but it seemed to be what he needed for his own peace of mind.

I tried to convince myself that the windstorm had been meant specifically for me as the trial of air and that it wouldn't return. And that it certainly wouldn't happen while my husband was crossing slower than a turtle.

It didn't help his progress that he kept looking back over his shoulder at me, as if to make sure that I was still there.

Stephanos joined me. "It's not like you to be so quiet."

"Watching him is stressful. He's scared of heights."

"I know," he said with a nod. "I thought that maybe you were trying to lure him back to your side with your beauty."

"What?" I asked with a laugh. "What do you mean?"

"That you were standing here stoically and quietly because of that old Sasanian adage about how to catch a man's attention. 'Women are only beautiful when they're silent.'"

My heart pounded so loudly that for a moment I couldn't hear, couldn't speak. "Where did you hear that?"

"It's something Dolion's always saying."

What?

I had only ever heard that once before.

No, no, no . . .

"Xander!" I screamed.

He stopped and turned toward me.

"Come back!"

Dolion rushed over with his broadsword and cut the rope closest to him, and that side of the wooden bridge sagged.

Xander's gaze never left mine, even though his brother was betraying him. Dolion ran over to the other rope and lifted his sword.

"Lia."

Panic surged inside me as I looked at my husband's calm face, and he smiled softly.

"I love you," he said as the bridge collapsed.

And then he fell.

CHAPTER FORTY-TWO

I felt a blinding, searing pain, as if an unseen blade were digging Xander's name directly onto my heart, putting him there permanently. I could feel him inside me, that thread connecting us that I knew could never be broken.

I screamed his name as he fell and heard when he smacked into the cliff face. Stephanos threw a spear at Dolion, but it went wide.

Rokh shifted, but two dozen people came out from behind trees and rocks. They all had their bows trained on us.

And then their leader walked out.

Artemisia.

I dropped to my knees. I had never felt so helpless in my entire life. There was nothing I could do to stop this. I could only watch.

Xander immediately started to climb the ropes attached to his waist. What if they cut those, too? If they didn't, he would go up there and kill every single person.

Was I about to watch my husband plummet to his death?

Dolion went over to the edge with a blowpipe and began shooting darts at Xander. I saw each time they hit, peppering his flesh, but it didn't slow him. He fought off whatever was in those darts and continued to climb, his muscles straining as he put one hand over the other, hauling himself up.

He had just gotten himself onto the top of the cliff and pulled out his broadsword. He took one step forward and then collapsed onto the ground.

I screamed his name again.

"Your precious husband's not dead. Just sleeping. I need him for my negotiations. Ilion will happily surrender and open their gates to get their king returned to them," Artemisia said.

I had thought I hated her before, but it was nothing compared to the raging inferno of loathing I felt for her now.

"But as for the rest of you . . ." Her voice trailed off as she raised her hand. "Fire."

We had no protection, no shields. No way to fight them off.

Every one of her soldiers loosed an arrow at us, but a gust of wind shot up from the chasm and blew all their projectiles away.

Artemisia frowned and told her men to fire again.

They did, with the same result.

Like we were being protected.

"That's a neat trick," Artemisia said. "I heard about your magic. Is this all it does? You can call up gusts of wind?"

I stood, ignoring the way my limbs shook. Dolion must have told her about our aspects. That snake. "I can show you exactly what I can do."

"Oh, I would advise against that. Because if you or any of your sisters try to use magic against us, I will kill your husband. We are going to leave, and you are going to let us."

"We can take her," Ahyana whispered to me. I wondered if they could hear her on the other side. "We can destroy all of them."

"No," I whispered back frantically. "We can't. She will kill him." Of that I had no doubt.

"Good decision," Artemisia said as she signaled to her men. Two of them went over and picked Xander up, putting him onto a litter. They lifted it and placed it on their shoulders and walked away.

It was like they had stolen my heart from my chest and there wasn't anything I could do to stop them.

"This isn't over," I told Artemisia.

"I'm sure we'll meet again," she said with a vicious smirk.

She was right. We would.

When I took my husband back.

She turned to leave, her soldiers following.

"Dolion!" Stephanos yelled out, and I heard the hurt, confusion, and anger in his voice.

"Don't come after us, Stephanos. I don't want to have to hurt you. And Rokh, if you fly after us, I will shoot you out of the sky." Dolion brought up the rear of the group as they left.

Then the Carians were all out of sight.

I remembered how that voice had urged me to tell Xander about Dolion and how he had kissed me. If I had listened, if I had done what it directed me to do, my husband would be safe right now.

Now I would have to live with that knowledge.

I could feel him, feel as he was pulled farther and farther away from me. It was like Zalira had said—I could track him. I would be able to find him with this connection. That thought briefly lifted my spirits.

Hope wasn't lost.

Ahyana came over and put her arms around me.

"I shouldn't have let him come," I told her, fighting off tears. "I should have insisted he stay in Troas."

"We aren't valuable hostages," Ahyana said. "She would have just killed us outright. The only reason we're alive right now is because they only wanted him."

"She's going to kill him," I said.

Rokh said, "No, she won't. If she planned on killing Xander, she would have done it immediately. Like she said, she needs him alive. She's going to use him as a bargaining chip."

Stephanos had his head in his hands. "I am such a fool. Dolion told me to give him all the arrows to carry. He said it would be easier if they were in one spot."

Zalira went over to him. "You were tricked. We all were."

Artemisia was the only other person that I'd ever heard use that phrase about women being silent. I had once asked Xander about it, assuming it was Ilionian, but he said it wasn't.

Because it was a Carian phrase. I thought of how Dolion had made himself seem like a hapless fool, pretending that he was behaving impulsively from one moment to the next when everything he had done had been deliberate and calculating. It hadn't been an accident that Dolion had come into the room when I was questioning Lysimache. He hadn't wanted to protect me. He had intended to stop her from giving me too much information. He had come in with his weapon deliberately, knowing what she would do.

Whenever I had watched Xander and his phratry train, the other men were all bare-chested, but Dolion never was.

It must have been because he had that hammer tattoo on his chest.

He had gotten a Sasanian tattoo on his wrist as a misdirection, to hide his true background. It was why Stephanos had assumed the phrase was Sasanian.

That red string I had seen on the tree this morning—Dolion had been leaving them for the Carians so that they could track us.

"We have to go after them," I said. "We have to get that bridge tied up so we can cross."

Rokh put his hand on my shoulder. "We can't. There will be traps. Ambushes. They'll be expecting us to follow."

"Then we fight!" I said, wiping away angry tears. "We have to rescue him!"

"We will," Zalira said. "But you know better than to walk into a trap. There will be another way to get to him."

I did know better. The problem was I didn't care. I would turn on my aspect and slaughter every Carian I came across to get him back.

"Let's stop discussing it," Ahyana wisely pointed out. "They might be just out of sight listening."

Stephanos agreed with her. "She's right. But if we're not going to cross the chasm, how do we get out of here?"

"I know how." Suri had woken up but looked groggy. "Fortification potions. Two."

Io reached into her pouch and pulled out two vials and handed them to Suri. She drank them quickly and walked over to the edge of the chasm. "I need help," she said.

We all went over and put our hands on her.

"Dea Chthonia," she said.

The rocks roared and groaned and I watched as a step formed in front of us. Then another, to the right and down farther. And another, and another.

She was creating stairs out of stone in the side of the mountain. She stayed in her magic, creating the steps, until it got to a point where she had to stop.

Suri turned her aspect off. "This kind of rock is much easier to manipulate. I'll make more when we reach the bottom step."

We ate and drank to get our strength back up. I had to keep myself from crying when I bit into the pasteli that Rokh passed out. Io also gave everyone fortification potions.

It restored my energy but I didn't feel like myself. I wasn't sure I would ever feel whole again without Xander.

Stephanos and Rokh got a rope and tied us all together. Rokh was in the front, with Suri, Io, Zalira, and Ahyana behind him. I was following Ahyana with Stephanos last.

"I have to stay close to you," he told me. "If you fall and die, Xander will kill me."

Another time it would have been a lighthearted joke. Now he just said it seriously. This was definitely a precarious situation. There wasn't a railing or any way to stop ourselves if we slipped or misjudged our steps.

"If one person falls, the others can dig in and help pull them back up," Rokh said, holding on to the rope.

"What if the wind starts blowing again?" Io asked.

"We'll have to pray that the goddess is with us," Zalira told her. "And that we can make it down safely."

I was glad Zalira had it in her to be comforting. Because if the wind did blow again, we were all dead.

But if we tried to follow after the Carians, Rokh was right. There would be traps. Artemisia was probably waiting and salivating at the idea of me coming after her. And if I had been alone, I probably would have done it. But I wasn't willing to risk the lives of my adelphia and Xander's brothers.

I would go after Artemisia, but it would be on my terms. Not hers.

Rokh and Stephanos made torches for everyone to carry. It wasn't dark yet, but it would be soon. And it probably wasn't the best idea for us to climb down these steps in the dark, but I didn't want the Carians to have too much of a lead.

And Stephanos was the one who pointed out that if we stayed put, the Carians might come back and launch an attack under the cover of night.

We needed to move and do as Zalira had suggested. We would have to pray that the goddess would be with us.

Rokh got on the first step and it held. He went to the next and we all started following. I had to focus all my attention on what I was doing. I couldn't let myself fixate on Xander and where he was and what they might be doing to him. Couldn't think about how terrified he must have been when he fell. That way led to despair and madness. I would get him back.

Darkness fell thick around us and we lit our torches. We were far enough down the mountain now that, even if the Carians did spot us, they wouldn't be able to reach us.

Except Dolion. He could have easily picked all of us off the mountainside. I hoped he wouldn't see us.

Everything became one step, then another, and another, keeping one hand on the craggy cliffside. It took all my concentration.

When we reached the last step, Suri had to make more on her own, with no one to lend her power. She would create ten more steps, call off her aspect, and then do it all over again.

It took hours but we eventually reached the bottom. I had never been so grateful to stand on solid ground as I was then.

As soon as Stephanos got to the ground, Suri turned her aspect on and destroyed about thirty of the stairs going up. I was about to ask her why she had done it, but then realized she was making it so the Carians couldn't follow us that way.

"Stay here," Rokh said after Suri had finished and turned off her aspect. "I'm going to look for where we left the horses."

"Be careful," Ahyana said, and to his clear surprise, she kissed him gently.

He couldn't stop himself from smiling before he shape-shifted and flew off.

Stephanos was winding the rope up, and I noticed how despondent he looked.

"Are you all right?" I asked him. It was probably a silly question, given that none of us were.

"Dolion was my best friend," he said. "I shared so much with him. He was the one I talked to about Zalira. How could I have not known?"

"Because he made sure you didn't."

Everyone had been tricked, including Xander. And now he was paying the price for trusting someone who didn't deserve it.

"He told me how he felt about you," Stephanos confessed, and I could tell that it wasn't easy for him to say. That even after what Dolion had done, he still felt like he was betraying a friend. "I should have told Xander. But I thought I was keeping my best friend's confidences."

"Dolion kissed me," I said, not wanting him to feel so alone. "And I didn't tell Xander, either. I didn't want to cause a problem in their relationship. Because I thought that if he felt about you all the way I feel about my adelphia, I didn't want to take that from him."

"I suppose Dolion took care of that all on his own."

It made me wonder whether any of what Dolion had said to me was real. Or if it had simply been part of his plan. Was he trying to drive a wedge between Xander and me?

And if he was, why? What was his end goal? It didn't make any sense.

Ahyana called on her aspect, and I went over to see what she was doing.

"I'm going to find Artemisia," she said, before I even asked. "They know to look for ravens, but I found a peregrine falcon. She flies so fast and sees so well."

She fell silent. I supposed she was watching through the falcon's eyes as she had with the bats.

Rokh flew into camp and shifted. "I found the horses. They're not far from here."

"We'll go as soon as Ahyana's done," Zalira said.

I saw the concern on Rokh's face and he went and sat next to her. She reached out and took his hand so that he could help power her.

Io approached and asked me, "Can I speak with you?"

I didn't feel ready to talk, especially not about her brother. I could feel him moving farther and farther away from me, a tiny light that grew dimmer with each passing moment.

"I'm sorry, but I would prefer not to hear a lecture right now." It was probably unkind, but I felt like a bowstring pulled too tight—I might snap if she applied more pressure.

"No, Lia. I want to apologize to you. I shouldn't have asked you to stay away from Xander. Or had you promise that you wouldn't hurt him. That was wrong of me."

I was so surprised that at first I couldn't formulate a response. But I did feel bad that I hadn't been able to do what she'd asked me. "I'm sorry that I couldn't stay away from him."

"Don't apologize. It was like trying to stop a waterfall from flowing," she said as she took my hand. "There was no way to prevent you and Xander from loving each other. I know better than anyone that we can't protect against pain. The price of humanity, of loving, is grief and hurt. We don't get to have one without the other."

I had to clear the lump in my throat before I could speak. "I know you did it because you were worried. You love your brother."

"So do you," she said.

And I didn't correct her.

"I found the Carians!" Ahyana called out. She turned off her aspect and stood, her limbs shaking. "But they aren't coming from the south. They're going around the mountain range. They're going to attack from the north!"

All of Ilion's defenses were being put up south of Troas.

Which meant that the city wouldn't be ready.

CHAPTER FORTY-THREE

"You have to go back and tell Thrax," I said to Stephanos. "Troas has to be warned and get ready for what's coming." Thrax and Xander led the army. Thrax was the only other person they would listen to. He had to be made aware of what was happening.

"I'm not going without you," Stephanos said with a shake of his head. I knew that it was primarily directed at Zalira but that he blamed himself for what Dolion had done and now felt responsible for all of us.

Which made me think he didn't quite understand that we were more than capable of protecting ourselves. "We have magic and we're strong. We will be safe and we will get Xander back."

"I can't leave her," he said to me quietly, his eyes pleading with me to understand.

And I did, all too well. "I know. But you have to. I promise to bring her back to you. There are so many innocent people in Troas at risk. The northern defenses need to be shored up to protect them."

As we walked to the horses, I continued attempting to convince Stephanos and Rokh that they had to go back to Troas.

"You don't need both of us to return," Rokh said. "I can stay here with you."

Stephanos said, "Xander needs you to be taking messages to nearby allies to get their help. We delayed for this mission, but that has to be a priority. You're the only one who can do it."

I took it as a good sign that Stephanos was now doing my work for me—I hoped that meant he would go to Troas. And it made me feel better to think that the two of them would be traveling together. I knew they could take care of themselves, but it would be good for them to watch each other's backs.

"Not to mention that Dolion will be specifically looking for you," I told Rokh. He had already said as much. Rokh wouldn't be able to fly undetected around the Carians.

The horses were right where we had left them. I wondered why the Carians hadn't scattered them or taken them. We untied them and grabbed their bridles and headed south.

Stephanos pointed out that the Carians might have known where the horses were and left them as another trap, hoping that we would return to them.

If that was their plan, we had avoided their scheme by reaching the horses first.

When we were far enough away that Rokh deemed us safe from accidental discovery, he led us into a large cave. Which meant that we only had one entry point to worry about. Rokh and Stephanos helped us make camp.

"Don't light a fire," Rokh said. "It will make you easy to spot. And take turns keeping watch."

"We know," I told him.

"Ahyana," he said, his heart on his sleeve. "Don't let us part in anger. Can you ever forgive me?"

She walked over to him and kissed him sweetly. I saw the way his body sagged with relief. Then she told him, "Lia was right. You are going to have to buy me a lot of pretty things."

A grin spread across his face. "Anything."

He kissed her again and I could tell that they were holding back because they had an audience. He rested his forehead against hers and whispered to her. It made my heart ache to watch them.

Ahyana wiped the tears from her face and nodded.

Then there was nothing left for Rokh and Stephanos to do but leave. They said their farewells to the rest of us and headed to the mouth of the cave with three of the horses.

"Happy tears?" I asked Ahyana.

"Very happy tears."

"Wait!" Zalira called out, and she ran over to Stephanos.

She threw her arms around his neck and hugged him. He hugged her back with his free arm.

When she stepped back, she said, "I should have told you this earlier. Stephanos, I love you."

He put his hand over his heart and I knew exactly what he was feeling, the way she had just burned herself inside him.

She cupped his face with her hands. "Now you will always find your way back to me."

"Is that the only reason you said it?" He was teasing, happy, but I heard the concern as well.

"Silly man, I said it because I love you. I always have and I always—"

He cut her off by kissing her, so deeply and passionately that I had to duck my head because I felt like I was infringing on an extremely personal moment.

The old Lia would have worried that Xander had said he loved me for the same reason—so that I would be able to track him. I might have thought that he'd never said words of love to me before.

But that wasn't true. All his words had been words of love—I just hadn't been able to see it.

And he hadn't said the actual words because he thought I was in love with someone else and he didn't want to end up with a relationship like his parents'.

He had said he loved me because that was how he truly felt.

The goddess would have struck him down if he'd said it falsely.

My heart throbbed with sharp aches as I thought about him, reliving over and over again the moment he'd told me he loved me. I desperately missed him.

I had to get him back.

Stephanos said with a smile to Zalira, "You do know that you just made it impossible for me to leave."

"We will be reunited soon. Go and do what needs to be done," she said.

He kissed her one last time and then he and Rokh finally headed out of the cave.

I went and put my arm around Zalira as she watched him go. She said, "If this is the end, I had to tell him. I would have regretted passing into the next life and never saying it. Because I do love him."

"You have to have hope," I said. "Believe that all will be well."

Ahyana joined us. "If we do live, then what are you going to do?"

Zalira shrugged. "If we're still standing when this is all over, we'll figure it out then."

"I never would have guessed that Rokh would be the last one to confess his true feelings," I said to Ahyana, teasing her a bit.

She blinked several times and then said with a sly smile, "You're right. He should have been the first. There's another thing he'll have to try and rectify to get back in my good graces."

"We should try and get some rest," Zalira said.

"I'll take first watch," I offered. I didn't think I'd be able to sleep. Not while I was this worried about Xander.

I was also afraid that, if I went to sleep, I might lose our connection. It was an irrational fear but I needed the constant, tiny pulse from his light.

The others settled in and I stayed up, watching the cave entrance. My mind was a jumbled mess of emotions and thoughts. I was glad that I'd asked everyone to keep hidden the truth of what we'd been looking for in the goddess's cave. Because it meant Dolion didn't know and wouldn't be able to tell Artemisia.

What had he told her? She knew that we could do magic. Did she have the specifics?

Thinking of her led me to Xander and wondering what she might be doing to him. I didn't expect that she would be treating him well. She would probably enjoy torturing him.

The thought made my stomach turn over. I had to stay calm. I had to deal with everything from a practical standpoint. Xander must have been terrified falling but he hadn't shown it. He hadn't allowed panic to take over. He had immediately sprung into action and been ready to fight his way clear.

I had to do the same.

Hours had passed when suddenly a glimmer of light happened near my feet and Luna appeared. How had she found us? We weren't where she had left us.

"There you are!" I loudly whispered, picking her up. "Where have you been?"

She stared back.

"I went looking for you. And then I fell down a hole and was nearly tossed off a wooden bridge and they took Xander . . ." Despite not wanting to cry, I started to. Quietly. I didn't want to wake the others.

She maneuvered herself so that she stood on her hind legs in my lap and put her front paws around my neck. Like she was hugging me.

That made me cry worse.

I felt the touch of her rough, slightly sticky tongue as she brushed it against my tears, like she was trying to clean my face.

"Thank you," I said. I wiped my tears away and told myself to calm down. I couldn't keep watch if my eyes were blurred.

She sat back down in my lap, looking up at me.

"Luna, did the goddess send you to me?"

Yes.

I thought of how I had acquired her—it had been because I'd helped that elderly woman during my marriage processional. Maybe that had been the goddess in disguise, giving me a test. One that I had passed.

"Are you a reward for me?"

No.

"Then why did the goddess give you to me?"

But she couldn't answer that question. She jumped off my lap onto the ground. She turned in a circle and then lay down and curled up like a cat, resting her head on her tail.

I heard movement behind me and turned slightly to see Suri coming over.

"You should be asleep after what you've gone through today," I said as she settled in next to me.

"I'm used to enduring a lot of pain," she said. "I can't sleep when Io's upset like this. She's so worried about her brother."

When Suri said that, when I heard the tone of her voice, it was like the scroll coming to life in front of my eyes, all the lines connecting to each other so that I could finally see the full picture. And I felt like a complete fool for not having realized it earlier.

"You're in love with her, aren't you?" I asked carefully, not sure how she would react.

I saw the misery in her eyes. She nodded.

"Oh, Suri. I would hug you but I'm afraid you'd punch me."

That made her smile slightly.

I sensed that she didn't want to discuss this further. I floundered for a moment, trying to come up with something else to talk about and finally asked, "Are you going to stop talking to us? If you do, that's fine. Talk, don't talk, it doesn't matter to us. You're our sister, no matter what."

She shrugged. "I haven't started screaming yet." I remembered in the goddess's cave how Suri had said she didn't speak because she was afraid she would start screaming and not be able to stop.

"What happened?"

"People who worship the goddess of discord are . . . not good."

"They hurt you," I said.

"In so many different ways. It made me wary of most men. Which is why I loved the temple. It was the first place that I ever felt at home. The first place I ever felt loved. The first place I belonged."

I wanted to ask her to give me the names of everyone who had harmed her so that I could hunt them down. They deserved to suffer.

But neither one of us should be dwelling on the past right now. It was something we could talk about further after Troas was saved. If Suri wanted to. So instead I said, "When you were performing magic, you were speaking."

"Yes. It's the only way it works."

That wasn't what Maia had thought. She had assumed that Suri saying it inside her mind was good enough for the goddess. "So you said your vows?"

"I whispered the words. No one heard me. When people don't expect you to speak, they don't catch when you do." Her gaze went back to Io.

"She did say that your light was brighter for her than the rest of us. That's how I see Xander. How Zalira and Ahyana see Stephanos and Rokh. Maybe you should talk to her. Tell her how you feel."

Suri shook her head, and I wasn't sure if that was a permanent no or if she just wasn't ready.

"It's important to tell the people you love that you love them," I said.

"I love you. In a different way."

That made me smile and I was grateful that I could. That there could still be some light and happiness amid all the darkness. "I love you, too, in a different way."

"You should take your own advice," she said after a few quiet moments. "Tell him how you feel."

There was no point in denying that I was in love with Xander. I didn't know when exactly it had happened, but I did love him. With every part of me.

And as I was ruminating about my feelings, I realized that something terrible had happened.

Xander's light had gone out.

CHAPTER FORTY-FOUR

A heavy stone dropped into my stomach, pressing me down.

"I can't . . . I can't feel him," I said to Suri, panicked. "There's a light and it's gone."

"Maybe he's too far away," she said.

Why had it gone out? I closed my eyes and tried to concentrate. To reestablish our connection.

It didn't work.

But for reasons I couldn't have explained, I knew he wasn't dead. I would feel it if he were.

Or maybe I was as delusional as Doria, who was forever insisting that my brother was alive and going to return home to her in Locris.

"Look for him," Suri said.

"I'm planning to."

"No, I meant night walk. Find him."

That could work. I could pull Xander into my dream. "What if he's not asleep?"

"Were your parents?"

She was right. They had been awake and I'd still been able to see them.

"Will you take over the watch?" I asked, and she nodded.

I went over to my bedroll and lay down, closing my eyes and focusing on Xander's face. "Dea Nyctipolus."

He was in a tent. He had been chained to a stake in the ground. My stomach filled with a mixture of anger and concern when I saw him. He had been beaten. He was covered in cuts and bruises.

I wished that Io hadn't severed our link. Artemisia had done this to him to hurt me. I deserved to feel every injury he had sustained.

But he didn't look as if they'd broken him. His expression was defiant, strong.

"Xander," I said, leaning forward to touch him. He didn't hear me and my hand passed through him.

I began to look around the tent to see what I could work with. Where were the keys? I would need those when I found him.

The flap opened and Artemisia walked inside. She had a massive war hammer, which she threw onto a wooden table. The hammer of Arion. I wished desperately that I could stab her where she stood. I even attempted it, but the blade couldn't make contact.

"King Alexandros, how have you been enjoying your accommodations?" she asked as she sat on a foldable stool.

"The service leaves something to be desired," he said.

"My men have a lot of aggression they wanted to work out. It seems you were the best option for them to do so." She crossed her ankles. "Dolion tells me that you and your wife are physically connected. I hope she's enjoying everything we inflict on you."

Apparently Dolion didn't know that Io had severed the physical link. Xander smirked, and I could tell it irritated Artemisia. She had hoped to get a rise out of him. "And the poison? Has that been to your liking?"

"I could do without it."

"What fun would that be?" she asked with a sneer.

"Poison is cowardly." I had once said that to him. "If you plan on killing me, you should just be done with it. This is tedious."

Panic clutched at my throat. He was going to provoke her into ending his life.

"Dolion told me about your special gifts. I need you weakened, and poison is the best way to do that. But I don't want you to die right away. First, I'm going to enjoy you."

Fury slithered through my gut. If she laid a hand on him, I was going to cut it off the first chance I got.

He shifted his gaze over to the table. "Is that the eye of the goddess that I see?"

Artemisia had somehow slotted the eye into the top of her war hammer. She seemed startled but quickly recovered. "And what if it is?"

"I know someone who is looking for it. And she'll take it from you."

"Your wife?" she asked, her voice dripping with sarcasm. "I'm not worried about her."

"You should be. You have no idea how powerful she is or how quickly you're going to die when she finds you."

"I'd like to see her try."

"You will," he promised.

"I welcome the fight. Things will be very different the next time she and I meet."

Yes, they would be. Because she wasn't going to survive the encounter. I would make sure of it.

Xander smiled.

"You don't believe me?" she demanded. "I am going to kill your wife."

The smile slid off his face. "If you harm anyone I care about, any of my people, I promise that I will kill you." He said it in that cold, calm voice that sent shivers down my spine.

It didn't have the same effect on Artemisia. "King Alexandros, I am going to harm every single one of your people. And I'm going to leave you alive to watch and then kill you last."

She leaned forward. "Carian ships are on their way. They're going to arrive the same time that we do. We will hammer Ilion from every side and destroy it and salt the earth behind us. Then we will cross the ocean and do the same to Locris. No eyes will be left to weep for the dead."

Artemisia was going to kill hundreds of thousands of people.

I had to stop her.

"What you don't seem to appreciate, King Alexandros, is how determined we are to destroy you and your people." She tilted her head to the side, as if taking his measure. "After the Great War, you sent your cowards to Caria. Your weakest men fled there. Your cruelest. Those who did not want pain for themselves but enjoyed inflicting it on others. The ones who would kill men and steal their families. Those wives couldn't fight back, but they refused to speak to their new husbands. Refused to eat with them. They taught their sons and daughters to hate the Ilionians. To bide our time until we could enact our revenge."

"Aren't you descended from those weak, cruel men?" Xander asked, taunting her.

Anger flashed in her eyes. "I suppose we both are. Which makes us what, family?"

"If we are family, then let Ilion repay the debt of those ancestors. We can try to recompense for what was done."

"Locris has paid a thousand years for a crime committed against one woman. How long should Ilion pay for a crime committed against thousands of women?" she asked calmly. "Your goddess demanded the sacrifice of Locrian maidens? My god demands death and destruction and to tear down all that his mother has built. The only payment I will accept is the blood of your people."

"Why take me prisoner if you aren't interested in bargaining in good faith?" Xander subtly pulled at his chains, as if probing for a weakness. I wondered if Artemisia noticed.

"Because I am going to negotiate with your beloved city for your 'safe return.' And as soon as they agree and open their gates, I'm going to slaughter everyone inside."

Part of me wished I hadn't sent Rokh off. This was information that Troas needed to have.

Although I supposed it didn't really matter because Artemisia wasn't going to get the chance to enact her plan. I would retrieve my husband and return to the city before she could arrive.

Armies moved slowly.

"It sounds to me as if you're not in a position to negotiate," Xander said. "Who is your commanding officer? Why don't you go and fetch him for me?"

A look of pure hatred crossed Artemisia's face before she called to one of the guards to find the general.

It was one of the rules of combat. A prisoner of war had the right to request an audience with the leader of an army.

They sat in silence until his arrival. He strode in with full armor on. When he removed his helmet, I saw that he was a middle-aged man, with gray strands lining his hair and beard. He looked like a military commander, his expression serious and sure.

"My apologies, King Alexandros," he said. "This is not a very civilized way to meet one another."

"I agree with you, General . . ."

"Enyalios," the man said. "Why have you called me here?"

"I wish to negotiate with you," Xander said.

"You are in no position to negotiate anything," Artemisia interjected with a snarl.

The general ignored her, as if she hadn't spoken. "What is it you're offering?"

"An end to your march on Ilion. Turn around and take your men home. And we can discuss what amount of gold you would need to make that happen."

"Why are you listening to this?" Artemisia demanded, standing up. "He is the child of liars and abusers."

Enyalios finally deigned to acknowledge her. "Because not everyone shares in your murderous enthusiasm. It was you who tricked the king into declaring war, and many of the men here do not want it—they would prefer to return home. If there is a way to negotiate a treaty between our two nations, then—"

"A treaty?" she shrieked. "We haven't waited a thousand years for a treaty! This is not what Arion wants."

"Do you speak for him?" the general countered.

"I am his hammer."

"Because you killed all your brothers. The hammer was only supposed to be wielded by the men of your family."

"None of them are left," she said through clenched teeth. "There is only me. And I will lead Caria to victory."

"Your plan is flawed and will not work. You lack the experience and knowledge necessary to lead," Enyalios told her. "The walls at Troas have stood for a thousand years for a reason. They are impenetrable."

"I have lived in Troas. I am very well acquainted with the city and its defenses," she said.

"You lived in the temple and only left the grounds a few times. You are all but useless. You did not learn anything of value that could help us."

"I captured their king!" she shot back, pointing at Xander.

"Dolion made it possible for you to take him. And Dolion is the one sharing information of actual consequence. You are dismissed, Artemisia. Leave."

Enyalios turned back to Xander. "Now, as we were saying, what are you willing to offer?"

"I will not be ignored!" Artemisia declared.

This seemed to make the general finally lose his temper. "Yes, you will! You have no authority or say here! You are a little girl playing with her toy, pretending at war—"

Artemisia picked up the hammer of Arion and flattened Enyalios's skull with it. I gasped as he fell to the ground.

"Does that seem like a toy to you?" she taunted his dead body. "Now I am the one in charge. I will lead us to victory!"

Xander made a sound and she whirled around on him, hammer grasped tightly in her hand. "Did you want to say something, King Alexandros?"

His expression was nonchalant, as if she hadn't just murdered a man in front of him. "How do you expect the army to follow you when you've killed their general? I don't think they'll like that."

Her chest heaved for a few moments before she answered. "I managed to take a great deal of gold when I left Ilion. From the statue of your goddess. I will pay them for their loyalty."

"Paid loyalty is not actual loyalty."

"It's close enough," she snapped. "And they all want Ilion destroyed as much as I do."

That wasn't what I'd heard from the general before he died, and I could see from Xander's face that he had come to the same conclusion.

"An army of deer led by a lion is more to be feared than an army of lions being led by a deer," she said, kicking the general's body. "They will follow me. It is the women of Caria who have stoked the fires of vengeance and hatred, waiting for this day. The generations of men who came before me were too cowardly to act. They wanted to wait until we were more powerful. Until the army was bigger, until we had more weapons, more money. Now the glory will be mine, and I will not wait for a man to decide whether or not I can take it."

Someone called the general's name from outside the tent, looking for him.

"It seems to me that you should go out and do some damage mitigation before your men find out on their own what you've done," Xander said.

A look of unease flashed briefly in Artemisia's eyes. She lifted the tent flap, as if she intended to leave. But she turned around and said to him, "You should be thanking my god that I still need you alive."

CHAPTER FORTY-FIVE

I stayed with Xander all night. There wasn't anything I could do to help him, and he couldn't hear me, but I could be there with him. Artemisia had guards remove the general's body, and she came in to personally administer more poison to Xander.

He didn't call out but I could see that it was affecting him. I wondered if it was interfering with our connection and that was why I couldn't feel him.

"Lia?"

I woke up to Zalira shaking me. "You were sleeping so deeply. I was concerned."

"Because I was night walking. I found Xander." I shared with my sisters everything that I had seen and heard.

I turned to Io. "Do you have poison antidotes with you?"

"Yes. I overpacked. And we'll give him some fortification potions, if we need to." She looked very worried but determined.

"Artemisia killed the general of her army?" Ahyana asked, wrapping her arms around herself.

Without hesitation. As easily as breathing. It didn't even seem like something she had considered—she had just acted and it had ended in a man's death.

A man who was trying to come to an agreement with Xander and stop this war before it even started. I nodded.

"Let's get ready," Zalira suggested, and we all moved off to change out of our shirts and pants back into our tunics, packing up our bags.

I took the goddess's sword and put it into the sheath strapped to my leg. I moved my xiphos to my waistband. I wanted to make sure I had access to both weapons when I needed them.

When everyone was dressed, I saw that Suri had removed the wrappings on her arms. We all knew about her scars because of the terawolf attack, when she'd been bitten, but she had still chosen to wrap her arms every day.

That had changed this morning.

And I was glad that it had.

I smiled at her and she smiled back with a nod.

Luna still slept and I had Io hand her to me once I climbed up onto my horse. I put my little dragon in front of me, keeping one hand on her so that she wouldn't slip off. Ahyana led the way, since thanks to the falcon, she knew where the camp was located.

Io brought up the rear. As the most experienced rider, she was in charge of bringing along Xander's horse for when we found him. He would need a way to ride back to Troas.

The hours we spent riding gave me time to think. I wasn't much of a planner, but an actual plan had started to come together in my mind. I had come up with a way to sneak into the camp and bring Xander back out without putting anyone else at risk and without alerting any guards.

I didn't want us to have to fight our way clear. I didn't think we'd be able to do it. Even with my power and his gift, there would be too many soldiers.

We came to a small village in the late afternoon. While my sisters procured some extra feed for the horses, I found a woman willing to sell me one of her outfits, a basket, and two sheets.

I put the sheets into the basket and then placed Luna on top. I lashed the basket to my horse so that I wouldn't have to worry about Luna accidentally falling.

Because I wanted to go faster. To push the horses to their limits. To get to the Carian camp as soon as possible.

But Io counseled against it. I knew she was right but I hated how long it was taking.

I spent all those hours solidifying my plan. I thought of what Quynh had said to me when she explained why she had chosen to become a kitchen maid.

Women are so often overlooked. Men don't believe that we could be smarter than them or that we're capable of defeating them, and so we're always perceived as not being a threat.

And it was Demaratus who had taught me about campaigning armies. They were always followed by a supply train that contained food for the soldiers and their animals, water for everyone, ammunition, carts for transporting spoils of war, a way to repair armor and weapons—it was essentially a mobile village.

He had been completely drunk while telling me about it, waving his arms about. "If you can destroy the supply train, you can take down the entire army!"

That wasn't the part that interested me. The supply train was usually well protected, as the army relied so heavily on it. No, the part that I was planning on exploiting was that the train was populated almost entirely by women.

There were hetaerae, of course, but also cooks. Laundresses. Healers. Seamstresses. Weavers. Foragers. They didn't fight and were only there to serve the army.

Servants who, in Quynh's words, were "unnoticed, unseen, forgotten."

It would be my way in.

We were also being slowed down by the terrain. Unlike the forests and grasslands near Troas, the area north of the Syrilline Mountains was full of hills and valleys, some with only one passageway. Ahyana had to call on some different birds to scout for her to find the correct paths.

We stopped to eat at dinnertime. I was eager to keep going, but Io told me that it was imperative that the horses be able to drink and rest because we didn't want to risk injuring them.

"So I think I'm ready to see that sword," Ahyana said. "If you'll let me."

I didn't see any reason why not. I took it out of the sheath and handed it to her. She took it gingerly, as if she half expected it to explode in her hands.

Ahyana swished the sword from side to side. "What do you think will happen if I say the words?"

"Third-degree burns," Io said.

"I want to try. I'm curious." Ahyana held the sword away from her body. "Dea Nikos."

Nothing happened.

She had squinted her eyes shut and opened them in disappointment.

"Maybe it's broken. Or maybe it only worked in the cave. You try," she said, handing the sword back to me.

"Dea Nikos." It immediately went up in flames. I hurriedly turned it off, worried that if Artemisia had scouts in the area, they would spot it.

"You do know that it's unfair that you can do that, don't you?" Ahyana asked with a smile and shake of her head. "All those abilities."

My eyes widened at her words. Maybe this was what the sphinx had meant. She had said I had "many."

Io came to the same conclusion. "Lia, you have many powers. Many aspects."

I had at least three so far. Did I have others? I wished I had a list of aspects in front of me so that I could say each one and see what happened.

"How? Why?" I asked.

"Do I have to say 'because you're the savior' again?" Io asked.

What else could I do?

When we resumed our travels, I went through the aspects that I could remember. It was difficult to recall them because my brain wanted to focus on Xander and freeing him.

But of the ones I did say, nothing happened.

It was nearly midnight when Ahyana turned to us and said, "We're here. They're just over this ridge."

We tied the horses to the base of the hill and climbed up to see the army. We crawled on our bellies to peer over the ridgeline.

The moon was full but we wouldn't have needed it. There were so many campfires dotting the ground beneath us—an ocean of people and fires, lighting up the landscape like the stars in the sky. We couldn't even see where it ended—the back part of the army was hidden behind some hills.

"By the goddess," Zalira whispered.

None of us had known how large this army was.

"What is—" Io reached down and pulled something out from underneath her ankle.

It was a black bird with an arrow through it. Ahyana took it from her and anger made her voice shake. "A raven. Dolion is killing them just like he said he would. In case any of them are Rokh."

Why couldn't I feel Xander? Maybe the poison was affecting him, but we were close enough now that I should be able to sense him again.

I would not allow myself to consider the possibility that he was dead.

"Let's go back down the hill," I said. I was sure we were far enough away not to be heard but didn't want to risk someone noticing us.

When we reached the bottom, Zalira asked, "What's the plan?"

"You think Lia has a plan?" Ahyana responded, elbowing her sister slightly.

"I do have one. And it involves me going in alone."

They all started to speak at once, even Suri, but I held up my hands. "This is not about me doing it alone or wanting to leave you behind. I know we're stronger together. This is about how getting in and out will be so much easier with one person than it would be with five. We will draw too much attention."

"She's right," Io said sadly as she sat on the ground.

"And I'm in the best position to fight my way out if something happens," I added, not wanting to leave out any of my arguments.

Zalira crossed her arms over her chest. "What if you do need our help?"

"Then I'll use the sword. I'll light it quickly and then put it out. Watch for it. If you see it, then come running." I said this to appease them. I had no intention of putting any of them at risk if I could help it.

"How do you plan on sneaking in and not getting caught?" Io looked up at me, and I sat down next to her before I answered.

"I'm going to dress up like one of the women following the army. I'm going to need a heavy rain from Zalira and I'll just walk in. And when I have him, I'll need a distraction when I'm coming out, so I'll need you to watch for me to help me escape. I thought you could do that, Ahyana. What can fly in the rain?"

"Everything can fly in the rain," she said. "But they don't like to. It's much harder; the water weighs them down and they have to fight against it. I'll probably call up wasps. Flying in rain infuriates them."

It sounded perfect.

Io reached into her bag and pulled out a fortification potion and passed it to me. "Why do you want rain?"

"It will mean fewer people will be out of their tents and those that are will be miserable. They'll be more concerned with their own discomfort than challenging me."

Ahyana took a potion from Io as well. "Are you going now? Under the cover of night?"

"No. The only people moving around the camp right now are guards. I would stand out. The women will be up early in the morning, getting ready for the day. That's when I'll slip in."

"How will you know where to go?" Zalira asked as she put her fortification potion in her pouch.

"My old battle master told me that generals were all different in where they would be in the camp—some insisted being in the middle so that they were the most protected. But others wanted to be up front, where the action would be if they were attacked. I think Artemisia will be in the front. But I need Ahyana to verify that for me."

She nodded, drank her potion, and called up her aspect. "Dea Karpophoroi." I heard the shriek of a bat in the distance and waited while she used it to scout.

When she turned the magic off, she said, "There is a tent, much larger than the others, near the front. It has a red banner with a picture of a terawolf on it."

The other symbol of Arion. "That's where they'll be."

We probably should have slept, but none of us could manage it. Instead we ran over my plan a thousand times, thinking of all the ways it might go wrong and what I could do to circumvent them.

The backup plan mostly consisted of "fight my way out."

When dawn began to approach, I changed into the outfit that I had bought from the villager, covering my head with a scarf. Io took the still-sleeping Luna, and I used the basket and sheets as a prop, hoping that people's eyes would pass over me as soon as they saw me.

We moved into position closer to the camp. My entry point would also be my exit point so that my sisters could easily see me.

"Ready?" I asked.

Zalira nodded and called on her aspect. The rain started falling immediately, dramatically. I was already soaked.

"I'll be back," I promised them.

I stayed among the trees to disguise my approach. I sucked in a deep breath before I headed out to the open area, where the guards would be able to see me. I hurried toward the camp, as one would if they had been caught in a downpour.

Demaratus had told me once that the secret to slipping behind enemy lines was that if I behaved as if I belonged, people would believe that I did.

I had reached the first tent when I heard a voice call out, “You there! Where are you coming from?”

My heart was thundering in my chest. “I was relieving myself,” I told the guard who came over to me. He poked at my basket with his sword.

“Back about your duties,” he said, dismissing me.

It had worked! Excited, I walked through the tents, heading toward my goal. The red dirt beneath my feet had turned to mud, and it coated my sandals. As I had suspected, these terrible conditions ensured that there was hardly anyone outside. They were all in their tents keeping dry.

Except . . . three people were headed toward me.

And I realized the one in the middle was Artemisia, flanked by two officers.

My vengeance told me that this was my chance. That I could easily kill all three, take the eye, and go.

But I decided not to.

I chose Xander’s safety instead.

Stupid girl, she’s going to recognize you! Hide!

Demaratus’s voice was like it had been in the temple—so clear that it sounded as if he were standing right next to me.

I darted into the nearest tent, hoping that it was empty. I didn’t see anyone and said a quick prayer that the goddess would keep me safe. I watched through the tent flap as Artemisia and her men passed by.

A weak, soft voice rose up from behind me.

“Euthalia of Locris, I have been waiting for you.”

CHAPTER FORTY-SIX

A woman was curled up next to the main tentpole, slight and shivering. I realized why I hadn't seen her initially—I had assumed she was a bag or a blanket. She seemed harmless enough, but the last time something told me it had been waiting for me, they had a giant rock-monster sister who wanted to eat me.

"Who are you?" I asked as I crept closer to her. My hand went to my xiphos, ready.

"You won't need that."

She had a bandage wrapped around her eyes. She couldn't see me. How had she known what I was doing?

"I am an oracle from Phocis. From a family of seers, but I was the most powerful. I was captured by the Carians, and they used my family to force me to prophesy for them."

As I crouched down I realized that she was tied up to the main pole. I reached for her bindings, but she said, "No."

"Let me free you," I said. I would get her out of here.

"You should hate me. I told them that the savior of Ilion would be a Locrian maiden. It was why they tried to take you from your ship before you reached Troas."

"But you just said they used your family to force you to comply." I couldn't blame her for that. I would have done the same thing in her position.

She hung her head low. "I went along with it until my youngest sister got sick and they wouldn't take her to a healer. I stopped doing what they wanted. I wouldn't give them more. That was when Artemisia joined the camp. She killed my entire family in front of me, saving my mother for last. Then she blinded me so that the last thing I ever saw was my mother's death."

That was so beyond horrific that for a moment I didn't even know what to say. "I'm so sorry. Come with me. My sister can help you."

She tugged down the corner of her tunic and I saw that her skin was mottled, bright red. Like she had a terrible rash. "I have a wound that is infected. My blood has been poisoned. I have been fighting death because I was waiting for you. I knew that when I heard your voice, I would die soon after."

"Why have you been waiting for me?"

"The god of prophecy wants me to tell you that his prophecies cannot be circumvented."

My heart flew into my throat, expanding so wide that I could barely breathe. I knew how things had to be, but to hear it like this . . . "Will Ilion win this war?"

"The future is always shifting, always changing from one moment to the next. But your sacrifice will be necessary if you want any chance of saving Ilion and Locris."

I nodded, wiping away the tears that fell down my cheeks. I was going to die.

All that hope I had told myself to have dissipated into the gloomy air surrounding us.

"Euthalia of Locris, remember that love is fire. Creation and destruction. It can be wielded either way—as a tool, or as a weapon."

I was about to ask her what that meant, but she spoke again. "You're running out of time. Go."

"Are you sure you don't want me to cut you loose?" I asked as I stood up.

"I'm sure. In a few minutes I will be joining my family in the next world." After a beat she added, "The tent you need is not the one you seek. Look in the smaller tent to the south of that one."

I didn't want to leave her. If she was going to die, I didn't want her to be alone. "Aren't oracles supposed to be mysterious?"

"We are. I'm tired," she said with a small smile. "Go, before it's too late."

I went back out into the rain, heading toward Artemisia's tent. I saw the red banner and followed it. I still wasn't sensing Xander, but I had to push that out of my mind and concentrate on what I was doing.

He was here, he was alive, and I would find him.

I located the tent the oracle had told me about and went inside.

Xander wasn't there.

It was another man, faced away from me. Chained to the ground with a gag in his mouth.

The oracle had been mistaken.

I was about to leave when the man turned to look at me.

The entire world came to a complete stop. White noise rushed in my ears and my lungs would not cooperate. I couldn't breathe.

All I could do was stare.

"Haemon?" I asked in disbelief.

My brother nodded.

With tears in my eyes, I knelt down and got the gag out of his mouth. "By the goddess, how is this . . . how are you . . . what's happening?" I asked.

"Lia." He sounded so weak. He was gaunt. His eyes were sunken. They hadn't been feeding him properly. I saw open sores on him, new bruises, and older bruises that had faded over time. There didn't seem to be an uninjured part of his skin.

I wanted to hug him, but I was afraid I would make his pain worse. "What did they do to you?"

"Look at you. You're so grown up." His voice. His smile. I had forgotten them. "Why is your hair red?"

As I sawed through the thick ropes at his ankles, I realized my entire family owed Doria an apology. Haemon had been alive the whole time and we hadn't believed her.

"This doesn't feel like a dream," he said.

"It's not. I'm here." I put my hands on his legs so he could see that I was real.

"How is that possible?"

"I came to rescue my husband and found you instead," I said.

"Who are you married to?"

"The king of Ilion." I clenched my teeth together as I resumed cutting. Why was this rope so difficult?

"Alexandros? He was here earlier but now he's gone."

That stilled my motion as my heart stopped. "What do you mean, he's gone?"

"He escaped hours ago."

The sigh of relief I let out . . . I had thought my brother was telling me that Xander was dead. "How do you know he escaped?"

"There's not much to do here besides listening. He got out of his chains and stole a horse. The guards have been panicking, not sure what to do. Artemisia doesn't know yet because she's been in war council all night and they're afraid to tell her."

She wouldn't take the news of her prize possession fleeing very well. Someone's head was liable to get flattened.

But I had seen her walking around a few minutes ago. Did that mean the war council was done? Would she come looking for Xander?

She would sound the alarm as soon as she discovered he was gone. Which would prevent me from sneaking Haemon out.

"Did he know you were here?" Xander would have saved Haemon, I was sure of it.

"No. We were kept in separate tents. Artemisia keeps me gagged most of the time."

Fury licked its way through me, igniting every cell in my body . . . I didn't care about all the recent resolutions I had made to be better. To do better.

I was going to gut Artemisia and watch her die slowly.

And I was going to enjoy it.

And then I would kill every other Carian I came across. Because this was long-term damage that had been done to my brother. Somebody else had been torturing him long before she had rejoined her people.

"Why didn't they kill you?" I was almost through the rope. Just a bit further.

"Because I'm Aianteioi. Not even the Carians would risk crossing that rule."

I had never been so grateful for the laws that governed how Ajax the Lesser's descendants were to be treated. "They're supposed to have ransomed you, not kept you locked up."

"Their king said that the law didn't specify when the ransom demand must be made," he said.

"So they were planning to just keep you as their prisoner forever?"

"No," he said with a shake of his head, which I could tell took effort. "I don't know what their original plan was, but Artemisia got their king to hand me over to her. She told me that she is going to use me in negotiations with our father. That if he will surrender Locris, he could have me back."

Our father would have done it without hesitation.

She had intended for Locris to be the ransom paid for Haemon's release.

And then without any kind of defense mounted, the Carians would have been free to slay every Locrian they came across. Just as Artemisia planned to do in Ilion.

She was so convinced her plan would work that she intended to do it twice.

I finally cut through the rope and pulled it free from his legs. He had so many sores and bruises. It made me angry all over again.

"The key is up there," he said, nodding toward a tentpole. "Artemisia liked keeping it just out of my reach."

I grabbed the key and used it to open the chains on his wrists.

"It was unnecessary for her to lock me up. I'm too weak to escape."

"Was she poisoning you?" I needed to know so that I could have Io take care of him.

"No. She didn't need to. Just constant deprivation."

I refused to let myself dwell on my anger. I needed to keep my wits about me so that we could escape. Calm. Rational.

When I had initially made my plan, I had assumed that there would be guards at Artemisia's tent. I planned to get past them by saying I had a delivery, making my way inside, freeing Xander, and then the two of us would take out the guards.

I'd planned for Xander to wear one of the guards' uniform and armor.

But there were no guards nearby, and even if I found one, I couldn't imagine that anything would stay on my brother. The armor would all slip off.

I helped him to his feet. He felt hollow, fragile. Like I wouldn't even need to call on my aspect if I had to carry him. He swayed to the side when he stood.

"Come on," I said, putting his arm around my shoulder. I would have to help him walk.

We went out into the rain and Haemon started to shiver. I felt terrible—he was suffering because of my plan, but there was nothing that I could do. I had to get him away from here.

When we rejoined the others, I wouldn't be able to let him warm up or rest. We would have to move out immediately because, at some point, the Carians would realize that both Xander and Haemon had escaped and they would come looking for them.

With all the potential scenarios I had gone through with my adelphia, none of them had included finding my brother.

And not once had I considered the possibility that my husband would have already rescued himself.

I could see where I had come in and made my way there. We were so close. I hoped Ahyana would spot me and unleash her angry wasps soon.

But a tall man stepped out in front of us, his sword drawn and pointed at me.

Dolion.

CHAPTER FORTY-SEVEN

He didn't speak.

My muscles tensed and my chest hurt. Like my heart would explode.

"Dolion, please," I said, the blood draining from my face and pooling in my gut. "This is my brother, Haemon. He's sick. I need to save him."

He still didn't speak, just kept his sword trained on me.

"Please, let us leave," I begged. I would have gotten on my knees if I'd thought that would sway him. I was so desperate to get Haemon to safety.

The screams started to the south of us. Ahyana must have released her wasps.

The three of us stood there, staring at one another. I tried to control the way my limbs were shaking.

Because even if I fought Dolion and won, at any time all he had to do was call for the guards and Haemon and I would be done for.

He slowly lowered his sword.

And then he said, "I would have been so good to you."

Was that a warning? Or was he going to let us go?

Dolion walked toward the screams, as if he intended to help with the wasp situation. I led Haemon away from it, going as quickly as we could. My lungs felt frozen—at every step I expected to hear someone call after us or order us to come back.

When we reached the trees and could no longer be seen by the guards, my trembling actually got worse as my adrenaline flooded out of me.

My adelphia was there, ready to help.

"That's not Xander," Io said, already reaching into her pouch for vials.

"Xander escaped. This is my brother, Haemon."

Ahyana put a blanket around his shoulders. "I thought your brother was dead!"

Haemon said with a smile, "So did Lia."

"We need to move," I said. "They're going to come looking for the escapees. And we have to find Xander, who is probably lying in a ditch somewhere, dying of poison. Instead of staying put and waiting for me to come save him."

Io poured some potions down Haemon's throat. "To be fair, Xander probably didn't expect you to rescue him."

After he'd told me he loved me? How could he not have expected it? I let out a deep sigh. I knew that I was covering up my concern and worry with annoyance.

Zalira turned her aspect off and Ahyana had to help her stand. She'd held that storm for a long time.

And . . . it was still going.

"How are you doing that?" I asked.

"I don't know," she said, sounding out of breath. "It's like I made it rain so much that it decided on its own to keep storming."

"You can do magic?" My brother sounded bewildered.

I helped him walk toward the horses. "We all can. I'll explain on the way."

"How is Doria?" he asked.

That should have been the first thing I'd told him, and I felt bad that I hadn't. "She lives with us at the palace. She never gave up on you.

She's been insisting this whole time that you were alive and she was right. She misses you so much."

He nodded weakly and I helped him up onto my horse. We would have to share because I didn't trust him not to fall off if I had him ride alone. I grabbed some food from my pack and gave it to him. "Eat."

Io used a rock to climb up on her horse. "How do we find Xander?"

Based on the scroll, I knew we had a large body of water north of us, mountains to the south, and the Carians to the east. Would he head directly west, back to Troas? Would he go in a straight line and try to put as much distance between him and the army as he could? Or would he attempt to disguise his tracks?

Or what if he went north to Cyzicus? He could have chartered a ship and traveled back to Troas that way.

Whatever it was, I had to decide immediately. I knew that the Carians would decamp and come this way. We had to reach him before they did.

Because while the army itself would be slow moving, they could send out hunting parties to search for him.

"Let's go west and see what happens," I said. I chose that because it was what I would have done.

Suri took Luna for me, although she didn't look pleased about it. Part of me wanted to laugh. If she hoped to have a life with Io, she was going to have to get used to small animals.

"What is that?" Haemon asked.

"Luna. She's an aether dragon."

"A what?"

"There is so much you don't know." I told him how our family was doing, that Quynh had fallen in love and was pregnant, and how Xander had broken Kallisto's betrothal.

It suddenly occurred to me that Haemon being alive changed everything. "You're going to be king of Locris," I said.

"If Artemisia has her way, I won't be king of anything." He took another bite of pasteli. "What have you been doing?"

I did my best to recount everything I had been through. I left out most of the details about my relationship with Xander. I didn't think my older brother would understand.

When I finished he was quiet for more than a minute. And then he said, "You're telling me that you're this savior?"

"She is," Io said.

"I just got you back. I don't want you to die," Haemon said, and I had to gulp back the burning lump in my throat.

Because I couldn't promise him that it wouldn't happen. The oracle had just told me it would.

And that there was nothing I could do to stop it.

The moment that Xander's light returned to me nearly knocked me off my horse. I put a hand over my chest, so intensely grateful to know that he was still alive.

"This way," I said, taking over the lead. "I feel him!"

My adelphia followed me for hours. Xander's light grew stronger and stronger. We were getting close.

I couldn't help myself. I urged my horse to go faster. I needed to reach him. Zalira called out after me, but they all followed.

The light took me down a dusty, unpaved trail that led straight to . . .

An inn.

Xander was inside.

With murderers, thieves, and cutthroats.

There was no way he would be there voluntarily. Someone must have captured him.

I let out a groan as I dismounted. Haemon moved to do the same and I stopped him. "Will you stay here with the horses?"

"There's no possibility that I will let you go in there without me," he said. He was doing better, thanks to the food and Io's concoctions, but he wasn't healed yet. There was no way he could fight. I would have been surprised if he'd been able to stand.

"If I have to worry about you, it will be harder for me to fight. I promise that I can take care of myself. And I will be out here in ten minutes or less with my husband. If I'm not, you can come in after me."

I handed him my xiphos, and this seemed to mollify him. He nodded curtly. I knew that Haemon was used to protecting me, but I didn't need him to do that anymore.

My sisters arrived and dismounted, bringing the reins of their horses over to Haemon.

I took out the goddess's golden sword and went first.

When I walked into the main room, there was a fire roaring in the fireplace against the far wall with wooden chairs and tables scattered about. A tired, older woman stood behind a bar getting her patrons what I presumed was beer, based on the smell.

There must have been two dozen men in this room who had been talking, laughing, and playing games before we came in.

And every single one of them pulled out their weapons and stood when they saw us.

"Who's in charge here?" I asked.

"That would be me." The man speaking had been standing near the fireplace and flirting with a hetaera. He left her to walk toward us. "I am Autolycus, king of thieves. Welcome to my home."

He was tall and had dark hair, dark eyes, golden-brown skin. His tunic was a bright red. He had several earrings in both of his ears, and every one of his fingers sported a ring.

"Usually we have to seek out beautiful women. They don't tend to wander willingly into our web."

The men laughed in a menacing way, and the sound sent chills of disgust racing along my skin.

"I hate spiders," I said.

He tsked. "That's a shame."

"Do you like your head?" I asked him.

My question surprised him, and he seemed delighted by the novelty of it. If he was the king of thieves, I was sure people didn't typically speak like this to him. "Very much. Why?"

"Because if you wish for it to remain attached to your neck, you will return to me what's mine."

"And what is it you think that I have stolen that is yours?" Autolycus asked, and the men laughed again.

"My husband. The king of Ilion."

"My apologies, my queen. I am the only king in this inn."

I lifted the sword. "Dea Nikos."

The sword ignited and every person in the inn took a step back.

Autolycus's entire demeanor changed. "Oh, you mean King Alexandros. He's right this way. Just follow me."

I kept the sword lit as my adelphia and I followed him. He took us up the stairs and led us to a room at the end of the hallway.

"He's in there," he said.

"If you or any of your men try anything, I will happily slaughter every person in this inn. Do you understand?" I asked him.

Autolycus nodded, looking a bit concerned while still retaining his debonair attitude. "Of course, my queen. No need to get all fired up."

"You should kill him just for that terrible joke," Ahyana said as the king of thieves left.

I opened the door, and there on the bed . . .

Xander.

My heart fluttered at the sight of him. I rushed over, with Io right behind me.

He cracked his eyelids open. "I don't know how I feel about you having a flaming sword of death."

I had forgotten. I turned it off. "It's going to make it much harder for you to beat me in a fight."

He smiled. "I still know how to disarm you."

Only my husband would be on his deathbed and saying flirtatious things to me.

That I secretly loved.

Io interrupted, directing him to open his mouth. She gave him at least six different potions.

After he finished drinking them, he turned his head toward me. "Your first act as queen was to launch a rescue attempt?"

I both wanted to throttle him for worrying me and hug him because I had missed him so desperately. "It would have worked if you had stayed put. You're the only person I know who would free himself while a rescue was underway."

That made his smile even bigger.

"Is the antidote working?" I asked. "Because if you die, I'm going to kill you."

"It's working," he said. "I'm feeling better already. How did you know I was poisoned?"

"My night walking. I saw you and Artemisia. And her former general." I moved closer to him so that only he would hear me. "I stayed with you all night. I couldn't bear to leave you."

"Wife, are you saying you were worried about me?" he teased, and I was again struck with the urge to punch him.

"Look at you. How could I not be worried?"

"I haven't seen a mirror recently, but I'm sure I look terrible."

"This is not the time for vanity. Oh no, the poor handsome man is not as handsome as he normally is. Whatever will you do?"

"You think I'm handsome?" he said flirtatiously, and sparks of heat pulsed through me.

What was wrong with me? He had nearly died, and all I wanted was to throw myself on top of him.

"Can you walk?" I asked.

"I can." He got up slowly.

When he stood, I hugged him. I couldn't help myself. He was so real and solid.

He kissed the top of my scalp. "I will be fine."

"You promised you wouldn't leave me."

"I wasn't given much choice in the matter." He sounded weary, but I also heard the laughter in his voice.

What would I have done if he had died before I reached him with an antidote? "I almost lost you."

"I never would have let that happen. I was about to rally and defeat the thieves."

That made me smile. "I know you were."

He put a finger under my chin to lift my face up to his. "Liar."

"You started it."

He leaned down to kiss me, and the sense of completion, of rightness, that I felt with his lips fused to mine . . . it overwhelmed me.

Zalira cleared her throat and I stepped away from him.

I had completely forgotten that there were other people in the room.

"We should probably go, what with all the criminals waiting downstairs," Ahyana said, her eyes dancing. She was going to tease me later.

And I would let her.

I might even enjoy it.

He held my hand as we left. Out of the room, down the hallway, taking the stairs, until we were in the main room with the thieves.

"Thank you for keeping him safe," I said. I could afford to be benevolent now that I had him back.

Autolycus bowed. "It was our pleasure. Thank you for allowing me to keep my head."

"You're welcome," I said.

"My queen, if you ever have need of me, please let me know."

"If I ever thought I needed you for anything, I would hit my head against the wall until that feeling went away," I said as sweetly as I could.

Autolycus laughed, as did his men.

Then I felt bad. He had kept Xander safe in his own way, so I added on, "There is a Carian army that will be marching through here soon. You might want to clear out."

"You do realize that they were planning to ransom me to the council in Troas," Xander said as we made our way through the great room. "You don't have to be nice to him."

"I know. I wanted to practice being magnanimous."

He chuckled as we walked outside, and I saw that Haemon was about to dismount.

Xander took my sword and pointed it at my brother.

"Stop," I said, pushing his arm down. "That's Haemon. The Carians had him. I found him when I went looking for you."

"Your dead brother?"

"Not dead," Haemon said cheerfully. "Thanks to your sister, I might even fully recover."

"Yes, Haemon can take a normal amount of medicine and heal. Unlike some people," Io said pointedly.

I made the introductions, and my brother jokingly said, "It seems fairly pathetic to me that you got taken down by a bunch of thieves. Aren't you supposed to be goddess-blessed?"

Xander grinned. "And how long did the Carians keep you captive for?"

My heart twinged as I watched two of the men I loved most in the whole world make each other laugh.

It felt so unfair that I had just gotten all this and it was going to be taken away.

CHAPTER FORTY-EIGHT

We put distance between ourselves and the inn. I could imagine that Autolycus would happily sell information about us to Carian search parties, and I wanted to be far enough away that it wouldn't matter if he did.

Xander rode next to me, carrying on a conversation with Haemon the entire time. As they exchanged their life stories, I was glad they got along so well and liked each other so much.

That they would have their friendship after I was gone.

My chest ached as I watched Xander laugh at something my brother said.

I love you.

For a moment I was terrified that I had spoken the words aloud, that I had done something I could never undo.

Because I had to be selfless where he was concerned. It wouldn't be fair to him to admit that I shared his feelings and then leave him to a lifetime without me. I didn't know how the love bond worked. Maybe if it was one-sided, not fully connected, he would be able to move on. Find someone new and love again.

And I found that I wanted that for him. Even though the fanged, jealous monster inside me roared to life, I shushed it. I wanted him to be happy.

To have a whole lifetime of happiness.

Something I wouldn't ever be able to give him.

After what had happened over the last couple of days, I also had a fear that even if I could move past everything else and admit my true feelings, something bad would happen if I did. That it would somehow cause his death.

I knew it wasn't rational, but I couldn't ever be rational where he was concerned.

Stupid girl, are you protecting him or are you protecting yourself?

I didn't have an answer. I wanted it to be the first one but worried that it was the second.

A few hours later Xander called for us to stop and rest. Haemon dismounted by himself and was able to walk a few steps and sit. I got down and went over to check on Luna.

Still sleeping.

Everyone set out to accomplish various tasks. I found myself drifting away from the group. I wanted to be alone for a moment, to take a chance to process everything that had happened.

Everything that was fated to happen in the near future.

I sat down on a fallen log and let out a big breath.

"May I join you?" Xander asked.

"That was so polite," I said admiringly. "All you needed to add was a 'please.' And yes."

If he had been anyone else, I might have asked him to leave.

But he was different.

He sat down next to me. "I'm so tired of being poisoned."

"I'm tired of saving you from being poisoned."

That earned me a grin. "I understand. It has been exhausting continually saving you from harm."

He rubbed his left arm where he had the scar—the one we had shared after I'd been attacked in our washroom and he had rescued me. Mine was gone but his remained.

"Why didn't you let the healers remove your scar?" I asked. I wanted to reach out and stroke the length of it but decided against it. I found that I needed to talk to him because there were still things I wanted to know before the end. If I touched him I knew what we'd spend our entire break doing.

He glanced down at his arm. "I wanted to keep it as a reminder of when I failed to be there for the woman I love. So that I would never let her down again."

I nearly choked on my own breath. When he'd said he loved me, I had assumed it was a more recent development. But he was saying that he had felt that way for a long time.

"It's also why I keep this one." He rubbed his finger along the scar I'd given him on his throat. "Proof of how much I love you and how desperate I was to be close to you."

He loved me then? I hadn't even known who he really was.

Then I recalled what he'd told me in one of our dreams.

I pledge you my sword, my body, my blood. I will protect you and keep you safe.

Then I'd asked him if he would lay down his life for me and he'd said, "Without hesitation."

Once I'd discovered his true identity, I had assumed he'd said those things to manipulate me, because they'd had a very real effect on me. Convinced myself that he was attempting to trick me into saying that I loved him first so that I'd be bound to him and have to marry him.

Even after the fact, when I knew he hadn't been trying to trick me, I'd realized that despite the amazing things he'd said, he had never said the actual words of love to me.

And as I sat there, I realized that if he hadn't known my real identity, maybe the reason he hadn't said it was because he knew he had to marry someone else. And it would have been wrong for him to give me those words instead of his future wife.

A woman who also happened to be me.

"Why did you come to Locris?" I asked. I knew he hadn't come to find me and scheme his way into my heart, but I'd never asked him why he'd made the trip.

"I came to see you. I wanted to know who I was going to marry."

That was why when he had seen Kallisto, he had asked me if I knew where the other princess was. He had been looking for me. "Did someone point me out?"

"No, your people are horrifically loyal. And I could only ask so many times before it would start to sound suspicious."

"When did you know who I was?"

"When Io told me the night of the harvest festival. Which is why I sent Thrax to retrieve you the next day. But with you being you, I should have known that I would have to come and get you myself."

"And extort me into marriage."

"A little bit."

I was glad the memories I had of him as Jason were pure and true, not calculated.

"There's something I need to tell you," I said. My pulse picked up. I wasn't sure how he would feel about it.

"You can tell me anything." From the encouraging tone in his voice, I wondered if he thought I was going to admit that I loved him.

But that was something I couldn't say. "Dolion kissed me."

He hadn't been expecting that. "What?"

"I immediately pushed him away and threatened him to not ever touch me again. He told me he had feelings for me, wanted me to run away with him. When he betrayed you, I thought that he had said those things because he was trying to drive a wedge between us. But after he let me go at the Carian camp . . ." It made me think his feelings had been real. That he hadn't been trying to ruin my and Xander's relationship as part of a plot to ruin Ilion, but had done it solely for himself.

"Why didn't you tell me?" His calm but deadly voice was not a good sign.

"Because I didn't want to harm your relationship. I know how much you care about your phratry brothers, and I didn't want to be the reason that got ruined. If I'd told you—"

"If you'd told me, I would have killed him," he finished.

"Yes. And there's more." I shared with him all the lies Dolion had told me—about why Xander had gone to Locris, that he had always known who I was, that he had set out to manipulate me.

"Now I know why you were so insistent that I had been tricking you."

"He also told me that you had feelings for Chryseis and had been having an affair with her."

"Then I went and kissed her deliberately in front of you." He shook his head.

"That didn't help things. But I know it was a mistake not to tell you about him. I'm sorry. I should have. If I had . . . maybe all this would have been avoided. But I thought he was my friend."

"So did I."

We sat in silence for a few moments. He seemed to be digesting what I had just told him.

"I'm sorry I kissed her," he said. "I'm not sure I ever said that to you."

While I understood why he had done it, it wasn't an image that I wanted to keep popping up in my head. "Could we not ever talk about it again?"

"Done. What other questions do you have?"

He knew me far too well. "What things are you keeping from me?"

His eyebrows rose. "I have been open with you."

"You don't remember? The other night I asked you if you were keeping things from me and you said you were. Things I didn't need to know."

"Oh. It was that I was in love with you."

I wanted to protest that I had needed to know that. That it had changed everything. But I also understood why he hadn't.

He took my left hand and brought it up to his mouth to press one soft kiss against it. He twirled my wedding ring around my finger. "Do you know why I picked Chalcidian steel for your ring?"

I had assumed that it had been some kind of slight, that I wasn't worth a precious metal like gold or silver. I shook my head.

"Because it reminded me of you. Made from the same material as your favorite weapon. Strong, resilient, permanent. You don't shatter under pressure. You endure. What other kind of ring could I choose for my favorite warrior?"

I ordered myself not to cry, but I still felt the lump in my throat that indicated I soon would.

"And it's engraved with the key pattern because the love I have for you is eternal."

I felt so small for dismissing the ring. For not understanding its true worth.

For not realizing that he had loved me for so long.

"Nothing to say, wife?" he asked.

"Why do you call me that when I told you it bothered me?" That was something safe. We could discuss that and I wouldn't dissolve into a pool of tears.

"Because I couldn't give you the words, every time I called you 'wife,' it was my secret way of telling you how much I love you."

My vision went blurry from the unshed tears that had arrived. "But you called me 'wife' when you were mad at me."

He kissed my hand again. "Even when I was furious with you, even when I was determined to tie you to our bed so that you couldn't do something completely foolish, I never stopped loving you. No matter how angry I am with you, and I am certain I repeatedly will be in the future, then, now, I always love you."

There was only one thing to say to that, and I couldn't. So instead I let the tears burn hot paths down my cheeks.

He reached up to wipe them away. "When I wasn't thinking of how to escape, I did nothing else but think of you and how I crave you. I crave your laughter. Your smiles—something you give to me so rarely that it is more precious to me than gold. I crave your thoughts. Your advice. Your opinions. I crave your touch. Your soft mouth on my skin, your sighs when I touch you. The desperate noises you make in the back of your throat when I kiss you and you want more."

Now my tears were mixed with pangs of desire and it was a strange but heady combination.

"Lia, I have seen your bitterness and anger, your desire for vengeance. And I have seen your delight and kindness and how you care for those you love. There is no part of you that I do not know, that I am not intimately acquainted with. And I love all of it—every piece. The dark and the light."

He laid his palm on the side of my face and I leaned into it. He ran his thumb over my lower lip and I shuddered in response.

His eyes were golden flames and I couldn't look away. "You are as vital to me as the air I breathe, the water I drink, the food I eat. I cannot exist without you. I would sacrifice my heart, give up all that I have, for the smallest hope that you might return my feelings someday. And if not, then I promise that I love you enough for the both of us."

He wasn't asking me to say the words, but I knew that it was what he wanted. To know that he wasn't alone in this, that he had as much power over me as I had over him.

Part of me wanted to forget the resolutions I had just made. I wanted to make that sacrifice for him, so that he would be able to move on. I should stay quiet.

But it felt like remaining silent . . . it was like I was about to lose something important.

"Xander, I—"

"Lia!"

Ahyana came running up, out of breath.

"Dragons," she said, panting. "Artemisia has earth dragons."

CHAPTER FORTY-NINE

"What do you mean, Artemisia has earth dragons?" I asked as Xander got to his feet.

"I connected to a common swift to see which way we should go, and then I sent it back to the Carian army to check on them. They're on the move. There are cavalry riders up front with bags attached to their horses that the red dirt is pouring out of."

"The dragons!" I reminded her.

"Yes, at the back of the army, there are earth dragons. They are massive." I remembered the drawings from my grandmother's book. Earth dragons were covered in impenetrable scales that resembled stones.

And they hadn't been seen in hundreds of years.

"How many?" Xander asked.

"Two dozen? Maybe more?"

By the goddess. "Do you have anything in Troas to fight dragons with?"

"No," he said, pressing his lips together in a thin line. "We were preparing for an army of people, not earth dragons."

Ahyana's eyes went wide. "Then what are we going to do?"

"I need to get back to Troas and warn them. I don't know that the walls will protect us. We should move everyone into the palace's lower caverns to keep them safe. But there's not enough time to do that."

"How much time do you need?" I asked him.

"Two days? Maybe three?"

"I'll get them for you," I said.

"How?"

"We'll use our magic to delay them."

A thousand different emotions flitted through Xander's eyes. He wanted to tell me no. He didn't want to leave me behind.

But I wasn't the only person he had to worry about. He was king. He had an entire nation he needed to protect.

"I will be fine," I promised him. "I saved you from a den of thieves, didn't I? Got my brother out of the Carian camp? You know that I can do this."

He grabbed me and pulled me close. He kissed my temple. "I know you can. I just don't want you to."

"You have to go," I said into his neck. "You're the only one they'll listen to. You have the authority to command the army. Let me do this for you."

Xander pulled back, his gaze intense. "You promise me that you'll come back to me."

"I promise." I infused as much conviction as I could into my voice. "And if there's one thing Locrians are known for, it's keeping our word."

He didn't smile at my joke. "How am I supposed to be parted from you?"

"There are hundreds of thousands of innocent lives that hang in the balance, and you are the only one who can get them to safety." I studied the lines and angles of his face, committing them to memory.

He was doing the same.

"Come on," I finally said, taking him by the hand. He had to leave as soon as possible. When we reached the others, we told them what was happening.

"Haemon, I'm going to need you to go back with Xander," I said.

"I won't," he said with a shake of his head.

"You will. You're not well enough to fight. And I don't want my husband traveling alone." The second one wasn't an actual reason, because Xander probably could have taken on the entire Carian army by himself, but I wanted my brother to feel like he needed to go.

"Your sister can take care of herself," Xander said as he started packing a bag to take with him. "You will distract her if you stay. She'll worry about you. She needs to know that you're safe so she can do what she has to."

The faith my husband had in me . . . his words were like warm honey spreading through my limbs. Infusing me with strength and confidence.

Haemon nodded, but it was obvious he didn't want to leave, either. He also packed a bag while Xander said a private goodbye to Io. She hugged him tightly.

Luna had woken up and I went over to her.

"You should go back to Troas, where it's safe. Xander and my brother are going now."

No.

Stubborn beast.

My brother had finished packing and I went to say goodbye. "I really will be all right."

He shook his head. "I just got you back. I don't want to lose you again. I love you."

"I know and I love you, too," I said. He pulled me into his arms and hugged me tightly. He still felt so fragile, like he might float away.

"And I promise that I'll protect your husband. I can see how much you love him."

Was it that obvious? I pulled away to see Haemon's smile, but I couldn't return it.

"What is it?" he asked.

"I haven't told him," I whispered.

"Why not?"

"Because right now the bond only goes one way. If I tell him, that will make it stronger, won't it? It will hurt him more if something happens to me."

"Lia, that is not how that works. If you didn't love him, when he said the words to you, no bond would have been created. Both people have to feel that way for it to work. I think it would hurt him more for you not to tell him."

My mouth hung open slightly. I'd had no idea.

"Haemon! Let's go."

Realizing that I was running out of time to decide who was going where, I approached my sisters, and Zalira said, "Before you say a word, we're obviously staying with you."

Everyone nodded and I again had to fight back tears.

"I didn't want to assume."

"You should assume," Ahyana told me. "Always assume that we are with you."

We decided that when we were done delaying the army, Suri and Io would share a horse so that Haemon and Xander could each have their own mount.

They climbed up onto their horses, and I went over to see them off.

"I'll take care of Io," I said to Xander.

"I know you will."

"Be safe," I said.

Say the words. Tell him.

But I didn't want it like this. I would tell him. When we could be alone and the words could be just for him.

He leaned down to kiss me fiercely. "Do not die," he ordered.

"I won't."

"I love you," he said, making the bond resonate in my heart, and then he made a sound and his horse leapt forward, with Haemon's close in pursuit.

Xander's light grew dimmer with each passing moment.

I love you.

"What now?" Ahyana asked.

I turned back to face my sisters. "Now we go and see what kind of damage we can do to the Carian army."

"Why are they using the earth dragons to pull up those trees?" I asked.

"Because that's the only way to kill an olive tree," Io said sadly. "Pulling it out by the roots. It takes a new olive tree so long to reach maturity—they are ruining the livelihoods of every Ilionian farmer from this area."

We were on a ridge where we could easily see the Carian army in the valley below us. I couldn't stop watching the dragons. They were so big, much bigger than I'd expected. Their scales resembled rocks and they looked like walking hills. Their long tails had a ball of spikes on the end, and I could only imagine the damage they could do with those.

What I couldn't tell was how the Carians were controlling the dragons. How did they get them to do what they wanted?

Xander had been right. Those dragons were going to knock down the walls of Troas like they were toys. I didn't understand why Artemisia's former general had been concerned about breaching the walls.

Unless there was something that would make it harder for them to control the dragons during battle.

"How are you supposed to stop a dragon?" Ahyana asked.

"With another dragon," Zalira responded.

But the only other dragon we had was Luna, who sat perched on my shoulder, even though she barely fit. She snorted derisively several times and it made me think she didn't like the earth dragons.

"Let's see what we can do to stop them," Io said. We had all drunk fortification potions and agreed not to power each other so that we would retain our strength. We would take turns trying to slow down the army.

Io knelt on the ground, putting her hands flat out in front of her. "Dea Khloe."

I watched as roots erupted out of the ground in the valley and wrapped around the dragons' legs. While it seemed to frighten them initially, they just stepped forward and snapped the roots.

"It's not working," Ahyana told Io.

"I know," she said.

Then she sent the roots after the infantry, and that caused a widespread panic that lasted for as long as Io did. She was trying to hold on, but this was taking an immense amount of power.

She turned it off and collapsed to the ground. She was still awake, but only barely.

That bought us several hours as the army hacked at all the exposed roots, making certain they wouldn't rise up and try to harm them.

Once they started forward again, Ahyana was ready for them.

"Dea Karpophoroi."

The ground hummed and shook around us.

"What is that?" Zalira demanded.

"Cicadas," Ahyana said with a smile.

Millions of large black bugs rose out of the earth. They made a deafening sound as they swarmed the soldiers, turning the sky dark.

I put my hands over my ears but it wasn't enough to drown out the high-pitched noise.

"Look at that!" I pointed at the back of the supply train. A large group of soldiers was heading east, back the way they had come.

They were deserting.

"They might be superstitious. Maybe they're taking this as a bad omen," Zalira said.

The Carians couldn't fight off the cicadas. The bugs were loud and they were everywhere, swarming endlessly.

The cicadas were bothering one of the dragons and it began to swing its tail in annoyance, or perhaps it was trying to bat them away.

The dragon accidentally hit several carts, spilling their contents onto the ground.

Ahyana lasted twice as long as Io had. Her body started shaking, and she made several sounds of pain.

"You've done enough," Zalira said. "Rest."

Her sister nodded and turned off her power. The cicadas stayed. They continued with their noises and flying around the area, but they began to settle. To find trees and plants to land on.

But the chaos they had created was immense.

It was twilight and the army had to stop. I couldn't imagine that they'd sleep very well with that constant shrill/whine the cicadas made.

"Time to move to our next location," I said. "We'll hit them with another round in the morning."

I hoped that what we had planned for tomorrow would be enough to make even more soldiers turn tail and flee back to their homes.

CHAPTER FIFTY

It had been a fitful night for me—I hadn't gotten much sleep. I was too worried about Xander and Haemon making it back safely to Troas and the approaching Carian army.

When I finally got out of my bedroll, I found Zalira watching the army from our vantage point. We had moved much farther west, beyond a choke point we hoped to utilize.

She had blanketed the valley with a dense layer of fog combined with a rain shower. The army was lighting torches but the rain kept putting them out. They couldn't see and the ground turned to mud beneath their feet, which made it almost impossible for the dragons to move, and most of their carts and siege engines were stuck.

"I didn't know you could do that," I said to her.

She turned off her aspect and sat back on her heels with a smile. "Neither did I. But it took a lot out of me. I'm going to need a few hours before I can go again."

The others woke up and we ate and observed. If this army hadn't been so intent on our destruction, it might have been entertaining watching them trying to dig out of the mud.

While I didn't have an aspect that I could use against the whole army, I wanted to keep my strength up in case something happened. Like if we were ambushed or hunted down by a group of cavalry. Because by now Artemisia had to know that we were responsible, and if I were her, I would have sent scouts out to locate us.

I needed to be ready.

Ahyana took a drink from her waterskin and then asked me, "Do you think there's a way to manipulate the sword's flame?"

"I don't know. And I'm not sure I want to attempt it out here." We were trying not to be spotted.

"I keep thinking about you having Dea's sword," Io said. "And how it means we're one step closer in the prophecy."

My sisters averted their faces at Io's words. Like Xander, it seemed they preferred to pretend that my death wasn't certain. I understood why they felt that way. I also wished that I could ignore what was coming.

But I didn't want to dwell on it. "Then let's be glad that there isn't any water or aether out here."

Although with my luck the earth would open and suck me down into a giant whirlpool while stars from the sky landed on top of me.

Eventually the sun overhead burned away the fog that Zalira had created and the army began to move west again.

The only way to continue was through a pass that had high, sheer walls on either side.

And it was right where Suri wanted them to go.

When the first line of dirt-spreaders entered the pass, she said, "Dea Chthonia."

She created a massive hole at the far end of the pass. It stretched from one wall to the other and looked deep.

Then . . . she began to push the hole forward, toward the army.

If Suri kept going, she would turn the entire pass into one giant pit.

I looked at her and saw the way that she was shaking. Her face indicated how much she was suffering.

"It's enough," I told her.

"Not yet." Her voice trembled.

"Aren't you in pain?"

She tipped her face up toward me. "Lia, I'm always in pain."

Suri went on, pushing the pit forward, her entire body racked with tremors.

Io came over and put her arm around her. "Let it go, Suri."

With a groan, she finally did and collapsed into Io's arms. Io stroked Suri's hair away from her face.

Suri had always been able to go longer than any of us when wielding magic. She could endure unspeakable amounts of torment and it broke my heart.

Some of the army attempted to go around the pass. We saw them break off from the main group. But the high hills ran north and south for miles, and the pass was the most direct route to Troas. Going around would add time to their march.

We had discussed having Suri try to break apart the hills and fill the pass with rocks, but she said making the pit would be better because manipulating that kind of rock from this distance would be difficult.

Unfortunately, after several hours the Carians came up with a solution. They brought two of the earth dragons over and had them hit the walls with their tails. Giant chunks of rock began to fall and fill up the pit.

And somehow they managed to do it in a controlled way that prevented the entire hillside from collapsing in.

Again I wondered how they were directing the dragons.

It was nearly nightfall when they finally filled the pit. They had to send their supply train north, to go around the hills. They would never be able to get all those wheeled carts and siege engines over the jagged terrain in the pass or over the hills themselves. The cavalry went with them.

Not all the riders left, though. Some of them stayed and walked their horses across the pit.

They were again forced to make camp as it had grown too dark to continue.

We had bought Troas another day.

The following morning we continued to keep an eye on the Carian army. They had been left without tents, as they no longer had their supply train. Zalira had sent a miserable rainstorm down on them that lasted most of the night.

But we expected them to be up and moving by this point and they weren't.

A lone figure walked out from the edge of the group.

"Lia of Locris!"

It was Artemisia, and she had some kind of metal cone in her hand that she was using to amplify her voice. In the other she held an olive branch with white linen attached to the top.

She wanted to arrange a conclave.

"I know you can hear me," she said. "And I know you've been harassing my men. We need to talk."

Io grabbed me by the arm. "You can't be considering this. It's a trap!"

Demaratus had taught me about the law of the conclave. Daemonians despised it because they saw it as a sign of cowardice. But the law was sacred—she would risk angering the gods if she broke it. She had to guarantee me safe passage to and from the field so that we could speak. "Not even Artemisia would break a conclave."

"The same Artemisia who slaughtered an entire temple of priestesses?" Io sounded slightly hysterical, and I understood why.

"What if she's willing to consider Xander's terms?" I asked. "If I could end this war here and now, I should do it."

"She's not going to stop her war," Zalira said.

"I still want to know what it is she wants. I'm going to go and find out."

They seemed to realize that they wouldn't be able to talk me out of it. And maybe this was a foolish decision. It could have been a trap that she knew would work because of who I was as a person. But Artemisia didn't know me well enough to have figured out how intense my curiosity was.

I had a feeling inside me that said this was what I was meant to do. That I needed to go onto that field.

Like it was fated.

"If she does anything, I'm opening a hole in the ground and dropping her into it," Suri said. "If she hadn't raised that flag, I would have done it already."

"Which I'm sure she's realized," I said. "She won't harm me because she knows we can harm her."

I walked over to my horse and climbed up onto it. Luna appeared on my right thigh. I picked her up.

"You can't come. It isn't safe. Stay here. I'll be back."

She made a disgruntled noise and then disappeared out of my hands, only to reappear next to Io.

I led my horse north from our position so that the angle from which I entered the field wouldn't reveal where my adelphia hid. As I rode, I drank a fortification potion and turned on my fury aspect. If someone shot at me, I'd be fast enough to avoid it.

Artemisia waited for me, still holding her makeshift flag. I stopped far enough away to keep myself safe while still being able to speak to her.

I stayed on my horse, planning to make a quick exit if necessary.

"What is it you want?" I asked.

She stared at me for a few moments before saying, "I should have killed you when I had the chance."

"I have been thinking the same exact thing."

"Really? I heard you were trying not to kill people now. Something about vengeance and anger."

"I'm willing to make an exception for you," I said. Dolion must have told her. "I don't have much patience for people who kill children."

"I killed Ilionians."

"Your sisters in the temple, who you vowed to protect. Maia." My voice caught, and I had to stop speaking. I didn't want to show any weakness to her.

"They were not my sisters. And I do not honor vows to a goddess I do not follow." She let out a short bark of laughter, and the sound was cold and empty. "I am not interested in rehashing the past. I invited you here to discuss you and I settling this the way the ancients did. In single combat."

This was what Demaratus had spoken about in the dream I'd had of him recently. Was that a sign that I should accept? "You and I fight and the war is over?"

"Yes. If you win, my army will return to Caria. If I win, Troas opens their gates and lets us in."

This didn't feel like it was my decision to make. I didn't have the authority to speak for Troas.

But maybe I didn't need to have that. Because with my god-weapon and my aspect, there was no way that I would lose to Artemisia.

"A fight to the death?" I asked.

She nodded. "Your goddess versus my god. Then we will see who is right and who is dead."

"I'll need to talk it over with my sisters."

"We'll meet here in an hour. If you are woman enough to show up."

I turned my horse around and rode hard, hoping that it would make me a more difficult target.

But no arrow or spear was launched at me. I again took a circuitous route to return to my sisters.

"What did she want?" Io asked as I dismounted.

"She wants to fight me one-on-one. To the death. When I win, the army will leave. And I will take the eye of the goddess from her weapon."

Ahyana shifted her weight from one foot to the other, like she was anxious. "What if you don't win?"

"Then she thinks we're going to open the gates of Troas to her. But I don't have the authority to make that decision, so I don't think it will be a problem to make that vow." I didn't lead Ilion the way that Artemisia now led the Carians.

"This seems like a terrible idea to me," Zalira said.

"If I fight her and defeat her, then the army will leave and I will have the eye." Which was why I had come to Ilion in the first place.

Zalira didn't seem to think that would be true. "What if the person who takes over after she's dead doesn't honor her deal?"

"Yes," Ahyana said. "What if that person is Dolion?"

That would be awful. "If that happens, we'll deal with it when we get there."

Io had Luna in her lap and was petting her. Luna's gaze followed me as Io asked, "I thought you were trying not to kill people. To honor life as the goddess would want."

It was the same thing Artemisia had just thrown in my face. And it was a little ironic coming from Io, who had taken quite a bloodthirsty turn recently. "I think killing one person to save hundreds of thousands is an acceptable price to pay. Besides, I was trying not to kill out of vengeance."

"Which this would absolutely be," Zalira pointed out. "You've wanted to take out Artemisia since the first time you met her."

That might have been a fair point, but I was still going to do it. And not because of my personal hatred for her. But to save Locris and Ilion. To get the eye. If I could get this army to turn around . . .

This was fated. I was supposed to fight her. I knew that as well as I knew anything else.

Artemisia had given me an hour, so I needed to head back. The route I had chosen was a long one.

I walked back to my horse and beckoned Suri over. She came with a disapproving look that I ignored. "If something goes wrong, you need to make them leave. Head straight back to Troas."

She nodded. "I will."

"Thank you." She was the only one I could count on to do so. The others would try to save me, but if I died, they would have to flee as quickly as possible.

I climbed onto my horse and my sisters came over. Ahyana said, "Please don't die. None of us wants to give that information to your husband."

"I'll do my best," I said.

Io wiped tears from her cheeks. "I feel like someone should say something. Something important."

Demaratus's old phrase appeared in my mind. "Breakfast here, dinner in the underworld."

That earned me a few smiles. I gave them one last, long look and then headed out. Once again I rode my horse farther north so as to not give away my adelphia's location.

As I rode I sent up a quick prayer.

Be with me. Please don't let me prove unworthy of my sisters.

Artemisia waited for me, surrounded by red dirt. She had her war hammer in her hands and looked eager to fight.

As eager as I was. I dismounted. "Swear it out loud. Swear on your god that if I kill you, your army leaves."

"I swear on Arion that if you kill me, the Carian army will leave."

"And I swear on Dea that if you kill me, Troas will open its gates to you."

She hefted her hammer, pleased. "This is going to be a short fight."

I planned to delay invoking my aspect until I was closer to her. I wanted to get as much use out of it as possible.

"It will be," I agreed as I began to head toward her. "You're not the only one with a god-weapon."

I started to run, and she did the same. Exhilaration and anticipation flowed through me. She had no idea what was about to happen.

"Dea Erinys," I said.

That was when everything went wrong.

CHAPTER FIFTY-ONE

I came to a stop. The magic sputtered inside me, as if struggling to surface. I tried the sword. "Dea Nikos."

Nothing happened.

Artemisia continued stalking toward me. "Did you really think you could stand on the soil of my god and use your goddess's powers?"

The dirt was everywhere. They had covered the entire valley floor in it. I would never make it back to my horse before she reached me. I would have to fight.

My aspect was there, but barely.

The fortification potion wasn't working, and the magic started to drain me immediately.

I wasn't going to last.

I wouldn't beat her.

I would die on this field.

A hysterical part of my brain reminded me that I was about to break my promise to Xander.

Artemisia slammed her hammer into the ground, and the shock wave of it swept me off my feet.

I lay on my back, trying to catch my breath, but the wind had been knocked out of me. My entire body ached, as if the soil were draining me even more.

She strode toward me with her war hammer.

My fury aspect was quickly fading, and I tried to turn it off but couldn't catch my breath to say the words. I struggled to keep my eyes open. I was going to pass out.

This was all familiar—I'd had a vision of this moment. Why had I felt like I was fated to go onto this field if this was how it would end? I hadn't even had my last two trials of the elements.

My heart beat faster the closer Artemisia got to me. I felt the sword of the goddess in my hand but I was too weak to lift it.

"Now you die, Locrian."

She raised her hammer over her head, intending to slam it into me.

Luna appeared on my chest.

That caused Artemisia to stop, to take a step back. "What is—"

My little aether dragon roared and shot silver flames at my enemy and I felt the intense heat of it.

Her roar set off something with the earth dragons and they all roared in return, making the ground shake violently beneath me.

Then I heard something that sounded like my sisters calling to me, and arrows began to fly overhead, toward my adelphia.

Five lightning bolts landed directly in the Carian camp and I heard the screams from the soldiers.

Suri started tearing the earth apart, creating another hole to eat up the army.

"This ends now," Artemisia said. She again lifted her hammer to bring it down on me.

But Luna made a circle out of her body on my chest.

Hold on.

It was like a giant hook had been inserted right behind my navel, and I was yanked backward into a black void that suddenly filled with sparkling stars. It felt like I was coming apart and being put back together again, wind rushing around me.

Then I was lying on the ground and looking up at my adelphia.

Luna had brought me here.

"What was that? And did you talk to me?" I asked as she flapped her wings and moved away from me.

I transported you. And yes.

"Lia!"

I sat up and saw that things had gone terribly wrong.

Ahyana was holding on to her ribs, her face racked with pain. Suri was still opening holes for the army to fall into.

And Io was breaking off part of an arrow that protruded from Zalira's shoulder.

I ran over to help. "What do you need?"

"Brace her other shoulder," Io directed. "It went straight through at the best possible spot. She won't have permanent damage, but we have to get it out of her right now."

The best possible spot? It made me think that Dolion was the one who had shot this arrow. Not only because he was the only one who could have made it over that distance, but because he still cared about Stephanos. Instead of killing Zalira, as he so easily could have, he injured her instead.

With an injury that could be healed and recovered from.

I held on to Zalira. She screamed when Io yanked the arrow out. Io poured a salve onto the hole to cleanse and close it and gave me a potion. "Have her drink this."

Zalira opened her mouth and I poured the healing potion in. "What happened to Ahyana?"

"The dragons roaring spooked the horses. She went over to stop them from fleeing, and one of them twisted and fell on her. I think she has some broken ribs," Io said as she wrapped a bandage over Zalira's shoulder.

I turned to look. "Where are the horses?"

"Gone."

That was very, very bad. We should have had about a half-hour head start on the army, but without the horses . . .

Suri finally called off her aspect and I went over to check on her. "When things went wrong, you were supposed to go."

She lay on the ground, panting. "Did you really think that we would leave you?"

Io was talking to Ahyana. "The healing potion doesn't work on bones. Your lungs aren't punctured, which is good. But there's nothing else I can do for you. It will take a few weeks to heal."

We didn't have a few weeks. We had to go now.

"Luna! Can you do that transport thing on all of us? Take us back to Troas?"

No. Too many. Too far.

Given the state everyone was in, we wouldn't get very far just by walking. I closed my eyes. "Dea, I know that I ask for more than my fair share of favors, but I need one now for my sisters. Please help me save them."

I felt a surge of power, and for a moment, I thought that Luna had moved me again.

But instead I turned to see five white horses trotting over to us. Their manes were silky and silver, glittering under the sun.

"What in the—" Zalira started to say.

"Asteria's sacred horses," Io breathed. "The goddess's daughter has sent us her horses."

"Everybody mount up," I said. It was a struggle getting everyone on their horses but we had no other option. We had to move.

Now.

Luna sat with me, and without a word, the horses all darted forward. I reached for the reins, but all they did was help me to hang on. The horses knew where they were going and shrugged off any attempt at direction.

The landscape around us was a blur. The horses ran so quickly it was almost like they were flying instead of running.

And the ride was the smoothest I'd ever felt.

They didn't have to stop to rest or eat or drink. They ran all through the day, straight for Troas.

It was nearly nightfall when I first spotted the high walls and I wanted to weep. We had made it.

Alive.

"The gates are closed!" Zalira yelled to me.

I heard Io behind me say, "And the horses aren't stopping!"

They were going to run us straight into a stone wall.

Just as I was about to throw my arms up to brace for impact, the horses leapt over the wall.

As if it were no more than a few inches high.

They ran for the palace, their gait never slowing. They ran through the labyrinth like they had done it a thousand times before.

Instead of taking us to the front of the palace, the horses went around to the back. There was an entrance there that I'd never seen—it was big and led down.

The soldier posted there saw us. "Hurry! We're about to seal this shut!"

We all climbed down from our horses. I quickly pet mine on the nose and told her, "Thank you."

The horse neighed in response, and as one, they all turned and ran off. I grabbed Luna, and my adelphia and I made our way into the entrance. The ground beneath our feet slanted down.

"You're the last ones!" the soldier told me. He had an axe in his hand. "Back up!"

We did as he said, and he cut a rope on one side and then moved across the path. When he hit the second rope, he turned and ran to us.

A moment later a rockslide sealed the entrance. No one would be able to get past that.

"The other citizens are down in the lowest cavern," he said. "They're gathered there for safety. You should join them."

"I know the way," Io said, taking the front.

Xander was here somewhere. I could feel him. I wondered if he would come looking for me or if I should track him down.

We went down, down, down. It became noticeably cooler and I was grateful that there were torches every few feet, lighting our way.

Io led us to the cavern the guard had mentioned. It was a massive, massive room filled with a sea of people, too many to count. Xander had done it. He had gotten everyone down here to safety. It was mostly women, children, and the elderly. I supposed all the men of fighting age had been called up to protect the city.

I became aware of the fact that water was pooling beneath my feet. I lifted my sandal as Ahyana asked, "Where is this water coming from?"

Io looked down and went completely pale. "No. This can't be happening. No."

She grabbed a torch and darted out of the room. We followed after her and she led us through several different tunnels. I would have gotten lost immediately but Io knew where she was going.

"What's happening?" I tried to ask her, but she kept running.

We came to a small room with a large hole in the middle. Water was gushing out of it.

"The cavern is under sea level. I told you that it could be quickly flooded to fight off an invading army who used the secret tunnels. Like what happened in the Great War, when the Achaeans used the tunnels to attack from inside the walls." Io's voice sounded detached and it was so unlike her that I wasn't sure how to react.

"This will take a while to flood," Ahyana pointed out.

"No. This is the first. Within the next fifteen minutes, a hundred more of these will all start pumping water down here. The engineers wanted to make sure that the Ilionian who set off the mechanism would be able to flee before it flooded completely. That's why there's a gate." Io gestured toward the circular latticed gate that was made to fit the top of the hole, but it looked rusted. "To shut it, lock it, and make sure the water kept flowing."

Zalira tugged on Io's arm to get her attention. "Then we have to get everyone out. You said that there were exits that only the royal family knew about."

"And those are tied to the entrance we just came in. Because the guard set off that rockslide, it will happen at every other entrance. Another defense. The only way to save people would be to lead them up through the palace itself, but that's a narrow path, so we'd only be able to get a few. The rest would die."

"What aren't you telling us?" Suri asked calmly. "How do we stop this?"

She had correctly sensed that Io was holding something back.

"There is a fail-safe at the bottom of the hole. A metal lever that must be pushed in the opposite direction. It will close a door and stop the water from coming in. But it's designed so that whoever pulls the lever will die. There's no way to make it all the way down there and back up before you run out of oxygen."

I looked at my adelphia as they questioned Io, trying to find another solution.

A sense of utter calm, of peace, settled through me. I knew what had to happen.

When I'd first met them, I'd taken a vow to give up my life for theirs. I had thought it strange at the time, but now . . . they meant more to me than I could have adequately expressed.

Quynh and her baby were in that cavern.

Haemon.

Xander.

I loved them all too much to let anything happen to them.

This was what Dea had created me for. I was made for this moment, for this purpose. To save these people and, by extension, my own.

I was Ilion's savior, no matter how much I had tried to fight it.

And I knew that meant I had to die.

CHAPTER FIFTY-TWO

It was a sacrifice I was more than willing to make if it meant all my loved ones would survive. I would give so much more than just my life to ensure their continued existence.

One for many.

I set Luna down and she immediately disappeared. I suspected she was going to find Xander, and I didn't know how much time I had before he came to stop me.

Unsheathing the goddess's sword, I put it in Zalira's hands. She immediately stopped talking and looked at me. "What are you doing?"

"It has to be me. I'm going down and switching the lever."

Silence.

Then everybody began to speak at once.

"That's madness! You can't do that!"

"What are you talking about?"

"You can't be serious!"

Io pleaded with me. "Wait. Let's talk about this. There has to be another way. I just haven't thought of it yet."

"There's no time," I said.

"I'll go." Suri started taking off her weapons.

"You can't swim. Io's not strong enough. And Zalira and Ahyana are both injured. Every moment has led us here. It's supposed to be me. This is what I'm meant to do. I swore in the temple to give my life to save yours, and that's what I'm going to do. We are bound by blood and love, in this life and the next. It will never be broken. I will see you again."

"No!" Io protested.

"The prophecy," I reminded her.

"You don't even believe in the prophecy!"

I took both of her hands, trying to give her what comfort I could. "You do. And I believe in you. Now I need you to believe in me."

She shook her head, tears streaming. "I take it back. You're not the savior."

"This is what's supposed to happen." I hugged her, and the rest of my sisters came over so that we could all hug each other, their bodies shaking as they cried.

Io lifted her head long enough to say, "There is a ladder built in on the left side, and you can use it to reach the bottom. When you get there, you have to pull the lever until you feel it click. That will seal the door and stop the others from opening. Then you need to swim as fast as you can for the surface."

I nodded. "Please tell my family how much I love them."

"We will." Ahyana's voice was broken.

"And always remember how much I love all of you." There wasn't time to say everything I wanted. Xander's light inside me turned brighter. He was getting close.

I went over to the gate and tried to pull it, but it was stuck.

"Why are you closing the gate?" Zalira asked.

"Because Xander's coming and he won't let me do this. It has to be this way. I can't explain. Please help me."

They all hesitated for a moment, and then they came over and began to pull with me. I didn't want to use my aspect yet. I was going to need it in the water. The gate groaned and protested but started to move. We pulled and pulled on the stiff metal, using all our strength.

I looked at the hole, and all I could think of was the dream I'd had, when I'd been told that my fate was in the water. I found the ladder, and the cold water was a shock to my skin as I climbed down. My sisters continued to push the gate closed over me until they finally fit it into the correct position.

"The trial of water," Io said miserably.

"Lock it," I said, my teeth chattering as I held on to one of the bars from the gate.

Suri did that for me, and Io let out a loud wail when the lock clicked into place.

Ahyana reached her arm through the bars and I moved over to her, taking her hand. My sisters all grabbed me, so that we were all touching.

"One for many," Ahyana said through her tears.

"Many for one," I told her. I was glad they were here. I didn't want to die alone.

"Lia?"

Xander came into the room and I immediately released my sisters and backed up. He moved them out of the way and reached for me, pushing against the gate.

"What are you doing? Give me your hand!"

"I can't do that."

"We will open this gate and I will go in your stead," he said.

"No, it has to be me." Xander needed to live. The goddess had blessed him as her warrior. He would fight Artemisia and do what I'd failed to accomplish. He would save everyone.

This was my task—to save him. "I'm doing this for you."

"You are *not* doing this for me! You're not doing this at all!" He strained against the bars, pulling with all his might. I heard a creaking sound. If he was able to get it open . . .

"Xander." I said his name calmly, quietly.

That got him to stop.

"It's going to be all right. You will be all right, and that's all that matters to me."

He was frantic, shoving his arm through the bars, reaching for me. "Lia, don't do this. Grab on to me! Take my hand!"

"Xander, look at me."

His eyes were desperate, his expression frenzied. I knew exactly how he felt—just as I had when Quynh had been pulled from my grasp. I understood why she had made that choice. She had done it to save me, and I was doing this to save him.

Because of how I felt. How much he mattered to me.

And I wanted him to know that.

"I love you," I said.

And I felt the moment our souls connected, my name permanently written into his heart. This could never be undone. I should have given him the words sooner. I should have spent hours, days, weeks, telling him the truth.

I had loved him for so long.

And I saw the moment when he realized why I was telling him now, and the desperation, the terror, I saw on his face was almost more than I could bear.

He stretched through the gate bars, as far as he could. More than anything I wanted to go over to him and take his hand, comfort him as best I could.

But I couldn't. I knew what he would do. He would hold on to me tightly and not let go. It's what I would have done had our situations been reversed.

"Swim over here and take my hand," he said, still reaching for me.

"Xander, you have to let me go."

"Please." The word was desperate and broken, as if it had been wrenched from deep inside him, frantically begging me not to leave him.

That single word, the way he said it—it very nearly broke my resolve.

"I will always love you," I said. "Find me in the next world."

He started hollering for Thrax to bring him something to tear open the gate, and I got ready to dive.

Xander yelled out, "No!"

"Dea Erinys," I said. And then I went under.

I heard the muffled sound of him screaming my name as I started swimming toward the bottom. The pressure of the water rushing past me was so intense that, even with the strength from my aspect, I had to use the ladder to pull myself down.

Part of me pleaded to turn around. Drowning was my greatest fear, and I was rushing into it headfirst. I thought of Demaratus's words—that only those who wanted to live would die with honor.

I would die with honor. And as he used to say, that was all I could ask for.

This was what had to happen. I was meant to lay down my life for my enemies. To protect Ilion. To make up for the sin that Ajax the Lesser had committed. I was Aianteioi—I would recompense for the sacrilege that had been done.

And I was doing it because of the love I had in my heart. The oracle had told me that love would be a tool or a weapon, and I had chosen for it to be a tool. It made impossible things possible, made me capable of things I didn't think I could do.

A silver light appeared next to me. It was Luna.

For one terrible moment I thought she was here to save me, to transport me out of the water, but she swam alongside me. Somehow she was causing her silver scales to light up, and that made it so I could see what I was doing.

My ears popped as my lungs began to scream for air. Begging me to take one breath, just one.

Sucking in water would be the worst thing I could do.

Down, down, down I went. My cheeks began puffing out as I tried desperately not to breathe. My lungs burned and burned, and my limbs started to feel heavy. My head pounded and my ears rang.

Little black dots appeared at the edges of my vision and then . . . there! I saw something shiny beneath me.

The lever.

I grabbed on to it and used the ladder for leverage so that I could push the lever in the opposite direction. Despite using my aspect, my strength felt nearly depleted. I fought against all my instincts to breathe, to swim up, so that I could finish this task.

Please help me.

Then I felt the click that Io had promised, and the water stopped rushing against me.

But it was still heavy as I struggled to swim. I tried reaching for Luna. She could save me and transport me out of here.

It had gone dark. I couldn't see her, couldn't feel her in the water.

Up and up I swam, my lungs feeling like they would burst as the water weighed heavily against me. It was like I was being burned alive, from the inside out. Everything hurt.

My arms and legs felt slow and clumsy. The black spots in my vision got bigger and bigger until I couldn't see at all. I was so dizzy.

I wished it had been anything besides drowning.

It would have been so much better if I could have—

CHAPTER FIFTY-THREE

One minute . . .

CHAPTER FIFTY-FOUR

Two minutes . . .

CHAPTER FIFTY-FIVE

XANDER

I had forced myself to stand on top of palace walls, despite my fear of heights. I had found my mother after she killed herself. I had been in battles where I was certain I would die. Where I was outnumbered, and it seemed that I had no chance of success.

But none of it had ever terrified me the way that watching the woman I love dive down into that hole did.

I'd never been so desperate, so frantic, so petrified as I was when she went under.

She'd told me she loved me. I knew she did. It wasn't something she had to say.

But she had given me the words.

For the same reason I had given them to her.

Because she thought she was going to die.

She had just told me how she felt . . . I wouldn't let things be over now. I was going to spend the rest of our lives showing her how much I loved her.

An insidious voice inside me whispered, *What if she's already dead?*

Erisa was responsible for this. She had pulled the lever to flood the lower levels. If she couldn't rule Ilion, she had decided no one could.

I had thought Erisa had already taken everything from me that she possibly could, but now she had taken my wife.

My Lia.

Thrax brought me a metal rod and I used it to pry the lock apart. It was stubborn but old enough and rusty enough that it finally broke when I twisted and applied all my strength to it.

I pushed the gate up far enough that I could jump into the water. It was freezing but I barely noticed. The only thing that mattered was getting to her.

She should have let me do this.

No. I wouldn't let myself think that way. I would find my wife and save her and all would be well, just as she had promised.

There was a silvery light ahead of me and I swam toward it.

Her lizard was shining, and the first thing I saw was Lia's red hair floating in that light. She'd made it halfway. I swam toward them as fast as I could, begging the goddess to let her be alive. As soon as I reached Lia, I grabbed her and pulled her close. I put an arm around her and began to swim up quickly.

When I surfaced, Thrax and Stephanos were there to help me get her out of the water. They laid her on the ground.

"She's not breathing," Thrax told me.

I climbed out of the hole and went over to her. I refused to accept that as a possibility. I put my ear against her lips, my hand on her chest.

My brother was right. She wasn't breathing.

There was no heartbeat.

Panic filled my chest. How could that be? How could I feel her burning in my own heart when hers no longer worked?

I would breathe life into her. I had seen an old sailor do it once. I would push the air she needed into her lungs. I sealed my mouth over hers, exhaling into her. Once, twice, three times.

Still she didn't stir.

"Xander." Stephanos put his hand on my shoulder but I shoved it away.

No. Lia would live.

"I forbid you to die," I told her. "And you have to obey me."

Some part of me hoped those words would anger her enough that she would come back just to argue with me.

"What if she has water in her lungs?" one of her sisters asked behind me. I turned Lia on her side and hit her back, the way I would if she had been choking.

No water came out of her mouth.

Frantic, I picked her up and held her in my arms. She was so cold. So, so cold.

"Come back to me. Please." Lia had taunted me about not using that word, but I would say "please" every day for the rest of my life if it would bring her back.

I rubbed her arms, her legs, her torso, trying to warm her up.

Thrax tried to reach for her. "Xander, it's been too long. She's gone."

A howl of anguish ripped out of my lungs, and I shouted at him, "No! Leave me!"

I heard Io crying, and I felt the tears in my own eyes as I hugged my beautiful wife to my chest, trying to give her my warmth.

"Lia, don't you know how much I love you? How I would do anything for you? That I have waited for you my whole life? We are going to have the most incredible future together. You will be my queen and we will rule Ilion side by side. We will have children. As many as you want. Io and Quynh will come and visit us. We will go to Locris and see your parents. We will laugh and we will dance and we will know nothing but happiness."

I was only vaguely aware that the crying behind me got louder.

Kissing her cold lips, her cold cheek, I kept trying to coax her back to me. "I will feed you pasteli every day and hold you in my arms every night. I will keep you safe."

My voice broke on the last word. I had promised her. Promised that I wouldn't let anything happen to her. That I would give up my life for hers.

And it was all gone.

My dreams of our future.

Our love.

Her light.

Gone.

The pain was unbearable. There was no way to survive this.

"Take me instead," I said to no one. "Let her live and I will take her place."

I had grown up knowing that the goddess existed. But she had been a more nebulous concept. Something I hadn't concerned myself with because, as far as I could tell, she didn't affect my everyday life.

But if she was there, she was the only being who could give Lia back to me.

"Dea," I said. "Please. You can't give me something so precious, so wonderful, so amazing, and then take her from me. I need her. I am not whole without her."

I sucked in a shuddering breath because my throat had gone tight, my chest constricted. "Our love bond surpasses death. I took your vows in our marriage ceremony and claimed Lia as my own. I promised to care for her and protect her. Please let me do that. Let me have another chance."

There was only silence, only my dead wife in my arms.

"Dea, I will offer you anything you want if you restore her to me. My kingdom, my crown, my life. All of it forfeit if you ask for it. I cannot do this without her. She is my light, my heart. Nothing else matters to me but Lia. Please."

I couldn't stop myself from muttering the word "please" over and over again, pleading, begging, as I rocked my wife back and forth in my arms.

Waiting for a miracle.

CHAPTER FIFTY-SIX

"Lia?"

I opened my eyes slowly. The first thing I noticed was that I wasn't cold anymore. The second, that I was dry.

The third? That I was outside, lying in a field of flowers.

I sat up and looked to my right. "Maia?"

She smiled brightly at me. "Welcome."

"Does this . . . mean I'm dead?"

"Yes."

That was not the answer I'd hoped for. I got up slowly, expecting to be injured, but nothing hurt.

I felt . . . good.

Maia walked over to me and held out her arms. I hugged her. "I never thought I'd see you again."

"Didn't I tell you that I'd always be here for you? You are my favorite acolyte, after all." That made me smile.

She released me and I asked, "Where are we?"

"Think of it as a world beyond our world."

"That didn't really answer my question."

"Always so curious," she said, tilting her head in amusement, and I realized she wasn't going to give me more details.

"That curiosity has helped. We've had to figure out so many things on our own."

"I know," she said with a nod. "I can't tell you how foolish I feel now. To find out that we could have had magic at the temple. Women carry the seeds of life within us, have an ability to nurture and create. Of course the goddess's power was always meant to be ours."

Confirmation wasn't necessary, but it was nice to hear. Maia speaking of when she'd still been alive dredged up some guilty feelings.

"I'm sorry I wasn't there to save you and your niece," I said, the words sticking in my throat. I would always feel guilty that I hadn't been able to help the women of the temple.

"Everything has happened the way it was supposed to," she said. "We are both very happy here. Free from pain, from death, from sickness. Living with our loved ones for all eternity."

"So is that what happens to me now? You're here to escort me to my family?"

"Your grandmother is here, and I could take you to see her. Or . . ." She turned to the right and a door suddenly appeared. "You could go through the door and see what waits for you there."

I was about to ask what was beyond the door but saw from her expression that she wouldn't be forthcoming. I would have to go on faith if that was what I decided.

"Which do you choose?" she asked.

"The door." There was no way I could spend eternity not knowing what was behind the door. It would have eaten away at me.

"I'm not at all surprised."

She stayed put, and I didn't know if there was something else or if I could go through the door. "So I just . . ."

"Yes. Walk through the door."

I hugged her again, not knowing if this would be the last time. "Thank you for everything."

"I'm so proud of you, Lia. I told you that you were capable of greatness. My faith in you was justified. Remember who you are and who you serve."

"I've tried," I said.

She took a step back and gestured toward the door. Gathering all my strength, I walked through the meadow until I stood in front of the door. I put my hand on the latch and turned it.

"Send Antiope my love!" Maia called out just before I walked through. I was about to ask her why she'd said that, but I was pulled through the door, as if by some unseen, giant hand.

It disoriented me, and I took a moment to get my bearings.

I was still in the meadow.

But instead of Maia, the goddess herself stood in front of me.

"Euthalia," she said with a smile so beautiful that I wanted to weep. She was so tall, her long golden hair hanging down to her feet. Her bright green eyes seemed to shine, her skin luminescent.

Her mouth had never moved before when I had seen her in my dreams. All her words had been in my mind. But she was speaking with me as one person would with another.

"Yes, I did speak to you in your mind. Almost every internal voice that you've heard has been mine. Demaratus was the one who got through to you the easiest, so I used it most often."

She had just read my mind. I supposed that shouldn't have surprised me, and yet it did.

But she was a goddess. Her glory was overwhelming. She was so beautiful, so bright, so loving. I was torn between wanting to fall at her feet and worship her and running the other direction so that she wouldn't see every dark thing I'd ever thought or done.

"Why didn't you just speak to me as yourself?" I asked, trembling at the idea of addressing the goddess directly. "Tell me what I needed to do?"

"Because mortals have free will. I would never force you to do anything. The choice is always yours. You have a spark of the divine inside you that can lead you if you let it. But the gods are not allowed to directly interfere in the lives of mortals."

From the stories I'd always been told, the goddess had certainly interfered. "You pulled Ajax into the earth and killed him."

"Yes, I killed him in anger and I was punished for it. The council of gods constrained me for a thousand years. And while I was bound, my son couldn't attack. We have rules."

That explained why Caria was attacking now. Her son had been forced to wait. "What good is it being a goddess if you can't do what you want?"

She laughed, and it was a musical sound that delighted my soul.

Then I realized that was why Lysimache had been able to do so many terrible things. She had said that when she cursed Locris, she could no longer feel the goddess.

"Yes," Dea said. "I couldn't protect my followers from what she chose to do. Mortals are allowed to make their choices, even when those choices hurt others. You can only know the sweet when you know the bitter."

"You should have swallowed her into the earth, too."

"Perhaps. Or perhaps I needed to let things play out to lead to this very moment." She paused for a moment before adding, "And you should know that Ajax paid for his own crimes with his life. I never wanted any Locrian maiden to be harmed."

I did know that. Lysimache had admitted as much. And I was also glad that I didn't have some generational sin that I had to make up for. That the goddess had already taken her retribution on the person who deserved it.

Thinking about Lysimache and her crimes led me to thoughts about the eye and what had happened when I tried to fight Artemisia.

"When I faced Artemisia, why couldn't I use my aspect? What happened?"

"My son's iron soil negates my magic. And mine does the same—Artemisia has taken my eye, but my son has no dominion over it. He can't draw power from it and neither can his followers, especially if they stand on the soil."

The thing that gave them power prevented them from accessing a greater one. At least I could enjoy my afterlife knowing that Artemisia wouldn't ever be able to use the eye.

"Why aren't you asking me the question you most want to ask?" she inquired.

I wasn't sure what she was talking about. "Which question?"

"The vow you took to me to remain celibate. You want to know whether that is something that I require for my followers."

"Yes. Is it?"

"I would never deny any of my daughters the opportunity to love and to have a family of their own. It was always permitted that priestesses and acolytes could marry if they wished for it. Lysimache changed it to make sure that no one would fall pregnant."

I recalled Lysimache's words to me when I had questioned her. "Because she couldn't risk them . . ."

Pregnant. She couldn't risk them getting pregnant. Why would that matter?

The goddess answered my question. "Lysimache was pregnant when she cursed Locris. She used the power her baby gave her. She miscarried soon after, and she connected the two events. They had nothing to do with one another. It was only a sad coincidence. But she believed that the only way to restore Locris would be with someone who was pregnant. It might make it a bit easier, but for the right person, it would be unnecessary. The chosen savior has the power within her to bring the land back all by herself. You'll just need the right words."

"Which are?" I prompted, hopefully.

"You already know them, and in this I cannot intervene."

Goddess save me from the gods and their rules.

She laughed and said, "I heard that."

I could feel my skin flushing. "So I could have . . . broken my vow and still remained worthy."

"I would not hold you to a vow that I did not require of you. It was not something I asked for, and you gave it against your will. I would have my daughters find love and joy in relationships, if that is their desire."

Which meant that I had held back for no reason. What a waste.

"Your worthiness was based solely on your heart. Your determination, your bravery, your perseverance, your kindness," she added, rubbing salt in that particular wound.

"Does that mean I wouldn't have had to keep my promise to you to reopen the temple in Locris?"

"That is different. Promises you freely offer are serious things," she said. "You would want me to keep my promises to you, so I would expect you to do the same. But there was a way that you could have had everything. A different path to keep your promise."

"And you're not going to tell me what that is."

Her lips twitched. "Correct."

It didn't matter now. I was dead. Even though I loved Xander, I might not have been allowed to have a life with him because of that promise. It made the love we had shared almost seem pointless.

The goddess's mouth turned down slightly. "Love is never pointless. It is always the answer. It heals all, restores all, binds all. It is the greatest of gifts and you do not need to do anything to earn it. I give it to you freely because you are mine. And you have given your love to so many."

"Not soon enough. I should have told him earlier."

"He knows how much you love him. And you showed that love in the most meaningful way—you laid down your life for his."

"I would do it again," I told her. "A thousand times over."

Her sweet smile returned. "I know you would. I know the woman you are, and you are so precious to me."

My heart suddenly started to ache. I felt as if my soul were being tugged, pulled.

"That is your husband, calling you back to him. Begging me to let you go. He keeps saying 'please.'"

"That doesn't sound like Xander."

"He has also threatened me several times if you do not return."

"Oh. That's definitely him," I said, and she laughed again.

I rubbed my chest. Would I always feel this way? Would I not be happy until Xander had finished his life and joined me? Would I always long for him?

"Euthalia, did you know that I made him for you? You are the savior, and I had to create a mate who could protect you. Keep you from harm. Someone who could take your burdens as his own, wear your scars on his body. Your husband is that person. It's why he's goddess-blessed."

Oh. That made my heart hurt worse. "Did you create me, too?"

"I knew that I needed a savior. Someone who could protect Ilion. So I made you in my image. To be like me. Which means you have my strengths, but it also means you have my weaknesses."

"You have weaknesses?"

"I have things I struggle with."

"Like what you did to Ajax," I said.

"Yes. I also have to learn and grow, just as you do." She turned her head slightly to the right. "Alexandros is calling me by name. He is claiming his rights as a husband to have you returned, telling me how much he loves you. The life he wants to have with you. Reminding me of your love bond. Saying that he needs you."

The ache in my chest only got worse.

"It has been a very long time since I have felt a prayer so pure and so powerful."

Tears fell down my cheeks. "I wish I could see him, one last time."

The goddess studied me thoughtfully. "There is a way for you to return to him, if that is your desire. You are the savior. You can save yourself."

CHAPTER FIFTY-SEVEN

My heart leapt with hope. It sounded too good to be true. "What do you mean?"

The goddess pointed at my left shoulder, and the imprint there began to warm slightly.

"You bear my mark, with all the leaf symbolizes. Fertility, hope, growth, life, abundance, peace. And, most importantly to you, rebirth."

My pulse quickened. "How?"

"There's still one trial of the elements left."

"I don't understand. You're saying I can be alive again? I thought I had to die to save Ilion and Locris."

Another indulgent smile from the goddess. "The prophecy did decree it to be so, yes. And my nephew is the god of prophecy, and his words must be fulfilled. But it didn't say anything about changing the order of events or about you returning after you had died."

There was a popping sound and then Luna appeared.

Lia!

She flapped her wings and landed on the goddess's shoulder.

"Luna? How did you get here? And how is it she can talk to me now?"

"Your aether dragon had to grow large enough that she could speak and access her other abilities. Sleeping expedites her growth. Which was important because aether dragons can portal to other places. Including moving between realms. Like this one and the one you just came from."

"Luna can take me back?"

Of course.

"It was you who brought Luna to me, wasn't it?" I asked.

"While I'm not allowed to directly intervene, we are permitted to test mortals from time to time while in disguise. And those found worthy can be given assistance."

What if I hadn't stopped to help that elderly woman? I wouldn't be able to return to Xander now. The goddess had set all this up. Every intricate step that led from one thing to the next and ended here.

"But it is up to you to direct Luna," she said.

"How do I do that?"

Dea put her hand over her chest. "Use the bond. Even now, do you feel it connecting you to Alexandros?"

"Yes."

"It's eternal. No matter what happens, the two of you are bound. Soulmates. One soul split into two bodies. You will always find each other. Follow that connection back to him, if that is what you choose. But also know that you could choose to stay here."

I knew what I would be going back to. War. Death. Pain. Destruction.

But all that paled in comparison to Xander.

"You have been worried," the goddess said. "About what you must do in your role as savior. In taking lives."

I nodded.

"All life is precious to me. Even those people who seem beyond redemption. But I have given my daughters the power of life and made them guardians of it. To create it, and to destroy it, if that is their choice. If that is what's needed."

Luna flitted over to me and I held her in my arms.

Are you ready to leave?

"Wait." I was going back to Xander. We could have a life together, but the goddess had told me that I had to fulfill my promise to her. "Can Io run the temple in Locris?"

Maybe she would be so happy that I was back she would be willing to do it.

The goddess walked over to me. She reached out with her hands and her fingers lightly brushed my forehead. Her touch filled me with such power, such love, that it was almost more than I could bear.

"Io will take over the temple in Ilion. She does not wish to marry a man, nor does she desire children of her own. Every living thing is her child. But she cannot go to Locris for you."

Could the goddess see my future as well? I didn't know if I was allowed to ask.

"You will have all the children you desire. Your husband promised that it would be so. Io will fulfill her calling in her own way, as will you. You both have very different paths in front of you."

Should I ask her about the others? About Xander's future? How was I supposed to get the eye back? What could I do to stop Artemisia and save Ilion?

She removed her hand. "It's not good for any mortal to know too much of what is to come. What I have shared will suffice."

"Thank you." It seemed an inadequate thing to say for all that she had done for me, all the love she had given me.

For all the ways that she had helped me.

"Remember who you are, Euthalia of Locris. You are my daughter."

I hugged Luna to my chest and closed my eyes. I thought of Xander.

Then I was flying backward in that same black void with the glittering stars, the wind rushing all around me. We stayed in that place for much longer than last time, presumably because it was a much farther trip.

But the darkness started to close in on me. It felt like I was suffocating.

Until I realized the reason why. My husband was crushing me to his chest and I couldn't breathe.

"Xander?" I mumbled against his neck.

He had been rocking me and went completely still. "Lia?"

"You're holding me too tightly."

"How are you alive? How did this happen?" I heard the awe and the remnants of fear in his rough voice. He shook his head. "It doesn't matter. I don't care how it happened. I only care that you're here. I'm never letting go of you again. I love you."

"I love you, and I still need to breathe."

His arms finally relaxed and I rolled back so that I could look him in the face. He had tearstains down his cheeks. My heart melted at the sight—that he had wept for me. I reached up to trace those tearstains, evidence of how much I meant to him. There was so much love in his eyes, so much joy.

And I knew that he would see the same in mine.

My adelphia gathered around us, all asking questions. Telling me how happy they were to see me.

Ahyana said, "When you said you'd see us again, I didn't know you meant a few minutes later!"

"Neither did I," I said, and she laughed.

Xander kept touching me, as if to reassure himself that I was really there. This went on for a little while. We both ignored everyone else talking and focused on each other.

"What did I tell you about dying?" he asked.

"Not to."

"You never listen. You are not allowed to die again. Do you understand?"

"I swear that I won't."

"My sweet oath-breaker," he said with so much tenderness that my heart ached. We both knew I couldn't promise him that. "Does this mean the prophecy has been fulfilled?"

"The part where I endure trials and die? Yes, that's over." The rest of it still needed to happen. I had to save Ilion.

Then he announced, "You need to rest. I'm taking you to our room."

I tried to get up, but he wouldn't let me. He stood with me in his arms.

"You can't carry me all the way back to our room."

"Don't impugn my manhood, wife."

"Put me down for a moment," I said. "Let me say goodbye to my sisters before we go upstairs."

He did so reluctantly, and I was surprised to find that my limbs worked well. I felt worn out, but good. I went over to hug my adelphia.

"I'm so glad you're alive," Io said.

"Me too."

Zalira handed me back the goddess's sword. "This belongs to you."

"Thank you." I took it and put it into my sheath. I looked over my shoulder and saw that Xander was being congratulated by Thrax and Stephanos, so I took the opportunity to lean in and say, "I saw the goddess. I spoke to her. I will tell you more about it later, but Lysimache made up the celibacy vow. We are allowed to love."

"Here's a restorative potion," Io said with a small smile, slipping a vial into my hand. "I think you'll need it."

I drank it and gave back the empty vial.

"And we should probably sleep in a different wing of the palace tonight," Ahyana teased.

Zalira grinned at me. "Or down here in the cavern."

"Or you could go find the people you love and tell them what I just told you," I said.

I saw their eyes light up with possibilities as Xander came back over and swept me up into his arms.

"Are you really going to carry me the entire way back?" I asked.

"Yes. Now hush. You're ruining my concentration."

He maneuvered his way through the tunnels easily, carrying me as if I weighed nothing. I reached up to stroke his face. "You were crying."

"You died."

"I don't recommend it," I said, making him smile. "I saw the goddess. She said you were begging for me to come back. And that you do, in fact, know how to use the word 'please.' All it took was me being dead."

He laughed and it sounded weaker than it usually did, as if his emotions were still too raw. "What else did the goddess say?"

"She said she created you specifically for me."

"Did she? I'm older than you, so it stands to reason that she created you for me."

I shook my head. "She also said we were fated. Two halves of a whole, longing to be reunited. That we would always find each other."

"She was right. Our souls are tethered."

"And she mentioned that you told her I could have as many children as I wanted."

He laughed again, and he sounded more like himself this time. "How did you come back? Did the goddess just send you?"

"No, it was Luna. Part of being an aether dragon is that she can move between realms and create portals that she uses to travel. I held her in my arms, thought of you, and she brought me back. Now aren't you glad you didn't throw her out a window?"

"That depends on whether she's going to get more of her sparkles on my floor."

"It's aether," I told him.

"It's still messy."

I laid my head on his shoulder. "Do you know who tried to flood the lower levels?"

"Erisa." His arms tightened around me.

"How do you know?"

"She killed the guards outside of her room. Poison."

That didn't surprise me. Pathetic.

He went on. "She also poisoned Kyros. He's dead."

"What?" That was horrible. What mother would kill her own child?

"I don't think she expects to survive, so I would guess that she killed her son to spare him from suffering."

"Where is she now?"

His arms tightened again. "I don't know. She has disappeared. I have my men looking for her. But she knew about the flooding mechanism, and I think she would rather see Troas destroyed if she can't rule it."

I had only thought her power hungry. I had never imagined that she was this evil. "She was desperate and didn't see a way to win, so she wanted to make sure that everyone else lost."

"And she very nearly succeeded. She almost took you from me."

Now I was the one wrapping my arms around his neck tighter. "You really can put me down. I can walk."

"What did I tell you about my stamina?"

That it was extensive. My stomach fluttered at the idea that I might soon get to test it.

And while my first seduction attempt had been successful in the past, my second had not, and it felt like everything had changed. Now that we had admitted our love, it was different and I was a bit out of my element.

We stayed silent as he continued his ascent up the stairs.

My heart began to beat louder with every step that we took. He didn't know what the goddess had told me, and I was trying to think of the best way to share the good news with him.

When we reached our room, he took me inside and then finally put me down. He locked our bedroom door. "You should take a bath," he said.

The idea of voluntarily getting into another body of water . . . a shiver passed through me. "I don't want to go into the water alone. Will you come and help me?"

He looked slightly confused but nodded. "Yes."

We walked hand in hand into the washroom. He stood in front of me and undid my belt, letting it fall. He then took my tunic, lifting it clear of my body.

And then he averted his gaze.

Which was both sweet and silly. It wasn't anything he hadn't seen before. I was about to say as much, but then I saw the muscle flicker in his jaw, the tension in his arms. He was trying to restrain himself.

Not sure of what to do, I took off my sword sheath and undergarments and then slid into the pool, sitting on the ledge and letting out a deep sigh.

"Were you hoping I would scrub your back?" he asked.

I leaned forward and looked at him over my shoulder. "It only seems fair since I did it for you."

He sat on the edge of the pool, his legs in the water behind me. The sponge made contact with my back and he rubbed it in slow circles. I sighed again, feeling relaxed.

He finished and moved his hand away. Then I heard him filling a pitcher with water, which he poured over my head. He worked soap into my hair, his fingers reflexively moving across my scalp, and it was the most luxurious thing I had ever felt. He was so tender, so gentle, so loving.

Then he rinsed me off and I felt him stand up.

"What are you doing?" I asked. "I wanted all of you in the water with me."

He did exactly as I asked, joining me while fully clothed.

I let out a little laugh. "You have your tunic on."

Xander agreed with me. "I do."

"Why?"

"Safer." The one word was his only explanation.

This was not what I'd had in mind. I moved over to put my arms around his neck. Wanting his fingers on my skin.

But he didn't touch me.

"What are you thinking?" I asked.

"The Great War was fought for the love of a woman, something I never understood until you. I would let every person in this city die if it meant you were safe and with me."

He wouldn't because he was far too honorable and too good of a king, but it meant so much to me that he would say it.

His gaze flickered off to the side. "A part of me feels that I don't deserve your love. I failed you."

"You didn't fail me. I made a choice. And no one *deserves* love," I said before kissing his cheek gently. "We're all flawed, broken creatures. We love in spite of what we deserve. And I see you, just as you see me. I know and love every part of you, Alexandros of Ilion. The good and the bad. The dark and the light. And I will love every side of you, every facet, every piece, no matter what."

The knot in his throat bobbed, and he said, "We should get out. I'll be right back."

He quickly stood and got out of the pool, dripping water all over the tile. He went into our bedroom.

A few minutes later he was back, in dry clothing, and I was very disappointed. He held out a linen for me to use to dry off with. I stood up and walked toward him. He kept his gaze on my face.

Then he wrapped the linen around me and used a different one to dry off my hair.

When he was done, he led me out to our room and had me get into bed. He kissed me on the forehead and said, "I'll be right outside."

He was nearly to the door when I finally registered what he had said. "You're leaving me?"

"I'm not going far."

"No. I want you to stay."

"Lia—"

"Xander, I want you to stay and make me your wife in more than just name."

CHAPTER FIFTY-EIGHT

"You just died," my husband pointed out.

"All the more reason to seize the day. Because now I'm alive and I feel good." Better than good.

He began to walk toward me hesitantly, almost as if he didn't intend to do so. "Your vow."

"The goddess told me that no such vow exists. Lysimache did it to prevent priestesses from becoming pregnant. She thought it would give them more power."

His eyes darkened at this information. I saw the way his chest began to move more rapidly as his breathing turned shallow.

"I came back for you. Because then, now, I always love you," I told him. I stood up, using one hand to hold on to the linen. "And you have me. All of me. My heart, my mind, my soul. And now I want you to have my body."

His hands involuntarily went to my shoulders, and I heard the stifled groan he made in the back of his throat. I reached up with my free hand to run my fingers along the contours of his face. "Yield to me, Xander."

I felt his fingers digging into my skin and the pressure was delicious. He didn't say anything to my invitation, didn't move.

"The last time I saw you speechless was when I told you I could do magic," I said.

"*You* are magic." The words broke free from his chest, rumbling and deep. "I have been under your spell since the day I met you."

"Xander . . ."

I saw him shudder in response. "It shatters me every time you use my name."

Leaning up, I pressed a kiss to the underside of his jaw and said, "I seem to recall you telling me that I would be calling it out over and over again."

Golden flames burned in his eyes. "I think I should make good on my promise."

Now I was the one trembling. "I do, too. I wouldn't want you to be an oath-breaker."

"You're not impaired in any way? The goddess didn't give you honeyed wine?"

I smiled. "No."

His voice turned hoarse. "I'm afraid that if I really touch you, you'll disappear. That this is some fever dream and you're not actually here."

I reached for his left hand and took it from my shoulder, placing it directly over my heart. "I'm very alive."

He left his hand where I had placed it. "This seems like such a momentous occasion, I feel as if I should make a speech."

"We have done enough talking," I told him.

My husband looked at me with such tenderness, such warmth, such love, that it made my heart overflow. He leaned in to kiss me. Brushing softly, sweetly against my lips. Kisses light as butterfly wings. Devastatingly sensual. He kissed me like I was a gift. Cherished.

Adored.

Every pass of his lips, every sweet and delicate touch, told me how he felt. They were all expressions of how much he loved me.

But he had lit a fire inside me long ago, one that was always simmering beneath the surface, waiting, wanting to be fed. It demanded more.

He moved his mouth from mine and I tried to follow after him. But he ran his lips along my jaw, stopping to press a kiss here and there. He moved to my earlobe and sucked it into his mouth, filling me with a shivery and trembly pleasure. Then he scraped his teeth along the skin, and this new sensation had me melting toward him.

"You like it when I talk. When I tell you how beautiful you are and how much I want you." He murmured the hot words against my wet earlobe, and my shivering got worse.

Then he nipped at my neck and moved his way down to the pulse point near my collarbone, which he sucked into his mouth, rendering me mindless.

"You like when I tell you how much I want you," he said. "And when I say how much I enjoy those breathless, erotic moans you're making right now."

I hadn't even realized.

Then he released me, taking a step back. I was panting, not understanding what he was doing. "Why—"

"Drop the linen," he commanded me.

That sent a lightning bolt of desire shooting down my spine. Without hesitation I released the linen, letting it fall to my feet.

I didn't try to hide myself. I wasn't embarrassed, wasn't shy. I welcomed his gaze. I wanted him to look at me. To watch the way his muscles clenched and tightened, how hungry his expression became, the way desire lit up his eyes.

It made me feel powerful.

"Do you know that you have the most perfect breasts in all of Ilion?" His voice was ragged, edged with want.

"You might be a little biased," I said, enjoying the way his gaze heated my skin, as if he were touching me. "I'm certain there are many people who would disagree with you."

"I will gut anyone who would dare to speak such a lie." Then to my great joy, his hands went to his belt, which he quickly removed.

His tunic was next, and I realized how much I loved watching him undressing, baring himself to me.

Then he started unwrapping his undergarment and the air in my lungs solidified. When he finished, my mouth went dry and my mind stopped working. He was magnificent. There was no other word to describe him.

We had been hiding from each other for so long, keeping secrets, telling each other lies, but now we were both totally vulnerable. Open.

Nothing between us.

There was an ache inside me that needed . . . something. "What do I do?" I asked.

"What is it you want to do?" His voice was silky and seductive.

"I want to kiss you. Touch you . . . everywhere. Do things that will make your eyes roll back in your head."

"If you knew how little effort that would take on your part to accomplish, I don't think I'd ever have a moment's peace again," he said with a strained laugh.

"Would you mind?"

"Not in the least."

When I took a step toward him, he held up his hand. "Stay there. Not yet. Give me a moment longer. I have imagined this so many times that I want to savor it. And I won't have your first time—our first time—be over too soon. I won't let you rush me."

"Have you seen yourself?" I demanded, impatient.

"Only in the mirror."

"I never would have imagined that I could be jealous of an inanimate object."

He laughed again. "I give you my royal permission to look upon me as often and as long as you'd like."

"I am going to take advantage of that offer."

"I'm glad that the way I look pleases you."

"It drives me to madness," I confessed.

"Good. It means we are suffering from the same affliction. Because I have not felt entirely myself since I first laid eyes on you. You've turned me into something new. Something better. The man I have always hoped I would be."

His words made me melt, had my heart expanding in my chest. I loved him so much that—

Then he reached for me and dragged me against him and I lost the ability to think. Our heated flesh pressed together . . . it was everything I had ever wanted.

"By the goddess," I murmured, reaching up to feel his muscles twitch and spasm under my fingers. This was what he'd said I should do—that I should touch him. I glided my fingertips down, across the ridges in his abdomen, heading toward—

He grabbed my wrist. "Not that."

"Why not?" That was the most interesting and different part of him.

"Because it will be over too soon if you do."

"But why—"

"Lia, I promise to answer all your questions later. For now, let me revel in the warm, naked woman in my arms that I need to kiss more than I need to breathe."

His mouth finally returned to mine, and the smoldering sensuality of kissing him with no clothing in our way was intoxicating. One kiss glided into the next, until my mind was coated with pleasure.

He deepened the kiss, his hand moving to the back of my head to maneuver me into the position he wanted. His tongue claimed mine, hot and wet, stroking, and I could taste his desperate desire. Despite all his claims about planning to go slowly, he was quickly unraveling.

I was no better—I was completely lost in the taste of his mouth, the feel of his body, the sound of his ragged breathing. He ignited me, drowning me in flames.

He began to guide me, leading me to our bed. When my knees hit the back of it, he picked me up by the waist and then laid me down. He followed, caging me with his body.

"Are you nervous? Scared?" he asked me.

I reached out to run my hand across his shoulder. "No. I'm with you. I'm more excited than anything."

"I'm nervous and scared," he admitted.

"You are? Why?" I asked, trying to hide my smile.

He still saw it and leaned down to kiss me quickly. "Because I want this to be perfect for you."

Each word melted into my skin like falling embers. "I'm with you. It already is perfect."

He smiled. "If at any point you want me to stop, tell me and I will."

"My king, that order will never come," I promised.

He made a raw and hungry sound that had my breath hitching and my pulse beating uncontrollably. Then his mouth was on mine again, kissing me into mindlessness, making me woozy and dizzy. There was so much pleasure not only in what he was doing, but in knowing that we didn't have to stop.

That we could be with each other fully, and in every way imaginable.

My hands ached with an incessant need to touch him, to hold him against me, to explore every inch of him that I could. Our bodies moved together, pushing and pulling, ebbing and flowing, and each time I brushed against him, my nerve endings lit up like a thousand fireflies.

Then he moved his lips away from mine and I whined in protest.

"The goddess was right," he said, punctuating each word with a kiss on a different part of my body. "I was made for you. Made to protect you. To serve you. To love you. To worship you. To pleasure you. To taste you."

My mind was so hazy and the things he was doing had me writhing under him. "You . . . you have tasted me."

"Not everywhere," he said with a wicked gleam in his eyes. He proceeded to kiss and nip and lick his way down my torso, his hands palming my breasts. He kissed my stomach and my muscles tightened under him.

"What are you—"

Then he put his hands on my hips to hold me in place and moved his face down. I felt his tongue brushing against me and I arched up in response. What was he doing? He couldn't!

I meant to reach for him to move him away but then he did it again and I didn't want him to stop because it was glorious. He had told me once that he could use his mouth on me, and if I had known . . . by the goddess, if I had known!

Being flame-kissed meant that I couldn't be burned, but this man knew how to burn me from the inside out.

My stomach knotted and unknotted as tension built and built inside me. I closed my eyes to better savor the threads of pleasure that shot through me. Liquid heat pooled in my core, making my entire body feel hot and tight.

"Xander, Xander . . ." I began chanting his name over and over as I arched my back, my body bowing, taut as a lyre string. The pleasure was too much. Overwhelming. I didn't think I could take more.

But he kept proving me wrong. He filled me with shooting stars and sparkling aether that spiraled and coiled inside me. My body sang with pleasure, feverish, yearning. I felt the same icy heat and fiery cold that I did while doing magic. It flooded into me, lifting me higher and higher.

Then suddenly, shockingly, the tension inside me snapped. I violently shuddered, quaking as I cried out—falling, falling, falling into an abyss where waves of pleasure and overwhelming sensations spread through me, cascades of soul-destroying delight turning me intangible so that I felt like I might float away.

He kissed one thigh, then the other, and kissed his way back up my body while I tried to catch my breath.

"So responsive." His voice was rough with desire. "So passionate."

"What . . . what was that?" I panted.

"What I promised you. The first of many."

I raised my limp arms to him. "I need you."

"Then you shall have me," he said. "In every way possible."

CHAPTER FIFTY-NINE

Xander's mouth crashed into mine. He kissed me, desperate and hot. Fiercely, wildly, with an unrestrained hunger. I was so greedy, so frenzied for more. Our mouths and bodies danced together, and it was like we were breaking down everything that had come before so that we could rebuild ourselves into something new.

Together.

I felt him moan deeply against my mouth. Pleasure coiled inside me, red and burning, leaving me in a prolonged heightened state where the tension seemed to endlessly build.

"Are you ready?" he asked, his breathing harsh.

"Yes." I wanted all of him.

He lifted himself up. "This will probably hurt. I wish that it wouldn't. But it should only be this first time."

I reached my shaky hands up to his face. "I know. I trust you. I love you."

His entire body tensed at my words and he swallowed, hard. "I imagined you saying those words to me for so long it doesn't feel real."

"It is real. I love you."

The look in his eyes stole the breath from my lungs.

"I love you," he said. He pressed himself into me and it felt strange at first. He moved extremely slowly, kissing me while he did so. As if to distract me.

And I soon realized why, because suddenly there was a sharp pinch of pain. I exhaled deeply against his lips.

"Are you all right?" he asked.

"Yes. Keep going." I had certainly dealt with worse than this.

"I'm trying so hard to take this slowly," he groaned, his words ragged. I saw the sweat on his brow, the quivering tension in his muscles, the tight cording of his throat. I heard his harsh breathing, as he held back.

Taking matters into my own hands, I lifted my hips up and pushed into him, until he was fully seated inside me, cringing at the way it hurt. He groaned, "So tight, so wet, so warm," and dropped his head on my shoulder.

My core burned, but I didn't care. This was like a sword being slipped into a sheath. I felt completed. Full in a way I never had before.

We were one.

I did my best to relax, to breathe evenly. To let my body adjust.

He kissed my shoulder, and then he began to whisper white-hot words of desire, of love, against my skin as he set about restoking the fire within me. He told me how good I felt, what I was doing to him, how badly he wanted me. The things he said thrilled me, and every pulse point in my body throbbed. My husband knew just as many ways to please as he did to kiss, and it didn't take long for my blood to simmer, my heart to thud, my breath to stutter.

"How does it feel?" he asked. There was so much care and concern on his face.

"It doesn't hurt nearly as much as the last time I was impaled."

He started to laugh and I joined him. I loved the way this felt—that in the midst of all this, we could laugh and tease and have this joy. I hadn't known it could be like this.

"I have never been this happy," I told him.

Again, the love in his eyes overwhelmed me. "Neither have I."

The pain had abated to the point that I was ready for more. "I have been led to believe that there is supposed to be some sort of movement involved."

He grinned. "There is, if you want it."

"Move, husband."

He did, going slowly. And at first it was pain and pleasure mingled together, until the pleasure crowded everything else out.

"I told you that you'd be my undoing," he breathed against my lips. "But I was wrong. You are my beginning. You are the making of me."

His thick, languid thrusts made me feel like I was coming back to life again, being reborn. Touching and kissing him, moving with him, with our love bond between us, intensified everything. Every kiss and touch was imbued not only with desire but with love and connection and intimacy.

I understood why he had demanded more than just my body. With our hearts, our minds, our souls . . . this was transcendent. Otherworldly.

"You are so beautiful like this," he said roughly. "I love you so much."

That caused an explosion of heat that radiated throughout my body until I felt like I might catch fire. All my feelings—physical, emotional—threatened to drown me.

And my whole life I'd been terrified of drowning. Had actually drowned. But this, drowning in his kisses, his touch, the pledges of his love . . . it was the best thing I'd ever experienced. No matter how hard the waves crashed against me, no matter how much the riptide pulled me under, he was there. He was my safe harbor.

He took my hands and put them next to my head. Then he laced his fingers with mine, our hearts beating in one rhythm, our breath low and hot, humid. And every time he thrust, every time we moved, sparks of need flashed behind my eyes.

My nerves were on edge, my skin feverish, and all the blood in my body throbbed low and liquid. Everything was heightened and it was nearly unbearable. There had to be a limit. Some boundary where the pleasure would cease. Where the sensations would ebb. But we hadn't reached it and all I could do was move and whimper beneath him, desperate for release.

He let go of my hands and I grabbed on to him. Then he slid his hand between us and said, "One more time, wife."

It was as if he had thrown oil onto a fire. It blazed up inside me, and I became a writhing mess, clawing at his back, my moans drowned out by his hot and frantic kisses.

"I . . . I can't . . ." I insisted. It was too much.

"You can. I have you. Come undone for me, Lia."

Waves of shocks, tingles, and excruciating, intense pleasure burst inside me and ripped a strangled sound from my throat. He tore my soul open and my brain whited out. I threw my head back, arching toward him and canting my hips up. I unraveled, completely shattered, riding a bolt of ecstasy that I couldn't have even imagined.

He sped up, thrusting with abandon three more times before his hips jerked and he went rigid, shouting my name as he found his own release.

This moment was ours, only ours. Our hearts, our bodies, our souls, our minds. It was everything.

His face was buried against my neck and we were both breathing hard. Just as he'd once promised, he had brought me to completion.

Because I was complete with him.

With his weight pressing into me, I felt connected to him in a way that I had never felt connected to another person. Everything felt right. Even though death and destruction waited for us beyond the city's walls.

"Are you telling me that we could have been doing that the whole time?" I asked when I was able to speak again. I had been so cheated.

His mouth curved into a smile. "Yes, my beautiful wife."

"I . . . I didn't know it would feel that way."

"Nor did I." He lifted his head and, while still joined with me, braced himself on his elbows to look down at me.

I smacked his side. "You are no novice."

He kissed me gently, tenderly. “It has never been like that for me before. You made it feel like my first time, too.”

This probably should not have pleased me as much as it did. “Let’s do it again.”

Letting out a soft groan, he slid out of me and rolled over onto his back. “Men need a recovery period before they are ready for the next round. I will need a few minutes.”

I propped myself up on my left elbow. “I didn’t need that.”

“Women don’t.”

“Oh. Well, I suppose that’s proof the goddess favors her daughters.”

He grinned. “I favor her daughter, too.”

Not wanting to be parted from him, I climbed on top of him, putting my hands on his chest and resting my face there. We were both sweaty and hot but I didn’t even notice. This was where I belonged.

He brushed hair away from my face and tucked it behind my ear while letting out a long sigh. “You know, you did promise that once I became king, you were going to kill me. I never imagined that you intended to do it in our bed.”

I laughed.

My husband continued to play with my hair, his heart slowing and his breathing evening back out. As if he intended to fall asleep.

Not wanting that I asked, “When did you know that you loved me?”

“When I saw you punch that goose at the library. You captured my heart that night, and I didn’t know what to do. How could a prince love a celibate priestess of the temple? There was no future for us but I didn’t care. I kept seeking you out.”

While it was incredibly sweet, it was also a reminder that there was still something I had to do for the goddess, something that could wreck all this. That we might not have a future.

I decided that was a problem for another day. I would have this night with him and wouldn’t allow anything to get in the way.

“When did you know you loved me?” he asked.

“It took me longer.”

"I noticed," he said with a knowing smile.

"Honestly, I don't know when the exact moment was. It just happened. But I think I started to have feelings for you the same night. When I found out that you had protected me and Quynh, had saved me, it unlocked something inside me that I tried to keep shut for so long. And no matter how hard I tried, I couldn't lock it back up again."

I leaned my head to the side, looking at him. How could I have ever thought that I hated him? That seemed unimaginable to me now.

"I'm going to be so furious if I just got this and I lose it because of Artemisia," I said.

"You and I will stop her. It's fated."

His fingers moved over to my face, tracing my jaw, down the line of my neck, across my collarbone. "I am going to explore every inch of you. I want to know every curve, every hollow, every freckle, every scar."

"That last one will take a long time," I warned, and he laughed.

"When I explore your scars, you will give me the story of each one."

I propped myself up and began running my fingers through the hair on his chest. "Do I get to do the same?"

"You may explore my body to your heart's content. But perhaps now we should sleep. There will be much to do tomorrow."

"Do you want to sleep?" I asked incredulously.

He nodded seriously. "I am very, very tired."

"So much for that incredible stamina."

I giggled when he poked my waist, and then I became aware of a delicious sensation. "The part of you that can't lie? It says you're not tired. And I thought you needed a few minutes."

"So did I."

It delighted me that I had that effect on him. "Good. Because I am owed many, many nights' worth."

He pulled me up to his lips. "I promise to spend the rest of this one making it up to you."

CHAPTER SIXTY

We made love twice more before finally succumbing to sleep, and then I woke him up early in the morning for another round. And every time I found completion, it felt like dying, but in the best possible way—as if I temporarily left my body. It was total bliss.

"Why don't people spend all their time doing this?" I asked him after. I was again lying on his chest while he caressed my back in soothing, swirling patterns.

"Because they have to do silly things like eating and working," he answered.

Both seemed entirely pointless at this moment. "I fear that you have created a monster. That I am going to become insatiable."

I felt the laughter rumbling in his chest. "I am always here to satiate your needs, anytime that you would like. You really are the woman of my dreams."

"More accurately, you're the man I brought into my dreams."

He laughed again. I propped my head up so that I could look at him and said, "It's hard to believe that I used to be frightened of this. Letting someone have this much power over me."

"If it helps, you have even more power over me."

"I don't think that's possible."

His eyes twinkled at me. "I promise you that it is."

The love and joy that I felt abated a bit as I remembered that there was information I still had to share with him. "I need to tell you something."

"Is there another prophecy?" he teased.

"I told you that I promised the goddess to go back and reopen her temple in Locris. Reinstate her worship there. She said she would hold me to that promise but that there might be another way to accomplish it. She wouldn't tell me what it was, though."

When I'd imagined telling him this, I had thought he might get upset. But he looked utterly serene. "Then we'll find out what the solution is. Together. I know that a king should put his people first, but they mean nothing to me without you. You have seared your name into my soul and I'll never be whole again if you're not with me."

"This is why I love you. Because you're so romantic."

"And here I thought it was because of my talented tongue."

Now it was my turn to laugh, and he chuckled along with me. "So you're not worried?" I asked.

"You are the one who said the goddess told you that you would have children. How would that be possible if I was in Ilion and you were in Locris?"

Oh. He was right. I hadn't thought of that.

"You know, Thrax told me what you wanted," he said.

It was such a strange thing for him to say that I wasn't sure how to respond.

"To be treated like the princess that you are, to never let you be unhappy, to make you feel loved and adored every day of your life."

Then I remembered. "I was talking about Quynh."

"I'm talking about you and how things are going to be with us. We will always be together, and I will give you everything you've ever wanted and needed."

"I love you," I told him.

"Not as much as I love you."

I smiled. Was he going to make everything a competition? I feared that I would welcome it.

"Unfortunately, there are things I have to do today," he said. "Training with the troops this morning and then war council in the afternoon, followed by a review of the defenses. Would you like to join me for the last two?"

"Yes."

"But first we should probably take a bath and clean ourselves up."

It was an excellent suggestion and we raced together into the washroom. Not much cleaning took place because, once we got into the pool, sliding against him in the water was every bit as pleasurable as I had once imagined it would be.

We finally did manage to bathe and get dressed, and it was disappointing that he had to wear clothing again.

A sentiment he shared. He pulled me into his arms to kiss me goodbye and said, "I'm looking forward to taking this off you later."

I shivered. "Me too."

"Where are you off to now?"

"My sisters need to know about what the goddess told me."

"And about the unimaginable, exquisite pleasure you've recently discovered," he added.

How could I still blush around him after all that we had done? He noticed and laughed, kissing me quickly before finally leaving.

I was still in a haze of bliss as I went next door to find my adelphia. The door was slightly ajar. I let myself in, but only Zalira and Ahyana were there.

"Where are Io and Suri?" I asked.

"Io wanted to go down and help the healers in the lower cavern and Suri went to watch over her," Zalira said.

I was glad that Io wanted to spend her time that way—getting back to what she had loved most from the beginning. Helping others.

"So . . ." Ahyana said with wide eyes. "Has anything interesting happened to you lately?"

She was teasing me, but I ignored it. Instead I told them everything that I had seen and heard in the world beyond this one, what both Maia and the goddess had said. I also told them about how the red soil interfered with our abilities when we stood on it.

"But Suri making holes, my cicadas, Zalira's lightning—that all worked against the enemy and their dirt," Ahyana pointed out.

"Right. Because you weren't standing on the soil. When we make contact with it, our aspects won't work right." I thought of how I had considered attacking Artemisia in her camp, when I'd been searching for Xander. The camp had been covered in that dirt, so it would have gone very, very badly for me.

"I'm just glad Artemisia can't use the eye," Zalira said, and I nodded.

"My fear is that she'll realize it and destroy it."

Ahyana shook her head. "I think she'll be too busy focusing on her attack to figure it out."

I hoped that was true. Then I told them about Luna, about how I could hear her speaking in my mind, that returning with her had been my trial of aether, which meant I'd completed all the trials of the elements. I also told them about her abilities.

Zalira tapped a finger thoughtfully against her chin. "So she has wings and can fly, she can swim in water effortlessly, and she breathes fire? You add in some big scales, and she has the abilities of all the other dragons."

She was right. I hadn't even realized that. "But Luna's so small I'm not sure what good that would do us in a battle." If she were full grown, she would be unstoppable.

Ahyana got up and moved to sit right next to me on the bed. "So can we now please talk about the best part? What happened with you and Xander last night?"

I had kept so much of my relationship with him to myself. Some of it because it was embarrassing and other details because they felt too personal. Our night together should have fallen into the latter category, but I found myself sharing more than I had intended to with my sisters.

They were both so giddy and thrilled that it was infectious, and every new thing I shared heightened their excitement.

"I can hardly wait for Rokh to get back," Ahyana said with a sigh.

Her sister looked down shyly before admitting, "I told Stephanos about the vow. We are going to get married as soon as this conflict is over."

"Zalira! Congratulations!" I shouted, and both Ahyana and I rushed over to tackle her into a hug. She was laughing, we all were, but I was so happy for her. She had been so completely miserable before and I was thrilled that she would be able to have the life she had always wanted.

So would Ahyana.

I glanced outside and realized that I had been in here so long that it was time for the war council meeting. "I have to go," I said as I stood up.

"We're going to go down and see if Io needs help. We'll tell her and Suri what you told us," Ahyana promised.

When my eyebrows shot up my forehead, she hurried to add, "Not the parts about Xander. Obviously. But everything else."

"That sounds good. I will see you both later."

I hurried off to the council chambers and immediately went over to Xander's side. He kissed me on the temple but was in the middle of arguing with an officer, so I sat quietly and listened. I had never defended a city before. I'd read about wars and sieges but hadn't gained any practical knowledge, while warfare had been part of Xander's basic education.

The entire war council was chaotic. People were arguing and fighting about what would happen and what we should do to defend ourselves. It made me worried. I had hoped there would be a clear plan. It would have made me feel much more confident.

When I said as much to my husband after the meeting had ended, he told me not to worry. "People want to be heard and to feel like their ideas are being considered. But this is my nation, and I will run the army and the defense of the city in the way I think is best."

He was taking me to the outer wall of the north gate.

"I forgot to mention it earlier," he said, "but your brother sends his love."

Guilt lacerated my heart. I should have gone and looked for him, checked on him, made sure that he was all right. I'd been so, well, caught up in everything happening around me. And to me. "Where did you see him?"

"He was training with the troops this morning."

I came to a stop, pulling on his arm. "Haemon shouldn't be training. He should be resting."

"He's doing much better," he said, tugging on my hand so that I'd keep walking. "Io's potions have worked miracles and he's been eating nonstop. I thought we had enough supplies for a long siege but your brother is making me reconsider."

Even if he was doing better, it still bothered me that Haemon was training and being with the army. I wanted him in the cavern with the others so that I would know he was safe.

Xander seemed to sense exactly what I was thinking. He stopped and put his hands on my shoulders so that he could look me in the eye. "I think after being a prisoner for so long he's enjoying being with the soldiers, doing something to fight back against the people who stole him from his loved ones. He feels like he's accomplishing something."

"I understand that," I said reluctantly. "I just want to protect him."

"Lia, you want to protect everyone, and it's one of the things I love most about you. Come on, let me show you the defenses."

We climbed a very high staircase that was built into the wall. When we reached the top, I realized that I could see everything. The fields surrounding the city walls, the docks, the harbor, the forest to the south.

Xander showed me how the outer wall was actually comprised of two parallel walls and that the space in between had been filled with rocks and stones to provide extra strength, and then concrete had been applied to the top so that the soldiers could walk along it. I wondered how this reinforced wall would hold up against the earth dragons.

He showed me an overhang with large slots. "So we can drop rocks and boiling oil on invaders below."

Then it was over to the artillery towers, where the archers and javelin throwers would be. He showed me the ballistae lined up with the window slots. They shot stones and arrows. He explained how it used torsion of a spring made of horse sinew to unleash artillery. I'd never seen anything like it.

"I've had the blacksmiths working on bolts big enough to pierce dragon hide. The problem is we don't have the right size ballista to shoot it, and that's also being constructed." I heard the edge in his voice, that he was worried these things wouldn't be done before the Carians arrived.

He pointed out the catapults along the wall, and the ones on the ground behind it that were even bigger. Men were using horses to drag massive boulders and stones to the catapults.

Xander explained that the goal of the sieging army would be to break through the walls. They would first focus their efforts on the gates, which was why they were currently being reinforced with massive wooden beams.

If they couldn't get a gate open or tear down a wall, then they would try using ladders to scale the walls. They would bring siege towers that would have ramps at the same height as the walls so that the soldiers could jump down and begin fighting.

"Those we try to hit with oil and flaming arrows," he said. "Same with their catapults and ballistae. Anything made out of wood, we want to try to catch on fire."

The Carians outnumbered us significantly. Even with the help of other nations, if they managed to overrun these walls . . .

Ironically, the walls that I'd once hated were now the only things that were going to keep my loved ones safe. "What about food and water? Are you sure you have enough?"

"The Great War lasted ten years. Troas learned their lesson. We have enough food and supplies in the caverns to last for years. We also have underground cisterns and water reservoirs. We will be fine."

I thought of how the Carians had blocked the water that ran to the temple. It had never made sense to me—why would they have done it?

Maybe Artemisia had guessed that my adelphia would be sent out to deal with it. The oracle had told her a Locrian maiden would be the savior, and they used it as a lure. So that they could release the terawolves on us.

What if they had more? For all I knew the Carians had been breeding them and planned on using them in the fight. I mentioned this to Xander and his mouth tightened.

"We need ditches surrounding the walls, but we don't have enough time to dig them."

"Suri can do that in minutes."

His eyes widened. "Describe to me in detail what each of you can do that would help with the fight."

I did, and how we could help power each other but that it drained us.

"But I didn't feel that way when you took my light," he said.

"That's because you're superpowered by a goddess."

"Can your sisters draw from me?"

"Io might be able to since you're her brother, but we only see the light around people that we love when we use our aspect."

He looked smug for a moment, probably thinking about how I saw the light on him long before I admitted that I loved him. "But you felt it with Quynh's baby."

"That I can't explain." I wasn't in my aspect when it happened. I thought of the goddess saying that women were the guardians of life and carried the magic inside us—maybe it had something to do with that. "And I've lost my chance to ask the goddess about it."

He folded his arms over his chest. "Yes, you have, because you're not dying again. Understood?"

"Yes, my king," I said, trying not to sound too mocking.

He growled and then pulled me to him. "Why do I like it when you call me that?"

"Because you're an arrogant, overbearing beast who relishes his power," I responded innocently.

That led to him tickling me and I giggled, trying to wriggle away. But he kept me in his arms. "I may need to punish you later for saying something so unbecoming of a queen."

My heart immediately sped up. "Do I get to pick the punishment?"

Desire flamed to life in his eyes. "What did you have in mind?"

"There is something I've been thinking about. What we did in the throne room." I glanced around. We were not alone—there were soldiers everywhere. So I decided to use a euphemism. "I have been thinking about what it would be like if we were to do that again, only this time I . . . impaled myself on your dagger."

A wicked grin lit up his face. "I know that you have no basis for comparison, but let me assure you, my love, it's a broadsword. And speaking of, aren't you sore?"

I pressed myself against him. "I'm a warrior. Soreness doesn't bother me. Or deter me."

"Yes, I have firsthand experience with that," he said, his hands traveling down my back. He was apparently unaware of the people around us. "So you wanted to go back to the throne room?"

"No. I wouldn't want someone to walk in."

"We could easily accomplish the same thing in our room. We can use a chair or our bed." He somehow managed to pull me even closer. "I used to curse your insatiable curiosity, but it has become my favorite thing. Please know that I am always available for any experiment you would like to conduct."

A man cleared his throat behind us. "King Alexandros?"

Xander reluctantly turned his head. "Yes?"

"Captain Thrax has specifically requested you and the queen join him at the docks."

My husband nodded and the soldier left.

"What could Thrax want?" I asked.

"I'm not sure. I suppose we should go and find out. But not quite yet. I need a moment to put my broadsword away."

Now I was the one grinning. I loved that I had that effect on him.

Twenty minutes later, we arrived at the docks. There were several large ships farther out, which surprised me. They had warned all the merchants and traders away because Artemisia had said they planned to attack by sea.

We found Thrax, who was beaming at us.

"What is it?" Xander asked.

"I have someone who claims to know the queen." Thrax stepped aside, and I gasped when I saw the man standing behind him.

"Demaratus?"

CHAPTER SIXTY-ONE

I was so stunned to see my former battle master that I couldn't speak.

"Stupid girl," he said affectionately. Then he did the most un-Demaratus thing imaginable and pulled me into a one-armed hug. If I hadn't been part of it, I never would have believed him capable of it.

"Good work on the not dying," he said gruffly when he released me. "Your hair is red. What did you do?"

I looked at him, still in shock that he was here. "Are you crying, Demaratus?"

"Daemonians do not cry. There was dust in my eye," he said as he wiped his face. "Let me call for the others."

He turned and shouted toward the boat closest to the dock. Thrax stepped behind Demaratus and pointed to his missing hand and delightedly mouthed, "Did you do this?" to me. I just shook my head at him and smiled.

"Cut off one man's hand and suddenly that's all you're known for," I whispered to Xander.

"To be fair, in this instance one is a lot."

Surprise at seeing Demaratus in person had impaired my manners. I should have introduced him to Xander, but my husband did it on his own. He offered Demaratus his hand and they shook.

"I am King Alexandros, Lia's husband. I love her more than my own life. I owe you a debt greater than you can possibly imagine. Thank you for teaching her how to survive."

Demaratus's face crumpled, and he turned his back to us while muttering about how terrible the dust in Ilion was.

It touched my heart how happy he was to see me, but I knew I couldn't say as much or else he might run back to his ship and sail back to Locris.

When he faced us again, I asked, "How are you here?"

"I had a dream where I was speaking to you and you said that you were going to war and needed help. It took some time to gather men and supplies. And to commandeer the Ilionian blockade ships in the middle of the night."

Oh no. "Did you—"

"Minimal loss," he said. "We have brought everyone back who surrendered to be reunited with their families. Ship fights are pathetic."

Soldiers walked toward us, and I realized that I recognized them. "Andronicus! Telamon! Linus! Polymedes!"

It was my regiment. I rushed over to hug them and they all talked at once, greeting me with grins. Then, almost as one, they took a step back from me.

"Who is that large man scowling behind you?" Linus asked me, his eyes wide.

"Oh, that's my husband. Xander. You'll get used to him."

This time I did make the introductions, telling Xander that this was the regiment who had helped me train to run the tribute race. That improved his jealous glower immediately and he thanked each of them for training with me.

"Is Quynh here?" Andronicus asked me, and I heard the hope in his voice.

"She is. That man right there, that's Thrax. Her betrothed."

I saw how Andronicus's face fell but I figured it was better for him to know right away. And it turned out to be a good thing, as Andronicus went over and introduced himself to Thrax and they had a very nice conversation.

“You were supposed to close the blockade,” I reminded Xander.

“I’ve been a bit busy,” he said. “It was on the list. But it’s a good thing I didn’t because if I had, the Locrians wouldn’t have had a way to get here.”

Behind the Locrian soldiers and the Ilionian sailors, there came a large group of men who wore armor similar to Demaratus’s.

“Daemonians?” I asked him.

He nodded. “We stopped in Olyer and recruited them to the cause.”

“We tried to contact them and they wouldn’t answer.”

“I owe this man a life debt,” a Daemonian officer said as he stood next to Demaratus. “He saved me in battle at the loss of his hand and eye.”

“Aristodemus is the commander of the outpost in Olyer,” Demaratus explained.

Saving his friend had cost Demaratus everything. It didn’t surprise me then that Aristodemus would be willing to join the fight if Demaratus had requested it.

We had a legion of Daemonians.

Artemisia had no idea what she was about to face.

Thrax came over. “We should take them to the barracks and find beds for them.”

“Agreed,” Xander said.

“I’m going to go with them,” I said to him. I wanted to keep talking to Demaratus. My husband kissed me goodbye and I walked with Demaratus and the men he’d recruited to join our cause.

“It’s strange that you’re married,” Demaratus said.

“It has been strange for me, too. Wonderful, as well.” He wasn’t going to care about my newfound happiness. “And speaking of relationships, I met someone I think you would like.”

“Oh?”

"Her name is Antiope. She's currently in a coma, but you two are essentially the same person. I think you should marry her. If she'll have you."

"Why wouldn't she have me?" He sounded indignant, and it made me laugh. I had missed him so much.

"How is my family?" I asked.

"About as well as can be expected," he said. "They miss you."

"Oh!" I exclaimed, suddenly realizing I hadn't told him the good news. "I found Haemon! He's alive!"

He grunted. "That will make your parents happy. And that mopey woman who was always at dinner."

"Doria." And they would all be thrilled. "Quynh is here, too. She's going to get married."

"You said you'd keep her alive and you did. I shouldn't have doubted you."

It was one of the nicest things he'd ever said to me. Pride welled deep in my chest.

We passed through the gate and he muttered, "Walls. I can't sit behind walls. It's humiliating."

"Can you do it for me so that I know you're safe?"

He let out a beleaguered sigh. "Fine."

Usually, when I made him sigh like that, he would take a drink. "Where's your wineskin?"

"Left it behind. I need a clear head for this."

He was so talkative that I had assumed he was already drunk.

"You should hate the walls, too," he told me.

"Why?"

"Because as I told you, in all but birth, you are Daemonian."

I smiled. "The walls are going to be helpful because there are earth dragons coming."

"So?"

"What do you mean, 'so?'" I asked.

"Do they bleed?"

I didn't actually know. "I would assume so."

"If they bleed, then they can die." He dismissed the dragons as if they were irrelevant.

We arrived at the barracks and spoke to the officer in charge, who showed the Locrians and Daemonians where they would be sleeping.

Xander rode up then and my heart fluttered at the sight of him. I couldn't keep the silly grin off my face.

"Did you miss me?" I asked him.

"Always." He kissed me. "Thrax told me the Thracian contingent arrived this morning and I came over to greet them. That must be them."

There were a bunch of ridiculously tall men and women, all with yellow or red hair and the same blue tattoos as Thrax, loudly singing and getting into drunken fights, swearing at one another in their native language.

But I was distracted by the sound of a woman yelling. And when I saw who it was, it was like getting punched in the stomach.

Antiope.

"Who is in charge here?" she demanded. She was carrying a sword that I could only assume she had liberated from some guard on her way down to the barracks. This was why Maia had said to send her love. She had known that Antiope was about to wake up.

I ran over to her. "I was just talking about—"

"Where is she?" Antiope demanded. "Where's Artemisia?"

"She's coming. She plans to attack Troas." I quickly filled her in on what she had missed while being in a coma, including Lysimache's treachery and the false vows she'd made us take. I told Antiope that she was going to get the chance to fight very soon.

This seemed to mollify her. "Who are all these people?"

"Ilionian, Locrian, Thracian, and Daemonian soldiers. All here to fight. Including my former battle master, Demaratus." I pointed him out to her.

Her eyes narrowed. "I noticed some of your bad habits when you first joined the temple. He and I need to have a word."

This was not how I wanted this to go. I thought they might like each other if given the chance, but Antiope looked like she wanted to fight somebody.

I hurried after her but my husband was there, pulling me to his side. "What is happening?" he asked me.

"Antiope is going to . . ." I didn't get to finish my sentence because she was already yelling at Demaratus. He kept responding calmly to her while she shouted about his bad training techniques.

I couldn't hear what he was saying, but whatever it was, Antiope ordered him to take out his sword. He did so with an amused smile on his face. I had never seen him smile before. It was strange.

She raised her sword and attacked. I put a hand over my mouth because I had seen her fight before, and by the goddess, she was going to cut off his other hand.

But to my shock, Demaratus was holding his own despite the fact that she was goddess-blessed. Antiope looked as surprised as I felt. Perhaps it was because she had just recently woken from a coma? They went back and forth, neither gaining the advantage, and even the drunk Thracians stopped their arguing to watch them. It was like when I'd seen Xander and Thrax fight during a training session. They had been like two immortal gods locked in an eternal battle.

That was exactly what watching Antiope and Demaratus fighting was like. I had known Demaratus was good. I had never realized that he was this good.

Would all the Daemonians fight like him? If they did, this war might be over quickly. Not even the Carians' red soil could give them the advantage over this level of skill.

Antiope was out of breath, something I'd never seen from her before. She stepped back and then dropped her sword on the ground.

And two seconds later she launched herself at Demaratus and kissed him.

My mouth hung open while the Thracians cheered loudly.

"That is the strangest and fastest courtship I've ever seen," I said.

"Lions mate the same way," Xander replied. "And isn't this what you wanted?"

I nodded. I just hadn't expected it to happen like this. I watched as Demaratus eagerly wrapped his arms around her waist, and then I turned away.

Because I did not need to see any of that.

It was like watching my parents kiss.

And it was strange to have these different parts of my world colliding. I thought of how Demaratus had called me Daemonian.

I was so many things now. A queen. An acolyte, a sister, a daughter, a friend. A wife.

A savior.

Locrian, Ilionian, Daemonian. I had once thought I had to choose one over the others. To make only one of those things matter, but it wasn't true. I was all of them, and it was time that I started blending the separate parts of myself into one so that I wouldn't feel as if I were being pulled in so many directions.

I could be many different things and they were all me.

And I was stronger because of them.

It was late when Xander returned to our room.

"The Carians have been spotted," he said. "They're not to the walls yet, but they will be here soon."

I had spent the evening with my adelphia. Ahyana had complained about Rokh for a good amount of that time.

"He wants us to wait because of my broken ribs. I told him I'm fine, but nooo, he wants to be considerate and caring."

"What a monster. Want me to kill him?" I asked her playfully, but she didn't respond to my joke. I knew she was frustrated. I had certainly been there.

Suri called us over and we moved into position so that we could power her. She dug massive trenches around Troas, which expended a great deal of energy. I made a comment about how we were using the magic so openly.

"Things are going to change at the temple when I reopen it," Io said. "The magic was intended for us, and that's how it's going to be going forward. All of Ilion will know."

The soldiers had gone out and put wooden palisades inside the trenches. The ends were sharp and they hoped to prevent horses or dragons from getting closer to the wall.

Xander telling me about the army's imminent arrival only served to remind me that both he and I could die. The fragility of our existence had become abundantly clear to me after losing my life.

And I no longer wanted to worry about it. I wanted to turn my mind off.

"If the Carians will be here soon, then we should make the most of the time we have," I told him. "Undress."

CHAPTER SIXTY-TWO

A mischievous look lit up Xander's face. "Another thing a man never says no to."

I watched him, my temperature rising with each piece of clothing he removed. When he was naked, he asked, "What now, my queen?"

"Over there," I said. "Sit."

I had placed a chair in the center of our room. He sat as I directed and I went over to lock our bedroom door.

He watched me with desire and amusement in his eyes as I walked back to him. "Does this mean you're ready for your punishment?" he asked.

Where I was in charge and telling him what to do, while seeking our mutual pleasure? "If this is the kind of punishment you plan on giving me, then you have my permission to punish me as often as you'd like."

His eyes darkened and I saw a muscle ticking in his jaw. "Wife, I adore you. I would worship the rain that waters the grass that grows under your feet."

He tended to wax poetic when he was aroused.

Which he most certainly was.

As much as I enjoyed looking at him, I got the distinct feeling that he enjoyed looking at me even more. I slowly undid my belt and then let it fall to the floor, watching the way his breathing quickened. I lifted my tunic up over my head and he growled a curse word.

"Have you been walking around all day with no undergarments on?" he demanded.

I hedged around his question. "I figured this would make things easier."

"It certainly makes them better," he said in a rough voice.

While he could reduce me to a senseless mess who did nothing but beg him for more, I could do the same to him. And I had loved exploring all the different ways to have him shuddering, swearing, and groaning.

"Come here," he commanded.

I tilted my head to one side and lifted my eyebrows.

"Please." He ground the word out.

Him saying that word was always going to be arousing to me. A fact he had quickly picked up on.

And I was so eager for him that I didn't want to delay. I went and climbed onto his lap and we both moaned when our bodies made contact. The way we slotted so perfectly against each other drove me to madness—my softness blending against his hardness. "This is not how this was supposed to go," I breathlessly told him.

"I am so overwhelmed by what I feel for you that I am mindless," he said. "I only want to touch and kiss you and be close to you and I can't think of anything else."

"That is how I feel, too."

"I know," he said before he kissed me. And while our kisses started out slow, unhurried, it didn't take long for them to ignite and turn hungry and deep. His hands never stopped moving on my body, never stopped lightly stroking, caressing, rubbing, and sending streams of fire through my blood. I shook from it.

Then his mouth was on me, sucking gently, and the soft, wet heat had me moaning.

"Will I always be this desperate for you?" I asked, my fingers in his hair, holding him close.

He pulled back to look at me. "Yes, always. As I will for you." The intent in his eyes was thrilling. It was primal and possessive and I welcomed it.

No longer able to wait, I moved into what seemed to be the correct position, and he put his hands on my hips, gripping me tightly. I slid down slowly and he guided me, his eyes never leaving mine. His stuttered groan was the only sound he seemed capable of making.

Once I had sheathed him completely, we both held still. Enjoying the feeling. Then his hands urged me to move. So I did.

He quickly went glassy-eyed, his pupils blown, his corded muscles straining in his shoulders and arms. His hips arched up several times, chasing me. Chasing the sensations we were giving one another.

The friction was exquisite. It quickly turned frenzied and carnal as we rocked against one another. Lightning coursed through me so that every cell in my body felt electric, alive.

I wanted to prolong this, to stay in this moment forever with him, but felt myself quickly unraveling.

"Xander, I'm . . ." I lost the ability to speak. I hurtled toward a violent bliss that felt unbearable, and when the wave hit, I let it take me and followed it down, calling out as I shattered into a thousand sparkling fragments.

My husband was only a moment behind me, his back bowing as if his release would break him in two, his body rigid and his groan so loud I was sure the entire palace could hear him.

But I didn't care.

I collapsed against him languidly, my bones having all turned to warm, liquid honey.

"That was . . ." I started to say, but he finished my sentence for me.

"Incredible. It always is."

"I love you."

He put his hands on the sides of my face and lifted it. "If the only thing I accomplish in this life is loving you, then it will be a life well spent."

Warmth filled my chest. We kissed and it was tender and sweet and beautiful.

He stood up and carried me over to our bed so that we could both lie down. When I lay on my back, something strange happened.

I felt a tiny pulsing light inside me. I put my hand over my womb, convinced that I was only imagining it.

But no, it was there. Was that from last night? Had we . . .

"I think the goddess gave me something very special," I said to him in awe.

"That was me, wife."

I laughed at his grumpy tone. "Not that. I just . . ."

It was too soon. I knew that. And perhaps I was only being silly. Or wishful.

If it was real, when I was certain, I would tell him.

Right now I needed to sleep.

"Geese!" I yelled, jumping out of the bed.

Xander was immediately awake. "What?"

"Geese are honking. Something is wrong. You need to call the alarm."

"Are you certain?"

Was I certain? "Do you think there's any possibility that I would ever mistake that sound?" The noise was faint but seemed so clear to me.

He ran over to the balcony doors and threw them open. He yelled out, "Alarm!"

The sound of the geese got stronger. They were agitated about something. I hurriedly got dressed, as did he, and I heard the word "alarm" being passed among various guards until horns started sounding.

We grabbed our weapons, ran down to the stables, and got on our horses.

"It sounds like it's at the northern gate," Xander said. We rode hard and got there as quickly as we could.

The geese were attacking intruders. Some of the Carians had managed to sneak over the wall. There were dozens of them. Maybe even a hundred. Where were the Ilionian guards?

The guard dogs?

It seemed we had caught the Carians before they started to spread their dirt.

"To me, to me!" Xander called out, and soldiers came rushing from every direction.

Horns continued to sound in alarm and I jumped into the fray to help.

"Dea Nikos!" My sword lit up, making it much easier to see.

These men were here to kill us. To take everything from us. To harm innocent people.

I wouldn't let them.

Yelling, I swung my sword and stabbed in the gut a man who was trying to kick a goose.

I hacked and slashed and hit and parried. I kept an eye on my husband, although I didn't need to. He sliced through the intruders like they were made of papyrus, and they fell quickly to the earth. I didn't even call up my fury aspect. I didn't need it.

Within a few minutes it was all over. Every single Carian lay dead. The geese honked their victory cheers.

Xander came over to inspect me, to make sure that I was all right. "I only have a couple of cuts. I'm fine."

He kissed me and then said, "They were trying to open the gate."

"Alexandros of Ilion!"

That was Artemisia. Her voice bellowed at us from beyond the wall.

My husband grabbed my hand and we ran up the staircase to the top of the outer wall.

I kept my sword turned on so that we could see. Artemisia stood alone in the field, too far away for an arrow or spear to reach her. The Carians had placed long planks over the trench Suri had dug. It was how those invaders had crossed over.

Artemisia held a torch in one hand and the metal cone that amplified her voice in the other.

"I am giving you this one opportunity to open the gates and surrender. If you do not, every man, woman, and child in this city will be killed. Lay down your weapons and your lives will be spared." She paused for a moment before adding, "After my men enjoy the spoils of war, as is their right."

She was so foul and twisted. I yelled back, "You want our weapons? Come and take them!"

Xander squeezed my hand to let me know that would have been his answer as well.

There was a thudding sound beneath us, off to the left, and I held my sword over the wall so that I could see.

A woman had climbed down one of the siege ladders the invaders had used to get over the wall. She was running toward Artemisia.

"Sanctuary! I seek refuge!"

"That's Erisa," Xander hissed.

What was she doing?

Erisa had nearly reached Artemisia when her body suddenly jerked and she fell back. Someone had shot her in the neck. Someone behind Artemisia, who we couldn't see.

"Down!" Xander told everyone on the wall.

"Aren't they too far?" I asked, crouching down.

"Dolion can reach that distance."

That made me think his former phratry brother was the one who had just killed Erisa.

And I wondered if he had done it because she was Ilionian, or if he had done it out of some small bit of loyalty he still had toward my husband.

Xander led me down the staircase, and at the bottom of the steps, Demaratus and Antiope were waiting for us.

They looked annoyed that they had missed the fighting.

"Your guards were killed by arrows, and then someone shot slabs of meat over the wall for the dogs, which distracted them," Demaratus said.

"We need to reward whoever thought of utilizing the geese," Xander said.

If the geese hadn't warned us, and the Carians had been able to open that gate . . . we would have been caught completely off guard. They would have run through this city like a raging river.

We owed our lives to the geese, who were still honking about their win.

I glanced back up to the top of the wall. Part of me wanted to ride out and confront Artemisia, but I knew I would end up like Erisa.

Artemisia had let a thousand years of her people's hatred warp her. I could have become like her. I might have, had it not been for the good people in my life. If I had stayed obsessed with destroying my enemy instead of wanting to help my own people—I knew how easy it would have been to let anger and vengeance rule me.

While I understood that Artemisia had to be stopped, not every soldier in the Carian army was like her. Her former general had seemed reasonable. There must have been people who would prefer to create a treaty and broker peace.

Because the alternative, that we would have to destroy their army down to the last warrior, was unthinkable.

"The enemy is at the gates," Demaratus said. "Tomorrow it begins."

CHAPTER SIXTY-THREE

Xander had ordered the men to stay off the wall—they were only to keep watch from the towers, which were enclosed except for narrow slits.

I was with my adelphia, my husband, and his military leaders in the tower near the north gate early in the morning. The Carian army spread out in front of Troas. We could see the supply train and the earth dragons off in the distance, traveling toward us.

It was meant to be a show of force. Meant to intimidate, to let us know that our destruction was about an hour away.

Io said quietly, "We are the olive tree. We can burn, be cut down, frozen, utterly ravaged, but we will rise again."

I knew that was why the olive tree was the symbol of Ilion, but I hoped we were not about to face all that.

The Carians were busy cutting down trees in the southern forest and using them to bridge the trench that Suri had created.

And every time they put down the wood to cross, Suri would expand the trench far enough to make the bridge collapse.

She had done this several times and we were all getting tired. Antiope was with us, helping us. She had tried out several different aspects, and to no one's surprise, her aspect was fury as well. She passed out after invoking it and had been angry about it when she'd woken up.

"I have spent enough time sleeping!"

Now she had Io's potions on her belt and was ready for a fight.

Suri turned off her aspect and we all breathed a sigh of relief.

There were Carian riders on horses who had large packs tied to their mounts' sides. The riders stabbed the packs with a knife and the red dirt went flying out. They were covering the entire area outside the wall with the soil, and most managed to evade the archers when they got close.

"Hitting a moving target is difficult for some people," Antiope remarked in a tone that made me think she wouldn't have missed if she'd had a bow and arrow.

Xander turned to Zalira. "I need rain to muddy the ground. But it has to be off by the time the towers and siege engines arrive. I don't want that wood soaked—it'll make it impossible to catch them on fire." He had told me earlier that the towers would also be covered in rawhide to make them fireproof. If the wood was wet as well . . .

Demaratus elbowed me, which, again, was so unlike him that I didn't quite know what to do.

"You were right. I do like her," he told me in a low voice.

"Yes, I noticed that yesterday, when you were kissing her," I teased, enjoying his slight embarrassment. We watched the Carian army together and I knew that Demaratus was itching for a fight. "Do you still think that cutting off the head of the snake would be effective here? If I capture or kill Artemisia, would that be enough to stop the assault?"

"It might. It would depend on how superstitious the Carians are."

"What do you mean?"

"See there?" He pointed toward the back of the army and we saw a group leaving, heading south.

Deserters? Or were they moving into a different position to attack?

"The rain from your friend is scaring some of them. They're leaving. If you took out their leader, they might see it as some kind of omen. A Daemonian wouldn't, but these are not Daemonians."

"Artemisia and I did take an oath on our gods that if I killed her, the army would leave." I didn't know if that would work, and it seemed ridiculous to pin all my hopes on it. Especially because I wasn't actually sure that I would be able to strike Artemisia down.

She certainly deserved it. And it would help save and protect others.

But I was so viscerally angry with her that I wasn't certain it would be a good idea. It still felt like a thin line that I could easily cross. I didn't want to go down a dark path again.

Stephanos was powering Zalira and she didn't even look tired. The rain was constant, steady, and it did turn the dirt to mud.

It would be so difficult for them to drag their wheeled war instruments through the muck.

"What is your . . ." Demaratus waved his right hand toward Zalira. "Thing you can do?"

"The same aspect as Antiope. Fury. Which means I can fight really well."

He gave me a look of approval, as if this pleased him, but then the corners of his mouth turned down. "That doesn't seem right for someone who is supposed to be a prophesied savior."

"What do you mean?"

"You have an aspect that tires you and drains you. From a military standpoint, that is a bad thing. If I were the goddess, I would give you an ability that was sustainable."

His words made me think. I already had two powers that I could invoke that didn't tire me out.

What if I had another?

Rokh came into the tower, out of breath. He had been grounded because of Dolion's threat and was only delivering messages inside the city. "We need Suri. Something is happening in the cavern."

Io asked, "What's going on?"

"Some of the city's engineers think that Erisa releasing the water did some damage to the main cavern. There are cracks forming and some rocks falling."

If that cavern collapsed, it would kill every innocent person in Troas. It had to take priority.

Xander echoed what I was thinking. "The structural integrity of the cavern is of the utmost importance."

"I'm going with Suri," Io said.

"Are you sure?" I asked her. We could use her here.

"I can power Suri and help her fix it. And going down there would allow me to join the healers. I think I would prefer to spend this fight saving people rather than harming them."

She was herself again. That made me happy. I hugged her tightly. "Be safe."

"You too. I will see you when this is all done."

"Yes, you will," I promised her.

Suri and Io left with Rokh. Ahyana turned her aspect on and stayed quiet for a few minutes. She turned it off and announced, "They're building a tunnel in the trench just outside the northern gate. I took care of it."

"How?" I asked.

"Angry bees."

Time somehow seemed to pass both slowly and quickly. Demaratus had remarked that we were killing time until it was killing time. There wasn't anything we could do that we weren't already doing. The troops were ready. The catapults and ballistae prepared. The ammunition piled up. Fires had been set up to boil oil, and torches were available to light the flammable arrows.

On our way to the wall earlier, Xander had told me that the labyrinth had also been made ready.

"What do you mean?"

"Why would you build a labyrinth unless you meant to use it to fight off invaders?"

"I thought it was just a maze to confuse them. So that they wouldn't know where to go," I said.

"No. There are all kinds of traps in there that can be sprung. Spikes, pits, fire. Entrances where doors can be suddenly dropped to contain attackers. Archers and shield bearers will line the tops of the walls and rain down destruction on everyone below them."

The labyrinth was another fail-safe—if the Carians managed to break down a gate or a wall, the Ilionians could withdraw and lead them into death traps.

"I'm glad none of that was used on me," I said.

"I wouldn't have let them," he responded.

The supply train drew ever closer.

"That's enough rain," Xander said, and Zalira turned off her aspect and collapsed into Stephanos's arms.

Thankfully, the storm disappeared and didn't stick around, like some of her earlier ones had. But the ground was incredibly muddy. They would have a difficult time maneuvering in it.

But the dragons were so massive. Would the mud affect them? I didn't think so. If they reached the walls, they would knock them down.

"It is fighters who make a city. Not walls," Demaratus said, making me realize I must have spoken my concern out loud.

The supply train made it through the mud because so many Carians went to help push and pull to move things into position.

They began constructing their towers and catapults, and Xander directed the archers to prepare their flame arrows.

But as soon as they did, a massive rainstorm appeared.

And it was only over the Carian army.

"Zalira?" I asked.

"It's not me," she said, her mouth open.

"Arion is an earth god," Ahyana said. "It seems that he has aspects similar to his mother."

The Carians had someone who could also control storms. They hadn't revealed it beforehand because they were waiting for this moment. They had let Zalira rain on them earlier, knowing that it would do her no good now.

The rain absolutely soaked the wood of the towers and siege engines. They would be impossible to light up.

And destroying them with fire was our only option. Otherwise they would use them to batter our walls down and get their soldiers inside Troas.

"Can you stop it?" I asked her.

"Dea Maimaktes," she said, closing her eyes. She held her hands out in front of her but then dropped them, turning off her aspect. "No. I can't do anything to it. I can't even sense it. It's like it's coming from a totally different source."

The construction continued and everything was coming together so quickly.

Ahyana went over to a window and turned to smile at me. "Do you know what they call a flock of ravens?"

"What?"

"An unkindness."

She called up her aspect and I heard the ravens before I saw them. There was an entire legion of them and they were dive-bombing and harassing the Carian soldiers. They managed to stall the construction as the soldiers tried to fight back or run away from them.

When Ahyana finally turned her power off, the ravens flew away. I saw another small group detach from the main Carian body and head south. And I was again left wondering if they were leaving or moving into a different position.

"I hate that all I can do is harry and delay them. I wish I could call down lightning like Zalira," Ahyana said.

Her sister shook her head. "I can only do it for so long, and it essentially turns into harassment, too. It's not enough to stop them."

The Carians finished their building and started moving things into position, despite the mud. The rain suddenly stopped and the sun was bright overhead.

Then one of the earth dragons began to roar, and the others took up the call. The stone under my feet rattled from the sound.

"What are they doing?" Zalira asked.

"It's a signal," Demaratus said. "Look!"

He pointed to the south, near the docks, and the entire ocean seemed to be covered in Carian ships. They had stayed out of sight until the dragon's roar and were heading straight toward the Ilionian navy.

"They'll be slaughtered," I said aghast. They were so outnumbered.

And the Carian navy was cutting off our one escape route. If things got bad, Xander had talked about trying to save people by putting them onto ships and leaving.

That wouldn't be possible now.

At the western gate, they had unveiled a battering ram that had a metal roof shielding it, so that it wouldn't catch fire and nothing could be dropped on the men holding it.

Then the dragons started toward the northern gate, where we were.

"Release the arrows!" Xander called out.

The archers immediately responded, and thousands of arrows struck the dragons and the towers.

Neither one was affected by the flames. It seemed as if nothing could pierce the dragons' scales.

The earth dragons moved into position and began battering the wall, not even bothering with the gate. They were going to bring the whole thing down.

"How are we supposed to set soaking-wet towers on fire?" Stephanos asked, throwing spear after spear at the men pushing the tower closer.

Dragon flame.

Luna suddenly appeared at my feet. I hadn't seen her since she had brought me back to Xander. "Where have you been?" I asked. "And what did you just say?"

Resting. I said dragon flame. Call the dragons.

"What?"

Call the dragons.

She meant for me to use the goddess's dragon aspect. I remembered learning about it at the temple and how incredible it had sounded. Was it possible? There was only one way to find out.

"Dea Drakones," I said, feeling the power surge into me, but it wasn't like my fury aspect. This one didn't take anything from me.

Luna smiled at me and then disappeared.

CHAPTER SIXTY-FOUR

Xander moved into motion immediately. "There are riders on the back of those earth dragons controlling them—shoot at them!"

Then he turned to Thrax. "Take the Thracian contingent and go open the western gate. Lead them into the labyrinth. We need to siphon off some of these soldiers."

Basileia stood next to her brother. "I'll come with you." Thrax nodded and they both ran off.

"Demaratus and Haemon?" Xander said. "I need you and the Daemonians and Locrians to go down to the docks. There are going to be Ilionian sailors and marines who will be stranded outside the wall. Provide them with safe passage."

"Finally!" Demaratus grunted.

I was worried about my brother's safety. I grabbed his arm. "I don't want anything to happen to you."

"Lia, if I am going to be the king, I have to fight alongside my soldiers. You understand that, don't you?" he asked. Physically he looked so much better, but it hadn't been too long ago that he could barely stand.

But I did understand that he needed to do this. I nodded and said, "Make sure you come back to us."

He kissed me quickly on the forehead and said, "I will." Then he went to join Demaratus and Antiope.

I wondered if this was how Xander felt whenever I went off to fight someone. My husband hadn't said anything to me this morning about not fighting today. Was it because he knew better or because he trusted me more?

A Carian catapult launched a large boulder but it wasn't aimed at the wall.

It had been directed at the palace. They knew the Ilionian citizens were down there. They were trying to kill them.

"We have to stop those catapults!" Xander yelled. "Fire!"

Nothing worked. No matter how many flaming arrows and javelins were tossed their way, they didn't catch fire. And when someone shot one of the operators, another soldier ran over to take his place.

Zalira held on to Stephanos and called up her aspect. She used lightning, making it fork in massive waves when it hit the ground so that it could do more damage. She struck the towers and catapults repeatedly, but nothing happened. They still didn't light.

She went until she passed out, trying desperately to help. Stephanos held on to her.

Nothing seemed to be touching the earth dragons. They kept hitting the wall, causing everything around us to shake continually. The archers managed to hit some of the riders, and those dragons stopped their work. One of them even seemed to go mad and went running through the Carian army, trampling people as it did.

"Keep aiming for the riders!" Xander shouted.

It again felt like everything was happening too slow and too fast all at once. We were running out of time. The Carian navy had hemmed in the Ilionians and fired repeatedly on them with stones and arrows.

Thrax had opened the western gate, and Carians poured inside. Even with the traps in the labyrinth, eventually their numbers would overwhelm us.

And these dragons were going to shake the ground out from underneath us.

A Carian catapult launched again, and this time it nearly hit the palace.

"Climbers!" someone called out, and I rushed to the door of the tower to see Carians on siege ladders. I ran over to kick one away, causing all the men on it to fall to the earth below us.

Everyone who had been in the tower came out to help fight off the invaders, to push their ladders away so that they couldn't use them. The archers joined us, firing like mad at everyone at the base of the wall.

This . . . this was too much. They were going to destroy us. We were going to be overrun.

Then Luna reappeared.

What do you need Dea's dragons to do?

I didn't know what she was talking about. Was this some kind of negotiation? "I need them to burn the towers, catapults, and siege engines. I also need them to destroy the Carian ships. And to get rid of Arion's earth dragons. What is—"

I was cut off by the sound of a dragon roar.

Coming from above my head.

It was an air dragon. Flying into battle, carrying a fire dragon. Flames erupted from the fire dragon, catching the nearest catapult on fire. The Carians began to scramble, running away.

Then there was another air dragon. And another. And another.

Dozens.

Some carried fire dragons that they used as weapons, to burn everything the Carians had constructed. Other air dragons swooped down and picked up the earth dragons with their claws, carrying them over to the ocean.

I looked in that direction and, in shock, realized that the water dragon I had seen on the *Nikos* when I'd traveled to Ilion had been a baby. These dragons were a hundred times larger.

They came up out of the ocean by the dozens and were so massive. They began destroying Carian ships, easily tearing them apart. When the first air dragon dropped an earth dragon, a water dragon opened its massive jaws wide to catch it and then pulled it down into the sea.

I turned back to see an air dragon pick up a catapult, fly to a great height, and then drop it on top of the Carian army.

Many of the Carians turned and fled. This wasn't an orderly retreat—they were utterly terrified by the destruction the dragons were creating. Their earth dragons were either taken and dropped into the ocean or they had run off on their own.

They had no way to fight Dea's dragons, no way to stop what they were doing.

Except for Artemisia. A fire dragon raced along the ground, shooting flames as it went. Artemisia rode up on a horse and used her hammer on the dragon, knocking it off its feet.

When it was down, she jumped off her horse and ran over to crush the fire dragon's skull. I gasped in horror, the fury and desire for vengeance rising up inside me.

She had to be stopped. And I knew deep in my gut that I had to do it. I couldn't send a dragon after her—they were sacred to the goddess. I wouldn't risk her doing more damage to them.

Not only that, but if an air dragon picked her up and dropped her somewhere in the ocean, I would risk losing the eye of the goddess, which was still embedded in her hammer.

Artemisia was using her red banner with a terawolf on it to rally her troops. Her killing the fire dragon seemed to encourage them, and they flocked to her. She got back up on her horse and led a large group of cavalry over to the western entrance. Who knew what she would do if she got inside the city?

"She's doing too much damage with that hammer," I said to Xander. "I'm going to confront her."

"I'm worried about her doing that kind of damage to your head."

"She won't. I will stop her." I had a glimmer of a plan and had to hope that it would work. I didn't know what else to do.

"Then I'm coming with you," he said.

I nodded. I wouldn't have wanted it any other way. I picked up Luna and then grabbed his hand. I closed my eyes and had Luna transport us to the wall near the western gate.

"Artemisia!" I called out. "Come and fight me, you coward! I'll be by the northern gate!"

She came to a halt when she saw me. She directed her riders to throw spears at us, but I used Luna to take us outside the northern gate. My poor husband looked ill from being transported twice, but he shook it off.

There was a group of soldiers just east of us that had not been there before.

I saw Dolion with them.

Turning on the goddess's sword, I waited for their attack.

But it didn't come. Dolion only nodded in our direction and led his men away from the city.

Xander had grabbed a spear from the ground and held it in his right hand.

"You're not going to throw that at him?" I asked.

"He saved your life by letting you leave the Carian camp. I grant him his life in return. But we are now even."

She's coming.

Luna's warning was unnecessary. I could see the horses riding hard toward us.

And I found myself thinking of Maia. Of one of the last things she had said to me when she was still alive.

About the acorn that had to be pushed down deep in the darkness, exposed to the elements, to try and root itself so that it could burst out in an attempt to become something new. Something better.

I had survived the darkness. I had been exposed to the elements. I had rooted myself deep in my enemy's nation.

Now I had to become something new to save them all.

"That's a lot of soldiers," I said to Xander.

He shrugged and then drank from his waterskin, which contained the fountain water. "You take Artemisia. I'll handle the rest."

"You can't fight them all by yourself!"

"To save you? Yes, I can. I already lost you once. I will never allow it to happen again. I will kill anyone who touches you."

"I know." Part of me wanted to look into his eyes, to make sure that I had that memory of him in case the worst happened, but I refused to let myself go to that place.

We had to survive. I wouldn't consider any other possibility.

"Stay alive," he told me. "I don't want to have to make good on my threats to fight the goddess to have you returned to me again."

I smiled at him, my heart beating quickly. "You stay alive, too. I love you."

"And I love you." He kissed me long and hard and then we turned to face our enemies.

Artemisia and her men drew ever closer.

My pulse pounded, my breaths coming quicker. I drank two of Io's fortification potions and Xander did the same. I ordered myself to calm down. I knew what I had to do.

Knew what I had to embrace.

It was time for me to do what I had been born to do.

CHAPTER SIXTY-FIVE

It looked as if Artemisia planned to try and run us down. I had expected she might attempt something like that, so I enacted the next part of my plan.

I called down an air dragon. She immediately responded and flew directly to me, landing on my left and towering over us. Xander was on my right, his broadsword drawn.

Artemisia pulled her horse to a halt and the riders behind her also stopped. "So it's not to be a fair fight?" she called out to me.

"No, it is."

The air dragon roared on my command, which terrified the horses, and they began to buck off their riders and ran in the opposite direction. Artemisia's horse remained somewhat steady while nervously shaking its head, and it gave her enough time to get down before it neighed and bolted.

Then I had the dragon flap its wings as hard as it could. It pushed Artemisia and her men back, but that wasn't why I had done it.

The wing flapping cleared all the red soil away so that it wouldn't interfere with my abilities.

Artemisia quickly realized what I had done. I had cut off her power source. She scowled at me. "I am going to kill you."

"We'll see."

The air dragon roared again and flew up, heading for the Carian soldiers. It grabbed several in its claws and took off with them.

Xander yelled and ran into the fray of the soldiers who still remained—far too many for my liking. Thankfully, the guards on the wall noticed what was happening and started calling out to one another, "The king! Protect the king!"

Archers began to fire on the Carians, thinning out the group.

Artemisa stalked toward me, ignoring all of it. "I am the hammer of Arion. I will destroy every person who believes in his mother and bring him eternal glory."

Then an Ilionian soldier ran toward her, with his sword over his head. He must have used one of the ladders to climb down. He was trying to protect me, but he was little more than a boy. Fourteen, fifteen years old.

"Stop!" I called to him.

But it did no good. Artemisia hit him square in the head and he went down.

Anger and fury pulsed through me so quickly, so sharply, that it made me feel sick. I was going to kill her. She was going to pay.

Then she slammed her hammer into the ground, and a shock wave headed straight toward me. I fell backward again, landing hard on my back, the wind knocked out of me.

"Dea Erinys," I said, turning on my fury. I immediately got to my feet and dodged just in time as Artemisia swung her hammer at my head.

I also noticed that my aspect felt shaky. I wasn't sure why—I had cleared out the dirt and taken a potion. I should have been strong.

But something was missing.

Or I was so angry, so filled with rage, that I was eating into my power. I was using it up too quickly.

I tried to tell myself to take control, to calm down, but I couldn't do it. All I could focus on was the need to end Artemisia's life.

I lunged at her but she met me quickly, using the handle of her weapon to block my blow. She shoved me back and I nearly stumbled.

What was happening? How was she still strong? I had gotten rid of the iron soil. Did some trace amounts remain that I couldn't see? Was she gaining power from her weapon? Did she have some other aspect like I did that she had invoked?

She came at me again, and though I tried to push her hammer away, it still ended up grazing my upper arm. It didn't cut me but I could feel the weight of it, realized how easy it would be for her to crush every bone in my body with her weapon.

My muscles had tensed and I could feel sweat pouring down my back. This was not how this was supposed to go. My aspect continued to slip away from me, causing me more and more pain.

Why wasn't the potion working? Had I taken them so often that I'd become immune? Or was it a faulty batch?

Was Xander suffering the same way I was? I glanced over at him but he was strong, fighting off the crowd of soldiers trying to get to him.

"Always so weak," Artemisia taunted me. "You care about your husband. And he's yet another weakness that will lead to your downfall."

"He's a strength," I said, trying to catch my breath. What was wrong with me?

"You cannot win," she said. "You are pathetic. Your goddess is pathetic. She speaks of love and goodness while Arion promises power. Victory. Wealth. The things that matter."

Her hammer hit my sword and she nearly knocked it from my hand. And then, despite me not turning the flame off, it went out on its own.

As if the hammer were stronger.

I again dodged at the last moment, nearly getting hit by that hammer. She slammed it into the ground next to my feet and I again fell back.

She raised her hammer over her head. "This feels familiar."

Luna suddenly appeared at Artemisia's side, flapping her wings. She breathed out a stream of silver fire, which Artemisia ducked. She turned to swing at my dragon.

"Look out!" I yelled to Luna.

She disappeared just in time, avoiding the hammer. She reappeared next to me, curling up on my chest just as she had when I'd faced Artemisia before.

Luna transported me a good distance away from where Artemisia stood. I heard my dragon's voice in my mind.

Remember who you are.

I stood and held up my sword, able to see my own reflection in the highly polished blade.

Remember who you are.

Now it was Maia's voice.

Remember who you are.

And then it was the goddess's.

Demaratus's voice added to the mix—I remembered how he had said earlier that if he were the goddess, he would have given me an aspect that was sustainable.

Not one that tired me out.

And maybe the reason my fury aspect wasn't working was because it was the wrong one.

It wasn't what the goddess had intended me to use when protecting her believers.

She'd had something far greater in mind.

I watched as Artemisia ran toward me.

Remember who you are.

I knew who I was.

And I let go of the anger. Of the need for vengeance. Calmness and clarity settled inside me.

"I serve Dea, the earth goddess. I am her champion and her savior, and you will not harm anyone in this city."

Then I invoked the aspect that whispered into my mind.

"Dea Soteira."

Savior.

And the savior aspect was unlike anything I had experienced so far. Power seemed to come directly from the ground through the soles of my feet until it filled my entire body. Green and swirling and mighty.

My sword immediately lit up again.

I wouldn't weaken. There wouldn't be any pain. I wasn't going to pass out. I knew, in a way I couldn't have explained to anyone else, that I could fight indefinitely with this ability.

It was the aspect I had been meant to wield.

Because this wasn't about vengeance. It was about me filling the role the goddess had asked me to. My job wasn't to get revenge. It was to save her people.

The power swirled into the sword and caused the flames to roar even higher, so strong that I had to momentarily look away. My hand was vibrating, trying to hold on to it.

"Luna, go help Xander," I said.

I wouldn't need her again.

She flew off and I began walking toward Artemisia. She swung her hammer up to deflect an arrow a soldier had shot at her.

She went to hit her hammer into the ground because it had worked so well for her before. But it was as if time were suspended—her movements seemed so slow to me. I remembered the words that Xander had said to me when we had sparred.

Rely on your senses, your instinct.

I did. I pointed my sword, and the flames shot straight at her. She had to jerk to one side to avoid being hit.

"Enough games!" she screamed at me. "You will die!"

"I've already died. I'm not worried about you."

"Your goddess will not protect you!"

She already was. "Your god has abandoned you."

Artemisia raised her hammer and brought it down quickly at me. I met her and blocked the movement with my sword. The two god-weapons were interlocked and responding to one another, power surging around them.

Then there was a release of kinetic energy that pushed both of us back.

She yelled and came at me again, aiming for my head, but I easily sidestepped out of the way.

Something Antiope had once said in training came to me.

The closer you are to the opponent, the smaller the weapon should be.

And it was easy to see why. The hammer was unwieldy, unbalanced. The heaviness of it cost Artemisia precious seconds to pull it back into an attack position, leaving her open.

My sword did the opposite. The weight was distributed perfectly, letting me swing it at her without having to compensate. She spent more time getting out of my way than she did trying to hit me.

Stupid girl, speed is the most important thing in a fight!

I knew better than to let that hammer make contact with my body. If it did, I was finished.

But it was so easy to avoid.

And so easy to take advantage of the openings Artemisia kept leaving me. I was able to stab at her, slashing into her skin. The smell of burned hair and burned flesh filled the air, but it didn't slow her down. She didn't seem to be feeling any pain.

Using a weapon that heavy would require a great deal of energy. She wasn't being powered by her god, and she was going to tire out.

While I felt like I could fight for the next fifty years and never miss a step.

My fury aspect gave me strength and power, but the savior aspect was a hundred times better. Stronger, faster, enduring.

It was simple to parry her attacks, to use the momentum of her swing to push her weapon to one side, again throwing her off-balance.

"Perhaps it is you who should lay down her weapon and surrender," I said.

"Be silent!" Artemisia seemed past reason. She was breathing heavily, holding the hammer lower than she had before. She didn't seem to realize how badly this was going for her. She was so bent on her revenge, so determined to kill me and everyone in Ilion, that she was willing to pay for it with her life.

She swung for my midsection and I pivoted out of the way, cutting a line up her right arm. She began to bleed heavily but didn't notice.

"Your tunic's on fire," I told her. "Time to give up, Artemisia."

Her eyes widened and she used her hand to put out the flames on her sleeve.

I heard Xander grunting, as if in pain. I quickly looked to the right to make certain that he was well.

Artemisia took advantage of my temporary distraction by coming at me, and I decided that this had gone on long enough. Xander might need my help. It was time to stop this.

I began to swing and lunge at Artemisia, driving her back farther and farther. She tried to use the handle of the hammer to block my thrusts, but she wasn't fast enough with it. Couldn't be. She was barely keeping up at all.

The advantage of speed became imminently clear to me. The flexibility that I had in my footwork and bladework, the ability to slash at her while still maintaining a cover for myself, the fluidity and precision I had to batter away at her without missing a step. Her exhaustion made her fall for my feints, and she didn't seem to register when my blade made contact with her body.

And when she tried again to swing her hammer at me, this time I used my speed to knock the hammer out of her hands. When it fell, I grabbed it and threw it as far as I could behind me.

Artemisia put up her hands, as if surrendering. She was panting but still managed to smile at me. "Is this where you take your revenge? Do you cut off my head for all the bad, bad things I've done? Have you lain awake at night dreaming of this moment?"

I thought of who I wanted to be. Who the goddess thought I was.

"Dea Nikos."

Her eyes widened when I turned off the flame.

"I'm going to lock you in a prison cell under that palace, and you are going to rot for the rest of your days," I told her. "You will live your life knowing how badly you failed and that I beat you. Knowing that Arion will never best Dea. You will think of me every minute of every day. But after today, I will never think about you again."

Her smile faded.

Xander made a sound of pain and I couldn't help but look to make sure that he was safe.

"You will remember me," she swore.

And I turned around to see that she had pulled a dagger from her belt and was going to throw it at my husband's back.

CHAPTER SIXTY-SIX

Again, time slowed. Without thinking, acting purely on instinct, I brought my sword down on her arm, cutting it above the elbow. She looked on in shock as her arm hit the dirt, still gripping the dagger.

Artemisia sank to her knees and began to laugh as blood poured out from her severed arm onto the ground below.

"Look, Lia. The soil is still red."

The smile froze on her face and she tipped over onto the dirt.

Artemisia was dead.

It was over. I had defeated her.

I had protected Ilion from her, had done what the goddess had created me to do.

And I had kept my husband safe as well.

There was a small sense of relief, and then I was glad that she wouldn't be able to hurt anyone else ever again. I waited a heartbeat to make certain that she was dead before I ran over to Xander. I lit my sword back up and half the soldiers fled.

The ones foolish enough to stay would meet their ends. I stood back-to-back with my husband, and together we fought as one, hacking and slicing and stabbing everyone who dared to oppose us.

We didn't have to speak, didn't have to warn one another. We moved in tandem, knowing what we needed to do. Keeping each other safe.

When it was over and the last Carian had fallen, Xander was breathing heavily and covered in blood. "Are you all right?" I demanded, trying to check him for injuries.

"It's not mine," he said. And I let him pull me into a sticky hug because I was so relieved that we had both survived.

The guards on the wall above us cheered, and the cheer carried through the city. The tide had turned. Artemisia had briefly rallied her troops, but with her gone, they were fleeing as quickly as they could.

"Do we chase after them?" I asked.

"We'll settle this diplomatically," Xander said. "There doesn't need to be any more bloodshed."

His gaze shifted over to Artemisia's body. "I thought you didn't want to strike her down in anger."

"I didn't. She was going to kill you. I struck her down out of love." The oracle in the Carian camp had told me that love could be a tool or a weapon. And I had used it here as a weapon to protect the man I loved more than my own life. I would never feel bad about or regret that choice.

I would make the same one again a thousand times over.

"That's two hands cut off," he pointed out. "You're never going to live that down now."

"Technically, it was almost her whole arm, so Thrax can be quiet."

He grinned at me.

There was a rumbling noise behind us, and we turned to see the hammer of Arion sinking into the earth.

As if Arion were reclaiming it.

"No!" I ran toward it, desperate to grab hold. The eye was still embedded in it!

But I wasn't fast enough.

It was gone, swallowed whole.

I started to dig, not knowing what else to do. Xander knelt next to me, helping me to scoop out piles of dirt.

"I can't save Locris without it," I said, trying not to cry. I had done all this with that goal in mind. Restoring my nation.

This couldn't be it.

This couldn't be how this ended. I whispered a prayer, asking for help.

A few seconds later Luna appeared next to me.

With the eye of the goddess in her paws.

This belongs to you.

"You are the best dragon in the entire world!" I told her as I took it. I kissed her little head and she looked annoyed.

The eye was larger than I had imagined, and I could feel the power swirling around inside it.

That is true. I am the best dragon in the world. And you should have me take the other dragons back to their homes. They grow weary.

Luna had transported them all here. I wondered how vast her powers had grown and what else she was capable of.

"Take the dragons back," I said.

With a nod she disappeared, and I said, "Dea Drakones," just to make certain that I had turned the aspect off. Followed by "Dea Soteira."

My husband said, "It is very disconcerting to only hear one side of your conversations with your lizard."

"She's transporting the dragons back because they're tired." I showed the eye to him. "She got it for me."

"May I?"

I gave the eye to him and realized what a huge moment it was. There was a time when I never could have imagined myself doing this. "Do you feel anything when you hold it?"

"No. Do you?"

"I do. There is a great deal of magic in it."

He handed it back to me.

"Now what?" I asked.

"Now we go and tell the Carians who haven't already fled to surrender. And then we set about fixing Troas and all the damage that's been done."

There was a long road ahead of us, one that I wanted to traverse with him. So long as we were together, we were on the right path.

Even though I still wasn't sure how we were going to accomplish it.

And I wanted him to have all the information as we worked to find a solution.

"Xander? There's something I want to tell you."

He blinked at me several times. "I can't even imagine what you might have to tell me in this moment."

"I think I'm pregnant."

There was immediate joy on his face, and he hugged me again. I was going to have to take a very long bath tonight and throw away this tunic. He swung me around in a circle.

"I'm going to be a father?"

"I think so. I feel this little light inside me. I suppose we'll have to wait a few weeks to see if I miss my monthly courses to be certain, but—"

"Your word is good enough for me," he said with a grin as he put me back on my feet and his hand went over my womb. "I can't believe it. We're going to be expanding our family."

His words swelled inside my heart until I almost felt like I wouldn't be able to breathe. I loved him so much.

"As soon as we figure out how to reopen the temple in Locris without me," I reminded him.

But he waved his hand, as if that were inconsequential.

"I can just imagine a tiny goddess-blessed boy with your dark hair and honey-colored eyes," I told him, "running around with Quynh and Thrax's baby and getting into trouble."

"Well, I see a smart, beautiful warrior princess who is the spitting image of her mother and is clever enough to wrap her father around her finger." Then his mouth turned down. "Wait. You mean to tell me you went into battle today knowing you were pregnant?"

"I wasn't sure, and I was perfectly fine."

"Wife, I don't ever want you to put yourself in danger, and now it's worse because—"

He was cut off by someone calling out to us. "King Alexandros! Queen Thalia! This way!"

The guards at the northern gate had opened it slightly for us to enter.

My overprotective husband gave me his hand and we walked back into Troas, ready to face what came next.

As my husband had predicted, most of the Carians either surrendered or fled. Those who surrendered were sent back to Caria as a show of good faith from Ilion. That we wanted our fight to be over and to find a way to work together in the future.

There wouldn't be a good deal of trust on either side in the beginning, but I was living proof that enemies could be turned into something else.

The first thing we had to do was gather the wounded Ilionians and bring them to the healers to be cared for. Then it was on to the dead bodies. Suri created a mass grave, and both the Ilionians and Carians were buried in there together.

Someone had suggested burning the Carians, but if we hoped to make peace with them, we couldn't treat their dead so disrespectfully. It would have been blasphemous to them—they worshipped an earth god and needed to be reunited with the earth when they died.

But we made an exception for Artemisia. My adelphia and I burned her together. I used the flame from the goddess's sword to accomplish it, and we all bore witness.

Both the Thracians and the Daemonians decided to depart immediately. With the fighting over, they didn't see a reason to stay.

Basileia told me she was going back with the Thracians, as she missed her home.

"Thank you for protecting Quynh," I told her. "You are welcome here anytime."

"It has grown quite boring here with no one trying to kill anyone else. Thrace at least knows how to maintain their enemies," she said with a wink, and we hugged.

Reuniting Haemon and Quynh was my favorite thing that had happened since the battle ended. They were beyond thrilled to see one another and couldn't stop talking. My family was coming back together.

And I was going to create a new one to add to that love.

The cleanup for the city would take months, if not years. We would have to reinforce and, in some instances, rebuild walls. The docks had been almost completely destroyed, and the harbor was littered with ship wreckage. Cleaning the sea was the priority because we needed the traders and merchants to return.

The citizens left the cavern and returned to their homes. Xander used the soldiers to set up a system to distribute the supplies from the cavern to make certain that everyone had enough food to tide them over.

Once the markets reopened and the traders returned, things would start to go back to normal.

We tried to carve out our own bit of normal by attending Quynh and Thrax's wedding. They married quietly in a simple ceremony, with only Xander, me, Rokh, Io, and Haemon as witnesses.

When I hugged her after, I said, "I have a present for you."

"You do?" she asked. I understood her surprise. Things were still so chaotic in the city that many traditions and niceties were being ignored.

I leaned in and said, "I think I'm pregnant, too."

"Lia!" She sounded so delighted and hugged me again. "That is the most incredible gift! Our babies will grow up together and be the best of friends!"

I wouldn't let the smile fall off my face. I was still trying to find a way to make that possible.

Several weeks later, we celebrated Zalira and Ahyana's double wedding to Stephanos and Rokh. As a gift, Xander gave them homes close to the palace, just as he had for Quynh and Thrax.

We watched them at the hearth of the palace, each woman accepting an apple from her new husband to finalize the ceremony.

"I got you a present today," Xander said.

"It's not my wedding," I said in amusement.

"Pelias and his family were asked to leave Troas."

It didn't make much of a difference to me either way, to be honest. I had kept Lykaon from Kallisto, and Chryseis was no threat to me or my happiness at all. "You exiled them?"

"I asked them politely," he said defensively.

I supposed it was better for Xander to have Pelias gone. He had been working with Erisa and was supremely untrustworthy. The council needed a better archon than him. "When you asked politely, did you say 'please'?"

He leaned in and nipped at my neck. "You're the only person I say 'please' to."

My breathing hitched, which he noticed. "Later," he promised.

We danced and celebrated until I felt a bit dizzy. I went out onto the patio to get some fresh air and came across Demaratus.

Who was drinking from a wineskin. "Is that Daemonian, or did you have to settle for the vastly superior Ilion wine?" I teased.

"I don't need to be clearheaded for this," he said, nodding toward the party. He hated this sort of thing.

"Why did you come?"

He jerked his head toward the hall and I saw Antiope there, talking to Zalira and Ahyana.

"Oh," I said knowingly.

"I asked her to come to Locris with me and she accepted." He was trying to hide it, but I could hear how pleased that made him.

"You did?"

He nodded. "I offered to stay here with her in Ilion, but she said there were too many shades, too many bad memories. She wants to start over."

"Are you going to marry her?"

"I get the feeling that I'm going to have to wait a long time before that happens, but I'm willing to do so. I've never met a woman like her before. She doesn't even care that I've been dishonored."

Because to any rational person, Demaratus had been brave and heroic in protecting his best friend in battle, and Daemonians had strange rules about honor.

Xander found us. "There you are. Come and dance with me, wife."

And despite the fact that dancing had just made me feel dizzy, I rushed back into his arms. As we danced he pulled me in close and said, "We should go upstairs."

"We are celebrating our dear friends and family," I reminded him with a laugh.

"Yes, but we need a redo of our wedding night."

"It's not our wedding night."

"But it is *a* wedding night," he pointed out.

"Excellent point," I said. He took me by the hand and we hurried out of the dining hall.

We were both laughing and kissing and stumbling around as we went up the stairs, so focused on one another.

Until Xander accidentally ran into someone on the landing and I turned to see Io and Suri.

Kissing.

CHAPTER SIXTY-SEVEN

They both blushed when they saw us. I grinned and decided not to tease them, even though I really wanted to.

My husband did not share in my sentiment. "The celibacy vow gets revoked, and what does my little sister do?"

"You're one to talk," she retorted. "How long after you found out did your wife become . . . uncelibate?"

He laughed and I had to press my lips together.

Io added, "There's something I want to show you."

"Oh, I think we've seen quite enough," he teased her.

She glared at him and told us to follow her. We all went to her room, where she picked up two books. "Suri and I went down to my mother's library and found these."

"What are they?" I asked as she handed them to me.

"They're manuals on how to operate the temple. The rules of what should be done. What the actual vows are. I think they came from Locris."

That made sense—Lysimache would have made sure to destroy any Ilionian copies.

"I'm going to send one of them to the scribes here at the palace so that they can make multiple copies," she said. She went over and put her hand in Suri's. "Suri and I are going to reopen the temple here in Ilion together, and we will run it the way it was always intended to be."

"Maia did say that so long as there was one priestess who still believed, the temple could keep going. And with a manual, anybody could reopen . . ."

A thought occurred to me, and I got excited.

I had the answer I had been looking for.

"Antiope is going to Locris," I said. "And now that we have a manual on how to run a temple—"

"You could ask Antiope to open the temple in Locris!" Xander finished, looking every bit as happy as I felt.

"Let's go ask her now!" I said, handing the books back to Io. I grabbed him by the hand and pulled him out into the hallway.

"Or we could ask her in about half an hour," he said.

"One hour," I countered.

He grinned. "Fine. Greedy little princess."

"That's entirely your fault."

"I know, and I thank the goddess for it every day."

Two weeks later we crossed the Acheron Sea to go to Locris. Xander and I were accompanied by my former regiment, Luna, Quynh, Thrax, Haemon, Demaratus, Antiope, Themis, and her youngest son, Adonis. I had thoroughly vetted him, and it seemed like he might be a good match for Kallisto.

I would leave it to my older sister to decide.

Antiope had quickly agreed to my proposal that she open the temple in Locris and reinstate worship of the goddess. "The chance to begin again, to do things the way the goddess intended? And to be able to have a relationship while doing so? I was worried about what I would do in Locris, and this is the answer."

Demaratus had already agreed to help her with the training since the manuals Io had discovered said that men were allowed onto the temple grounds to worship.

It wouldn't be easy—Locrians had so thoroughly removed the goddess from their lives that I was certain there would be some resistance. I found myself feeling a little sorry for anyone who tried to cross Antiope.

We drew ever closer to Locris. Unfortunately the ship went over a high wave, and I gripped the railing so tightly that my knuckles turned white. I was most certainly pregnant. The light inside me grew stronger with each passing day, and my monthly courses hadn't ever come. I had also started vomiting every morning. My husband held my hair back and told me how much he loved and adored me while I threatened him with an ever-growing list of ways that I wanted to torture him for doing this to me.

The voyage to Locris nearly did me in. Seasickness combined with pregnancy sickness was one of the worst things I had ever endured.

"Worse than drowning?" Xander asked me teasingly.

"Have you not learned that you shouldn't provoke your temperamental, pregnant wife?" I took the gingerroot he offered me, but it didn't seem to help much.

I was on the deck when Mount Knemis came into view. A lump rose in my throat. I had promised myself that I would see it again, and now here I was.

When we pulled into the harbor, I saw my family waiting for us at the dock. Xander had sent them a letter saying that we were coming to visit, but I asked him not to mention our surprises. I wanted to see their faces.

Xander and I went in the first rowboat with Quynh, Thrax, and Luna, and I had Haemon go with the others in the second.

When we pulled up to the dock, my father was there with tears streaming down his face. "My girls! My flowers!"

I started climbing the ladder, but my father reached for my hand and pulled me up so that I could hug him. His embrace was so comforting, so familiar, that I started to cry.

My mother's arms went around us, and I pulled her into the hug.

Then my father let go so that he could reach for Quynh. Doria and Kallisto joined us and we stood there on the dock, reunited at last. Xander and Thrax got out of the boat and waited for us to finish.

"I have a surprise for you," I said, my voice muffled.

"What kind of surprise?" my father asked.

I pulled away and said, "Look."

The second rowboat had arrived.

No one in my family moved or breathed. They all stared.

"Is that—" My father stopped speaking, unable to believe what he was seeing.

"Is that how you plan to greet your long-lost son?" Haemon asked with a wide smile as he climbed the ladder.

Doria pushed through us, going straight to Haemon. "I knew it," she said, tears falling down her cheeks. "I knew you were alive."

He pulled her into a long kiss and then said, "I love you. I missed you so much."

"I love you," she said.

My parents' tears only got worse. They fell on Haemon's neck with loud sobs, and a moment later Kallisto was there with them, crying every bit as hard.

My entire family was together again. I had returned Haemon to them, making us whole.

Xander came over to put his arm around me. "This must make you happy."

"It does," I said, wiping my own tears away.

When they finally released Haemon, I took the opportunity to introduce Xander and Thrax to my parents, explaining that Quynh and I were married to them.

They got pulled into the family hug. Thrax was delighted, while Xander looked uncomfortable but endured it for my sake.

We all went back to the palace and nobody even asked about Luna—they were so focused on Haemon's return and our marriages.

I knew that we would have time during our visit to explain everything. I could be patient.

My father declared that we must have a feast, as I knew he would. I had made sure that the ship was packed with supplies so that we could celebrate. Everything was brought to the palace, and I took the opportunity to take my husband on a tour of my first home.

When we got to the courtyard with the ancient olive tree, he laughed and brought me over to it.

"Who could have guessed that we would come full circle like this? Back to where it all began," he said, pressing soft kisses to my neck.

I leaned my head back to give him better access, tingling from his touch. "Not me."

"You aren't going to try and stab me again, are you?"

"For your own safety, I would advise you not to ask me that question when I'm vomiting in the morning."

He chuckled and then moved to my side to hold me in his arms. One of his hands went to my womb and he kissed my temple. I felt so loved, so complete.

This was everything I had ever wanted.

Xander was everything I had ever wanted.

I would always be so grateful to the goddess for making him for me.

Then I realized that this was the vision I'd had on the day of our wedding.

And I silently thanked the goddess for him, and for letting me have this.

We had celebrated well into the night, trying to catch my Locrian family up on everything that had occurred since we had left.

While obviously leaving out many details that I knew would upset my parents.

Early the next morning, I lay in my husband's arms, thoroughly satiated.

"You should pass a law," I said, "that everyone should spend all their time making love."

He laughed. "I don't have to pass a law for that. It's already happening. Besides, if I legislated it, it would bring the nation to a grinding halt."

"But think of how happy everyone would be."

"You make me happy," he said, kissing me. "And I love you more than you could possibly imagine."

"I don't know," I told him. "I have an excellent imagination."

"I'm well aware," he said with a smirk before he kissed me again. "So should we follow my new impending law again?"

"Actually, I want to take the eye and try to fix Locris. Will you come with me?"

"Of course," he said. "Aren't you going to tell your family what we're doing?"

"No. I don't want them to be disappointed if it doesn't work."

"It will work," he said confidently. "I believe in you."

Every time I thought I couldn't love this man more, he said something to prove that false.

We got dressed and grabbed something to eat, which I promptly threw up, and then walked out of the palace, through the city, and toward the mountains.

Luna insisted on accompanying us and alternated between flying and walking along the ground.

"I don't know that I can build an enclosure big enough for your lizard," Xander said. It was true—Luna had grown again and was now the same size as a dog.

I am an aether dragon, Luna said indignantly in my mind. She could understand other people now, but I was the only one who could hear her.

"She doesn't like it when you call her that."

Luna emitted a stream of silver flame, as if to prove her point.

"Fine, dragon," he conceded, and she looked satisfied. "But I don't know how I feel about her growing an earth dragon tail."

It was true, her tail had begun to change. The end had rounded and tiny flexible spikes surrounded it. I was certain they would harden as she grew. "Then it's a good thing she's on our side."

When we were far enough away from Naryx, I knelt down. "Here will work."

I took the eye of the goddess out of my bag. Lysimache had mentioned that she had buried it in the earth, so I assumed I would need to do the same.

"Before you do anything with that, perhaps we should keep it and then we can live forever, together," he said.

"We will have that in the next world," I told him. I very much planned on having him all to myself for all eternity.

I put the eye into the earth, covering it up. I put my hands flat over the top of it.

"Do you know what to say?" Xander asked, and I nodded.

The goddess had been inadvertently instructing me on what to say since I'd first dreamed of her.

I intended to rely on my instincts here. Fortunately, I knew the right aspect to use.

"Dea Euthalia," I said. The green, swirling magic came up through my hands, filling my entire body. I pictured Locris the way that the goddess had shown me in my dream. Full of trees, grass, bushes, flowers.

I started to tremble under the weight of it, but then Xander was there, touching me so that I could take power from him. It was like swallowing a bolt of lightning.

Our baby also tried to help, but I didn't draw on her light.

I didn't need it.

This was also what I had been made for. I closed my eyes.

The ground violently shook around me but I took the magic and directed it out, coaxing the earth to come back to life.

I felt it happening all around me, felt the magically dormant roots in the ground stirring to life and pushing up through the soil. The pain started but I held on. I would finish this.

Then . . . it was done.

Panting, I turned off the aspect and opened my eyes.

I had expected new growth.

But everything around me was as it had been in my vision. The trees were full size, the flowers blooming. We were in a forest, surrounded by a green paradise.

It was beyond beautiful. It was everything that I had hoped for, everything that I had dreamed about. No one in Locris would suffer from starvation again. We would grow our crops, and life would return.

Locris was saved.

I had saved it.

The enormity of it threatened to overwhelm me.

Fortunately, my husband was there to be my anchor. "Your own name?" he asked.

I nodded. "The goddess told my mother to use it for me." The goddess had put this into place before I was born—she had named me after this aspect so that I would know to use it to restore Locris. "'Euthalia' means well blooming, flourishing, flowering."

"You certainly did that. If I hadn't seen it with my own eyes, I wouldn't have believed it. I'm shocked that you're still awake."

"With you by my side, I can do anything," I told him.

He kissed me and then helped me to stand. I was a little wobbly, but not too much.

We had begun to walk back to the palace when I suddenly saw a woman watching us. She was extremely tall, with silver hair and purple eyes.

Xander drew out his sword and put himself between us. I went down on my knees and tugged on his tunic to do the same.

After a moment he did so, and I said to her, “Thank you for the horses.”

Asteria, the daughter of the goddess, smiled so much like her mother that for a moment it took my breath away. “You were worthy of them because you asked for help for your sisters, and not for yourself.” She glanced around. “You did excellent work. My mother was right to choose you.”

Luna flew over to the goddess and landed at her feet. “Good morning, precious one,” Asteria said. “Aether dragons belong in my realm, with me.”

My heart froze inside my chest. “Have you come to take Luna?”

“She has bonded with you. I suspect that even if I did try to take her, she would just come straight back to you.”

Yes, Luna strongly affirmed in my mind, and I smiled.

But if she wasn’t here for Luna, then why else would she . . .

Oh.

“The sword,” I said.

“Yes. I have been sent to retrieve my mother’s sword.”

I took the sword out of its sheath and walked toward her with Xander right behind me. I handed it to her.

When she took it, the sword went back to its original size. She slid it into a sheath on her back.

“If you ever need the sword again, you may call on me. But I visited with my cousin, the god of prophecy, before I came here. He said you will never have need of it, and that you both are going to live a long, happy, and peaceful life. Loving and being loved in return. And his prophecies must come to pass.”

Tears welled up in my eyes as I realized what she had done. What she had given us. I didn’t even know what to say.

“Thank you,” I said, wishing there were another way of conveying the gratitude I felt for this gift. “And thank your mother.”

"I will. Take care, Euthalia of Locris."

She shimmered into silver sparkles and then was gone.

Xander exhaled deeply. "This has been an extremely strange morning."

I completely agreed. We resumed our walk back to the palace, and I said, "What do you think of the name Asteria?"

"For what?" Realization hit him quickly. "Wait, are you saying that you know we're having a girl?"

I nodded and he let out a whoop of excitement and pulled me into his arms.

What about Luna?

I told him what my dragon had said, and his response was, "I think one Luna is quite enough."

She made a huffy sound and then disappeared.

"You did it," he said. "I knew that you would. You restored your home."

"This was my home," I told him. "It's not anymore."

"Oh?"

I smiled. "My home is with you. And it always will be."

He kissed me for a long time, with so much tenderness and passion that he had to hold me upright.

Eventually we walked hand in hand back to the palace. I knew there would be so many questions about what I had done this morning, and I was ready for them. I had wanted last night to be about Haemon, so Quynh and I had decided to give my parents the news that they would soon become grandparents this morning. We would stay for a few more days, long enough to see Haemon and Doria married, and then we would return to Ilion.

My husband and I had a nation to rule together. And I needed to meet with the archons about bringing on a new council member, preferably a woman, and how to implement our plans to send Ilionian girls to school.

I also had a dinner planned next week with my adelphia that I didn't want to miss.

Xander smiled at me, his happiness infectious.

Asteria was right. I was going to have a future that was filled with joy and peace.

And most important of all—love.

AUTHOR'S NOTE

I am so, so sad that this trilogy is over. I can't begin to tell you how much I love these characters and this story, and I really hope that I'm able to find a way to write about them again! Thank you for coming on this journey with me. I hope you are satisfied and happy with the way the series ended. Thank you to everyone who left reviews and posted about their love of these books. It means the world to me.

If you want to find out what I'm doing next, be sure to sign up for my newsletter (on my website at www.sariahwilson.com).

And I would love it if you could leave a review on Amazon and Goodreads. It will help other readers to find this story. Thank you!

ACKNOWLEDGMENTS

Thank you to everyone who has hyped up this series and DMed and emailed me to say how much you loved it. Your kind words are what kept me going through this process!

Thank you to Megan Sakoi for your suggestions and input. I'm thankful for your support and enthusiasm—I so appreciate them! I'm grateful for the entire Montlake team—Kris Beecroft, Angeline Harjono, and Angela Elson. This wouldn't be possible without all of you! Thanks so much to Charlotte Herscher. At this point I'm not sure how I would write a book without your input, which again means you're stuck with me indefinitely.

For Sarah Younger—thank you for always being there. I'm so grateful to have you on my side.

Thank you to the copyeditors and proofreaders who track down my mistakes and continuity errors. The cover for this book is gorgeous, and so I have to thank Elizabeth Turner Stokes for creating something so fantastic. (And it's my favorite color!)

As always (and I'll keep putting it in books until he returns), #BenSoloDeservedBetter and #SoDoesRey.

For my kids—I'm so thankful for you and so excited by the people you're becoming.

And for Kevin—then, now, I always love you.

ABOUT THE AUTHOR

Photo © 2020 Jordan Batt

Sariah Wilson is the *USA Today* bestselling author of more than two dozen romantic fantasy and contemporary romance novels, including *A Tribute of Fire* and *A Vow of Embers* in the Eye of the Goddess series, *The Chemistry of Love*, and *Roommaid.* She happens to be madly, passionately in love with her soulmate and is a fervent believer in happily ever afters—which is why she writes romance. She currently lives with her family and various pets in Utah, and harbors a lifelong devotion to ice cream. For more information, visit her at www.sariahwilson.com.